My Favorite Thief

"A beautiful love story . . . a unique tale of unconditional love found in the most unusual circumstances . . . *My Favorite Thief* stands alone and is a story worthy of a high recommendation."—*Romance Reviews Today*

"Monk has created a band of colorful characters, keeping this fast-paced story an entertaining read. Harrison and Charlotte are a joy to watch as they discover each other . . . Monk continues to write wonderful stories filled with adventure, where her characters find love in the most unexpected places with the most intriguing people."
—*The Oakland Press*

The Wedding Escape

"With its clever, witty writing, deftly plotted story and superbly crafted, subtly complex characters, Monk's latest historical is a deliciously romantic delight."—*Booklist*

"You'll be utterly captivated by the charm of this winning love story."—*Romantic Times*

"The fast-paced, fantastic story will captivate your heart."
—*Reader to Reader*

The Prisoner

"*The Prisoner* is Karyn Monk at her finest . . . [It] will fill your heart with joy."—*New York Times* bestselling author Virginia Henley

"A remarkable and heartwarming tale of boundless love, redemption, and the courage of the human spirit . . . Once again Karyn Monk gifts readers with a love story to cherish."—*Romantic Times*

"An enthralling love story . . . Monk proves again she knows how to entice and entertain her readers."

—*The Oakland Press*

The Rose and the Warrior

"*The Rose and the Warrior* is an absolutely delightful read, with an inspiring hero and heroine, and an enchanting cast of characters. With her gifted pen, Karyn Monk provides passion, medieval flavor, comedy, suspense, intrigue and hope, all the necessary ingredients for a memorable read."—*The Midwest Book Review*

The Witch and the Warrior

"Monk has created an absorbing, atmospheric drama."

—*Publishers Weekly*

"Monk spins a fascinating, readable story of passion and magic that will charm readers who like their historicals laced with humor and appealing characters."

—*Library Journal*

Once a Warrior

"Karyn Monk has created another soul-searing, wondrous read that combines sensuality, emotional intensity, and even a dash of humor. She is truly a bright light in the genre that shines brighter with each new novel . . . Readers will share in the joy and enchantment of this magical story."—*Romantic Times*

Surrender to a Stranger

"Karyn Monk brings . . . the romance of the era to readers with her spellbinding storytelling talents."

—*Romantic Times*

Also by Karyn Monk

EVERY WHISPERED WORD

KARYN MONK

BANTAM BOOKS

EVERY WHISPERED WORD
A Bantam Book / March 2005

Published by
Bantam Dell
A Division of Random House, Inc.
New York, New York

This is a work of fiction. Names, characters, places, and incidents either are
the product of the author's imagination or are used fictitiously.
Any resemblance to actual persons, living or dead, events, or locales is
entirely coincidental.

Bantam Books and the rooster colophon are registered trademarks
of Random House, Inc.

ISBN 0-553-58442-1

Printed in the United States of America
Published simultaneously in Canada

www.bantamdell.com

OPM   10   9   8   7   6   5   4   3   2   1

FOR

GENEVIEVE

WITH ALL MY LOVE

Every Whispered Word

PART I

THE SOUND OF HER HEART

CHAPTER
1

London, England
March 1885

If only she'd had her pickax handy, she would have made bloody good use of it.

She kicked the black door in frustration instead, then stifled a curse as pain shot through her foot.

I hate this bloody place.

The door groaned and retreated slightly, exposing a narrow view of the entrance hall beyond. She stared at it a moment, swiftly analyzing her options.

No doubt the proper thing to do would be to pull the door firmly closed. People in London probably didn't expect their doors to be kicked open in broad daylight, she reflected, especially by relatively respectable-looking young women. But what if Mr. Kent was actually at home, and had simply not heard her knocking? Perhaps he was engaged in some area of the house where it was difficult to hear someone pounding incessantly upon the door. Then again, she mused, a man of his social stature probably employed a butler. Well then, why had this servant not responded to her knocking?

Because he was old and deaf as a post, she promptly theorized. Or maybe he was a secret tippler and had collapsed on his bed, utterly foxed. Or suffered a dreadful attack of some sort and was lying helpless upon the floor, too weak to call for help. How tragic it would be if she just callously closed the door and left, abandoning the poor old, deaf butler to suffer alone and die.

"Hello," she called, flinging the door wide open. "Mr. Kent? Are you in?"

A banging sound thundered from somewhere within the house. It was eminently clear why no one had responded to her knocking. Someone had to be in the house to be making such a racket, although what activity he or she was involved in she could scarcely imagine.

"Mr. Kent?" She stepped into the entrance hall. "May I come in?"

The foyer was strangely void of furnishings, as if the owner had only just moved in. A battered, spindly-legged stool stood at the side of the hall, upon which a precarious tower of books and papers had been carelessly erected. More stacks of worn leather-bound volumes and notes were scattered in untidy hills across the floor and up the staircase, forcing her to step carefully as she navigated her way further into the hall.

"Mr. Kent," she called again, trying to be heard above the clamor, "are you all right?"

"That's it!" shouted someone, triumphant. "I knew it! *I knew it!*"

The voice was coming from the kitchen below, suggesting that it did not belong to Mr. Kent, but to one of his servants. That was better, really. A servant could tell her if Mr. Kent was in the house. If so, Camelia could then be issued into the drawing room to wait while the servant formally announced her. A formal presentation was much more desirable than having the renowned Mr. Simon Kent suddenly come upon a strange young woman standing uninvited in his home amidst the clutter of his personal books and papers.

Assuring herself that she was actually pursuing the more socially acceptable course of action, she closed the front door. Then she straightened her hat and brushed her gloved hands over the emerald-and-ivory-striped fabric of her skirt. There was no mirror handy for her to check the state of her hair, but the multitude of pins she had clumsily poked into place were already working their way loose, causing her inexpertly crafted chignon to droop against the nape of her neck. Zareb was probably right, she realized in frustration. If she was going to stay in London much longer, she would probably have to resort to the hiring of a lady's maid. The thought of such a frivolous expense irritated her. She jammed several hairpins back into place and marched through a door leading off the entrance hall, then descended the narrow flight of stairs leading to the kitchen.

"Yes, yes, that's it, that's better now!" shouted the deep voice, ecstatic. "Bloody hell, you've got it!"

A man of considerable height stood in the middle of the kitchen with his back to her. He was dressed in plain dark trousers and a simple white linen shirt, the sleeves of which were carelessly shoved up to his elbows, and the fabric of which was sodden and clinging to him. This was not surprising, given the extraordinary heat and moisture suffusing the kitchen. A fine, silvery mist wafted about, giving the chamber a faintly ethereal quality. It was a bit like being in the jungle after a heavy summer rain, Camelia thought, wishing she wasn't dressed in so many suffocating layers of rapidly wilting feminine attire.

A loud banging and gasping roared from an enormous apparatus beside the man. *A steam engine,* she realized, feeling a surge of excitement. It was turning a massive crank, which was facilitating the movement of a series of revolving wheels. These gears were part of an intricate structure that was connected to a large wooden tub, but Camelia could not make out exactly what the extraordinary piece of machinery was doing.

"Wait now, bide a bit, steady, steady—not too fast, now, you've got to keep it steady!" coaxed the man, speaking to the contraption as if it were a child learning a new skill.

He braced his lean, muscled arms against the rim of the wooden tub and stared inside, intently focused upon whatever was taking place within. "A little more, a little more—that's it—yes—that's it—brilliant!"

Intrigued, Camelia moved closer, making her way through a maze of long tables which were crowded with strange mechanical devices. Stacks of books were piled everywhere, and the tables, floor, and walls of the kitchen were covered with intricately drawn sketches and notes.

"A little faster," urged the man, excited. "No, no, no," he scolded, raking his hand through the damp waves of his coppery hair. He began to swiftly adjust a series of levers and valves on the steam engine. "A little more—a little more—come on now, we're almost there—that's it—"

A deafening blast of hot vapor belched from the apparatus. The crank began to turn faster, which in turn caused the gears to rotate with rapidly increasing speed.

"That's it!" he shouted, elated. "Perfect! Brilliant! Marvelous!"

The wooden barrel started to shiver and shake. Water sloshed over its sides and onto the floor.

"Too fast." Shaking his head, he frantically worked to readjust the changes he had made to the steam engine. "Hold now, slow it down— slow down I say, do you hear me?"

Camelia watched with mounting concern as the enormous barrel shivered and shook and sent waves of soapy water spraying through the air. Whatever the contraption's purpose might have been, it was clearly not meant to completely drench the person operating it, as it was now doing.

"Stop now, hold, cease, do you hear?" the man commanded, blinking water from his eyes as he scrambled to readjust the settings on the machine.

The crank and wheels were spinning at an alarming rate now, and the great barrel was quivering and quaking as if it might break apart.

"Hold, I say!" the man shouted, banging upon the recalcitrant contraption with his wrench. "Stop this nonsense before I take a bloody ax to you!"

Suddenly, sopping wet garments exploded from the barrel in every direction. A sodden pair of drawers smacked hard against Camelia's face and she stumbled backward, momentarily blinded. The table behind her gave way, toppling the one behind it. A dreadful crashing filled the room as she landed hard upon her backside.

"*Stop, you worthless piece of junk!*" roared the man,

who was still frantically trying to get his contraption under control. *"That is enough!"*

Camelia pulled the wet drawers from her face just in time to see the machine give a final, defiant huff. The man stood before it, dripping wet, his legs apart, wielding his wrench like a menacing sword. His shirt was unfastened nearly to his waist, exposing the taut contours of his chest and belly, and the considerable breadth of his shoulders was clearly defined beneath the virtually transparent mantle of linen. Camelia thought he looked like a mighty warrior poised for battle—except for the limp stocking dangling from the top of his head.

He waited a long moment, breathing heavily, watching to see if the machine was going to give him any more trouble. Evidently satisfied that it was not, he slowly lowered his wrench and turned, shaking his head in disgust. He glowered at the sight of the overturned tables, the smashed jumble of inventions, and the litter of notes and books strewn across the sopping wet floor.

Finally his dark gaze fell upon Camelia.

"What the devil do you think you're doing?" he demanded, incredulous.

"I'm trying to get up," she returned, hastily pulling her wet skirts over her legs. Her bruised dignity marginally restored, she held out her hand and regarded him expectantly.

"I mean what on earth do you think you're doing *here*?" he clarified, ignoring her outstretched hand. "Are you in the habit of just marching into people's homes uninvited?"

She struggled to maintain an air of polite formality, which was enormously difficult, given the fact that she was sprawled on the floor and the man was glaring at her as if she were a common thief. "I knocked," she began primly, "but no one came to the door—"

"And so you decided to just force your way in?"

"I most certainly did *not* force my way in." Since it was clear he lacked the basic manners of even the most inexperienced butler, she decided her interrogator had to be one of Mr. Kent's apprentices. While she could appreciate that it was probably difficult to find reliable assistants who were sufficiently skilled in mathematics and science, that did not excuse his utter discourtesy. "The door was already open."

He yanked the wet stocking from his head and threw it aside. "And so you decided that meant you were welcome to sneak in and spy on me?"

As it was obvious he was not going to assist her in getting up, she pushed herself to her feet with as much dignity as she could muster, given the challenge of managing her bustle, petticoats, reticule, and awkwardly tilting hat. Once she was upright she met his gaze with cool disdain.

"I can assure you, sir, that I did not sneak in, but rather walked in after knocking upon the door for several long minutes, and then calling out loudly to announce my presence. The door was open, as I have already mentioned—a careless oversight of which I'm sure your master would not approve, were he to hear of it from me."

The man's blue eyes widened.

Good, thought Camelia with satisfaction. *I can see I have your attention.*

"As it happens, I have an appointment this afternoon with Mr. Kent," she continued crisply, affecting an air of supreme importance.

She was only embellishing the truth a little, she assured herself. In fact she had written to Mr. Kent asking for an appointment exactly five times. Unfortunately, he had not responded to any of her letters. But she had been advised by certain members of London society that the esteemed inventor was a bit odd, and could sometimes go for weeks without either being seen or responding to any of his mail. And so instead of waiting for Mr. Kent to write back, she had taken matters into her own hands, penning a note in which she informed him that she would be calling upon him on that particular day, at that exact hour.

"You have an appointment with Mr. Kent?" The man arched a skeptical brow, which only served to further irritate her.

"Indeed I do," Camelia assured him firmly. Obviously Mr. Kent wasn't at home or he would have come rushing in by now, to find out what had made such a tremendous racket in his laboratory. "Regarding a matter of great import."

"Really?" He folded his arms across his chest, unimpressed. "What?"

"Forgive me, sir, but that is not your concern. If you will just advise me as to when you expect Mr. Kent to be in tomorrow, I shall call upon him then."

She had decided that she should not wait for the inventor to appear. Although there was no mirror in the kitchen, she was certain the effect of being hit in the face with a wet pair of men's drawers was not estimable. She could feel her enormous hat listing dangerously to one side, and her hair was falling in a tangled damp nest beneath it. As for her carefully selected outfit, which she and Zareb had labored so hard to iron into a state of neat perfection, it was now a soggy, wrinkled disaster. If Mr. Kent were to take her proposition seriously, she could hardly appear before him looking like a waif who had just blown in from a gale.

"I'm Simon Kent," the man informed her brusquely.

Camelia stared at him in disbelief. "You're not."

"Am I not quite what you expected?"

"To begin with, you're too young."

His brow creased. "I'm not sure whether I should be flattered or insulted. Too young for what?"

The barest flicker of amusement lit his gaze, making it clear to her that he was simply making sport with her. Well, she was not that gullible.

"Too young to have earned several degrees in mathematics and science from the University of St. Andrews and St. John's College in Cambridge," Camelia pointed out. "And to have lectured extensively on the subjects of Mechanisms and Applied Mechanics, and to have written two dozen or more papers published by the National Academy of Science, and to have registered patents for some two hundred and seventy inventions. And obviously, too young to be responsible for all of *this*," she finished, gesturing to the room full of scientific activity around her.

His expression was contained, but she could see that she had surprised him with her knowledge of his employer's accomplishments. *Good*, she thought, perversely satisfied that she had managed to put him in his place.

"Given the disastrous results of the experiment you just witnessed, I fear I have forever damaged your too kind opinion of me. However, since you just barged into my laboratory uninvited and unannounced, I'm afraid I cannot be held responsible for that. I don't customarily permit anyone to see what I am working on until I am relatively confident it is not going to explode and start shooting undergarments about."

Camelia stared at him, speechless. He was not so young after all, she realized, suddenly noticing the furrows in his forehead and between his brows, which suggested countless long hours spent in study and deliberation. He was certainly thirty-five, or perhaps even a year or two more. While that was relatively young for a man to have accomplished all that she had just described, it was not impossible. Not if the man was exceptionally brilliant, disciplined, and driven. A terrible sinking feeling enveloped her as she realized she had just insulted the very man she had so desperately hoped to impress with her visit.

"Forgive me," she managed, wishing that the floor would open up suddenly and swallow her whole. "I did not mean to intrude. It's just that I very much wanted to meet you."

He tilted his head to one side, his expression wary. "Why? Have you come to interview me for one of those irritating rags that takes such inestimable pleasure in dismissing me as a mad inventor?"

His tone was sarcastic, but Camelia detected a thread of vulnerability that suggested he had not been impervious to being described as such.

"No, nothing like that," she assured him. "I'm not a writer."

"Not a writer, and not a spy. That's two counts in your favor. Who, then, are you?"

"I'm Lady Camelia Marshall," she said, grabbing her hat as it started to slide off her head. "I'm a great admirer of your work, Mr. Kent," she added earnestly, holding fast to keep the heavily flowered confection from flopping over her face. "I've read several of your papers and have found them to be most intriguing."

"Have you indeed?"

If he was impressed by the fact that a woman had actually read some of his work, or claimed to find it intriguing, he gave no sign of it. Instead he walked behind her and lifted the first table that Camelia had knocked over.

"What a bloody mess," he muttered, bending to pick up some of the dozens of tools, pieces of hardware, and wads of notes that lay strewn about the wet floor.

"I'm terribly sorry about knocking your tables over," Camelia apologized. "I hope nothing is broken," she added, stooping down to assist him.

Simon watched as she awkwardly picked up a small metal box. She gripped it with one soiled, gloved hand while the other held fast to the enormous monstrosity of her sagging hat. That done, she started to rise. Unfortunately, her balance was compromised by the heavy weight of her wet bustle. She abandoned her grip on her bonnet and flailed around with one hand, her expression suddenly panicked, still holding his invention safe against her breast.

Simon reached out and grabbed her as her hat dropped in a riot of wilted roses over her face. As she toppled against him the scent of her flooded through him, an extraordinary fragrance unlike any he had ever known. It was exotic yet vaguely familiar, a light, sun-washed essence that reminded him of wandering in the woods on his father's estate during a summer rain. He held her fast, drinking in her fragrance and acutely aware of the delicate structure of her back, the soft gasp of her breath, the agitated rise and fall of her breast as it pulsed against the damp linen clinging to his chest.

"I'm so sorry." Horrendously embarrassed, Camelia wrenched her hat up off her face. Finally free of its pins, the treacherous headpiece fell to the floor, dragging whatever semblance of a coiffure she might have retained down with it, until her hair was spilling across her back in a hopeless mass of tangles.

Simon stared down at her, taking in the smoky depths of her eyes, which were wide and filled with frustration. They were the color of sage, he realized, the soft green shade of wild wood sage, which grew in the dry, shady heaths of Scotland. A fine fan of lines surrounded her lower lashes, making it clear that she was well past the girlish bloom of her early twenties. Her skin was unfashionably bronzed and sprinkled with freckles, and her honey-colored hair was streaked with the palest threads of gold, indicating she was well accustomed to being in the sun. That he found surprising, given the quality of her attire. In his experience most Englishwomen of gentle breeding preferred the protection of either the indoors or shade. Then again, he reflected, most women of gentle breeding didn't march boldly into a man's house, uninvited and unescorted. He was vaguely aware that she no longer required his assistance to stand, yet he found himself strangely reluctant to release her.

"I'm all right now, thank you." Camelia wondered if he thought she was incapable of staying upright for more than three minutes. Not that she had given him much reason to think otherwise, she realized miserably. "I'm afraid I'm not accustomed to wearing such a big hat," she added, feeling he must require some kind of explanation for her inability to keep the confounded thing on top of her head. She declined to mention that a wet pair of drawers had knocked her in the face, challenging the integrity of her awkwardly arranged hairpins.

Simon didn't know what to say to that. He supposed a gentleman might reassure her that the hat was quite fetching on her, but he thought the bloody thing was ludicrous. There was no denying she looked much better without it, especially with her sun-kissed hair loose and curling across her shoulders.

"Here." He picked her hat up and handed it to her.

"Thank you."

He turned away, suddenly needing some distance from her. "So tell me, Lady Camelia," he began, trying to focus on his disaster of a laboratory, "do we actually have an appointment today of which I am unaware?"

"Yes, absolutely," Camelia replied emphatically "We most certainly do." She coughed lightly. "In a matter of speaking."

Simon frowned. "Meaning what, exactly?"

"Meaning that our appointment was not confirmed, exactly. But it was certainly set, there can be no doubt about that."

"I see." He had no idea what she was talking about. "Forgive me if I seem obtuse, but just how, precisely, was this meeting arranged?"

"I wrote you a series of letters asking you for an appointment, but unfortunately, you never replied," Camelia explained. "In the last letter I took the step of informing you that I would call upon you today at this time. I suppose that was rather forward of me."

"I believe it actually pales in comparison with marching into a man's house unannounced and unescorted," Simon reflected, slapping a sheaf of soggy notes onto the table. "Are your parents aware that you are wandering around London without a chaperone?"

"I have no need for a chaperone, Mr. Kent."

"Forgive me. I did not realize you were married."

"I'm not. But at twenty-eight I'm well past the age of coming out, and I have neither the time nor the inclination to be constantly arranging for some gossipy elderly matron to follow me about. I have a driver, and that is sufficient."

"Aren't you concerned for your reputation?"

"Not particularly."

"And why is that?"

"Because if I lived my life according to the dictums of London society, I would never get anything done."

"I see." He tossed a wooden pole with a metal attachment onto the table.

"What's that?" asked Camelia, regarding it curiously.

"It's a new type of mop I'm working on," he said dismissively, bending to retrieve something else.

She moved closer to examine the odd device. "How does it work?"

Simon regarded her uncertainly, not quite believing that she was actually interested in it. Few women had ever ventured into his laboratory. Of those that had, only the women in his family had demonstrated a genuine appreciation of his often outlandish ideas. Yet something about Lady Camelia's expression as she stood there tempered his initial impulse to simply brush off her question. Her sage green eyes were wide and contemplative, as if the odd tool before her were a mystery that she genuinely wanted to solve.

"I've attached a large clamp on the end of a mop-stick, which is operated by this lever," he began, picking it up to show it to her. "The lever pulls this rod, which tightens this spring, causing the clamp to close tightly. The idea is that you wring out the string end of the mop without ever touching it, or even having to bend over."

"That's very clever."

"It needs work," he said, shrugging. "I'm having trouble getting the tension on the spring right, so that it squeezes out the mop sufficiently without snapping the lever." He placed it back on the table.

"And what is this?" Camelia indicated the metal box she was holding.

"A lemon squeezer."

She regarded it curiously. "It doesn't look like any of the lemon squeezers I've ever seen." She opened it to reveal a wooden fluted nob surrounded by a ring of holes. "How does it work?"

"You put the halved lemon on the mount, then close the lid and press down firmly, using the handles to create more pressure," Simon explained. "The hollow in the lid squeezes the lemon hard against the mount, extracting the juice without the need for twisting. The juice flows through the holes into the chamber below, free of pits and pulp, which get trapped in the chamber above. Then you pull this little drawer out and there you have your lemon juice."

"That's wonderful. Are you planning to manufacture it?"

He shook his head. "I made it for my family because I'm always trying to find ways to lighten their work a little. I expect others would think it was a piece of nonsense."

"I believe most women would welcome anything that makes their household tasks easier," Camelia argued.

"Have you at least registered a patent for it? Or for the mop?"

"If I stopped to register patents for every little thing I came up with, I'd spend my life buried in paper."

"But you have some two hundred and seventy patents."

"Only because some well-meaning members of my family took it upon themselves to take my drawings and notes on those particular inventions and submit the necessary documents and fees to the patent office. I have no idea what has been registered and what hasn't. Frankly, it doesn't interest me."

She regarded him incredulously. "Don't you want to know that your ideas have been properly registered, so you can receive credit for them?"

"I don't invent things for the sake of receiving credit for them, Lady Camelia. If someone else wants to take one of my ideas and improve upon it and invest the time and the capital necessary to put it into production, so be it. Science and technology would never advance if all scientists hoarded their theories and discoveries as if they were gold."

He hoisted the second table back onto its legs and began to pile onto it more of the wet papers, tools, and various inventions that had fallen to the floor. "So tell me, Lady Camelia," he said, shaking the water out of a tangled nest of wire, "what is it that led you to write all those letters asking to see me?"

Camelia hesitated. She had imagined conducting her meeting with Mr. Kent seated in a richly velvet-draped drawing room, where she could expound at a leisurely pace upon the importance of archaeology and the evolution of man, perhaps while being served tea on a silver service by some suitably deferential servant. It was now abundantly clear to her that Mr. Kent didn't employ a servant, given the numerous stacks of greasy dishes piled high upon the stove and in the sink on the other side of the kitchen. She considered suggesting that she return on another day, when he might not be preoccupied with the task of restoring his laboratory to some semblance of order, then quickly rejected the idea.

Time was running out.

"I'm interested in your work on steam engines," she began, bending to pick up a few more items from the floor. "I have read one of your papers on the subject—in which you discussed the enormous benefits of steam power when applied to the pumps used in coal mining. I thought your thesis that steam power has yet to be used effectively was most compelling."

Simon couldn't believe she was serious. Of every possibility that might have explained her presence, the subject of steam engines and coal mining would have struck him as amongst the least likely. "You're interested in steam engines?"

"As they apply to the challenges of excavation and pumping," Camelia explained. "I am an archaeologist, Mr. Kent, as was my father, the late Earl of Stamford. No doubt you have heard of him?"

A glimmer of hope flared in her eyes, which for some reason Simon was loathe to extinguish. However, he disliked the idea of lying to her.

"Unfortunately, Lady Camelia, I'm not very well acquainted with the field of archaeology, and I don't typically attend functions where I might have had the pleasure of meeting your father." His tone was apologetic.

Camelia nodded. She supposed she couldn't really expect him to know of her father. Given everything she had heard about Mr. Kent, it was apparent he spent most of his time cloistered in his laboratory.

"My father dedicated his life to the study of the archaeological riches in Africa, at a time when the world is almost exclusively interested in the art and artifacts of the Egyptians, Romans, and Greeks. Very little has been done in terms of recording the history of the African people from a scientific point of view."

"I'm afraid I don't know very much about Africa, Lady Camelia. My understanding is that its people are basically nomadic tribes who have lived extremely simple lives for thousands of years. I didn't think there was anything of value there—except diamonds, of course."

"Africa does not have the abundance of ancient buildings and art that have been found elsewhere in the world," Camelia allowed. "Or if it does, we have not yet found them. But my father believed Africa was home to civilizations far older than those existing anywhere else in the world. When Charles Darwin proposed his theory that human beings may have descended from apes, most of the world laughed. My father, however, grew more convinced of Africa's singular importance in the evolution of mankind."

"And how does that apply to my work with steam engines?"

"Twenty years ago, my father discovered an area of land in South Africa in which there were many indications that once an ancient tribe lived there. He purchased some three hundred acres and began an excavation, which produced many exciting artifacts. I am now continuing my father's work and I need your steam-powered pump to assist me."

"I thought archaeological digs were basically carried out with a shovel, a bucket, and a brush."

"They are. But excavating in South Africa has unique challenges. Once you get below the first layer of relatively soft ground, the crust becomes extremely hard and difficult to break. Then you have the problem of water seeping into the hole as you approach the water table. And then there is the rainy season, which can last from December through March. At this moment my dig is completely flooded, making it impossible for my workers to continue."

"Surely there are steam-powered pumps available in South Africa," Simon suggested.

"They are actually somewhat difficult to come by."

Camelia was careful to keep her tone light. She did not want Simon to know about the extraordinary problems she had encountered in trying to secure a pump for her site. If he knew that her previous equipment had been sabotaged, or that she believed the De Beers Company had instructed the pumping companies not to lease her any more machinery, he might decide it was too risky for him to supply her with his own unique pump.

"There is a water-pumping monopoly in existence, which is controlled by the De Beers Mining Company," she continued, "and its priority, understandably, is providing services for pumping the diamond mines. At this point, I am unable to either purchase or lease a pump, which has brought the work on my site to a halt. But after reading your article, I am convinced your pump would be far superior to anything currently in use in South Africa. That is why I have come to you."

"And just what makes you think my pump is better?"

"In your paper you dismissed current steam turbines as extremely inefficient. You proposed that far greater energy could be harnessed if the steam could expand gradually, instead of in just one step, enabling the turbine to move at an extraordinary speed, which would in turn result in a much more powerful and rapid pumping action. Since the artifacts I am excavating can be damaged by prolonged exposure to water, and because I am extremely anxious to progress with my work, I believe your new steam pump is the best solution for clearing my site."

So she had actually read the article, Simon reflected. Even more surprising, she apparently had understood it. He raked his hands through his hair and gazed about the room, trying to remember where he had put his notes and drawings on steam engines. He began to rummage through several piles of drawings scattered on the floor, then moved to one of the tables that had not been upended by Lady Camelia's spectacular fall and continued searching.

"Why were you making this engine shake this tub?" Camelia asked while he searched.

"The engine wasn't supposed to shake the tub. It was supposed to turn the paddles inside, which in turn would force the water through the clothes. Unfortunately, it didn't work as well as I had hoped."

Camelia stared at the enormous contraption in astonishment. "You mean this is a giant washing machine?"

"It's an early prototype," Simon told her. "Current machines employ a wooden tub and paddles that are turned by a crank. I'm trying to make a machine that will operate with steam power, freeing women from the exhausting job of turning the crank by hand."

Although her experience with washing clothes was limited, Camelia could certainly appreciate that for a woman in charge of an entire household's attire, a steam-powered machine would be of enormous help. "That's a marvelous idea."

"It needs a lot of work," he admitted, casting an irritated glance at the soaking wet garments strewn about the kitchen. "A steam engine is difficult to operate, and I'm having trouble getting it to give me a good, steady rotation. Also, it's too large and expensive. Gas power is another option, but few homes are connected to gas. Electricity is also a possibility, but most homes don't have it yet." He began to burrow beneath a towering stack of unwashed dishes, which looked as if they might come crashing down upon his head at any moment. "Here it is," he said, extracting a crumpled sketch from beneath a frying pan.

Camelia moved closer as he cleared some space on a table and attempted to smooth out the badly creased, stained drawing.

"The basic premise of a steam engine is that it places steam under enormous pressure, then permits it to expand, creating a force which can be converted into motion," Simon began. "Using a piston and cylinder, a pumping effect is created, which can be used for many tasks, including pumping water from coal mines and pits. I was trying to improve the engine's efficiency by having the steam expand through a series of stages, thereby significantly increasing its pressure."

"Did you succeed?"

"I managed to break down the movement of the steam

and intensify its pressure. Unfortunately, it was not enough to make a substantial difference in terms of the pump's efficiency."

Disappointment filtered through her. "Did the pump you built work well enough to clear water out of a pit?"

"Of course," Simon assured her. "I made a few adaptations to it, so that the action was better than what most pumps can achieve. It just wasn't enough to warrant manufacturing it on a large-scale basis. The materials I used were costlier than what is generally employed, and the machine takes longer to assemble, which means no manufacturer would consider the design economically viable."

Camelia supposed that a somewhat improved pump was better than nothing. "Would you be willing to lease it to me?"

"Unfortunately, there is nothing to lease. I dismantled most of it, because I needed the pieces for other things."

She stared at him, crestfallen. "How long would it take you to build another one?"

"More time than I have right now," Simon replied. "I am currently working on too many other projects. Besides, that machine had several problems which I couldn't seem to solve."

"But that is what should compel you to devote more time to it," Camelia argued. "As a scientist, you should be motivated by challenge."

"Look around you, Lady Camelia. Do you honestly believe I don't have enough challenges already demanding my attention?"

"I'm not saying the other inventions you are working on are not important," Camelia assured him. "But you can scarcely compare lemon squeezers and washing machines to something that will help me unearth a vital piece of human history."

"That depends entirely upon one's point of view," Simon countered. "For people who collapse on their bed every night exhausted by the overwhelming burden of their daily chores, any invention which makes a task easier to perform is an improvement on their life. Potentially improving the lives of thousands strikes me as far more important than digging up a few disintegrating bones and broken relics in the wastelands of Africa."

"Those disintegrating bones and relics tell us about who we are and where we came from," Camelia returned, infuriated by how he was denigrating her work. "The discovery of our history is of critical importance to all of us."

"I'm afraid I am more interested in devoting my time to inventions that will make the present and the future better. While I respect the field of archaeology, Lady Camelia, it is a rarefied area of interest mainly for a few privileged academics. I don't believe you are about to discover anything that will improve the lives of thousands of people. Since my time is extremely limited, and I am already working on far more projects than I can manage, I'm afraid I cannot help you." He began to pick up more of his scattered inventions and papers from the floor.

"I will pay you."

He paused and eyed her curiously. Her expression was composed, but her hands were gripping her reticule so tightly her soiled gloves were stretched taut against her knuckles. Clearly, pursuing the work of her father meant a great deal to her.

"Really? How much?"

"Very well," she assured him. "Handsomely."

"Forgive me if this seems somewhat uncivilized, but I'm afraid you will have to be a little more precise in your terms. How much, exactly, does 'handsomely' mean?"

Camelia hesitated. Her financial resources were severely strained. She had scarcely enough funds in the bank to keep the handful of loyal workers who had remained on her site from quitting over the course of the next two months. But Mr. Kent mustn't know that. The disheveled man standing before her appeared to be having financial troubles of his own, given his modest, sparsely furnished home and his apparent inability to employ anyone to assist him, either with his inventions or with the avalanche of crusted pots and greasy dishes piled around the stove and sink.

"If you will build me a pump immediately, Mr. Kent, then I am prepared to offer you five percent of my profits over the next two years. I believe you must agree that is very generous."

Simon frowned. "I'm sorry, Lady Camelia, but I'm not clear on what that means. Profits on what, precisely?"

"On whatever I find at my site."

"I wasn't aware there was a flourishing market for bits of bone and broken pots."

"There is if they are of archaeological significance. Once I have had the opportunity to study and document the pieces, they are sold to the British Museum for its collection, with the understanding that I am to have continued access to them should I ever wish it."

"I see. And just how much you have managed to earn in the past five years while engaged in this pursuit?"

"What my father and I earned in the past is of no consequence," she informed him firmly. "At the time of his death six months ago, my father was on the verge of an extremely important discovery. Unfortunately, rain and water seepage have made progress on the site extremely slow, and my workers have had difficulty accomplishing much."

Actually, most of them had become convinced that the site was cursed and fled, but she saw no reason to share that particular piece of information with him.

"With the help of your steam pump," she continued, "I will be able to excavate the site a hundred times faster than I could using only manpower for removing the water and mud. Then I will finally find what my father spent so many years looking for."

"And what was that?"

Camelia hesitated. There had already been rampant fear amongst her own workers as to what it was she sought. When the accidents occurred, that fear had ignited into a firestorm of panic. Of course, Simon Kent was an educated man of science, who probably didn't believe in curses and vengeful spirits.

Even so, the less he knew, the better.

"My father was searching for the artifacts of an ancient tribe that inhabited the area of our site some two thousand years ago." That was certainly true, she assured herself. It just wasn't the entire truth.

Simon looked decidedly unimpressed. "A few smashed bits of ancient tribal artifacts? No secret stashes of gold or diamonds? No mysterious ancient powers trapped in a jewel-encrusted chest?"

"The value of these particular artifacts will be enormous." Camelia struggled to keep her temper in check. "My father spent his last twenty years on the cusp of an important scientific discovery, which is certain to open the door to an entire new area of archaeological study."

"So what you are offering me at present is essentially five percent of nothing," Simon observed bluntly, "given that you and your father have so far failed to find this so-called 'significant discovery.'" He began to gather up the sopping wet garments strewn about the kitchen and toss them back into his washing machine. "Forgive me if I seem ungrateful, Lady Camelia, but as marvelously tempting as your offer is, I'm afraid I shall have to decline."

Camelia glared at him in frustration. Simon Kent was nothing like she had imagined. She had envisioned him as a refined, elderly man of science and letters, who was driven by an insatiable thirst for knowledge, as her father had been. She had believed Mr. Kent would welcome the extraordinary opportunity to participate in her exploration, in which one of his inventions would be used to further the world's understanding of its own origins. She had convinced herself that he would be nothing like the other British men she had met upon her return to England, most of whom seemed to think that South Africa was nothing but a scrubby plot of dirt inhabited by barbarians, a land just waiting to be ravished for diamonds and gold.

"Ten percent then, over two years," she offered stiffly as he continued to hurl garments back into his infernal washing machine. She hated the fact that she needed his assistance so desperately. "Will that satisfy you?"

"It isn't just a matter of the money." Simon was impressed by her obvious determination. Clearly her desire to honor her father's life's work and succeed where he had failed was admirable. "Even if I built another steam-powered pump for you, which would take several weeks at the very least, who would operate it for you once it was shipped to South Africa? You have already described the significant challenges of the geography and weather. The steam pump I would build would be different from anything currently in use. It would have to be adapted to address the problems that would undoubtedly arise. Someone would have to be trained to operate and maintain it, otherwise you would find yourself saddled with a completely useless piece of machinery."

He was right, Camelia realized. The one steam engine she had managed to lease for her dig right after her father died had suffered countless breakdowns during the few brief days it had actually worked. Then it had mysteriously fallen over and smashed its gears, destroying it completely. The leasing company had demanded that she pay for the ruined machine, then refused to lease any equipment to her again.

Mr. Kent's machine would be useless unless someone with adequate knowledge of such a piece of equipment could be engaged to run it.

"Would you be willing to come to South Africa and train someone to use it? You would only need to stay a week or two," she hastily assured him. "Just long enough to demonstrate how the machine works and familiarize someone with its maintenance."

"Someone might be able to master operating it in two weeks, but learning to maintain it and repair it would take weeks or even months beyond that," Simon pointed out. "I'm afraid I don't have the time or the inclination to sail to Africa to do that—I have far too many other projects demanding my attention at this time."

"Of course I would offer you more, to compensate you

for your time," Camelia added. "I would increase your stake in the profits to ten percent over five years—surely this would satisfy you for the time I am asking you to invest."

"Lady Camelia, I'm afraid I do not share your fascination with scrabbling around in the African dirt. I hope you understand."

Camelia pressed her lips tightly together. What a complete and utter waste. She had spent two weeks poring over his articles in *The Journal of Science and Mechanics* while writing him letter after letter, politely asking him for a visit. In that time she had convinced herself that she would be able to persuade the reputedly odd but brilliant Simon Kent to provide her with the steam pump she so desperately needed. Two precious weeks lost, with absolutely nothing to show for it. Panic flared within her.

Her gaze fell to the greasy sketch on the table before her.

"Of course I understand," she said calmly. "I hope you will forgive me for entering your home unannounced, Mr. Kent, and I thank you for your time." She placed her enormous hat on her head. "Oh, dear," she exclaimed, feeling about helplessly at the back of it, "I seem to have lost my pearl hat pin. It must have fallen on the floor—do you see it anywhere?"

Simon scanned the littered floor. "Here are some hairpins," he said, bending to pick up a half dozen wire fastenings strewn amidst the remaining debris, "but I'm afraid I don't see—"

"Oh, here it is! It was just caught in the top of my hat." She jabbed the pin into the loose tangle of her hair and moved swiftly toward the stairs leading to the main floor.

"I'll see you out," Simon offered.

"That won't be necessary," Camelia assured him airily, mounting the staircase as quickly as her damp, heavy skirts and bustle would permit. She strode across the entranceway and flung open the front door. "I hope I have not caused too much of a disruption to your day, Mr. Kent."

She gave him her sweetest smile, then turned and proceeded to make her way down the stone steps to the street.

Simon watched as she hurried along the sidewalk toward an elegantly appointed black carriage, her crinkled skirts swishing heavily about her, her pale blond hair falling in a tempest of waves beneath the wilted roses of her ridiculous hat. He wondered why her driver had not waited with her carriage directly outside his door. Perhaps she had instructed him to park a little further down the street so that she might enjoy a brief stroll. Whatever the reason, her stride was quick and determined as she walked, her beaded reticule swinging from her gloved wrist. The mauve and pewter colors of early evening swirled in a dusky veil around her, and as she reached the carriage she turned and waved.

Then she opened the vehicle's door and climbed inside, evidently so anxious to depart that she did not wait for her coachman to climb down and assist her.

Simon closed his door and stood in his front hall a moment. The leaden light had fallen like a caul over the barely furnished area, making it seem unusually oppressive and gloomy. He debated lighting the gas lamp fixture on the wall, then decided against it. He rarely ventured from his laboratory until the middle of the night anyway, and with all the straightening up he still had to do, he would probably be down there until the early hours of the morning. As he headed back down to the kitchen he noticed that his trousers were wet and clinging to him, and his sodden shirt was open nearly to his waist.

Wonderful, he thought dryly. Now on top of being labeled reclusive, absentminded, and profoundly eccentric, he could add being an exhibitionist to his list. Lady Camelia had not seemed to mind his state of undress, he reflected, or if she had, she had been extremely adept at masking her discomfiture. Perhaps her time in the wilds of South Africa had desensitized her to the proprieties of English society. It was doubtful that the native workers she employed labored in the scorching heat in a starched shirt, waistcoat, and jacket.

He lifted his experimental mop from the table and set to cleaning the floor, trying hard not to think about her sage green eyes, and how gloriously soft and warm she had felt in the achingly brief moment he had held her.

"Good Lord, madam, whatever do you think you're doing?" demanded the beefy-faced gentleman staring at Camelia from the opposite side of the carriage. "This isn't your carriage!"

"It isn't?" Camelia looked about its wine velvet interior, pretending to be confused. "It certainly looks like my carriage—I recognize the curtains—are you certain you haven't made a mistake and climbed into the wrong one?"

"Quite certain," the man returned adamantly, "since I've just returned from the country and have been sitting in this very seat for the last three hours. I was just about to disembark when you climbed in."

She cautiously peered out the carriage window, watching as Simon went back into his house and closed the door.

"Then I must beg your forgiveness, sir," she apologized, opening the door. "I told my driver to wait for me here, but it appears he must have moved a little further down the avenue. I regret causing you any inconvenience." She disembarked and fled down the street, tightly clutching her reticule.

Her heart pounded against her ribs as she raced along, fearful that at any moment Mr. Kent would discover she had stolen his drawing and chase after her. A heady mixture of triumph and fear kept her breaths shallow and her steps swift. She might not have Mr. Kent's newfangled steam-powered pump, but she had an extremely detailed sketch of it. She would find someone else to build it for her—someone who would share her vision of advancing the field of archaeology. There were other inventors in London—men who were interested in loftier pursuits than trying to use steam power to launder underclothes or wring the last bit of juice out of a lemon.

She came to the end of the street and crossed, then slipped down a narrow alley that ran behind a row of homes, weaving her way back to where she had left Zareb with the carriage. Her African friend had argued vehemently with her when she had insisted that he could not drive her directly to Mr. Kent's home, but ultimately he had relented. They couldn't afford to rouse any attention, and Zareb by his very appearance never failed to draw a fascinated audience wherever he went.

She held her hat with one hand and her reticule safe against her chest with the other, despising the iron grip of her corset and the cumbersome cage of her bustle and petticoats. When she finally got back to Africa, she would take great pleasure in burying them both. Some archaeologist a thousand years hence would no doubt think they were instruments of torture.

"Hello there, duckie." A heavyset man appeared suddenly in front of her, blocking her path. "Where are we off to in such a hurry?"

Before she could respond, an enormous hand clapped roughly over her mouth, cutting off the enraged protest in her throat.

CHAPTER 2

"For cryin' out loud, Stanley, will ye hold her steady?" The short, round dumpling of a man in front of Camelia regarded the giant who had grabbed her with exasperation. "I ain't lookin' to get poked in the blinker."

"She's in a fair pucker, Bert," Stanley explained apologetically as he tried to restrain Camelia's flailing arms while still muffling her mouth. "I think she's scared."

"O' course she's scared, ye great lumberin' oaf," Bert snapped. "An' so she should be," he quickly added, his dark, woolly eyebrows furrowing into a menacing scowl as he sauntered closer to Camelia. "A fine lady like this ain't accustomed to dealin' with a couple o' dangerous cutthroats like us—are ye, me fancy dove?"

Camelia kicked his shin as hard as she could.

"Gawdamighty!" screeched Bert, hopping about on one leg. "Bloody hell—did ye see that? Kicked me right in the shanks, she did—I'll be lucky if she ain't broken the skin!" He doubled over to gingerly rub his throbbing leg. "Can't ye hold her better than that, Stanley, or do ye need me to do it for ye?"

"Sorry, Bert," Stanley apologized, valiantly trying to hold Camelia still as her enormous hat fell to the ground. "I can't hold her arms an' gob an' keep her feet steady, too—shall I take my hand off her gob?"

"No, don't take yer hand off her gob, ye bloody clod pate—do ye want her screamin' for half o' London to come runnin'?"

"Maybe she won't scream if we ask her not to."

"Oh, that's a bang-up idea, that is," sneered Bert, rolling his eyes in exasperation. "Sure, Stanley, let's just free her bone box an' ask her ladyship nice and pretty not to make a cheep."

Stanley started to take his hand away from Camelia's mouth.

"Stop, ye great big lobcock!" shouted Bert, flapping his arms like an addled chicken. "I didn't mean it!"

"Then why'd ye say it?" asked Stanley, confused.

"I was bein' sarky—ye know, when ye say somethin' ye don't really mean."

Stanley shook his head, bewildered. "Ye say things ye don't mean? Then how am I supposed to know when ye mean somethin', and when ye don't?"

"Godamercy—I'll tell ye, Stanley, all right?"

"Will ye tell me before, or after ye say somethin' sarky?" persisted Stanley, troubled. "I want to be sure I know when ye're doin' it."

"For the love o'—I'll tell ye right after, all right? Will that suit ye?"

"It'd be better if ye tell me before," Stanley reflected. "That way I'd be sure not to do whatever it was ye was tellin' me to do but not really meanin' it."

"Fine, then, I'll tell ye before—I'll say 'Stanley, I'm

about to say somethin' sarky,' so ye ain't to pay no mind
to it—all right?"

Stanley shook his head, thoroughly confused. "If ye
don't want me to pay no mind to it, why bother sayin' it
at all?"

"Sweet Mary an' Joseph—fine, then!" Bert looked as
if his dark little eyes were about to explode from their
sockets in frustration. "I won't say nothin' at all, all
right? Now if it ain't too much trouble, can we please get
on with it?"

"Sure, Bert," said Stanley amiably. "What do ye want
me to do now?"

"Just hold her still so she can't kick me in the gams
again," Bert instructed, glaring at Camelia.

"I can't hold her legs without lettin' go o' somethin'
else," Stanley explained.

"Then put yer leg across hers, so she can't move
them."

"That ain't proper, Bert," Stanley told him soberly.
"Why don't ye just stand a bit aways from her, so she
can't reach ye with her foot?"

"Because I want that bag o' hers that she's got on her
arm."

"I'll get it."

Camelia writhed fiercely against Stanley, fighting to
keep her arm pinned tight against her body, but she was
no match for her enormous captor. Keeping his calloused
hand against her mouth, Stanley used the rest of his massive arm to hold her fast as he pulled her reticule off her
wrist and tossed it to Bert.

"Well, well, what 'ave we here?" clucked Bert, opening it. He withdrew the crumpled sketch Camelia had
hastily crammed into her bag and examined it. "Aha!"

His eyes bulged triumphantly as he looked up from the precious piece of paper. "This wouldn't happen to have somethin' to do with yer precious dig in Africa, now would it, yer ladyship? Did that dicked-in-the-nob inventor friend o' yours give ye this?"

Camelia regarded him serenely, as if she didn't give a whit whether he took that particular piece of paper or not.

"I thought so," said Bert, shoving the sketch into his pocket. "What else 'ave we got in here?" he muttered, peering down into the reticule. "Ye got any brass?"

"He didn't say nothin' about takin' brass from her, Bert," Stanley objected.

"He didn't say nothin' about *not* takin' brass from her, neither," Bert pointed out pragmatically as he fished a small leather purse out of Camelia's reticule and quickly counted the coins inside. "We done a bang-up job, and we're entitled to a share o' the whack—that's just good business." He shoved the coin purse into his pocket.

"Are we finished then?" Stanley eased his grip upon Camelia slightly, not wanting to hold her any tighter than necessary now that she had stopped struggling.

"Not quite. I've a message for ye, yer ladyship," Bert drawled, inching his way toward Camelia. "Stay out o' Africa," he hissed, pulling a pistol out of his coat, "unless ye want to see more o' yer precious workers snuff it. That land ye're on is cursed, as sure as I'm standin' here. Best thing for a fine lady like ye is to stay away from it— or else ye'll find yerself snuffed too—got it?"

"Excuse me," drawled a heavily slurred voice suddenly from the end of the alley, "can either of you gentlemen tell me the way to the Blind Pig?"

"No!" snapped Bert, glowering at the drunken man

staggering down the alley. "Now bugger off, ye bloody soaker!"

"It's a tavern," the man explained thickly, as if he thought that piece of information might help them give him directions. "With the primest doxies this side of London. One of them's a real rum piece—Magnificent Millie, they call her, and I'm not ashamed to say I've given her my heart—my soul—an' most of my money, too!" He hiccupped loudly.

Bert leveled his pistol at him. "On yer way, jingle brains, or I'll blast a hole in yer arse."

"Forgive me." The man lurched unsteadily toward them. "I think I'm goin' to be sick." He doubled over and braced his hands against his knees.

"For the love o' Christ," muttered Bert, wincing as the man began to make horrific retching sounds. "Could ye turn yer head, at least?" He lowered his pistol.

"He ain't feelin' well, Bert," said Stanley, sympathetic. "Maybe he ate some bad bubble an' squeak."

Seizing upon the distraction, Camelia let out what she hoped was a convincing swooning cry and went limp in Stanley's arms.

"Here now, what's the matter with her?" Bert demanded, alarmed. "What the hell did ye do to her, Stanley?"

"I didn't do nothin'," Stanley said defensively as he awkwardly tried to keep Camelia from collapsing onto the filthy ground. "She must o' got scared an' fainted—I told ye she was scared, Bert! All yer bluster about snuffin' it—ye ain't supposed to talk to ladies like that!"

Doubled over like a rag doll, Camelia jerked the knife sheathed in her boot free while her captors argued over which of them had caused her to swoon. One deep thrust into Stanley's thigh would force the giant to release her. Then she would yank the blade out and hurl it at Bert, causing him to drop his pistol while she raced away.

One ... two ... three ...

An ear-splitting blast pierced the air, then another and another. Balls of fire exploded around them.

"*Help!*" shrieked Bert, tearing down the alley as fast as his stout little legs would carry him. "He's shootin' at us—come on, Stanley—run for yer life!"

"Come on, yer ladyship." Stanley swung Camelia up and shielded her with his body. "That soaker's gone off his head!"

"Put me down!" All thoughts of stabbing poor Stanley were eclipsed by the realization that the giant was now apparently trying to save her.

"Release her!" Simon commanded, "or we'll blow you into bits so small, the rats will be licking you up for a week!" He hurled several more firecrackers at their fleeing forms, which exploded in a deafening blaze of red, green, and orange light.

"Godamighty, it's a bloody army!" yelped Stanley, cradling Camelia tightly against him as he lumbered along, oblivious of the fact that she was now holding a knife.

"For Christ's sake, Stanley, toss her down!" shouted Bert, who was wheezing and gasping for breath. "It's her they want, not us!"

"They are trying to save me, Stanley," Camelia explained, struggling against his massive chest. "Just put me down."

Stanley frowned, worried. "Ye sure ye'll be all right, yer ladyship? Ye ain't feelin' faint no more?"

"I'll be fine," she assured him.

"All right, then." He planted her roughly on her feet, holding her steady until he was certain she was able to stand on her own.

Another series of explosions blasted through the alley.

"Come on, Stanley, for the love o' Christ, *run!*" yelled Bert.

Stanley obligingly loped down the alley to join his terrified cohort

"After them, men!" bellowed Simon dramatically as he reached Camelia. "Don't let them get away!" He continued to hurl lit firecrackers in Stanley and Bert's direction until their terrified forms reached the end of the alley and disappeared. Finally he turned to Camelia.

"Mr. Kent," she gasped, astonished. "What on earth are you doing here?"

Simon stared down at her, swiftly taking in the dark smudges on her face, the wild tangle of her hatless hair, the tear in the shoulder of her gown, fighting to control the fury coursing through him. When he had first ventured down the alley and seen that enormous ox holding Camelia captive while that puffed up piece of filth threatened her, he had been consumed by a rage unlike any he had ever known. Fortunately, his customary logic had kept him from racing in like an idiot. He was alone, he had no weapon, and he did not flatter himself by imagining that he would be able to single-handedly take on a giant like Stanley—especially with little Bert waving a pistol in his direction.

Then he remembered the firecrackers stored in the coat he had put on before leaving his home.

"It suddenly occurred to me, Lady Camelia, that the carriage you had climbed into bore the crest of Lord Hibbert, who happens to be one of my neighbors. I was somewhat perplexed by this, especially when I looked outside again and found the carriage was still there, apparently waiting to drive Lady Hibbert to visit one of her friends. Lord Hibbert told me that you had mistakenly climbed into his carriage and then bolted down the street. My curiosity was sufficiently aroused that I decided to go looking for you—just to find out if you ever did manage to find your own carriage." He arched a sardonic brow.

"Thank you for your concern—although I can assure you I would have been able to deal with those two thieves." Camelia raised the hem of her skirts and slipped her dagger back into her boot.

"Do you customarily go about with a blade in your boot?"

"London can be dangerous," she remarked. "That is one of the reasons why my father came to dislike it so—there are thieves everywhere."

"Those men didn't strike me as common thieves."

"Of course they were," Camelia insisted. Not knowing how much Simon had overheard, she decided it was best to downplay the incident. "All they wanted was my reticule and—sweet saints—they took my reticule!"

"Is that where you put the drawing you stole from me?" His expression was impassive.

"I was only borrowing it. I didn't think you would mind, since you weren't using it anyway. I had every intention of bringing it back to you."

"After you had given it to someone else to copy and use as the basis for your steam pump? I believe the law would rule that removing my drawings from my home without my consent is stealing, Lady Camelia, however you may wish to paint it otherwise."

"But you said you weren't interested in protecting your inventions and ideas—you told me science and technology would never advance if scientists hoarded their discoveries," Camelia argued. "And since you didn't have the time to invest in that steam pump, I saw no harm in borrowing the sketch from you—just for a little while. But now it's gone—this is terrible!"

"If it makes you feel any better, I don't really need the sketch—that particular steam engine design is engraved in my mind."

"But now they know I'm in London to arrange for a steam pump!"

"Who?"

"Those two ruffians," she hastily replied. She did not want Simon to know that she was being watched. "I'm just worried that now they will sell your invention to some other scientist, who will build it and take the credit and make lots of money from all your hard work."

"I'm touched by your concern," Simon reflected dryly. "What I don't understand is why your charming friends Stanley and Bert are so interested in your movements, and why you are clambering into carriages that don't belong to you and skulking down dark, deserted alleys with a stolen sketch and a six-inch dirk sheathed in your boot. Do you actually have a carriage waiting for you somewhere, Lady Camelia, or is that just another one of your charming fabrications?"

"My driver is waiting for me over on Great Russell Street, in front of the museum," Camelia told him. "I felt it best that he wait for me there."

"Let me guess. You had him park there while you went into the museum, making it seem as if you would be there for several hours—a perfectly credible way for the

daughter of an esteemed archaeologist to spend an afternoon while she is visiting London. Then you slipped out
of the museum via a different door and made your way to
my house, thinking no one would suspect you had left
without the benefit of your carriage."

"It was a sound plan."

"I suppose it was, right up until the moment your
friends Stanley and Bert descended upon you. Evidently
they are not as easily duped as you think. The question
is, why are they so anxious to keep you out of Africa? Is
there something about your excavation that holds a special fascination for them?"

"I told you, I am on the cusp of a very significant discovery. There are many archaeologists out there who
would love to take over my dig and receive credit for
what I find."

"Those two didn't strike me as the archaeological
type."

"Of course not—they are just thugs who have been
employed by someone else—someone who has instructed them to watch my movements and try to scare
me off."

"I had no idea the field of archaeology was so cut-
throat. Do you have any idea who this rival archaeologist
might be?"

"No. Everyone in the British Archaeological Society
pretends to scoff at the idea that there is anything of consequence to be found in South Africa, but I believe someone understands the magnitude of the find I am about to
make. They think if they can scare me away, I will be
willing to sell my land for whatever I can get to the first
bidder. They are wrong. I will never leave Africa. And I

will never leave my dig until I have unearthed every last relic that is there to be found."

"I admire your determination."

A sliver of hope lit her eyes. "Then will you help me?"

"No. I am as committed to pursuing my own inventions as you are to finding your African relics, Lady Camelia. I will, however, escort you to your carriage." He strode down the alley and retrieved her hat.

"I don't need you to escort me," Camelia informed him briskly, annoyed that he was still unwilling to help. "I can assure you I am quite capable of getting to my carriage on my own—I do it all the time."

"Indulge me," Simon urged, handing her hat to her. "Surely that is the least you can do, to repay me for stealing my sketch?"

"You just said you didn't need it anyway." Camelia jammed the wilted, grimy headpiece onto her head. "You said you had it committed to memory."

"Then indulge me as a way of repaying me for gallantly coming to your rescue when you were in distress," Simon suggested. "I must say, I thought my performance as a lovelorn drunkard was particularly brilliant."

"I appreciate your concern, Mr. Kent, but I didn't actually need your help. I had the situation well in hand."

"I suppose if you think being held captive by a seven-foot-tall giant while another man threatens to snuff you and waves a pistol in your face is having it well in hand, then yes, I'd have to say you had the situation going beautifully."

"I was just about to stab that big man in the thigh when you staggered down the alley."

"Really? Have you ever done anything like that before?"

"I have hunted and helped to butcher large game countless times. I'm quite sure I could slash the muscles of a man's thigh without any trouble."

"Thank you for the warning." He extended his arm to her.

"Forgive me, Mr. Kent, but are you not concerned about being seen in your relative state of undress? You seem to have forgotten your hat and tie, and your shirt is unfastened."

"I left my house rather quickly." Simon was amused by her sudden sense of propriety. "I'm afraid I often leave my house inappropriately dressed—it is one of the consequences of being almost constantly preoccupied. Does my lack of a hat bother you?"

Camelia watched as he slowly closed his rumpled shirt over the chiseled curves of his chest. "Not at all," she returned, meeting his gaze evenly. "I'm well accustomed to seeing men without their hats."

"Good. Then you won't object if I take you back to your carriage?" His shirt now properly fastened up to his neck, he offered his arm once more.

She sighed. "If it makes you feel better, I will indulge you, Mr. Kent." She laid her hand lightly upon the thin fabric of his coat sleeve. His arm was surprisingly hard, and heat permeated the cotton of her glove, making her palm tingle.

They walked along in companionable silence, trading the charcoal dankness of the alley for the smoky gray light of the streets. Men and women in elegant evening attire were strolling and passing by in carriages, making their way to parties and suppers and the theatre. Camelia knew she and Simon made an odd pair as they walked along, she in her pitifully crushed day gown with her tangled hair and drooping hat, and Simon in his damp trousers and rumpled coat. People cast them disapproving glances, evidently thinking they had no right to be walking amidst their betters, or worse, assuming they meant some mischief like picking pockets. Their censorious stares irritated her. She glanced at Simon, wondering if he was also bothered by the attention they were drawing.

To her surprise, his expression was almost cheerful as he walked along. Either he didn't notice the way people were frowning at him, or he was wholly unbothered by it.

"I had forgotten how extremely pleasant an evening stroll can be," he remarked. "I really must try to get out of my laboratory more."

"How did you make those explosions in the alley?" asked Camelia, curious.

"I used some firecrackers that I had made for the amusement of my younger brother and sisters, which I had left in my coat pockets. I was planning to set them off for them the next time I visited."

"Those huge balls of fire were just firecrackers? They sounded like gunfire."

"I like to make my firecrackers big and noisy," Simon told her. "I add metallic salts and a chlorinated powder to intensify the colors and make the explosions burn even brighter. My mother is always complaining that one day I'm going to blow something up, but my brother and sisters think they're grand."

"How many brothers and sisters do you have?"

"There are nine of us all together, but only three of them are still young enough to be impressed by a big brother who can make explosions. The rest of them remember all the fires I nearly started when I was a lad, when I was trying to discover how much gunpowder it would take to blow the lid off the roasting pan, or see how much light could be generated from an oil lamp stuffed with five wicks instead of just one."

"And did you ever start any fires?"

"A few," Simon admitted, shrugging. They turned down the street where a half dozen carriages were waiting in front of the British Museum. A small crowd of children and adults was clustered in front of one of them, laughing and pointing at something. "But fortunately I never managed to actually burn the house down, though our butler, Oliver, was always sure that I would."

"That's my carriage." Camelia indicated the modestly sized plain black vehicle that the children were pointing at.

"What are those children looking at?"

"My driver. He tends to draw quite a bit of attention wherever he goes."

Simon walked with Camelia toward the front of the carriage, to see just what it was about this fellow that the children were finding so fascinating.

Seated upon the coachman's bench was a lean African man of some fifty years or more. His skin was as dark as coffee and deeply lined from years of exposure to the harsh African sun. His jaw and forehead were squarely cut, his cheeks sculpted but also slightly hollow, indicating that there had been times in his life when food had not been abundant. He sat with his back straight and his head high, staring straight ahead, his demeanor proud to the point of arrogance, betraying a nobility and strength of spirit that Simon found immensely compelling. A magnificent swath of fantastic robes was wrapped around him, woven of the most brilliant scarlets and sapphires and emeralds. On his head he wore a simple leather broad-brimmed hat, which seemed at odds with the rest of his exotic attire, but was eminently more practical than the glossy felt hats that fashion dictated the gentlemen of London wear. His rich, dark skin color, extraordinary robes, and strange hat would have been more than enough to invite the curiosity of everyone passing by, but it was none of these things that was causing the children in the crowd to yell and squeal with laughter.

It was the monkey bouncing up and down on his head, tossing cherries at them.

"Zareb, I asked you not to let Oscar out of the carriage," chided Camelia.

"He wanted to see the children," Zareb explained.

"More like he wanted to feed them," Camelia muttered. She held her arms out to the monkey, who screeched with delight on seeing her and flew off Zareb's head, landing safely in her embrace. "Really, Oscar, if you want to come out with me you're going to have to learn to stay in the carriage."

Oscar chattered in protest and wrapped one slender, furry arm around Camelia's neck.

Zareb's currant-colored eyes swept over Camelia, swiftly taking in her disheveled appearance. Then he shifted his gaze to Simon. He stared at him a long moment, as if he were trying to delve beyond the matter of Simon's own rumpled appearance and see what lay beneath. Finally he turned his attention back to Camelia.

"Can we return now?"

"We can return to the house," Camelia said, knowing that wasn't what Zareb meant. She turned to Simon.

"Thank you for escorting me to my carriage, Mr. Kent, and for coming to my assistance. I do apologize for causing so much disruption to your day, and for losing your sketch."

"No apology is necessary." Now that the time had come once more to say good-bye, Simon again found himself strangely reluctant to leave her. "Are you sure you'll be all right?"

"Of course," Camelia said, trying to restrain Oscar from pulling out the last few hairpins that remained in her sun-streaked hair. "I'll be fine. If for any reason you change your mind, Mr. Kent, I'm staying at number twenty-seven Berkeley Square. I'll be there for another few weeks—after that we'll be returning to South Africa."

Simon hesitated. He wasn't quite sure how to properly take his leave of her. A gentleman would kiss her hand, but given the fact that she was now using both hands to keep her monkey from playing with her hair made that somewhat impractical.

"Well then, I'll see you again, Lady Camelia," he said awkwardly, as if he thought he might just bump into her one day on the street. He opened her carriage door and extended his hand, preparing to assist her into it.

Oscar scampered up his arm and plopped himself down on his head, startling him.

"Oscar," said Camelia, "come down from there at once!"

Oscar squawked defiantly and shook his head, holding fast to Simon's hair.

"Come down now, Oscar," Camelia began in a warning tone, "or there will be no ginger biscuits after dinner."

The monkey flashed her a cheeky smile, causing the crowd of people still gathered around the carriage to laugh.

"Down, Oscar," Zareb said. "Patience."

Oscar hesitated, as if thinking about this. Then he patted Simon on the head and leaped onto the worn velvet seat of the carriage.

"I'm sorry about that," Camelia apologized. "He doesn't usually do that—he's fairly well-behaved." That wasn't even remotely true, but she saw no reason for Simon to think otherwise.

"That's all right. Do you always take him out with you?"

"Not always, but I'm afraid he finds staying in the house rather confining. He is accustomed to having much more freedom when we are home, but I can't let him wander about London on his own. He is supposed to stay in the carriage when we go out, but he doesn't like it. He is not used to being locked up."

"I can appreciate that." Simon assisted her up into her carriage and closed the door.

Camelia regarded him hopefully. "Do you think you might reconsider my offer, Mr. Kent?"

Simon hesitated, torn by the imploring look in her extraordinarily green eyes. For one brief moment, he was tempted to say yes. Unfortunately, he also was painfully aware of his obligations. He had sworn to his brother Jack, who owned a rapidly growing shipping company, that he would devote as much of his time as possible to the development of a better engine for marine propulsion. Jack wanted North Star Shipping to boast the fastest ships in the world, and Simon was determined to make that happen. Then there was the myriad of other inventions he was working on, including his clothes-washing machine, which had to be ready for unveiling at the Society for the Advancement of Industry and Technology fair in just six weeks. Much as he disliked the business side of his profession, there were, unfortunately, practical financial matters that he could not ignore. So far several of his inventions had been manufactured on a limited basis, but that had not generated sufficient income for him to continue his work.

Even if he wanted to just abandon everything and run off to Africa with Lady Camelia, he simply couldn't afford to.

"I will make some enquiries and see if I can find someone else to help you," Simon offered. "I'm sure there is a manufacturer of pumps in London who will be willing to lease you a pump and ship it to South Africa."

Camelia nodded, trying not to let him see her disappointment. She had already discreetly approached every pump manufacturer in London. They had all turned her down, citing a lack of available equipment or problems with her credit. Camelia knew that was not why they were refusing her.

As suppliers to the monopoly that controlled the pump market in South Africa, they had been instructed not to furnish Camelia with a pump, unless they wanted to see their contracts disappear.

"Thank you. That is most kind."

Zareb snapped his reins and set the carriage rolling forward. Oscar leapt up to screech at Simon as they pulled away, causing the crowd still clustered nearby to laugh once more.

Simon watched as the carriage ambled down the street before turning and disappearing into the rapidly cooling shadows of night. Finally he turned and began to slowly make his way home, feeling strangely alone.

He smelled smoke long before he saw it.

He rounded the corner of his street to see dozens of people crowded before his house, staring in awe at the brilliant orange flames dancing from the windows.

Sweet Jesus.

Dread fisted in his chest. He was vaguely aware of clanging bells ringing in the distance, signaling that the horse-drawn pumps of the Metropolitan Fire Brigade were on their way. A group of about twenty men had formed a line and were swiftly passing sloshing buckets of water to each other. A heavyset man on the end was valiantly heaving them onto the house. The water splattered uselessly against the brick walls, unable to reach the smoke and flames pouring from the rooms within.

"Let me pass!" Simon shouted, fighting his way through the mob of fascinated bystanders choking the smoke-filled street. "That's my house! Let me through!"

"It's him!" yelled someone. "The inventor—Kent! He isn't in the house!"

The crowd gasped and parted, creating a narrow path for him to advance toward his home.

"Always knew he'd burn the bloody place down," someone muttered as he passed. "What with all those bloody foolish inventions of his."

"We'll be damned lucky if it's just *his* house," added another.

"If the wind stirs it'll take the whole street," snapped someone else. "Just look how high those flames are."

"We should have thrown you out!" a woman shouted furiously. "Ought to be a law against it, if you ask me."

Simon ignored them, focusing on the sight of his flaming home. He had always known his neighbors didn't relish having an inventor living in their midst. Especially an inventor with a rather unsavory background. The heat was more intense now, and the air was thick with smoke and ash. A noxious plume of black spewed from the open front door, but the hallway and stairs beyond were dark, indicating the flames had not yet spread there. Simon whipped off his coat and held it to his face as he ran toward the steps leading from the street down to the servant's entrance off the kitchen.

"Don't try to go in!" yelled one of the men passing buckets. "It ain't worth it for a few bloody pieces of junk!"

Simon barely heard him as he looked inside the windows to see his laboratory burning. Squinting against the scorching heat and smoke, he saw the remnants of nearly eleven years' work lying strewn about the floor. His books and papers were burning everywhere, and all of the tables, which had held countless prototypes, works in progress, and assorted flights of fancy, had fallen over. His precious clothes-washing machine, which he had anticipated in just two months would forever revolutionize the way garments were laundered, was lying uselessly on its side. The enormous wash barrel had snapped from its frame and rolled away, leaving the flames to lap at the steel construction of his steam engine.

"Excuse me, sir, but you'd best come away now," said a voice. "It's not safe to be so close—the windows might shatter any minute. There's nothing more you can do."

Simon turned to see an earnest young fireman standing behind him. Three horse-drawn pumps had arrived, and thirty-some firemen were clamoring to get set up and start spraying the house with water. Even though they were moving quickly, Simon knew they had absolutely no hope of saving the house, except perhaps for its shell. All they could do was focus on the task of keeping the flames from spreading to the houses beside it.

"Ever hear of a fire knocking over tables and a heavy piece of equipment that weighed in excess of five hundred pounds?"

The fireman regarded him in confusion. "No, sir—not unless there was an explosion of some type."

Simon cast one last, rueful look into the ruins of his laboratory, fighting to control the helpless fury surging through him.

"Neither have I."

CHAPTER 3

Zareb walked slowly toward the dining room, holding the precious envelope in his aged, dark hand.

It had traveled all the way from South Africa, this envelope, and it bore scars, stains and creases that betrayed its long, arduous journey. By horse, by train, and by ship it had come, traveling for nearly four weeks across the rough swells of the ocean as it moved steadily toward them. He held it tighter, wishing he could feel the heat it had once known. He missed the cleansing caress of the hot African sun, which burned like a magnificent circle of molten gold against the brilliant blue sweep of sky. In London the sky was usually veiled with clouds, and a perpetual caul of ugly, stinking smoke hovered everywhere, the result of tens of thousands of coal fires burning from morning to night. All the houses seemed to be built on top of each other, forming an ugly grid of brick and stone that reminded Zareb of a prison, and the people inside confined themselves in dark chambers choked with heavy draperies and overstuffed furniture. There was no space, no air, no light, and from what he could see, no joy in this place called London.

The sooner he took Camelia home, the better.

He found her seated at the dining room table, her head bent, her brow puckered into a worried frown as she contemplated the letter she was writing. Oscar was seated on the table beside her, munching greedily on peanuts and littering the table and carpet with broken shells. The monkey had had little to do except search for mischief and eat since they had come to London. Zareb supposed if he were eating, that at least meant he wasn't getting into any trouble. He only hoped that his little friend didn't make himself sick in the belly, or thicken himself with so much fat that he couldn't move with his typical ease. Camelia's Grey Lourie, a spectacularly vain bird named Harriet, sat perched upon the back of one of the dining room chairs, admiring herself in the oval mirror Camelia had hung from the chandelier for her amusement. The bird squawked and ruffled her feathers as Zareb entered, announcing his presence.

"A letter has come, Tisha," Zareb told Camelia, calling her by the African name he had given her as a child. "From Mr. Trafford." He paused a moment, waiting to see if she wanted more.

"And?"

"There is a dark wind blowing." He would not have told her if she hadn't asked. He disliked burdening her even more. "That is all I feel."

Camelia nodded. Of course there was a dark wind blowing. These past few months there was always a dark wind blowing, as far as she could tell, so why should that day be any different? She sighed and laid down her pen. Maybe Zareb was wrong. She could not actually remember a time when he had been wrong, but sometimes the things he said were sufficiently vague that they were probably open to interpretation. A dark wind blowing. *Fine,* she said to herself, shoving aside the trepidation tightening in her chest. She accepted the envelope from Zareb and tore it open. *Let's see what the dark wind is bringing me today.*

"There has been another accident at the excavation," she said quietly, swiftly scanning the letter from Mr. Trafford, her foreman. "They've been trying to take the water out by hand, but the site is still flooded, and the walls we created at the southeast end have become unstable. One collapsed suddenly, killing Moswen and injuring four others. Nine more workers quit."

She laid the letter on the table and swallowed thickly. He had been a good man, Moswen. He had worked for her for only two months, but he had been strong and willing, and he had seemed genuinely pleased when some small artifact was found. Now he was dead because of her. And four others injured. Mr. Trafford did not say how badly they had been hurt, but Camelia could well imagine that the force of a collapsing wall would have been terrible. She raised her fingers to the flash of pain that began to pulse at her temple.

"There is more," said Zareb. It was a statement, not a question.

Camelia nodded. "The remaining workers are even more convinced now that the site is cursed. They are telling Mr. Trafford they will quit unless I increase their wages, to compensate them for the danger they are bringing upon themselves and their families by working on a cursed site. He has promised them more money will come, as a way of keeping them working until he hears from me. He wants to know what he should do."

Zareb waited.

"I will write and tell him to offer each of them an additional fifteen percent, to be paid at the end of their contracts."

"That will not satisfy them, Tisha," he pointed out quietly. "They are only men, and they are afraid. They fear they may not live until the end of their contracts. You must give them something now, as a show of faith. You must remind them that their loyalty will be rewarded."

"How can I pay them more now, when I don't even have the money to pay them what I already owe them?"

"You will get the money. It is coming."

"When? How?"

"It is coming," Zareb insisted. "You will get it. This I know."

Camelia sighed. "I appreciate your faith in me, Zareb, but so far I haven't been able to secure any of the help we need to keep the project going. My father's oldest friends have refused to invest any more money in it, because now that he is dead they don't believe I have the ability to succeed where he did not. None of the pump manufacturers in London would agree to provide me with equipment. They said I posed a credit risk, or claimed to not have any equipment available, but I know it is really because the De Beers Company has told them not to deal with me. My last hope was Mr. Kent, and he refused to help me."

Actually, her last hope had been Simon's drawing, but even that had been a faint one. She did not know of anyone else in London who might be able to build a steam-powered pump who wasn't already employed by one of the manufacturers that were refusing to do business with her. She had not told Zareb that she had stolen Simon's drawing from him. Zareb was a man of uncompromising honor.

However much he loved Camelia and wanted her to succeed, he would not approve of her resorting to common thievery to do so.

"Mr. Kent did help you," Zareb countered. "He came to your assistance in the alley."

"I didn't need his assistance in the alley," Camelia protested. "I had the situation under control."

Her disheveled appearance when she had reached her carriage had left her no choice but to tell Zareb what had happened with the two men who tried to frighten her the previous day. She had described the incident as a simple robbery by two pitifully inept thieves. She had assured him that they had succeeded in surprising her only because she had not been alert to her surroundings as she walked—a mistake she would not make again. She could not let Zareb think she was in danger. Her old friend already worried about her incessantly, which was why he had refused to let her come to England without him in the first place. He would not have responded well to the thought that someone had hired common thugs to frighten her into abandoning her dig.

He already thought London was filthy, uncivilized, and teeming with barbarians.

"Mr. Kent will come again," Zareb insisted. "He does not want to, but he will."

Camelia regarded him skeptically. "How do you know?"

"I know."

She sighed. She knew she could not question him further without the risk of insulting him. Once Zareb claimed to know something, he clung to his pronouncement with the stubbornness of a lion protecting his kill.

Someone pounded suddenly upon the front door, causing Harriet to squawk in fright and flap low across the dining room table. Startled, Oscar bounded toward Camelia, knocking over her inkwell as he leapt onto her shoulder.

"Oh, no—my letter!" Camelia snatched up the letter she had been writing, watching in frustration as black droplets rained from it onto the scratched surface of the table. "It's ruined."

Oscar hurled a torrent of blame in Harriet's direction, then buried his face meekly against Camelia's neck.

"This place is not good for Oscar," Zareb observed. "He feels trapped." He turned from the room, his magnificently colored robes rustling as he went to answer the front door.

"That's all right, Oscar," Camelia murmured, stroking the contrite monkey's back. She laid the ruined letter on the table, then pulled a wrinkled linen handkerchief from her sleeve and began to vigorously mop up the ink to keep it from spilling onto the carpet. "It was an accident."

"Lord Wickham to see you, my lady," announced Zareb solemnly.

A tall, handsome young man with sandy hair and eyes the color of molasses stepped into the dining room.

"Elliott! How good it is to see you!" Camelia hurried over to him and eagerly clasped his outstretched hands. "Oh, no," she moaned, looking with dismay at the black mess she had made of his skin with her ink-stained fingers. "I'm so sorry!"

"Don't worry, Camelia." Elliott quickly withdrew a crisply folded white linen square from his fashionably tailored coat pocket and wiped as much of the ink as he could from his hands, until his skin was restored from black to merely dirty gray. "There, you see? This time I was prepared." His voice was lightly teasing.

Still clinging to Camelia's neck, Oscar screeched irritably at him.

Elliott frowned. "Oscar still doesn't approve of me, I see."

"He doesn't approve of many people, actually," Camelia said, trying to disengage the clinging monkey from her shoulder. "He's worse, here, I think. Everything seems so foreign to him."

"He's known me for years, Camelia, so I'd hope that I would seem familiar to him."

"Well, I don't think he likes being closeted in this house so much of the time," Camelia added, wincing as Oscar stubbornly dug his little fingers into her shoulder. "That's enough, Oscar," she scolded, pulling his fingers free. "Go to Zareb." She held him out so Zareb could take him.

Elliott regarded Zareb expectantly, waiting for the servant to excuse himself.

Zareb tranquilly returned his gaze and remained where he was.

"Perhaps we could have some tea, Zareb," Elliott suggested.

"Thank you, Lord Wickham, I'm not thirsty."

Elliott's mouth tightened slightly. "Not for you, Zareb. For Lady Camelia and me."

Zareb turned to Camelia. "Would you like some tea, Tisha?"

Camelia sighed inwardly. The tension between the two men had existed from the time she was a little girl of thirteen, when Elliott had first come to South Africa to work with her father. "Yes, Zareb, that would be nice, if you wouldn't mind making some."

"Very well, Tisha." Zareb turned to Elliott. "Would you also like some tea, your lordship?"

Camelia watched as Elliott nodded, evidently satisfied that he had gotten Zareb to do his bidding. Poor Elliott did not understand Zareb's ways, so he could not appreciate that Zareb had, in fact, just offered Elliott tea as a host, instead of bringing it to him as a servant. The difference was subtle.

For Zareb, it was critical.

"You should have listened to me and left him in Africa," Elliott said after Zareb left the dining room. "I told you London was no place for that old servant. He just doesn't understand how he is expected to behave here."

"Zareb isn't my servant, Elliott," Camelia pointed out. "He was my father's friend, and he has devoted his life to looking after me. He would never have let me come to London by myself."

"He was your father's native servant," Elliott countered emphatically. "The fact that he and your father established some kind of strange friendship over the years doesn't change what he is. Although I understand he's fond of you, Camelia, Zareb doesn't have the right to influence your decisions. You should never have brought him—or that ridiculous monkey or bird, either, for that matter. It only makes people talk, and I dislike it immensely when I hear the kinds of things they say."

"I'm not interested in what people say about me," Camelia returned. "I couldn't leave Zareb behind. And since I didn't know how long we were going to be here, and there was no way of making poor Oscar understand that we would be coming back, I had no choice but to bring him here, too. If I had left him in Africa, he would have tried to follow me and ended up lost."

"For heaven's sake, Camelia, he's a monkey. How on earth could he get lost in Africa?"

"Even monkeys have homes, Elliott. Oscar's home is with Zareb and me. If we had both left him, he would have felt abandoned, and he would have done everything possible to find us." Her gaze shifted to the carpet, then snapped back up to Elliott. "Why don't we go into the drawing room," she suggested with sudden brightness, grabbing his arm, "where we can sit down while we wait for our tea?"

Perplexed, Elliott glanced at the floor.

"Good God!" he swore, leaping away from the orange-and-black snake slithering up his boot. "Camelia, stay back—it could be poisonous!"

"Only a little." Camelia bent to pick up the two-and-a-half foot-long creature. "Rupert is a tiger snake, so his venom isn't particularly harmful to humans. I think he was just a little intrigued by your boots—normally, he likes to keep to himself."

Elliott regarded her incredulously. "Don't tell me you brought him here as well."

"I didn't actually intend to bring him—he slipped into one of my cases when I was packing. By the time I discovered him, we were already at sea. He hasn't been any trouble, though. As long as he's well fed and has a warm place to curl up, he's perfectly content."

"I'm delighted to hear that," Elliott managed, eyeing the snake warily.

"There now, Rupert, you stay in here with Harriet and behave yourself," Camelia instructed, laying the bulbous-eyed snake on one of the faded velvet dining room chairs. "I'll be back in a little while to give you some lunch." She closed the dining room doors behind her, then led Elliott upstairs to the drawing room.

"I'm worried about you, Camelia," Elliott began as she seated herself on the sofa. "You simply cannot go on like this much longer."

"Like what?"

"Living here in this house alone, with that wild menagerie of yours. People are talking about you. The things they are saying are not acceptable to me."

"First of all, I don't live here alone. I live with Zareb."

"Which is a problem. As an unmarried woman you shouldn't be living here with a man, even if he is just your servant. It isn't seemly."

Camelia refrained from pointing out yet again that Zareb was not her servant.

"Seemly or not, that is my living situation. You know Zareb has been taking care of me since I was a little girl, Elliott, so I'm surprised that you would think that there is anything inappropriate about the fact that he still lives with me after all these years. Nothing has changed."

"Your father died, which changes everything," Elliott insisted. "I know it's difficult for you to understand, Camelia. You've spent most of your life following your father around on his excavations, living in tents amidst dozens of natives, without a proper governess or chaperone to watch over you. And while your father was willing to indulge your desire to be with him and let you live such an inappropriate life for a young girl, now that he is gone you really need to think about your reputation."

"The only reputation that interests me is my achievement as an archaeologist. If people must talk about me, then they should focus their attention on my work, not whom I live with or what animals I brought with me from Africa. I really can't understand why those things should be of any interest to them."

"What people should do and what they actually do are two entirely different things. Whether you like it or not, your reputation as an unmarried woman also affects your reputation as an archaeologist. You came here to try to raise more funds for your expedition—but have you succeeded?"

"I have been somewhat successful. I'm not finished yet."

She did not want Elliott to know the enormous difficulty she was having raising the money she needed to continue her work. From the moment her father died, Elliott had tried to convince Camelia that she should just give up on the site and sell it. Elliott had worked the site for fifteen years alongside her father. Although his love of Africa and his loyalty to Lord Stamford had kept him there over the years, he had gradually become convinced that there was little of value there. Elliott's deep fondness for Camelia made him protective of her, and Camelia knew he did not want to see her use up what little money her father had left her, and devote what could be many years of her life, only to fail as her father had.

"How much money have you managed to raise?" he asked.

"Enough to keep us going for a while," she replied vaguely. Of course it wouldn't keep them going much longer if Camelia had to pay her workers more to keep them from deserting her, but Elliott didn't need to know that. "I expect to secure more shortly. I plan to approach the members of the British Archaeological Society at their ball this week to tell them about the excavation. I'm sure once they hear about the extraordinary new cave paintings we found last October, they will be very anxious to give their support."

"Cave paintings can't be moved to a British museum," Elliott pointed out. "The society members are more interested in supporting ventures that will give them a handsome return on their investment, which means finding objects that can actually be removed and sold to a collection."

"Which I'm certain we will find, once we get the site cleared of water and continue digging."

"Have you managed to find a pump?"

"I will."

"Have you heard anything from Trafford?"

"I had a letter from him this morning. They are still trying to take the water out by hand."

"Is that all he reported?"

"Unfortunately, a wall collapsed and one of the workers was killed—a lovely, hardworking young man named Moswen. Four others were injured."

Elliott ruefully shook his head. "Now the rest of the workers will be even more convinced that the site is cursed."

"Which you and I both know is nonsense. There's no such thing as a curse."

"It doesn't matter what you and I believe, Camelia—

what matters is what the natives think. If you can't get anyone to work the site, the land is virtually worthless." He regarded her soberly. "You should seriously consider the De Beers Company's offer to buy it, Camelia. They have made you a very reasonable offer, considering the land has not proven to be of any value."

"I believe the land is of extraordinary value, Elliott."

"In twenty years your father never came across a single diamond."

"My father wasn't looking for diamonds."

"I'm just pointing out that given your current financial situation, you are fortunate that the De Beers Company is interested in acquiring it simply because they want to expand their holdings around Kimberley."

"I've told you, Elliott, I will never sell the land to De Beers so they can eventually destroy it in their search for diamonds—whether they plan to do so next year or fifty years from now. That land is a precious window into the past, and it needs to be protected. Which is why I have to get back to it as quickly as possible. When I'm there, the workers are not so afraid. I suppose male pride makes them think if a white woman is willing to work the site, then they should be at least as brave."

"Pride has nothing to do with it. I know you hate to hear this, Camelia, but the Kaffirs see you as a source of money, nothing more. Once that money is gone, they will abandon the site and you will be left with nothing."

"Then I will dig the site by myself," Camelia insisted. "For as many years as it takes."

"You are as stubborn as you are proud. Just like your father."

"You're right. I am."

He sighed. "Very well, Camelia. Have it your way. As I

also had planned to attend the Archaeological Society ball, I will escort you."

"That's very kind of you, Elliott, but it really isn't necessary. Zareb will drive me."

"Zareb will only cause people to talk," Elliott argued. "Everywhere he goes people are drawn to your carriage because of the ridiculous sight he makes, wearing those outlandish African robes of his. You shouldn't permit it, Camelia—you must instruct him to wear something more appropriate to a servant, at least for the time he is here."

"English clothes are meant for the English."

Camelia and Elliott turned to see Zareb standing at the doorway. His expression was composed, but the taut line of his mouth told Camelia that he had not missed Elliott's reference to him as a servant.

"I do not make the mistake of thinking that being in England makes me one of them," Zareb continued, "any more than being in Africa makes an African out of you, your lordship." He set the tray he was carrying down on the table in front of the sofa. "Your tea, Tisha."

"Thank you, Zareb." Camelia doubted Elliott understood that Zareb had just insulted him. Elliott would never think any white man would want to be like an African.

Oscar leapt onto the table and snatched a ginger biscuit from a plate, knocking a pitcher of milk onto the floor in the process.

"Oh, Oscar," sighed Camelia, scooping the monkey up and drying his milky paws with a linen napkin, "must you always get into everything?"

Content to be in her arms, Oscar began to ravenously eat his biscuit.

"I must be going, anyway, Camelia," Elliott informed

her. "I hope you will reconsider my offer to take you to the ball."

"Thank you, Elliott, but I really would prefer to go in my own carriage," Camelia assured him. "I know you enjoy those kinds of affairs, but I find them tiresome. I would hate to think that I was forcing you to leave early on account of me. I'm sure you are eager to talk to the members about your new importing business here."

A hint of frustration shadowed his elegantly chiseled face. However much he would have liked to further argue the issue with her, Camelia knew he would not do so in front of Zareb. Despite all the years he had spent in South Africa, Elliott still held the rules of British society in the highest esteem.

One did not argue in front of servants. Ever.

"Very well. I will see you there."

He bent forward to kiss Camelia's hand, but the fact that it was still ink-stained and now damp with milk from Oscar's furry paws made him reconsider. Instead he opted for a small, formal bow, then followed Zareb downstairs to the front door.

Heat radiated from the heavy brass door handle as Zareb laid his hand upon it. It warmed his palm and seeped into the stiffness of his fingers, which had been aching since he had arrived in the wretched dampness of England. Something was about to happen, he realized. Something powerful.

Slowly, he opened the door.

"Good afternoon, Zareb," drawled Simon. "I'm here to see Lady Camelia."

Zareb regarded him calmly, assessing the anger emanating from him. It was powerful, but not intense enough to have caused the warming of his hand. No, the energy radiating from the disheveled white man standing before him was not attributable to his barely contained fury. There was another force embracing this peculiar looking inventor, whose tongue suggested a gentleman, yet whose attire and mannerisms betrayed a casual contempt for the trappings of his kind.

"Certainly, sir," Zareb said, opening the door wider. "Please enter."

Simon marched into the front vestibule.

Elliott took one look at his rumpled jacket, wrinkled shirt and trousers and assumed he was some sort of deliveryman. "Forgive me," he began in a polite but unmistakably patronizing tone, "but deliveries are not normally made to the front door."

Simon regarded him with curiosity. The man before him was exceptionally handsome and impeccably dressed, two attributes which for some strange reason only served to irritate him. "I'll keep that in mind the next time I'm arranging for a delivery."

Elliott frowned. "It seems I have made an error. My apologies. I am Lord Elliott Wickham," he said, attempting to mitigate his insult. "And you, sir, are...?"

"Simon Kent."

A flicker of surprise lit Elliott's gaze. "The inventor?"

At that moment Oscar bounded into the hallway, shrieked with pleasure, and scurried up Simon, planting his bony little rump firmly on his head.

Simon scowled.

"Mr. Kent!" Camelia regarded Simon in surprise as she descended the stairs. His expression was taut, which she supposed was understandable given that Oscar was now rooting through his red hair, happily looking for bugs. "I didn't expect to see you quite so soon."

Simon stared at her, momentarily unable to respond. She was wearing a simple day gown of pale green silk, which served to accentuate the extraordinary sage shade of her eyes. The gown clung to the curves of her breasts and hips like rainwater pouring across the supple bend of a fern, and a delicate frill of ivory lace trimmed the tantalizingly low scoop of her neckline. She wore no bustle, suggesting that she did not enjoy enduring the mandatory discomfort of feminine attire when she was not out in public, and her honey streaked hair was only loosely arranged on her head, giving her a charmingly soft and disarrayed look. The scent of her flooded his senses once more, that summery rain-washed fragrance of sweet grass and citrus. Heat shot through him as she met his gaze with those wide, clear green eyes, making him feel aroused and strangely off balance.

What the devil was the matter with him?

"We need to talk, Lady Camelia," he announced, manfully attempting to regain control of his reeling senses. "Now."

"About what?" asked Elliott.

"Mr. Kent is an inventor, Elliott," Camelia explained. "I went to see him yesterday to discuss a business matter."

Elliott regarded Simon with interest. "Are you planning to sell Lady Camelia a pump?"

Simon gave him a second assessing look, which did little to contest the preliminary conclusions of the first. The man was an exceptionally fine example of the species known as the pampered English gentleman, from the patrician arch of his querying brow to the impossibly glossy sheen of his expensively cobbled chestnut leather boots. Simon felt an immediate and overwhelming dislike for him, which seemed just a bit unfair, given the fact that other than mistaking him for a deliveryman, his lordship had not done much to invite his aversion.

"My apologies, Wickhip, but this matter is between Lady Camelia and me." Simon shifted his gaze back to Camelia.

"It's Wickham," Elliott corrected mildly. "And I believe Lady Camelia will tell you that as I am one of her oldest friends, she will not object to your discussing whatever you came here to discuss in front of me."

"I doubt that." Simon's blue eyes were hard and penetrating, making Camelia feel exposed and uneasy. "However, if you insist—"

"Actually, Lord Wickham was just leaving," Camelia interrupted.

She couldn't imagine why Simon was apparently so angry with her. After all, he already knew she had stolen his sketch. Perhaps she had accidentally destroyed something of great import when she had knocked over all those tables in his laboratory the previous afternoon.

"I'll see you later this week, Elliott," she said, laying her hand on Elliott's arm and guiding him to the door. "And I'll be sure to let you know of any developments— all right?" She gave him a reassuring smile.

"Very well." It was clear to her Elliott was reluctant to leave Camelia with Simon, but he knew he couldn't very well force his company upon her. "Mr. Kent." He politely nodded his head.

"Wicksted."

"It's Wickham."

"Of course." Simon was bemused by his ridiculous desire to needle him. "Forgive me."

"Good day to you, your lordship." Zareb ushered Elliott out and closed the door behind him.

"Oscar, come down from there at once," ordered Camelia, holding her arms out to the monkey.

Oscar smiled and shook his head defiantly at her.

"Is he always quite this friendly?" wondered Simon, reaching up to detach the stubborn monkey from his hair.

"Oscar likes you." Zareb nodded with approval. "It is good."

"I'm flattered," said Simon dryly. He finally managed to free the obstinate little wretch from his stinging scalp and set him firmly on the floor.

"Why don't we go upstairs to the drawing room and have some tea, Mr. Kent?" Camelia suggested.

"It is already prepared," Zareb added, trying to entice him. "With fresh ginger biscuits. They are quite good, I believe. I made them only this morning."

Camelia looked at Zareb in surprise, wondering what on earth had suddenly come over him. He had not been nearly so hospitable to poor Elliott, and Zareb had known him for years. Couldn't he sense the hostility radiating from Simon toward her?

Simon hesitated. All night anger had burned within him as he struggled to come to terms with the fact that years of his work had been completely destroyed. But he was also hungry, despite having eaten a substantial breakfast of oatmeal, kippers, sausages, and toast at his parents' London town house.

"Come, Mr. Kent," urged Zareb, gesturing up to the open doors of the drawing room.

"Very well." Simon followed Camelia, trying hard not to focus on the softly swaying movement of her hips.

"Please sit down." Camelia gestured to a threadbare chair as she seated herself upon an equally worn sofa.

"Yes, sit. Have some tea." Without bothering to ask how he took it, Zareb dumped three heaping spoonfuls of sugar into a cup and added a generous splash of milk, then filled it with tea. "And a biscuit." He held a plate before Simon.

Simon accepted the tea and glanced at the blackened lumps Zareb was offering to him. "Thank you." He took one just to be polite.

"Would you like some currant cake?" asked Zareb.

Camelia could not imagine why her old friend was making such an effort to be nice to Simon. He had not extended such a display of hospitality to anyone since they had arrived in London. Perhaps he thought Simon had changed his mind about helping her.

From the angry expression on Mr. Kent's face, she knew he was not there to offer her any assistance.

"Currant cake would be good with tea," Zareb informed Simon. "I'll get some." He hurried from the room, his robes rustling in a riot of brilliant color behind him.

There was a moment of awkward silence.

"I had not expected to see you again quite so soon," Camelia began cautiously.

"I had a rather eventful evening after you left. My home burned down."

Camelia gasped. "Oh, no—was everything destroyed?"

Her surprise seemed genuine, Simon noted. But he couldn't be sure. Some people were capable of extraordinarily skillful performances when they needed to be. Something told him Lady Camelia fell into that category. "Unfortunately, yes."

"How did the fire start?"

"I was hoping that you might be able to shed some light on that."

Her brow puckered in confusion. "Surely you don't believe I had anything to do with it."

He said nothing.

"I can assure you, at no time when I was in your laboratory did I do anything that might have started a fire. I can hardly see how I could have, since you were watching me the entire time."

"Given the fact that you managed to steal one of my sketches from me, it seems I was not watching you closely enough."

Anger flared within her. "I did not set your home on fire, Mr. Kent," Camelia informed him flatly, "What possible reason could I have for doing such a thing?"

"I made it infinitely clear that I could not make a steam pump for you because I had too many other projects demanding my attention. Today, every one of those projects has been burned to rubble, instantly wiping my agenda clean. Does that not strike you as an extraordinary coincidence?"

It was rather strange, she reflected. In South Africa such an occurrence would have been blamed on bad spirits, or the curse that she and her father had supposedly released during their excavation. Or maybe this was part of the dark wind that Zareb had warned her about.

Unease pricked her spine.

She did not believe in curses, she reminded herself firmly. Everything that happened had a logical, scientific explanation. Her father had taught her that from the time she was a little girl, and it was a lesson she had clung to fiercely over the years.

Even when she had desperately wished for a bit of good luck, or the comfort of some loving spirit watching over her.

"What I find extraordinary, Mr. Kent, is that a man of your apparent intelligence would come to such an irrational conclusion," Camelia began coolly. "When I went to you yesterday, I hoped you would be willing to provide me with a pump. But I also made it clear that I respected your work, even though I was disappointed that you would not temporarily set it aside to help me. As an archaeologist of some standing in the academic community, and as an employer who currently has a number of men dependent upon me for their livelihood, I can assure you that I would never risk my name, or the welfare of those who have come to depend upon me, by engaging in illegal activities. There is much I am willing to do to expedite my excavation. Arson and the destruction of property are not among them."

She swept regally to her feet, her back ramrod straight, her chin set high. "Now that I have been able to clarify that for you, I'm afraid I must excuse myself, as I have a number of urgent matters to attend to. I trust you can find your way to the door."

"Whatever you do, don't move," Simon managed in a low, strained voice.

Confused by the sudden pallor of his face and the alarm in his eyes, Camelia turned.

"Oh, Rupert." She sighed, plucking the fierce-looking snake off the sofa and setting him down on the carpet. "Why can't you behave yourself and stay in the dining room? I promise I'll feed you shortly."

Rupert eyed her mournfully with his bulging, lidless

eyes and curled into a brilliant orange-and-black coil at her feet.

Simon regarded her in disbelief. He inhaled a deep breath, forcing himself to relax. "Is he yours, too?"

"I don't own him, if that's what you mean. He was injured when I found him last year, and once he got better he seemed to decide he liked living with me."

"I see."

Immensely relieved that he was not going to be required to wrestle a three-foot-long snake into submission, Simon set down his cup and biscuit and studied him from a respectful distance.

"I've always been fascinated by snakes." He tried to make it sound as if the sudden appearance of the terrifying creature had not been anything out of the ordinary. "They have the most amazing strength and fluidity of movement. Is he a coral snake?"

"No—a tiger."

Simon nodded. "I should have known by the bands. Not so poisonous, then."

That was a bloody relief. Even so, if his memory served him well, tiger snakes could strike out and land a vicious bite when agitated.

"I spent some time studying snakes as a lad," he continued. "What made you decide to bring him with you?"

"He decided for me. He made his way into one of my trunks when I was packing. By the time I discovered him, Zareb and I were already at sea."

"A stowaway, then." If Simon had found a snake in his trunk, he would have slammed down the lid and bolted from his cabin, satisfied to wear only the clothes on his back for the rest of the voyage. "And Oscar?"

"Oscar could not have endured being left behind

without me and Zareb. Since he could not be made to understand when I would be returning, I had little choice but to bring him with me. I also brought my Grey Lourie, Harriet. I expect you think that's rather ridiculous of me." Her tone was slightly defensive. "Apparently most of London does."

"Families come in all shapes and sizes, Lady Camelia. Even my own." He continued to study Rupert, not moving any closer to the serpent, but not retreating from him either.

Camelia said nothing. In her research on Simon she may not have adequately noted his age, but she had managed to glean a few details about his childhood. Apparently he was a Scottish orphan who had been taken in by Haydon and Genevieve Kent, the Marquess and Marchioness of Redmond. While he had obviously fared well for himself, attaining a first-class education and becoming a respected lecturer on a number of subjects, Camelia sensed he had not been unscathed by the life he had led before. For some part of his childhood he had been alone and afraid.

As she knew only too well, those wounds might heal, but the scars remained forever.

"Why did you come here to see me?" she asked quietly. "Did you really think that I was feigning my admiration for all that you have achieved? That I was the kind of person who would selfishly destroy everything you have fought so hard to create to achieve my own ends?"

It sounded appalling when put like that, Simon realized. But while he might have entertained that thought the previous night, deep down he had known it wasn't possible. Whatever Lady Camelia's failings might have

been, it was clear to him that she was someone who loved
to discover and preserve, not destroy.

"No."

"Then why are you here?"

He continued to study Rupert, avoiding her gaze. In
truth he didn't really know why he was there. All night
long he had been overwhelmed by the grip of fury and
despair. He could start again. He understood that.
Genevieve and Haydon were, as always, unwavering in
their support of him. They had already offered to find
him a new house to lease, and Haydon was transferring
funds to his bank account that day so he would be able to
purchase whatever equipment and supplies he needed to
go forward. This was a dreadful setback, but not necessarily an insurmountable one. His sketches and drawings
were lost, but the information was still etched relatively
clearly in his mind. With a great deal of time and exceptionally hard work, he could regain what had been taken
from him.

Why, then, was he wasting time in Camelia's house,
letting monkeys riffle through his hair and contemplating the locomotion of a bloody snake?

"I suppose I'm trying to make some sense of why a
lifetime of work has just been reduced to twisted metal
and ashes," he reflected. "This was no simple accident,
Camelia. Whoever set my laboratory afire intended to destroy it—and my entire house with it."

"What makes you think that?"

"When I returned I was able to get close enough to
look in the kitchen windows. The tables I had righted
were overturned once more, and everything was scattered all over the floor. The washing machine I had built
had been destroyed, and the engine itself was knocked

onto its side. That steam engine must have weighed over five hundred pounds. It could not have been turned over by a few flames."

"But you must have had explosives in your laboratory, which you used to make your fireworks," Camelia pointed out. "Perhaps they ignited and caused an explosion, and the force of that turned the engine over."

"I never keep more than enough to make a few firecrackers, for that very reason. A few accidents in my youth taught me that potassium nitrate is not to be treated carelessly. Even if my entire inventory of gunpowder had been ignited, it would not have been enough to do more than cause a very loud bang and a fantastic amount of smoke. There is also the question of how the house itself burned."

"What do you mean?"

"When I got home, the bedrooms of the upper story were burning, and so was my laboratory, which as you know was on the lower level. Yet the main floor and the staircase had no flames—only smoke, which must have been coming up from the kitchen stairs."

"But that makes no sense," Camelia objected. "How could the bedrooms be in flames if the fire started in the kitchen and had not yet taken the staircase?"

"My thoughts exactly. The only logical answer is that someone ransacked my laboratory and set fire to it, and then decided to ignite the upper level—or perhaps there were two of them, and each one set fire to one floor. They probably realized that between the two floors, the rest of the house would take care of itself."

"Even if someone did cause the fire in your home, what makes you think it had anything to do with me? It could just as easily have been a jealous inventor who wanted to destroy everything you have achieved."

"I'm flattered you think my work might have attracted such a dedicated admirer. But as I told you, I have always been fairly free with my ideas, and not terribly organized about my patents. The idea of some demented rival destroying my laboratory so he could gain time for his own work strikes me as rather implausible."

"Maybe he wasn't just trying to compromise your work. Maybe he actually stole one of your sketches, and then ruined your lab so he would have time to complete a prototype and register a patent for whatever he stole from you."

"Then I hope he gets the tension right on that mop, or else he's in for a lot of complaints."

Camelia regarded him in exasperation. "This is not something to joke about."

"I don't think this was the work of some cake-headed inventor, Camelia. My sense is that this had to do with you." He regarded her seriously. "What did those men in the alley really want from you yesterday?"

She shrugged dismissively. "I told you, they were probably employed by a rival archaeologist who is trying to scare me away from my site."

"I know what you told me. Now I'm asking for the truth."

She met his gaze evenly. He had promised her nothing, she reminded herself. Yet as she stared into the depths of his silvery blue eyes, she sensed a faint shifting from his flat refusal to help her. As he had said, in a matter of hours every one of his projects had been destroyed. His agenda was wiped clean. Perhaps he could be convinced to help her after all.

"I have told you the truth," she insisted. "There is nothing more."

She was lying to him, Simon realized. Her brow was set in an earnest line, her sage green eyes shimmering with an enticing mixture of feminine determination, graced with the slightest touch of fragility. It was as if she were struggling to keep him from seeing the fragment of hope she was nurturing within her breast, because her pride and her independence prevented her from letting him see anything that might be perceived as weakness. It was a remarkably genuine performance, which would have easily convinced any other man. But Simon was not just any other man.

Years of fighting to survive as a beggar and a thief had seen to that.

"I have changed my mind, Lady Camelia," he announced suddenly. "I am going to build a pump for you."

Camelia regarded him in surprise. She had not expected him to change his mind quite so quickly. "Why?" she asked, wary.

He shrugged. "It will take years for me to rebuild all the inventions I was working on. Now that you have reminded me of the issues I had with that steam engine, I suppose I feel challenged to see if I can solve them. This is as good a time as any to begin."

"And you'll come with me to Africa, to make sure that it works?"

"Absolutely. I will even see to it that several of your workers are trained sufficiently that they will be able to operate it long after I have left. I am most curious to see this dig of yours, and find out what it is about your excavation that is so important it was worth those men attacking you and threatening you with death."

His tone was faintly facetious. Camelia had the distinct feeling that he was mocking her.

"I shall arrange for our passage to Cape Town on the next available steamship."

"That would be a bit premature. I need time to build the machine first."

"But you can do that in South Africa," Camelia objected. "Just bring everything you need with you and assemble it there."

"Unfortunately, it is not quite that simple. I am going to alter my design, which means some things will work and others will not. I need to be in London, where there are numerous reliable manufacturers I can trust to make pieces for me to my specifications. That will take time."

"How long?"

"I should think I would be able to build a reliable pump within a period of about eight weeks."

Camelia's expression fell. "That's too long!"

"Those relics you are searching for have presumably been buried in the earth for thousands of years. Surely it won't matter if they stay there another few months."

"But I have my workers to consider," Camelia pointed out. "At this time, all they can do is attempt to remove the water with buckets. Regardless of how little they accomplish I have to pay them for their work, and unfortunately, my funds are not limitless. To pay them for two months and have them accomplish virtually nothing will be a significant strain on my finances."

"Then send a letter instructing them to go home for eight weeks," Simon suggested. "Tell them to come back once we have arrived with the pump."

"These men come from tribes that live many miles away—sometimes hundreds of miles," Camelia told him.

"They travel for weeks or even months on foot to find work, and then they agree to stay for an established period of time, after which they are very anxious to go home to their families. They cannot just pack up and go home and then return. Couldn't you manage to build something faster?"

"If I work at it day and night, and my manufacturers are able to keep within my deadlines, perhaps I could build a pump within six weeks."

She regarded him imploringly. "Do you think if you worked even harder you might be able to do it within four?"

"It's unlikely."

"But you'll try?"

Simon sighed. "Yes. I'll try."

"Wonderful! When do we start?"

"I'll be starting tomorrow, by finding another house in which I can set up a new laboratory."

"Why don't you set it up here?" offered Camelia. "You could have either the dining room or the drawing room—or even both, if you like. We don't use them much—I rarely have visitors, and Zareb and I really prefer to eat downstairs in the kitchen."

"That's very generous of you, but somehow I don't think you want your neighbors talking about the fact that you have a strange man wandering around your house day and night."

"I don't trouble myself overmuch about what other people choose to say about me. As it is they all dislike the fact that I'm staying here with my animals, so I can't really see how your presence would make much of a difference."

Simon didn't know whether he should be insulted by

the fact that she equated his presence with that of a monkey, a bird, and a snake, or concerned that she seemed to have so little awareness of how cutting the gossip of London society could be.

"I will be able to make other arrangements for my laboratory," he assured her. "But thank you. Once I have set myself up in a new space, we will have to meet again. There are a number of things I will need to discuss with you as I work on the pump's design. As you pointed out, the harsh African environment presents some unique challenges."

"You may call upon me any time, day or night. I am very anxious to assist you in any way I can, so that we can return home as quickly as possible."

"Excellent. Good day, then, Lady Camelia." He moved to the drawing room doors, maintaining a safe distance from Rupert, then stopped. "There is just one more thing: We neglected to discuss the issue of my compensation."

"Of course, forgive me." Camelia frowned, pretending to think for a moment. "I believe yesterday we discussed five percent of my profits over two years."

"Actually, I believe by the time you had finished your extremely impressive efforts to recruit me, you had offered me ten percent over five years."

She regarded him coolly, irritated that he remembered. "Very well."

"Unfortunately, that was yesterday. Since then my circumstances have changed considerably, and therefore I am compelled to set my price at twenty percent over two years."

"I can't afford to pay you that much!"

"Actually, you are getting something of a bargain. If

you are truly on the cusp of an important discovery, then it will generate a fortune, and twenty percent will be insignificant. But if it turns out the site does not bear the riches you foresee, or if they cannot be successfully removed within two years, then you will have had my services and expertise for nothing, for I do not intend to accept a percentage of a few hundred pounds from you. In the meantime I will be devoting all my time and energy to the creation of the pump, as well as paying for all the necessary labor and materials. I think anyone would agree that the venture is far more of a risk for me than it is for you."

"He is right, Tisha." Zareb stood in the doorway, holding a small cloth package. Oscar was perched upon one broad shoulder. "You must agree."

"Fine, then," Camelia said tightly. The amount was exorbitant, but she was hardly in a position to bargain. "I accept your terms, Mr. Kent. Shall we commit them to paper?"

"Your word is good enough for me, Lady Camelia. Zareb is our witness."

"Then it is done." Zareb smiled.

"I shall call upon you in a few days, Lady Camelia, so we can go over the details of my sketches. Good day." Simon gave her a small bow.

"Here, Mr. Kent. I wrapped your currant cake so you would be able to take it with you."

"Thank you, Zareb." Simon thought the old servant was remarkably thoughtful.

"It is my pleasure. I will see you to the door."

Camelia watched as Simon followed Zareb and Oscar down the stairs to the front door. Then she scooped up

Rupert from the floor and settled back against the sofa with him curled upon her lap.

"Four weeks, Rupert," she murmured, caressing his little scaly orange head. "That will give me some time to raise some more money to keep paying the workers. Then we can finally go home."

Rupert stared back at her, silently enjoying her gentle stroking.

"It will go by quickly," Camelia promised, more to reassure herself than Rupert. "You'll see. In the meantime, why don't we go downstairs and see if we can't find you something to eat?" She draped him around her shoulders and rose from the sofa. Four more weeks of living in London.

It seemed an eternity.

"He's leavin'," Bert reported as Simon climbed into his carriage. "Come on, Stanley, we're off."

Stanley emerged from behind a tree, a fistful of greasy spiced meat and pastry dripping down his hand. "I ain't finished my pie."

"Godamighty, Stanley, I told ye not to snaffle that pie—do ye want the hen that's made it to cry beef on us?"

"I'm hungry," Stanley said innocently.

"Ye're always hungry, ye great simkin," Bert snapped. "Ye just crammed down a plate o' sugar-sops an' mash, an' ye've been lettin' off roarin' cheesers ever since. Can't ye stop stuffin' yer gob for a minute?"

"Sure, Bert." Stanley regarded him sheepishly. "Do ye want some? It's right prime, it is."

Bert glowered at the mangled mess of pie in Stanley's enormous hand. He was about to say no, just out of irritation, and make Stanley toss it on the street. After all, how was the poor clod pole ever to learn what's right and what ain't, if Bert didn't show him? Sometimes he was worse than a bloody baby, and that was the sad truth of it. The pie did smell prime enough, though, despite the fact that Stanley had made such a muck of it. Must have been nice and juicy and warm when he first nicked it. Which he never should have done, since Bert had told him plain as a pikestaff to leave it be.

"Give over," Bert muttered. "One day ye'll get nabbed by the peelers an' where will ye be then?" He shoved the remainder of the crumbling meat and pastry into his mouth.

Stanley regarded him in confusion. "In the coop—right, Bert?"

"Aye, in the coop, for Christ knows how long, an' do ye think they'll serve ye hot sausage pies an' mash when ye're there?"

Stanley frowned, considering. "They might. Lots o' people like them."

"They ain't servin' what people like in the coop," Bert told him, rolling his eyes. "'Tis all runny gruel an' sour soup with scarce more than a bone in it, an' bread so dry it breaks yer teeth when ye bite into it. Ye'd starve to death in less than a week, ye would, an' there'd be nothin' I could do to help ye, on account of I'd be starvin' as well—do ye understand?"

Stanley smiled. "Sure, Bert. I understand."

Bert stared at him in frustration, positive he didn't understand at all. How could he? The poor chub was too weak in the head to mind the ways of the world. Bert didn't know whether he'd been born that way or whether he'd had the sense knocked out of him in a brawl. He supposed it didn't really matter.

Nearly five years they'd been thick, and in that time Bert had done his best to keep Stanley with a roof over his head most nights, and enough food in his belly most days. That wasn't easy, given how much he could eat. Like feeding a bloody horse, it was. The minute Bert had a bit of brass in his pocket, Stanley's belly started groaning. At this rate, they'd be working 'til doomsday and still have nothing to show for it but the rags on their backs and a cold sausage in their hands.

Bitter frustration pulsed through him.

"When I say ye ain't to do somethin', ye must mind me—got it? That means when I tell ye not to nick a pie, ye don't, no matter what yer belly tells ye—right?" He licked his fingers.

"Right, Bert," Stanley said, anxious to please him. "Ye ain't mad at me, are ye?"

Bert sighed. "No, I ain't mad at ye. I just want ye to mind what I say."

Stanley nodded. "What are we goin' to do now, Bert? Are we goin' to follow his carriage?"

"Too late for that now, ain't it? All this time I had to waste tellin' ye to mind me, an' now his carriage is bloody gone. We've no way of knowin' what he's about now."

"Maybe he's gone home," Stanley suggested.

"Oh, sure, Stanley, that's a rare fine idea, that is. The only problem is, his home's burned to a cinder, so he can't go there now, can he?"

"Not that home," Stanley clarified. "His da's home. That carriage had a fancy crest on it, which means 'tis his da's carriage, most like. That's where we should go.

Unless ye think we should stay here an' watch her ladyship. Whatever ye think is right, Bert. Ye're the one with the brains."

"That's right, I am." Bert knit his dark brows together, considering. "We'll head over to Bond Street an' ask about in some o' the fancy shops if they know where Lord Redmond lives," he decided. "We'll explain we've a note to deliver, only we're confused about which street his house is on. Once we got the street we'll mention a number, an' they'll say 'Here now, that's wrong, it's number such an' such.' An' then we'll know where to go."

"That's a rum bite, Bert," enthused Stanley, impressed.

"It is that," said Bert, pleased with himself. "Come on, then, Stanley. The old puff guts said there'd be some extra brass in it for us if we could give 'im a full report next time we see 'im. I'm thinkin' if we can keep this job goin' a while, we'll soon have enough to get a bigger flat—an' maybe get ye yer own bed, too."

"Really?" Stanley's eyes widened. "With a feather pillow?"

"We'll see," Bert said, trying to manage his expectations. "If we stop her ladyship from goin' to Africa, who knows what the cakey old toast might pay? As long as she's here she needs watchin', an' who better to keep their peepers on her than us?"

"I like watchin' her," Stanley declared happily. "She's a real spanker."

"A spanker that's goin' to see us well breeched," Bert promised, narrowing his dark gaze on Camelia's house. "As long as we keep her penned."

CHAPTER 4

"Then I place the coin like so, wave my hand in the air, say the magic word, and—the coin is gone!" Simon wiggled his fingers to show his enraptured audience he wasn't hiding the shilling anywhere.

Byron knit his little red brows together in confusion. "You forgot to say the magic word."

"Honestly, Byron, what does it matter if Simon says it or not?" asked Frances, rolling her enormous sapphire colored eyes. At fourteen she was emerging from the last vestiges of childhood, and she was most anxious to demonstrate that she wasn't a little girl any more. "It isn't really magic—it's just a trick."

"But it's a very clever trick," Melinda declared loyally, not wanting Simon to think they didn't appreciate his gallant attempts to entertain them. Melinda was seventeen, with the same elegant cheekbones and brilliant red-gold hair that graced her mother. She bore the slender, slightly coltish demeanor of a young girl who would very shortly blossom into an exquisite young woman. "Didn't you think so, Eunice?"

"Canna see what's so grand about slippin' a bit o' brass up yer sleeve," Eunice returned as she pummeled a floury hillock of bread dough into submission. "Ye'd all be better off helpin' me make my Scotch collops," she added, tucking a strand of snowy hair back under her crisp white cap. "Miss Genevieve and his lordship will be home soon, and ye'll all be cheepin' for yer supper."

"When I was yer age I was fleecin' swells all day long, an' there's nae that ever saw so much as a penny cross my palm," boasted Oliver, gripping a tarnished silver spoon in one wizened hand while he rubbed at it vigorously with a blackened cloth. "'Course I didna skitter about waitin' to see if they'd notice they'd just been made a wee bit lighter—I was quick as a rabbit in those days, so all they'd feel was the wind on their arse. Now there's a bit o' magic for ye!" He snorted with laughter.

"Why don't ye teach the duckies how to turn one coin into three," suggested Doreen, her lean, withered face drawn even tighter as she savagely beat some thinly sliced veal with a rolling pin. "At least that would be practical."

"You mean like this?" Simon placed his right hand flat on the kitchen table, knocked upon his knuckles three times with his left hand, then raised both to reveal three shiny shillings.

"That's splendid!" squealed Byron. "Now turn them into six."

"I'm afraid three is my limit for today," Simon admitted. "Maybe next time."

"Only six?" Oliver scoffed. "On a good day I'd make two dozen coins or more—that's what I call magic!"

"That's what I call pinchin'," observed Doreen wryly.

"'Tis an art all the same, an' wee Byron here has

shown a real talent for it." Oliver's eyes crinkled with pleasure as he gazed fondly at the boy. "Maybe after dinner I'll put on my coat an' we can play pinchin' in the park. What say ye, Frances and Melinda? The last time we played, Melinda nicked my snuff box from me so nice an' quiet, I didna feel a thing."

"Aye, and his lordship had somethin' to say about it afterward when Melinda went to give him a hug and nipped his best gold watch right from his pocket without his knowin'," Eunice reminded him sternly.

"He said he didna understand why all his bairns had to be trained as pickpockets afore we was willin' to send them off in the world," added Doreen, slapping the veal slices onto a frying pan.

"Just because ye have the skill doesna mean ye need to use it," Oliver said philosophically. "Simon here has turned out all right, but if he hadna been able to steal when he needed to, the poor lad would've starved, an' that's the sad truth o' the matter."

Byron regarded his older brother with awe. "Were you really starving, Simon?"

"No," Simon assured him. "Oliver just likes to exaggerate."

Byron was only eleven—barely two years older than Simon had been when Genevieve rescued him from a filthy cell in the Inveraray jail. But his little brother had lived his entire short life safely ensconced in comfort, privilege, and unconditional love. Although Genevieve had tried her best to help her three youngest children understand that there were much less fortunate people who struggled every day to exist, eleven-year-old Byron had no real understanding of what that meant.

Simon saw no reason to enlighten him.

"Now that ye've finished yer magic, I'd like ye to squeeze those oranges for my orange cream." Eunice waved a plump, floury hand at the bowl full of oranges on the counter behind her. "I'm makin' it special tonight on account of Simon stayin' here—I know 'tis one o' yer favorites. Melinda, ye can help me peel these tatties for the pot. Frances, ye can chop those onions over there."

"What can I do?" asked Byron.

"Ye come over here an' give this silver teapot a polish with this piece o' leather," Oliver suggested. "Rub it hard 'til ye can see yer face in it."

Simon rose from the table, removed his jacket, and rolled up his sleeves. "You should have seen the lemon squeezer I made for you, Eunice—I think you would have really liked it," he said as he took a knife and began to cut the oranges in half. "You put the halved orange in a box and all the juice was extracted instantly, without any wringing or pressure on your wrist. Then the pits were strained from the liquid, and you took out a drawer and poured the juice wherever you wanted it."

Eunice looked at him in bewilderment. "Ye put the juice in a drawer?"

"A small one. It had a little spout on one end, to make pouring easier."

"An' where did the pits go?" wondered Doreen.

"They stayed in a sieve in the box."

She frowned. "Forever?"

"No, just until you cleaned them out and washed it."

"Now that's a fine idea," Oliver declared, sensing that the two women were having trouble envisioning Simon's contraption. "I canna tell ye how many times I've wished there was a machine just like that, to save me the trouble o' fishin' out the pits with a spoon."

"I'm sure 'twas a fine invention, lad." Eunice didn't sound terribly convinced as she piled her dough into a bowl and covered it with a clean cloth.

"I'll make you another one, Eunice," Simon promised as he set to squeezing the oranges on a plain glass juicer. "Then you'll understand how much better it was than this old thing."

"That old thing has served me well enough for more than twenty years," Eunice informed him. "An' 'twould serve ye well, too, if ye remembered to roll the oranges hard against the table afore ye cut them. That's what makes the juices run sweet."

Simon took the next orange and slowly rubbed it against the table. "I'd forgotten about that. I wonder if I could make something that would roll them for you?"

"Have ye any thoughts for cleanin' silver?" asked Oliver. "'Tis one job I wish could be made easier."

"I tried making a machine where you put the silver item inside covered with hartshorn paste. Then you turned a crank which caused round brushes to remove the polishing paste and tarnish."

"That sounds brilliant," said Melinda. "That means you would never have to get your hands all blackened and dirty."

"Unfortunately, it also removed most of the silver plate," Simon confessed. "I ruined more than two dozen forks and spoons before I finally gave up on it."

Oliver chuckled. "Dinna fash yerself, lad—if there's nae silver on it, there's nae reason to polish it!"

"Some things are best done by hand," Doreen reflected.

"Nae sweat, nae sweet," added Eunice, nodding.

"Still, I've grown very fond o' the tattie masher ye made for me—it smashes them 'til they're just like pudding."

"An' dinna forget about the eggbeater ye made for me last Christmas," said Doreen. "It whips the eggs so light an' fluffy, ye'd think they might float away."

"I'm sure if ye took that idea to someone in the business of makin' such things, ye'd soon have a fortune on yer hands," Oliver speculated.

"Simon doesn't want to have a fortune on his hands," Genevieve observed fondly as she entered the kitchen. "He just wants to invent."

Simon looked up and smiled at her. Although his mother was nearing fifty, she still maintained the extraordinary beauty that had overwhelmed him from the first moment he had seen her. He had been a ragged, rawboned lad of barely nine years, who had scraped by on nothing more than his quick wits and even quicker hands from the time he was about five or six. He had thought his life was over when they put him in prison. He was tough for his age, but after he had been caught and given a dozen lashes for stealing, he had felt small and broken and ready to die.

Then Genevieve had walked into his cell, with her brilliant red-gold hair and those magnificent chocolate brown eyes. She had knelt down beside him and gently laid her hand upon his cheeks and forehead, her expression filled with outrage and concern.

And for the first time in his life, he had believed that just maybe God had not forgotten about him after all.

"But he's sure to make a fortune anyway, Mummy," Byron informed her seriously. "Simon knows how to make money appear just by knocking on his hand."

"Now that's a skill I'd like to learn," Haydon joked as he joined his wife.

The Marquess of Redmond surveyed the busy, crowded kitchen with pleasure. Before he met Genevieve, he had never spent any time in his kitchen, even when he was a lad. Now he found it was one of his favorite places.

"Eunice and Doreen, whatever you are preparing smells absolutely wonderful," he said appreciatively, lifting the lid off the pot heating on the stove.

"We'll be havin' Scotch collops with onion an' sherry, baked salmon with caper sauce, tatties with peas, spinach dressed with cream, and date pudding with sticky toffee sauce an' orange cream for dessert," Eunice informed him. "I'm thinkin' that should be enough to keep yer bellies full 'til mornin'."

"I'm helping to make the potatoes," Melinda told her father.

"And I'm chopping onions," said Frances.

"Then I'm sure supper will be even more delicious than usual. What are you up to, Byron?"

"I'm polishing this teapot," Byron informed his father seriously. "Can you see yourself in it?"

Haydon took the smeary-looking teapot in his hands. "Indeed I can," he assured him, gently ruffling his son's hair. "Well, Simon, you will be happy to know that as of tomorrow you will be back in business inventing things in your own laboratory."

Simon regarded him with excitement. "Did you get the lease on that house we looked at yesterday?"

Genevieve smiled. "Yes."

"The owner was a bit hesitant when he learned we were taking it for you," Haydon reflected. "Unfortunately, it seems most of London has heard about your house burning down."

Simon had known the fire would make it difficult for him to find a house, which is why he had asked Haydon to arrange the lease for him. "Did you have to offer to pay him more?"

"A little."

"I'm sorry, Haydon. Whatever the amount is, I'll pay you back just as soon as I'm able."

"I don't want you to worry about the money, Simon. Genevieve and I just want you to have a place where you are comfortable and can concentrate fully on your work. I know the loss of your laboratory has been a serious setback for you, but hopefully you will be able to recover from it quickly."

"Jack has told me he's very anxious for you to come up with a better steam turbine for him to try in one of his ships," Genevieve added. "He's trying to make all of his routes even faster, and with the right engine, his shipping company will be able to expand its market and take over even more of the routes from his competitors."

"Jack's engine will have to wait a bit," Simon told her. "I have another project I'm working on at the moment that I have to finish first."

"Is that the clothes-washin' machine you were telling me about?" Eunice asked, curious.

"No, that is going to have to wait as well. I have been approached by Lady Camelia Marshall to build her a steam-powered pump."

Oliver frowned. "Ye mean for fillin' the bath?"

"No. Lady Camelia is an archaeologist. She needs a pump to clear the site she is working on of water."

"Isn't that Lord Stamford's daughter?" asked
Genevieve.

"You've heard of her?"

"Yes. She has only been in London a short while, but
she has already commanded quite a bit of attention."

"I can well imagine that," said Simon wryly.

"What kind of attention?" demanded Eunice, wondering if she should disapprove.

"The kind of attention a beautiful, intelligent, unmarried woman is bound to attract if she goes about unescorted, trying to raise money for her dig in South
Africa."

Oliver drew his wiry brows together, perplexed. "Is
that all?"

Doreen snorted, unimpressed. "That's nothin' com-
pared to what the lassies in this family have done. Not
that I want to hear about you lassies gettin' into any
trouble, mind," she added, casting a warning look at
Melinda and Frances. "Yer mother an' Annabelle, Grace,
an' Charlotte have done quite enough already," she finished, referring to their older sisters.

"Lady Camelia is not only renowned for the fact that
she goes about on her own," Genevieve reflected. "She is
something of a curiosity because she travels with an
African servant who dresses in very flamboyant robes,
and usually takes her pet monkey with her."

Oliver slapped his knee, amused. "Now that's a lass
with spirit!"

Byron regarded his father suspiciously. "You told me I
couldn't have a monkey because it was against the law to
keep one for a pet."

Haydon glanced at Genevieve for help.

"Lady Camelia probably has some sort of special

permit," Genevieve quickly improvised, "because the monkey is only here temporarily. I'm sure when she returns to South Africa she will be taking it with her."

"She will," Simon affirmed. "Along with her bird and her snake."

"Can I have a snake?" Byron asked his father excitedly.

Haydon shrugged. "Ask your mother."

"I don't think a snake would make a terribly good pet," Genevieve objected, frowning at her husband. "You can't play with it, and it isn't warm or cuddly."

"But you *can* play with it," Byron insisted stubbornly. "You can build an enormous tower of blocks and then put it inside, and let it be the horrible serpent fighting to get free of the castle. You can also wear it around your neck—or you can let it loose and then play hide-and-seek."

"Aye, an' the next thing I know 'tis curled up in my bed an' I've dropped dead from fright," muttered Doreen. "Better for ye to get a nice, quiet cat, which will be good for catching mice."

"Snakes eat mice," Byron pointed out.

"I'm nae havin' a snake slitherin' around my kitchen searchin' for mice," Eunice said flatly.

"Fine, then," he huffed. "What about a lizard? They don't slither."

Oliver scratched his head. "The lad has a point."

"Where did you meet Lady Camelia, Simon?" asked Genevieve, trying to change the subject.

"She came to see me the other day, because she had read about my work on steam engines," Simon replied. "She offered to pay me to build a pump for her, and I agreed. Oliver, would you mind driving me over to the new house first thing in the morning? I'm anxious to get my lab set up as quickly as possible."

"Doreen and I canna leave 'til after we've cleaned up the breakfast dishes an' set the house in order," Eunice interjected. "If that doesna suit ye, Ollie, ye'll have to come back for us."

"We'll be packed and ready to leave by ten o'clock at the very latest," added Doreen.

Simon regarded them in confusion. "Packed?"

"Aye—ye didna think we'd be leavin' ye to clean and set up yer new house all by yerself, did ye?"

"That's very kind of you," he quickly assured them. "But it really isn't necessary for you to sleep there. I'm certain you'll be much more comfortable staying here—and Haydon and Genevieve will need you tomorrow night."

"Actually, Haydon and I are planning to return to Scotland with the children tomorrow," Genevieve told him. "We only stayed on here a few extra days because we wanted to be sure we had found you a place. And since Lizzie and Beaton will be back tomorrow from visiting their families," she added, referring to the housekeeper and butler who lived at their London home, "Oliver, Eunice, and Doreen have very kindly offered to stay in London with you, to help you get your new home organized." She smiled fondly at the elderly trio. "While we will miss them, we do have enough staff at home to keep things running relatively smoothly until they return."

"I'm goin' to make sure ye eat enough, lad," Eunice informed Simon flatly. "Ye look like nae but skin and bone. 'Tis time to fatten ye up with some lovely haggis an' sticky toffee pudding."

"An' I want to see ye're sleepin' on a real bed with clean linens," added Doreen, "instead of falling asleep in a chair or on the table like ye've been known to do. I'll also see that yer clothes are kept neat an' pressed. Ye look like ye just dragged yerself in from a gale."

"I'll just be makin' sure ye dinna burn yer new house down," Oliver finished baldly. "An' come night, I'll be blowin' out the lamps an' hidin' the matches—do ye hear?"

Simon regarded Haydon helplessly.

"Don't look at me—this is Genevieve's idea."

"It's just until you get settled, Simon," Genevieve told him gently.

Ever since he had arrived at their house in the middle of the night several days earlier, Genevieve had been deeply concerned about him. Although Simon had insisted that the fire was caused by an unattended candle, and promised that he would take greater care in the future, Genevieve was worried that such an accident might occur again. Next time he might not be so lucky. She knew Simon became extremely distracted when he worked, often forgetting to eat, or sleep, or even to step outside and take a breath of fresh air to clear his lungs. He seemed pale to her, pale and somewhat agitated, which was how he often got when he was working on one of his inventions. She didn't like the fact that he insisted upon living alone, even though he assured her he preferred it that way. She and Haydon had offered to hire a servant for him countless times, so that they could at least know that he had food in his house and someone to talk to now and again. But Simon always refused, insisting he couldn't work when there were people around to distract him.

"Eunice, Oliver, and Doreen aren't quite ready to go back to Scotland yet, and they find there just isn't that much for them to do at home anyway," Genevieve continued, trying to make it sound as if it was really for their benefit that she was suggesting this. "So it makes sense for them to stay with you for a while, and help you to get your home organized."

"Ye'll like havin' us with ye, lad," Doreen assured him.

"I'll prepare all yer favorite dishes," Eunice promised, setting a plate of warm shortbread in front of him.

"An' I'll keep ye from burnin' yer house down." Oliver's eyes twinkled with amusement.

Simon sighed. "You'll stay only until the house is organized?"

"O' course, lad."

"Once the kitchen is to my likin' an' I've managed to put a bit o' meat on ye, I'll be on the first train back to Inverness," Eunice added.

"The minute yer clothes are washed an' pressed an' the house is clean, I'll be gone, too," Doreen promised.

"Very well." Simon took a piece of shortbread and bit into it.

"Shouldna take more than a couple o' months at the very most."

Simon choked. "A couple of months?"

"Dinna fash yerself, lad," Oliver said, whacking him hard on the back. "I promise ye, after a day or two ye'll scarce even know we're there."

If one more person told her how much they admired her for her dedication to her work, she would throttle them.

Instead Camelia smiled and tried her best to maintain

an expression of ladylike calm, or at least some variation of what she thought ladylike calm might look like. Occasionally she glanced at the women crowding the stifling ballroom, searching for some hint as to how she was supposed to act at this spectacularly tedious affair. The young girls swirling gracefully upon the ballroom floor all bore the same vacuous expression, like beautiful china dolls with their lips painted into taut little bows. The other unmarried women standing in clusters around the dance floor waved their fans and fluttered their eyelashes at the nervous young men brave enough to attempt a conversation with them.

Some of the girls looked as if they wanted to bolt, and rightly so, Camelia thought. One only had to look at the wretched assortment of gangly-legged, bran-faced young suitors around them to understand. A faltering dance or two, a sickly cup of tepid punch and a plate of stringy chicken, and the next thing they knew their mamas would be declaring it a match.

She turned her attention back to the droning voice of Lord Bagley, eternally grateful that she was well past the age of eighteen, when some of her father's friends had tried to convince him that he needed to find her a husband.

Fortunately, her darling father had not believed his only child needed to be married off the instant she came of age. And since Camelia had assured him that she had no interest in marriage, but wanted to be working alongside him, the matter had been swiftly put to rest.

"... and then we packed them on a ship and sent them on to the British Museum, where they have been the very core of its Greek Antiquities Collection ever since," finished Lord Bagley, triumphantly running his fat, gloved knuckle underneath the yellowing gray swath of his moustache. "I told your father then that he should have come with me, but he always was too stubborn for his own good. Said he believed there were extraordinary riches to be found in Africa, and he was the man to find them." He chuckled and shook his head, as if there was something marvelously amusing about Lord Stamford's devotion to his work in Africa.

"He was right." Camelia disliked immensely the way Lord Bagley was dismissing her father's work.

"Certainly—as long as he was talking about diamonds and gold," Lord Bagley agreed. "But your father wasn't talking about minerals. The last time we spoke, some six months before he died, he did nothing but complain about the big mining companies."

"He said they were destroying the land," Lord Duffield added. A thin, dour-looking man of about sixty, he wore what little remained of his graying hair combed over in a thin mesh across his liver-spotted scalp. "He insisted that if they were allowed to continue they would completely destroy Africa."

"He was right about that, too," Camelia insisted. "Tell me, Lord Duffield, have you ever seen firsthand the devastation wrought on the earth by the process of diamond mining?"

"Mining is a messy business," he returned dismissively, absently patting down a few stray strands of his hair. "I'm afraid that's unavoidable."

"Surely you must agree, my dear, that diamonds have put Africa on the map," Lord Gilby added, stroking the fastidiously trimmed point of his wiry gray beard.

"Africa was on the map for millions of years before that wretched white pebble was found near the banks of the Orange River barely eighteen years ago," Camelia replied evenly.

"But what was it?" Lord Pendrick twisted his fleshy, alcohol-flushed face into a scowl. "A barren, miserable piece of cracked earth and rock, peopled only by ignorant, naked savages, wild beasts, and those ridiculous Dutch Boers. Nobody cared about Africa until the diamonds were discovered—it was wild, uncivilized, and virtually uninhabited."

Lord Duffield nodded vehemently. "Absolutely right."

"Now, thanks to the mining, they are laying railroads and telegraph wires, building towns, and establishing governments. I've heard they are even installing electricity at Kimberley, where the biggest mine is."

"They are trying to bring some sort of civilization to the place—and they'll do it, too, as long as they can get those savages to get up and do an honest day's work." Lord Gilby laughed, making it clear he believed such a feat was nearly impossible.

"It is difficult to get natives to work when they haven't been raised with a proper Christian work ethic," reflected Lady Bagley, the abundant folds of her face nearly swallowing up her pious little eyes. "I'm afraid they would rather sit around in the sun all day and do nothing."

Camelia clenched her fists, preparing to let the ignorant, patronizing group before her know just what she thought of their disgusting bigotry. She felt Elliott move a little closer to her, not quite touching her, but making his reassuring presence felt all the same. He was trying to help her keep her temper under control, she realized. Elliott had always been far more adept at playing this game than either she or her father, and he knew it. She inhaled a shallow breath, which was all her painfully tight corset would allow, and fought to calm her anger. Nothing would be gained if she launched a scathing attack on her audience. She would only succeed in insulting them and alienating the members of the British Archaeological Society, thereby destroying any possibility of eliciting support from them.

If she couldn't manage to raise more contributions, she had no hope of seeing her father's precious dream realized.

"South Africa is a beautiful country that is currently undergoing some extremely exciting developments," Elliott began, smiling as he smoothly shifted the conversation onto less treacherous ground. "In the fifteen years I worked alongside Lord Stamford I came to appreciate all of its riches, however simple some of them may be. Lord Stamford was convinced Africa held the key to the history of humanity, and I believe he may have been right."

"He was right," Camelia insisted. "It is just a matter of time before we prove it. The site we are excavating has already revealed hundreds of fascinating artifacts that I believe date back thousands of years. I'm certain within the next few months we will find even more pieces of major significance."

"Really?" Lord Bagley regarded her curiously over the rim of his brandy glass. "Just what, exactly, is it that you are about to find, Lady Camelia?"

Camelia opened her mouth to answer, then stopped. Despite his casual demeanor, a sudden intensity had flared in Lord Bagley's eyes, causing a prickle of unease to creep along her spine.

Stay out o' Africa, unless ye want to see more o' yer precious workers snuff it.

Was Lord Bagley the man who had hired those two ruffians to frighten her? she wondered. It was certainly possible. Lord Bagley was an esteemed archaeologist with a long and distinguished career, but he was not the kind of man who would devote years of his life to digging in the earth with no guarantee of finding anything. His lordship's approach had always been to simply take what was already there, even if that meant carving up a beautifully situated temple or knocking down some glorious sculpture so it could be boxed up and shipped to the British Museum. It had been years since Lord Bagley's last find, Camelia reflected. And despite his professed scepticism of her father's work, he had always been extremely eager to talk to Lord Stamford about the progress of his African dig when her father went to London.

Had her father managed to actually convince Lord Bagley of his site's extraordinary importance before he died?

"I'm convinced we will find more artifacts illustrating the rich and ancient history of the African people," Camelia replied vaguely as she held his gaze. "Perhaps there will even be some evidence to support Mr. Darwin's theory regarding the evolution of the species."

"I'm afraid I find this idea that we all came from apes as distasteful as it is ridiculous." Lady Bagley flapped her ostrich-feather fan vigorously over her enormous, diamond-draped bosom as she concluded, "Everyone knows man was created by God."

"From what I understand of it, Mr. Darwin leaves open the possibility that God created apes first, then watched over them as they gradually changed into human beings," Lord Duffield said. "It took thousands of years."

"That is absurd," Lady Bagley countered. "If God wanted human beings on the earth, why would He start by making apes and then changing them into humans? He has the power to make whatever He wants, and that is exactly what He did, by creating Adam and Eve."

"There are many things about how we came to be where we are today that we simply do not understand, Lady Bagley," Elliott diplomatically pointed out. "As archaeologists, it is our mission to ask questions and keep searching, to try to put together some of the many pieces of that puzzle."

"If mankind truly began in Africa, as Mr. Darwin claims, then it begs the question: What on earth have those Negroes been doing all these thousands of years?" demanded Lord Gilby.

Lord Bagley nodded in agreement. "Why do we not see any great buildings, or splendid tombs, or spectacular works of art, like those left by the ancient Egyptians and Greeks and Romans? Where are the accomplishments of so many years of existence?"

"The people of Africa have no need to aggrandize themselves with the construction of enormous pyramids and temples," Camelia explained, struggling for patience. "Their spiritual beliefs are inextricably tied to the land and the animals, which means they believe that when a person dies their spirit remains part of the land around them. They see no need for elaborate burial rituals or gravesites. As for the construction of permanent dwellings, this makes little sense in a nomadic society. The land and weather can be harsh, forcing the tribes to move on when the need for food becomes great."

"Or they were all just too lazy to build anything of import," quipped Lord Duffield.

"They didn't have the intelligence," asserted Lord Bagley. "Not their fault, really. There are scientific studies proving it is just a matter of brain size."

"And tell me, Lord Bagley, just how big exactly are we to assume your brain is?" Camelia's tone was acrid. "I only ask because I'm not aware that you have built anything of particular note in your lifetime."

"Camelia—" Elliott began in a warning tone.

"I'll have you know, Lady Camelia, that I am one of the major archaeological contributors to the Greek and Roman Antiquities Collection of the British Museum," Lord Bagley huffed, insulted. "I am responsible for the installation of an entire Greek temple within the museum, which is widely regarded as one of the collection's most important pieces. My work in the field of archaeology is, as I'm sure every member here will agree, of foremost significance."

"You went to Italy and Greece and hacked down some magnificent temples and works of art and carted them away before anyone had the sense to try to stop you," Camelia retorted. "Were you not just tearing down what others had built?"

Appalled, Elliott moved even closer to her. "What Lady Camelia is trying to say is—"

"I know what Lady Camelia is trying to say," Lord Bagley assured him, his chalky, deeply lined face flushed with indignation. "And I must say, I find her comments to be not only ill-informed, but extremely offensive."

Camelia opened her mouth to retort that she found his comments about the African people to be equally offensive, but Elliott was now squeezing her hand, imploring her to be silent.

"Don't let it be said the Lady Camelia doesn't share her father's passion for a rousing debate!" he declared, laughing heartily. "Lord Stamford never cared particularly which side he argued—so long as it was a direct challenge to whatever point I was trying to make. I can see that his daughter is the same way—aren't you, Lady Camelia?"

His face was a carefully contrived mask of amusement. Beneath the playful merriment in his dark brown eyes, Camelia could see he was pleading with her to stop insulting her host and go along with Elliott's explanation.

She returned his gaze evenly, unwilling to apologize for her comments. She detested the puffed-up little group of arrogant ladies and gentlemen around her, all of whom were so thoroughly convinced of their own superiority. She wanted to lash out at them, telling them in no uncertain terms what she thought of their ugly ignorance and bigotry.

Still smiling, Elliott raised an expectant brow.

Apologize, he instructed her silently. *Now.*

Frustration welled within her. She needed the support of these people, she realized. Without their funding or endorsement, however grudgingly it was given, she couldn't continue her work. It was that simple.

And that infuriating.

"I am like my father," Camelia murmured, trying her best to sound somewhat contrite. "Sometimes, in the heat of the moment, I'm afraid I may go too far." She regarded her audience impassively.

There was a moment of strained silence.

"There now, my dear, no apology is necessary," Lord Bagley assured her.

Good, because you aren't getting one. She regarded Lord Bagley innocently.

"No doubt things are somewhat different for women in South Africa," Lady Bagley added, as if she were grappling for some kind of excuse for Camelia's outrageous behavior. "I suppose because it is such a young country. I can't imagine living in such a hot, wild place."

You wouldn't last a day there, Camelia assured her silently. *You would shrivel up in the sun or be eaten by a ferocious animal.* She smiled, taking perverse pleasure in the thought.

Misinterpreting the nature of Camelia's smile, Lady Bagley smiled back.

"If you will excuse us, I have promised to show Lady Camelia the gardens," Elliott said, eager to remove Camelia from the group now that a brittle calm had been restored. "I understand they are simply magnificent."

"Oh, they are indeed," enthused Lady Bagley. "It is said that our rose garden is one of the finest in London!"

"Then I am most anxious for Lady Camelia to see it." Elliott offered Camelia his arm, which she took. "Excuse us." He bowed slightly, then quickly led Camelia away.

"Young Wickham is in for a surprise if he thinks he can tame that one," remarked Lord Bagley after they were gone.

"Nothing wrong with the girl having a bit of spirit," remarked Lord Duffield appreciatively. "Even if her arguments are totally ridiculous."

"A bit of spirit is fine, but Lady Camelia has gone completely wild," fretted Lady Bagley, briskly waving her fan over herself. "Her father should never have permitted her to go to live with him in Africa after her mother died. He should have put her with relatives in England,

and then arranged a marriage for her the minute she came of age. It's shocking for a young, unmarried woman to be working on a dig in the middle of Africa surrounded by dangerous beasts and naked native men."

"She won't be doing it much longer," her husband assured her. "She claims to be on the brink of some important find, but everyone knows the only things of any importance to be found in Africa are diamonds and gold. Unless she can find some of that, and quickly, she'll be forced to abandon this fool-headed dream of her father's."

"How is it that she has managed to go on for as long as she has?" wondered Lord Pendrick.

"Stamford left her a modest inheritance, along with a fair amount of debt," Lord Gilby explained. "Some members of the society have generously forgiven their loans to him. A few have even given her money over the last little while, out of respect for her father's memory. Unfortunately, I'm afraid their sense of charity is wearing thin."

"It's well known she's had trouble at her site, though she doesn't like to admit it." Lord Duffield stroked the tip of his beard as he added, "A few of her workers have been killed in accidents, and many have fled. I understand the site is flooded from all the rain, and she can't get it pumped out. The natives believe the land is cursed."

"The natives always believe their land is cursed," Lord Bagley scoffed impatiently. "That is part of their ignorance. If I stopped excavating every time someone told me about some idiotic curse or other, I'd never have discovered anything."

"Quite right, dear," agreed Lady Bagley. "But I think

you must agree, it is different for a young woman. Lady
Camelia should abandon the site at once."

"I know young Wickham is praying she'll come to her
senses soon and sell the land," reflected Lord Pendrick.

"Apparently the De Beers Company has made her an
offer, although I can't see what earthly use the place is to
them." Lord Duffield shook his head. "There's never
been so much as a diamond chip found there."

"They're trying to consolidate their holdings around
Kimberley," Lord Gilby speculated. "As long as they own
it, no one else can do anything with it."

"The land may not be worth anything now, but thirty
or forty years from now, who knows?" Lord Pendrick
added. "I suppose the De Beers Company reasons that
even if there aren't any diamonds to be found, one day it
may be useful just to have it for farming or housing."

Lord Bagley laughed. "That's an extraordinarily long-
term investment. You wouldn't catch me putting money
into something with such a faint hope of a return. I like
to know that I'll be getting something back long before
I'm too old to enjoy it."

"Then let us hope that Lady Camelia comes to her
senses quickly, before she completely bankrupts herself," mused Lady Bagley.

"I'm sure she'll come around before long, my dear.
Cursed or not, if she cannot pay her workers, then she
will have to sell." Lord Bagley paused to take a sip of his
brandy before cryptically adding, "It is that simple."

"You shouldn't have spoken to Lord Bagley like that,
Camelia," Elliott admonished as he led her down a path
of crushed cream-colored gravel. "You offended him."

"He deserved to be offended," Camelia returned heatedly. "They all did. Their comments about the African people were disgusting. Did you really expect me to just stand by and let them say those things?"

"I know it is difficult for you, Camelia, but you have to learn that sometimes it is better to say nothing," Elliott said. "You won't change their opinions by challenging them the way you did, but you will insult them, which will only make them less apt to want to help you. And since you need their help, you have to be careful in how you act around them."

"I don't need their help so much that I have to tolerate listening to them denigrate an entire race of people who work harder in one day than most of the people in that ballroom do during the course of an entire year."

Elliott sighed. "Have you managed to secure any contributions so far this evening?"

"Lord Cadwell indicated he would be willing to give me something. He was a good friend of my father's, years ago."

"Did he say how much?"

"Not precisely—but I'm sure it will be a generous amount. He seemed to be very interested when I described the latest bones we have found, and of course he is quite keen to learn more about the rock paintings."

"Any others?"

"Not so far."

He regarded her with grim resignation.

"The evening isn't over yet, Elliott."

"No, it isn't, Camelia, but surely you must see that there seems to be a pervasive unwillingness on behalf of the society to continue its support of your father's work."

"They are just somewhat reluctant to give their

money to a woman," Camelia argued. "I have to work on convincing them that the fact that I am a woman is of no consequence—what matters is the importance of the site itself."

"It's more than that, Camelia, and you know it. Even when your father was alive, he was finding it increasingly difficult to convince people to invest in his work. Despite his enthusiasm and dedication, wherever he went, he never managed to discover anything of great consequence."

"This time is different. Pumulani is going to be of vital importance."

"You can't possibly know that for certain, Camelia. Your father and I worked on Pumulani for fifteen years before he died, and you have been working tirelessly on it for six months since. All we ever managed to find were some bones, beads, a few primitive tools, and the rock paintings, which, although interesting, hardly constitute a major archaeological find—at least in the minds of the Society," he quickly qualified, seeing she was about to argue.

"There is more there, Elliott," Camelia insisted. "I know you got discouraged after Father died, which is why you decided to pursue establishing your exporting business instead. I don't blame you for that."

"My leaving Africa was not just a case of being discouraged, Camelia," Elliott objected. "You more than anyone know I loved living and working at Pumulani, regardless of how much or how little we found. I went to Africa by choice, against my entire family's objections, because I loved archaeology, and because I believed in your father and wanted to learn from him. And the years I spent there were incredible. Unfortunately, my own father's death has left me with other responsibilities—responsibilities which I simply cannot meet without a steady source of income. Our lives have changed, Camelia." He gently laid his hand over her arm as they walked. "And even though it is difficult, we must accept those changes and move on."

"I truly believe there is something vital waiting to be discovered at Pumulani, Elliott," Camelia told him earnestly. "If I can just hold on long enough, I will find it."

"The best thing you could hope for is to find diamonds there," he mused. "Then the De Beers Company would offer you even more for the land than they already have. As it is, they are just trying to acquire as much land around the Kimberley mine as they can, as a way of protecting their interests." He paused a moment before quietly adding, "You really ought to give their offer serious consideration."

"I will never sell to the De Beers Company, or to any other of the mining companies," Camelia vowed. "That land is a precious archaeological link to the past, which must be protected and preserved. I will not permit anyone to start digging and blasting away at it with dynamite until it is a great, ugly pit, like the horrible hole they have made at Kimberley."

"But what if we have already exhausted the site?" Elliott argued. "I know your father dreamed there was a great burial chamber to be found there, but there is no evidence to suggest such a chamber actually exists, and even if it did, it probably only holds a few disintegrating bones and some broken pieces of shell. It isn't worth bankrupting your entire life for such a find, Camelia." His voice softened as he moved closer to her. "It isn't worth giving up your chance for a real home, with a husband and children, here in England."

"England is not my home," Camelia protested. They had wandered into one of the pretty hedged "rooms" in the garden, and Camelia now found herself with a dense wall of green at her back. "Africa is."

"England could be your home," Elliott insisted, his voice low and coaxing. "I know you find it strange here, but eventually you would learn to like it. And I promise you, I would do everything within my power to make you happy, if you would only let me." He reached out and gently placed his hands on her shoulders, drawing her closer.

"In all the years we have known each other, I don't think I have ever seen you so sad, Camelia, and it pains me. All I want is for you to be happy again—the way you used to be when I would bring you a new book from Cape Town, or a special dagger that you had never seen before."

Camelia gave him a wistful smile. "It isn't that simple anymore, Elliott. I'm not that same carefree young girl who can be distracted for hours with a new book or knife—even if it comes from you. I'm an archaeologist in charge of a flooded dig in the middle of South Africa, with dozens of workers dependent upon me for their livelihood, and a score of debts that I am fighting to keep from swallowing up everything I own."

"Then let me help you find a way out of this mess," Elliott pleaded. "I know once you set your mind to something you hate to let go—you've always been that way, and I've always admired you for it—but it hurts me to see you struggling so to keep your father's dream alive."

"It is my dream also, Elliott," Camelia reminded him. "My father and I shared the same vision."

"Your father was a man—however much you hate to hear it, it was different for him. You cannot spend your life living in filthy, dust-filled tents in the middle of nowhere, surrounded by dozens of natives, scratching away at the ground looking for bones and stone tools. You belong here, in London, living in a magnificent home, raising children and playing hostess to the cream of British society."

"Somehow I don't think the cream of British society would appreciate my attempts to play hostess," she countered. "I'd serve them all a heavy supper of roasted antelope and plantain pudding, all the while arguing that humans come from apes while Oscar, Harriet, and Rupert leapt, flew, and slithered over and under the dining room table. I doubt anyone would want to visit me after that!" She laughed.

"Then they are all fools." Elliott reached out and brushed a wayward lock of hair off her cheek.

Camelia regarded him in confusion. His fingers lingered upon her skin, his touch gentle, yet filled with a masculine possessiveness she had never sensed in him before. In that instant she was aware of something shifting between them, quietly yet absolutely.

Holding her gaze steady, Elliott began to lower his head toward hers. "You belong with me, Camelia." His lips were barely brushing against her mouth as he huskily finished, "You always have."

Camelia stood frozen, her breath caught in her throat, her heart pounding like a trapped bird against the tightly corseted cage of her ribs. Elliott's lips pressed against her mouth, warm, firm, dry. His hands were rest-

ing upon her shoulders, his hold tender but insistent.
There was restraint in the kiss, she could sense that even
as he increased the pressure of his mouth slightly, trying
to elicit some sort of response from her.

A swirl of emotions eddied through her. Elliott was an
old and beloved friend, who had been a part of her life
since she was thirteen years old. From the moment he
had arrived in Africa as a handsome young man of
twenty-one, Camelia had adored him. Filled with energy,
intelligence, and determination, Elliott had seemed wonderfully independent and daring to Camelia—a viscount's son who had brazenly defied his father's wishes
and left England to pursue his love of archaeology. For
years a flame of innocent desire and admiration had
burned brightly for him in her utterly inexperienced
heart. There had even been a brief moment in which she
had fantasized about one day marrying him. But Camelia
was not a little girl anymore. She was a woman, and her
feelings for Elliott had long ago faded into a warm and
comfortable friendship. Elliott was part of her family. She
cared for him deeply, but she didn't belong to him. She
didn't belong to anyone.

Did he really believe she could leave Africa and live in
England with him as his wife?

His kiss grew harder and more insistent.

The evening air was suddenly thick and hot, just as
the air in the ballroom had been stifling. It was always
like that in London. Elliott would put her in a dark,
dusty, velvet-choked house, in which she would be expected to raise children and manage servants and make
decisions on ridiculous, impossible things like draperies
and menus and gowns. He would never let her return to
Africa, except perhaps for a brief visit every few years,

and after she had children, he would likely put an end to even that. She couldn't do it, she realized, feeling as if she couldn't breathe. She knew nothing of children and fashion and entertaining, but she knew enough about herself to know that she would wither and die if she were forced to stay in England and play the role of some man's wife. She flattened her hands against his chest, trying to push away from him, but he misunderstood her touch and drew her closer, his mouth opening as he deepened his kiss.

"Sorry to interrupt," drawled a low, faintly mocking voice. "I didn't realize you were engaged."

Startled, Camelia shoved herself away from Elliott and stumbled back, to see Simon regarding her with what appeared to be amusement.

"Mr. Kent," she managed breathlessly, trying hard not to sound like a woman who had just been in the throes of some sort of romantic kiss.

Simon studied her, taking in the scarlet swath of her evening gown, which dipped tantalizingly low around the ivory skin of her shoulders. Her sun-streaked hair was drifting in playful strands along the column of her neck and into the pale swell of her breasts, leading him to wonder if she ever managed to secure it properly with pins, or if there was something particular about those silky strands that simply defied constraint. Her mouth was drawn into an embarrassed coral line, the lips flushed but not swollen, suggesting that whatever had been taking place between her and Wickham had not been going on for very long.

He felt a stab of satisfaction that he had interrupted them, although he couldn't imagine why that should make any difference to him. After all, Lady Camelia was a grown woman, who was certainly entitled to make her own decisions about whom she kissed. Nevertheless, the anticipation he had felt as he had rushed over to the Archaeological Society's ball to find her had been shattered, leaving him feeling hollow and a bit irritated.

"What the devil are you doing here, Kent?" demanded Elliott, annoyed that his moment alone with Camelia had been ruined.

"I have some drawings for you to look at, Lady Camelia," Simon said, his gaze still fixed on her. "I thought you would want to see them as quickly as possible."

Camelia stared back at him, transfixed. Simon was taller than Elliott, she realized, somewhat surprised that she had not noticed this before. He was dressed in a wrinkled day coat, waistcoat, and shirt, and although he had actually managed to wrap a tie around his neck, it was hopelessly floppy and uneven, suggesting that he had put it on in a great hurry, as a last minute addition to his utterly rumpled ensemble. The loose waves of his red-gold hair were curling slightly against his shoulders, which seemed far broader than Camelia had previously realized, and while his trousers seemed to be of a good fabric and cut, they had long ago lost whatever pressing they might once have enjoyed. His strong, lean hands were gloveless and generously ink-stained, indicating that he had been working for hours upon the sheaf of papers he held, and some of the ink had seeped into the white of his shirt cuffs. A powerful, relaxed confidence emanated from him as he stood there staring at her, which was rather extraordinary given the inappropriateness of his attire and the fact that he was completely disheveled. It was clear that Simon Kent didn't particularly care what people thought about what he was wearing.

"You can't just come charging in here because you happen to want to see Lady Camelia," Elliott informed him tersely. "This party is only for people with invitations."

"I'm sure I probably had an invitation, somewhere," Simon reflected, shrugging. "It must have been lost in the fire. I'm afraid my house burned down a few nights ago. Surely you must have heard about that?"

"But you aren't dressed properly," Elliott pointed out, wholly uninterested at that moment in Kent's problems. "Guests are required to wear evening clothes."

"I'm sorry, Wickhip, but I'm afraid I don't have time to stay and dance," Simon returned amiably. "I just need to have a word with Lady Camelia, and then I'll leave both of you to get back to doing whatever it was you were doing."

"We weren't doing anything," Camelia hastily assured him, embarrassed but also profoundly grateful that Simon had arrived when he did. "What was it that you wanted to ask me?"

Moonlight was spilling over her in a veil of silvery light, turning her sun-kissed skin into the palest silk. Her eyes were like two glittering pools of green, and although she was trying her best to appear calm, Simon could see anxiety swirling within their celadon depths.

What the hell are you doing with a dull, pompous lobcock like Wickham, when you are so full of fire? he wondered.

He could see she was embarrassed, which was understandable given the fact that he had come upon them at such an inopportune moment. What he couldn't understand was why she had been in Wickham's arms to begin with. He supposed the viscount was handsome enough in a flat, unremarkable sort of way—the kind of standardized male beauty that he had seen glorified countless times in paintings and sculptures. Simon could certainly appreciate that most women would find Lord Wickham appealing, with his sandy brown hair and his elegantly chiseled features, and his painstakingly pressed and relentlessly fashionable clothing. But Camelia was not like most women. She was a woman of unique curiosity and determination, who had dedicated her life to studying the world around her, and presumably analyzing and assessing the most infinitesimal of details.

Could she really not see that beneath those rigorously tailored clothes and painfully polished boots, Lord Wickham was a posturing, arrogant idiot?

"I have been working on some sketches for your pump, Lady Camelia." Dismissing Wickham, Simon moved toward a stone bench and spread a series of wrinkled sheets upon it. "Although I have some ideas about how it will have to be adapted, I need you to tell me more about the density of the soil that mixes with the water, the amount and size of the rocks we are likely to encounter, and the availability of fuel for the pump—"

"Really, Kent, I'm afraid I must protest," Elliott interrupted. "Lady Camelia is here this evening to enjoy a social event, not to conduct some sort of business meeting with you. This is entirely inappropriate."

"Forgive me, Wickhip—"

"It's Wickham," Elliott corrected in a taut voice.

"If you prefer," Simon said agreeably. "Lady Camelia and I are partners in an archaeological project, and she told me that time was of the greatest essence in this matter. She assured me I could speak to her about any questions or concerns at any time, day or night."

"I hardly think she meant you were to track her down at a private party and corner her in the garden," Elliott retorted.

"Actually, I believe she was already cornered."

"I did tell Mr. Kent he could call upon me at any time," Camelia swiftly interjected, seeing Elliott's jaw twitch.

Elliott turned and regarded her incredulously. "Calling upon you at your home is one thing, Camelia, but seeking you out at a party to discuss business matters is completely improper."

"You're probably right," Simon agreed, carelessly gathering up his wrinkled sketches. "I should go."

"Why is it improper, Elliott?" demanded Camelia, suddenly annoyed by the way Elliott was interfering.

"First of all, Mr. Kent wasn't invited—"

"Actually, I believe I was—in fact, I'm almost certain of it," reflected Simon, scratching his head. "I'm afraid I just have trouble keeping track of such things. Not just invitations, you understand, but dates and correspondence in general. Lady Camelia can attest to that."

"It hardly matters whether he was invited or not, Elliott," Camelia argued, "since he didn't come here to enjoy the party. He came here to see me about a business matter."

"But that in itself is inappropriate, Camelia," returned Elliott. "You should not be discussing business matters at a social function."

"You know that is the only reason *I* came, Elliott," Camelia reminded him. "And my understanding is there is nothing wrong with that, given that men delight in discussing business at virtually every social function they attend. Or is the fact that I am a woman the reason you seem to think I don't deserve the same right?"

"That isn't what I said," Elliott protested, realizing he had roused her anger.

"No, it isn't," agreed Simon, nodding. "He specifically said *you* should not be discussing business matters," he told Camelia seriously. "I sure Wickhop here feels other women can do whatever they please—isn't that right, Wickhop?"

"It's Wickham," Elliott managed, his teeth clenched.

"Since you find it so unseemly for me to be conducting a business discussion here, perhaps the best thing would be for me to leave." Camelia turned to Simon. "Why don't you come over to my house, Mr. Kent, where we can continue our discussion without the risk of offending anyone?"

"That's an excellent idea," Simon declared enthusiastically. "I can follow you in my carriage. There, you see, Wickhop? Now we won't be in any danger of offending anyone."

"You can't be serious, Camelia." Elliott regarded her as if he thought she had gone mad. "It is practically the middle of the night."

"That's very kind of you to be concerned, Wickhop, but I'm not tired in the least," Simon assured him jovially.

"That's not what I meant," Elliott managed tautly. "Camelia, you should not be entertaining Mr. Kent in your home in the middle of the night."

"I'm hardly entertaining him, Elliott. We will be discussing business."

"Even so, it isn't appropriate."

"I'm sorry, Elliott, but if I spent my life trying to observe these apparently endless British rules of what is appropriate for women and what isn't, I'm quite certain I would never accomplish anything."

"Then I'll come with you."

"That's very kind of you, but I wouldn't dream of pulling you away from this ball. You have a marvelous time, and I will speak with you again in a few days to let you know how things are going."

"Really, Camelia, I insist—"

"And I insist that you stay, Elliott," Camelia countered emphatically. "Your time would be far better spent here, seeing if you can get anyone interested in investing in your new business venture. Maybe you will even indulge in a dance or two—the music sounds lovely. I'm sure there are lots of young ladies in there who would very much enjoy the opportunity to dance with you." She gave him her sweetest smile.

Elliott regarded her helplessly. He could hardly force his company upon her.

"Shall we, Lady Camelia?" Simon gallantly offered her his arm.

Feeling as if she had just been granted a reprieve, Camelia laid her hand upon Simon's heavily creased sleeve.

Heat shot through her hand and streaked up her arm, causing her fingers to clench.

"Is everything all right?" asked Simon, frowning.

It suddenly occurred to him that perhaps it was not terribly wise for Camelia to be marching out of the ball with him as her escort. After all, he was fairly certain he had not actually been invited. Although he was not in the habit of caring what people thought of either him or his attire, he disliked the idea that Lord Bagley's guests might make disparaging comments about Camelia because of him.

"If you prefer, I can leave on my own," he suggested, "and meet you out by your carriage."

"That won't be necessary," Camelia assured him. She sensed that he was trying to protect her from the curious stares they were certain to attract in the ballroom. The sight of her leaving with the likely uninvited and hopelessly underdressed Simon Kent would undoubtedly set their tongues wagging for days. She smiled brightly at him as she finished, "I came in through the front door, and see no reason why we should not leave by the front door."

A smile pulled at the corners of Simon's mouth. Camelia certainly wasn't afraid of scandal. In fact, as far as he could tell, she didn't seem to be very much afraid of anything. He found himself idly wondering if she was still carrying that wicked-looking dagger somewhere beneath the copious layers of her stunningly simple evening gown.

"As you wish, Lady Camelia. Good night, Wickhip," he added, bowing slightly to Elliott. "I do hope you enjoy the rest of your evening."

Elliott watched in pained frustration as Camelia made her way back down the ivory path on the arm of her ridiculously disheveled, addlepated inventor.

He was a patient man, he reminded himself forcefully.

When the rewards were so exquisite, patience was essential.

CHAPTER 5

Something was wrong.

It was a curse, sometimes, to have the power to sense things when others had no inkling of the forces churning around them. It was a burden he bore with stoic resignation, as his mother had before him, and her mother had before that.

For generations it had been assumed that the power was particular to the women of her line; for as far back as any of them could remember, only women had been given what his mother had quietly assured him was a gift. But on the day she had finally recognized that the power did not dwell within any of his thirteen sisters, but burned only within Zareb, he had sensed her heart was torn. A woman was accustomed to pain and disappointment and joy, she had told him, and therefore women could more easily bear the heavy weight of feeling these things before they actually happened. To endure it, he would have to be stronger than the most powerful lion, and wiser than the most ancient shaman. He had been a young boy at the time, proudly descended from the mighty Waitimu, one of the greatest warriors the tribe had ever known. Youthful arrogance had left him no doubt that he would have ample strength and wisdom to easily carry his gift.

He had been mistaken.

"I will open the house and light the lamps for you, Tisha," he said to Camelia as he quickly disembarked from the driver's seat of the carriage.

"Don't be absurd, Zareb, we can all go up to the house together," Camelia protested. "I don't mind if the house is dark."

"Mr. Kent is our guest, and he should not enter a black house." Zareb tried to make it sound as if he were only trying to observe some British code of conduct. "It will only take a moment."

"Which is exactly why it is silly for the two of us to sit waiting in our carriages, when we could be going in together," argued Camelia. "I'm quite sure Mr. Kent isn't afraid of the dark."

"I'll be fine as long as your snake keeps his distance," Simon quipped, appearing beside Zareb. "I don't particularly warm to the idea of him dropping suddenly on my head." He went to open Camelia's carriage door.

Zareb placed his weathered hand on Simon's arm, stopping him.

Simon frowned. "Is something wrong, Zareb?"

Heat flooded Zareb's hand where it touched the white inventor's sleeve. He held his hand steady a moment, wanting to be sure.

Perhaps his senses were wrong, he mused, confused by the warmth now pulsing through him. The white inventor regarded him quizzically, his blue eyes wide, not angered by the fact that Zareb had taken such a liberty with him, as Lord Wickham would have been. It was good, Zareb decided, trying to temper the unease that had gripped him moments earlier. There was darkness, but there was also light.

He hoped that light was strong enough to counter whatever was coming.

"I will do it," he said with quiet dignity, reaching for the door handle of the carriage. And then, perhaps because he wanted to make it clear to the white inventor that Camelia was his alone to guard, he solemnly added, "It is my duty."

He opened the door and held out his hand to Camelia, supporting her as she stepped out of the vehicle. He held fast to her hand a moment longer than necessary, his long, coffee-colored fingers closed protectively around her small, gloved palm.

"Is everything all right, Zareb?" Camelia regarded him curiously.

"It is nothing," he assured her, hoping that might be true. "Come."

He wanted to keep holding her hand as they walked to the house, as he had when she was a child, but he understood that this was no longer acceptable. Reluctantly, he let go of her. He thought she might reach for the white inventor's arm, but she did not.

Somehow, that made him feel a little better.

"That's strange," murmured Camelia as they mounted the steps to the front door. "The door is ajar."

Zareb moved in front of her, blocking her from stepping closer to the door. "Wait."

He swiftly scanned the windows at the front of the house, searching for any signs of light or movement behind the drawn curtains. He saw nothing. But the door was open a finger's length.

Zareb knew he had locked it.

"There's no evidence that anyone forced their way in," mused Simon, examining the edge of the door and its frame. "Is it possible you just didn't close it securely, and the wind blew it open?"

"The door was locked," Zareb said quietly. "And there is no wind."

Fear tightened Camelia's chest. Oscar, Rupert, and Harriet had been left in the house alone. She ducked around Zareb and raced inside.

"Wait, Tisha!" called Zareb, rushing after her. "You do not know what lies ahead!"

"Oscar!" Camelia stumbled through the darkness of the entrance hall, trying to see through the shadows. "Oscar, where are you?"

"Wait a moment, Tisha," urged Zareb, fumbling with a match. "Do not go anywhere until I have made some light." His voice was uncharacteristically firm. It was the same voice he had sometimes used on her when she was a little girl, when she would do something impulsive and dangerous.

Camelia waited anxiously as Zareb coaxed a flame from the match. A thin veil of orange light spit across the room, then grew stronger as he transferred the flame to a lamp and turned up the wick.

"Oh, God," she whispered. Slowly, she walked into her father's study.

Her father's desk and chairs had been overturned, and their worn leather upholstery had been viciously slashed, causing reams of dry, dusty gray horsehair stuffing to spill forth onto the faded carpet. The bookcase and a small side table had also been heaved over, then attacked with an axe, until the pieces had been reduced to firewood. Every one of her father's precious oil paintings, rare sketches of ancient buildings, and antique maps had been torn down from the walls and ripped from its frame. Irreplaceable artifacts, masks, and statues gathered from his many journeys lay smashed upon the floor. And his beloved books, which Camelia had kept in stacks around the room just as he had left them on his last visit to London, had been torn to pieces and strewn everywhere.

She stood there a moment, staring at the destruction, overwhelmed with a sudden, suffocating despair.

And then she turned abruptly and went into the darkness of the dining room.

Zareb quickly followed, carrying the lamp. Coppery light splashed across the broken dining room table and chairs, and illuminated the overturned buffet. A white and blue sea of smashed china plates, cups, and crystal glasses littered the carpet. Camelia's eyes fell upon the flurry of gray feathers scattered around the room.

"Harriet!" Her voice was edged with panic. "Rupert! Where are you!"

"I don't think they are down here." Simon fought to control the rage boiling within him as he surveyed the ravaged rooms. He held out his hand to Camelia. "Come, Camelia," he said, his voice gentle and markedly calm. "We will probably find them upstairs."

Numbly, she nodded and took his hand. His strong fingers closed around hers, warm and firm and reassuring.

"Of course we will," she said, trying to slow the

violent pounding of her heart. "They were scared and have probably gone upstairs to hide."

She turned her back on the demolished dining room and followed Zareb up the staircase, still holding fast to Simon's hand.

"Come out, Oscar," called Zareb. "All is well, little one."

"I'm home, Oscar," Camelia added tautly. "You have nothing to fear now."

Dread swelled in Simon's chest as they slowly mounted the stairs. There was no sound coming from the floors above, where the drawing room and bedchambers were located, but the light from Zareb's lamp revealed that these levels had not fared any better than the ground floor. Whoever had done this had been thorough. They had known that Camelia was out for the evening and they had taken their time, going room by room, smashing and slashing and destroying. Simon wondered if they had found whatever it was they were looking for.

In that moment, all he really gave a damn about was finding Camelia's precious animals.

"Oscar," called Camelia, fighting to keep her voice steady as she surveyed the ruins of her drawing room. More of Harriet's gray feathers lay spread across the carpet. "Harriet!" Camelia suddenly let go of Simon's hand and raced up the next staircase.

"Wait, Tisha!" Zareb moved as quickly behind her as his voluminous robes would allow. "You mustn't go up without me!"

Ignoring him, Camelia tore down the hallway, then threw open the door to her bedroom. Silent blackness greeted her.

"Oscar?" she whispered, her voice breaking.

A small, dark form shrieked with relief and hurtled toward her, landing hard against her legs. Camelia cried out as she scooped him up and held him tight against her chest.

"Are you all right, Oscar?" She swiftly ran her fingers over his head and arms and legs to see if he was injured. "Are you hurt?"

Oscar chattered happily and nestled against her, his little arms wrapped tightly around her neck.

"We have found Harriet," said Zareb, appearing in the doorway with Camelia's bird clutching his shoulder. "She has lost many feathers, but otherwise she is unharmed. I don't believe she will enjoy looking at herself in the mirror quite so much until they grow back again."

Camelia held out her arm, and Harriet instantly abandoned Zareb to fly to her.

"Oh, Harriet, you're still a lovely girl," Camelia crooned, stroking the bird's soft gray breast. "We'll put all the mirrors away until your feathers are fully restored." She shifted Harriet onto her shoulder. "Now we just need to find Rupert."

Simon frowned. "Is it my imagination, or is that pile of clothes moving?"

Camelia glanced at the slowly shifting garments spilling out from her overturned wardrobe

"Rupert!" she cried happily, bending to unearth him from the mountain of satins and silks. "How clever of you to hide in my clothes!"

Rupert eyed her with his bulbous, glassy stare, then shot his slender tongue out at her.

Camelia picked him up and tenderly kissed his cold, smooth head.

Simon stared at her, transfixed. The deep lines of fear

that had been etched in her face moments earlier had vanished, replaced by unmitigated relief. These strange African creatures were everything to her, he reflected, unaccountably moved by the realization. An ugly orange-and-black snake, a mischievous, undisciplined monkey, and an apparently neurotic exotic bird. These animals, and Zareb, were Camelia's only family.

He swallowed, profoundly relieved that whoever had broken into her home and vandalized it had not managed to harm any of her animals.

"Let us leave this place, Tisha," Zareb suddenly urged, gesturing toward the door. "Now that we have found the animals we must go."

It was faint, the thread of urgency that colored Zareb's tone. So faint that anyone else might not have noticed it. But Camelia had known and loved Zareb for far too many years to not recognize it. Confused, she turned, sensing there was something he was trying to protect her from.

Her gaze fell upon her bed.

"Bring the lamp closer, Zareb," she said quietly.

"We should look in the other rooms, Tisha," Zareb insisted, trying to draw her away from it. "There is nothing here—"

"Bring the lamp," she repeated, moving slowly toward her bed. And then, because she knew he was only trying to shield her, she softly added, "Please."

Reluctantly, Zareb moved closer to her, carrying the lamp.

A warm glow fell over the dagger embedded in her pillow.

It was her father's favorite weapon, she realized, a heavy throwing dagger that had been made by a member of the San people, who were also known as Bushmen by whites in South Africa. It was a fine example of exceptional craftsmanship, with its heavy shaft of hammered iron, welded to a deadly sharp blade of painstakingly polished steel. It was not ancient, but it was elegantly crafted and precisely balanced— an impressive piece of weaponry, for anyone who wanted to use it as such. She told herself that whoever had taken it from its hook above the mantle in her father's study and used it to spear the note beneath it to her pillow could not possibly have known that a shaman had gifted the blade with dark powers.

She stared at it, fighting to leash her fear. She did not believe in supernatural curses, she reminded herself firmly. Even so, she felt cold, as if an icy wind had suddenly whipped around her.

"That's a braw-lookin' dirk," observed Oliver cheerfully from the doorway. "That poor wee cushion didna have a chance."

Simon sighed. "Lady Camelia, may I present Oliver, who is supposed to be outside waiting for me in my carriage. Oliver, this is Lady Camelia, and this is Zareb."

"Pleased to meet ye." Oliver tipped his snowy head at them. "And ye canna blame me for comin' in to see just what in the name o' Saint Columba is goin' on here," he continued sternly to Simon, "when I see nae but one light movin' through the house like a ghost, after ye've already been in here long enough to set the whole house afire—with lamps, I mean," he quickly qualified, casting a reassuring glance at Camelia. "I expect ye've heard that the lad burned his house down the other night, but 'twas the first time he let a fire get quite that out of hand—I'd nae want ye to think he makes a habit o' such things. O' course there was that time he near set Miss Amelia's house afire with a smoke bomb," he reflected, scratching his head, "but that was on purpose. As a lad he was always blastin' the top off o' somethin', or stuffin' too many wicks in a bottle an' settin' them ablaze. He'd tell us he was just tryin' to see if he could fix us a better way of lightin' a room." He snorted with laughter as he finished bluntly, "We always thought we'd wake one day an' find the house burnin' around our ears!"

"I'm not responsible for the recent fire at my house, Oliver," Simon said, anxious to put an end to the old man's rambling. He didn't think that was particularly the right moment to regale Camelia and Zareb with tales of his boyhood antics. "I didn't tell Haydon and Genevieve because I didn't want them to worry, but someone purposely set fire to my laboratory. I think the same people are responsible for vandalizing Lady Camelia's house this evening."

"'Tis nae the work o' proper thieves, that's for certain," Oliver reflected, gazing soberly around the room. "I was a thief myself," he told Camelia and Zareb proudly, "and I'd have nae left a house in such a muck. What's the point o' lashin' the cow that gives the milk?" He scowled as he finished furiously, "'Tis only spineless scalawags that would do such a thing, an' if I ever get my hands on them, I'll whip them 'til they canna sit for a month!"

Somehow Camelia took comfort from the ancient little Scotsman's outrage. "Thank you, Oliver." She wasn't entirely sure what to make of him, with his wiry shock of snowy hair and his boasts of being a thief. Simon had inferred that he was his driver, but it was clear to Camelia he was in fact much more than that. "That's very kind of you."

Oliver beamed at her, then frowned. "Do ye know ye've a wee beastie wrapped around yer neck?"

"That's Rupert," Simon told him. "Lady Camelia's snake."

"Ye mean like a pet?" Oliver regarded Rupert dubiously. "Should he nae be in a cage?"

"I'm afraid Rupert wouldn't like being caged very much," Camelia told him. "He is quite accustomed to moving about as he pleases."

"The note, Tisha." Zareb indicated the paper speared by the dagger. "What does it say?"

Camelia slowly pulled the dagger out of her pillow, then held the note closer to Zareb's lamp. Struggling to keep her voice steady, she read:

"Death to those who disturb the sleep of Pumulani."

"What's Poo Moo Lanee?" asked Oliver.

"That is the African name of the land where my archaeological site is in South Africa," Camelia explained. "It means 'rest' or 'resting place,' in the Nguni languages. About a hundred years ago it was settled by a family of Dutch Boers, who established a farm there. My father bought the land from the grandson of the original Boer owner, and he began to excavate it about twenty years ago. Since his death six months ago, I have continued with his work."

"Sounds to me like someone disnae want ye there."

"My father believed the land is the site of an extraordinarily important archaeological find," Camelia explained. "Over the years we have found many artifacts indicating a thriving community once lived there, and a number of rare rock paintings support that theory. I believe there are rival archaeologists who want to frighten me into abandoning my site. They think if I give up, then they can buy the land at a fraction of its value and excavate it themselves."

Oliver frowned. "Are ye sayin' this is nae the first time they've tried to scare ye?"

"No."

"What else have they done?" demanded Simon.

"A few things," Camelia said, dismissive. "It doesn't matter. They want to frighten me away, and they are not going to succeed. That land is mine, and I will continue to excavate it until I find what my father was looking for."

"And what was that?"

"Evidence of an ancient civilization."

Oliver scratched his chin thoughtfully. "Seems like a lot o' fuss over a few bits o' bone."

"You're right, it does." Simon regarded Camelia intently.

"I suppose it does to people who have not devoted their lives to the field," Camelia allowed. "But to those who spend their entire lives hoping to make just one discovery of major historical significance, it could prove to be extremely important."

"We must leave here, Tisha." Zareb's expression was grim. "Now."

"We cannot leave, Zareb," Camelia countered. "Mr. Kent has not had time to finish his work on the pump."

"I don't mean we should return to Africa tonight," Zareb qualified. "I mean it is no longer safe for you to stay in this house. We must go."

Camelia shook her head. "This is my father's house. I have no intention of letting some common ruffians frighten me out of it. We will clean up and we will stay."

"That's a stouthearted lass." Oliver nodded at Simon with approval. "Wet sheep dinna shrink—they shake off the water."

"Sheep get killed, Oliver," Simon muttered.

"Well, sometimes," Oliver reluctantly allowed. "I was tryin' to be positive."

"And I appreciate that, Oliver," Camelia assured him. "This isn't the first time someone has tried to drive me away from my work, and I don't expect it will be the last. But I will not be frightened away."

"There's a braw lass." Oliver smiled at her. "'Tis nae the size of the dog in the fight, but the fight in the dog."

"Lady Camelia is not a dog," Zareb objected. "She has been threatened by her father's own dagger—a blade that has been given dark powers by a very great shaman. She cannot stay here any longer. We *must* leave this house tonight."

"Dark powers, ye say?" Oliver frowned and scratched his head. "Well, now, that's a different kettle o' kippers."

"We cannot leave tonight," Camelia objected. "We have nowhere else to go."

"Ye could stay with us," Oliver amiably offered.

Simon regarded him in disbelief. "I don't think that's a good idea—"

"Why not? We've more than enough room for the lot o' them—although ye may have to work a bit on Eunice to let ye have that snake slitherin' about. Eunice is nae fond o' slitherin' beasties."

"Rupert can stay in Lady Camelia's room," Zareb quickly suggested. "He will not mind that."

"I cannot keep Oscar and Harriet locked in a bedchamber all day and night," Camelia protested. "They have to have room to move about. We will stay here."

"Well, now, I'm sure Eunice and Doreen will be fine with them, as long as they behave themselves and dinna make too much of a mess," Oliver reflected.

"I will see to it that they behave well," Zareb assured him before Camelia could say anything. "And I will feed them and clean up any mess. Your Eunice and Doreen will not notice they are there."

"Well, then, it's all settled," Oliver said happily.

"I really don't think this is a good idea," Simon began once more.

"Ye've nae need to be worried about the lass's reputation," Oliver added, ignoring Simon as he spoke to Zareb. "Eunice an' Doreen are well accustomed to watchin' over young lassies—they've done it time an' again, over the years."

"The only honor that matters is that which burns within the heart," Zareb stated solemnly. "Lady Camelia's honor is safe wherever she goes."

"O' course, that goes without sayin'," Oliver agreed. "But with all of us under one roof, there will always be a pair o' eyes to make sure her ladyship is safe. I can tell ye, if the scalawags that came here tonight try to get into my house, they'll be feelin' the kiss o' my boot right up their scabbit arse—"

"Thank you, Oliver, I'm sure Lady Camelia appreciates your desire to help," Simon interrupted. "However, I'm not entirely sure this is the best solution—"

"Now, lad, ye'll still have plenty of room for playin' about with all yer inventions," Oliver assured him. "It doesna look to me like Lady Camelia will be bringing much with her."

"Only some clothes," Zareb said. "And I do not need a room for myself. I can sleep anywhere."

"There now, ye see? 'Tis all worked out." Oliver beamed at Camelia. "Why don't ye just gather up a few things, lass, and me and Zareb here will take them down to yer carriage?"

Camelia looked at Simon uncertainly.

In truth, she was shaken by this latest assault. Her father's home and everything in it had been ruthlessly attacked, and she had been powerless to stop it from happening. All that really mattered was that her animals had not been hurt, she told herself firmly. But what happened the next time she and Zareb went out, and Oscar, Harriet, and Rupert were left alone? If whoever was trying to frighten her succeeded in harming one of them, how would she ever forgive herself?

"Is this all right with you, Simon?" She hated the fact that she and her animals were being forced upon him. But the sight of her father's dagger buried in her pillow disturbed her more than she wanted to admit. "It would only be for a short while."

Simon sighed. Oliver and Zareb were right. It wasn't safe for Camelia to stay at her house. He didn't believe in evil curses, but someone was determined to frighten her into abandoning her dig.

The next time they might not limit themselves to just destroying her furnishings.

"I would be pleased to have you, Zareb, Oscar, and Harriet stay with me," he told her.

Camelia started to nod, then frowned. "What about Rupert?"

Simon warily eyed the serpent wrapped around her neck.

"Rupert can come, too," he reluctantly conceded, "as

long as you absolutely promise to keep him in your bedroom. I don't want Eunice shrieking in terror every time she comes upon him." He refrained from mentioning that he didn't particularly relish the idea of stumbling upon the ugly creature in the middle of the night, either.

"I don't think Rupert will mind terribly staying in my room," Camelia mused, protectively stroking the snake. "But are you sure you won't mind having Oscar and Harriet roaming about?"

"Of course not, lass," Oliver quickly interjected. "They're sure to bring a bit o' life to the house."

Camelia looked at Simon. "Simon?"

Her eyes were lit only by the sheer wash of gold spilling from Zareb's lamp, but Simon could see uncertainty shimmering in their depths. She was strong and determined, yet it was evident to him that this latest incident had had a profound effect on her. She had been terrified as she tore through the house calling for her animals. She had told Simon she didn't believe in curses. Perhaps that was true.

Even so, there was no question the sight of her father's dagger buried deep into her pillow had torn away a strip of her bravado.

"I'm sure Harriet and Oscar won't be any trouble at all," he lied.

"There, ye see, lass?" Oliver beamed. "Now why don't ye gather your things an' we'll be on our way."

"Oliver and I will make sure all the windows and doors are secure while you and Zareb pack. Call us when you are ready to leave." Simon turned and left the room.

"Ye'd best tell Eunice an' Doreen about the monkey an' the snake last," Oliver suggested in a hushed voice as they descended the stairs. "I'm nae sure they'll be quite as bobbish about it as I said."

"I'll let you tell them, Oliver," said Simon calmly. "Since this was entirely your idea."

"Now, lad, I know ye well enough to ken that ye'd nae have left that lassie alone in this mess, with great dirks stickin' out o' pillows an' evil spells waftin' about. All I did was help ye make up yer mind to take her home."

"She isn't a pet, Oliver."

"Ye're right, she's a braw lassie—an' rare bonny too. Reminds me of Miss Genevieve, when she was a lass." He chuckled. "They'll get on right quick when they meet."

"They aren't going to meet. I'll be working night and day to get her pump built over the next few weeks, so we can get Lady Camelia back to Africa as quickly as possible."

"Africa, ye say? Now there's a place I've nae thought to see. I wonder if 'tis really as hot as they say."

"You aren't going, Oliver."

"I imagine that's a long voyage, even on one of Jack's fastest ships," Oliver reflected, ignoring him. "We'll have to pack plenty of Eunice's oatcakes."

"Oliver—"

"A bloody shame, what they've done here." Oliver's expression was sober as he looked at the smashed relics in the study. "But even in a fallen nest, ye may find a whole egg," he added cheerfully.

"I think whoever ransacked this place did a fairly thorough job," Simon reflected, his gaze sweeping over the floor.

"They didna break her, though, did they?"

"No."

"So there's yer egg." He smiled and went off to check the windows in the dining room, leaving Simon to contemplate the ruins around him.

CHAPTER
6

Her heart clenched when the carriage finally came to a stop.

Like most London houses Simon's new home was narrow and tall, in an attempt to make the most out of the limited land available. When Camelia was a little girl she had thought all houses were made that way, except for her family's dilapidated country estate. Her mother had not cared much for that drafty, ramshackle house, with its mouldering walls and its incessantly leaking roof. Lady Stamford had far preferred the lights and bustle of London to being sequestered for weeks at a time in the middle of a field, as she put it. Since Camelia's father was away most of the time on one or another of his expeditions, her mother chose to remain in the city, where she could amuse herself with shopping, attending the theatre, and visiting friends.

Camelia had adored those rare occasions when her father returned home and insisted they go to the country for a few weeks. She loved lying upon the grass in a meadow staring at the sky, with the sun warming her skin and the soft whisper of the wind shivering through the trees. She even liked the house, with its old, mossy smell that permeated every room, and the faded draperies and shabby furniture that spoke of generations of people living their lives within. Her father had filled every conceivable nook and cranny with artifacts he had collected on his travels. Some were ancient and fairly valuable, while others were merely common, everyday objects he found either beautiful or interesting. Camelia would listen rapturously as he wove her some splendid tale for each piece, describing how he had nearly died in his quest to find it, or from what incredibly dastardly or colorful character he had bought it. He would urge her to run her fingers over the piece as he spoke, trying to get her to feel its warmth, its spirit, its secrets.

Best of all was when he would bring home some new piece of weaponry. Her father loved weapons, not because of the injuries they could inflict, but because he was fascinated by the fact that craftsmen in virtually every civilization labored to make them as beautiful as they were deadly. He would hand Camelia heavy spears, sharp daggers, cumbersome swords, and intricately decorated shields, instructing her to test them for balance and weight. Sometimes, if she pleaded with him enough, he would let her take them outside and try her hand at wielding them. He would stand close to her as he demonstrated the proper way to hold a sword, throw a spear, and hurl a dagger, his huge bronzed hand clasped firmly over her small soft one, his deep voice resonating with quiet pleasure as he gave her instruction.

One day her mother had startled them while Camelia was tossing a dagger at a tree. The blade slipped and cut deep into her palm, causing a brilliant stream of blood to leak down her arm. Nearly hysterical, Lady Stamford had grabbed Camelia and whisked her back into the house, furiously accusing her husband of all but killing their only child. Camelia was not permitted to touch a weapon again for the rest of her mother's life.

She shifted uncomfortably against the crushed silk of her evening gown and crinoline, suddenly aware of the tautness of the strap fastening her dagger to her calf.

"Come, Tisha." Zareb opened the carriage door and extended his hand to her.

"Thank you, Zareb."

She felt a little better as she placed her hand in Zareb's. Although she was trying hard not to show it, the sight of her home ransacked and her father's precious possessions and books destroyed had shaken her deeply. They were only objects, she reminded herself firmly. The fact that some of them had been rare artifacts made this argument bittersweet.

What bothered her most was that someone had managed to drive her from the only place in London where she felt at least somewhat at home.

"Why don't you carry Harriet's cage, and I'll take Oscar and Rupert?"

"Perhaps we should leave them here a moment," Zareb suggested, "until Mr. Kent has had a chance to warn Eunice and Doreen about them."

"I don't think Oscar will stay in the carriage without me after his ordeal," Camelia reflected, feeling Oscar tighten his hold on her. "And I'm afraid if he gets upset it will only alarm Harriet and Rupert. We should all go in together."

"As you wish." Zareb reached into the carriage and

picked up Harriet, who had been put into her cage for the trip.

Simon watched as Camelia and Zareb joined him on the front walk leading up to his newly leased house. They made an odd pair, she in her scarlet evening gown and he in his spectacularly colorful robes, carrying a monkey, a bird, and a basket between them. Yet there was an extraordinary dignity to them as they made their way toward Simon and Oliver.

"Here now, lass, let me take that basket from ye," offered Oliver, rushing forth as Simon unlocked the door. "Ye've enough to carry with that monkey holdin' fast to ye."

"Thank you, Oliver." Camelia smiled. "You're very kind."

"We're home," Simon called, pushing the door open.

"An' high time, too." Eunice bustled through the door that led down to the kitchen with Doreen following behind. "Me an' Doreen was all but ready to send the peelers lookin' for ye—sweet Saint Columba, that lass has a hairy beast 'round her neck!"

"That's Oscar," Oliver told her brightly. "An' this here is Lady Camelia, an' that's Zareb, an' that's Harriet in the cage."

"Pleased to meet ye, I'm sure." Doreen regarded Oscar warily. "Does he bite?"

"Only apples," Zareb assured her. "Not people."

"Lady Camelia and Zareb have had some trouble in their home this evening," Simon explained. "They are going to be staying with us for a while before they return to South Africa."

Eunice looked at him in surprise. "What sort of trouble?"

"Some ruffians broke into her ladyship's house while she was out an' tore it to bits," Oliver replied. "Plunged a dirk in her pillow an' left a note sayin' wicked things— an' if I ever find the soddin' priggers, I'll give 'em a basting they'll nae forget!"

Eunice regarded Camelia sympathetically. "Ye take nae mind of it, lass—ye're here now, safe an' swack."

"'Tis the way of thieves today—there's nae honor in it anymore," Oliver continued angrily. "'Tis all pistols an' dirks and spineless threats—I ask ye, where's the honor in that?"

"What happened at Lady Camelia's house was not the work of ordinary thieves," Simon pointed out. "They were purposely trying to frighten her."

"That's even worse, the filthy curs." Doreen pounded her bony fist against her palm as she railed. "They'd best nae try such a thing here, or I'll be crownin' them with a pot and puttin' a broom to their arse afore they know what they're about!"

"Hopefully the authorities will be able to find them before they know where Lady Camelia has gone," Simon said. "I'm going down to the police station now to make a report."

Camelia regarded him with alarm. "The police mustn't know about this."

"Why on earth not?"

"If the police investigate, it will be reported in the newspapers, which means the members of the Archaeological Society will hear of it. The handful of members who have been reluctantly willing to give me financial assistance will then have cause to worry about me, which means they will withdraw their support—thinking they are only doing so for my protection." She adamantly shook her head. "No one must know my home was ransacked or that I have been threatened."

"If we don't contact the police, we have no hope of finding the men who did this," Simon pointed out.

"Seems to me there's nae much hope o' that anyway," reflected Oliver. "Unless they make a habit of breakin' into homes and smashin' everythin' they can lay their hands on."

"The men who destroyed Lady Camelia's home will be found when it is time for them to be found," Zareb observed. "The police will make no difference in that journey."

"If the lass doesna want the peelers to be told, then we won't tell them," Doreen decided. "No point in stirrin' up the wasps when ye've already got bees chasin' ye!"

Camelia smiled. "Thank you for understanding, Doreen. I hope Zareb and I are not imposing upon you too much." Like Oliver, it was clear to her that these two women were far more to Simon than just servants. She liked that.

Hopefully, it meant they would have a better understanding of her relationship with Zareb.

"Ye're nae imposin' at all," Eunice swiftly assured her. "'Tis a big house with just the four of us rattlin' about—there's plenty of room."

"Why don't ye take this basket while me an' Zareb here go out to the carriage and collect the rest of their things?" Oliver suggested to Eunice. "Ye an' Doreen can show Lady Camelia to her room an' help her to get settled."

"I'm thinkin' ye'd be happiest in the room with the green paper," Eunice decided, taking the basket from Oliver. "'Tis nae fancy but it's clean, an' if ye like I can bring ye some—*sweet saints!*" she shrieked as Rupert popped up from the basket. *"Help!"*

She heaved the basket into the air and threw herself against Oliver, mashing his face against her plentiful bosom. Camelia and Simon both ran to catch the basket, in which Rupert was now a most reluctant passenger. Suddenly the snake shot upwards, freeing himself from it. Simon caught the basket while Camelia jumped up to catch Rupert.

At that point Oscar decided he'd had enough of Camelia. Screeching wildly, he leapt off her and onto Doreen's head. Thrown off balance, Camelia crashed against Simon. They toppled to the floor, losing the basket along the way, while Doreen screamed and tried to pull Oscar off.

"Got you!" said Zareb triumphantly as he caught Rupert.

"Help!" shrieked Doreen, staggering drunkenly about the room. *"Get this wild beastie off me!"*

"Come down from there, Oscar," commanded Zareb.

Oscar gladly leapt from Doreen's wobbling head to Zareb's firm shoulder.

"I canna breathe." Oliver's voice was muffled against the plentiful pillows of Eunice's bosom.

"Oh, Ollie," she cried, easing her terrified grip upon him, "I thought I was goin' to snuff it for sure!"

Simon looked at Camelia, who was lying on top of him, her legs twined intimately against his. "Are you all right?"

Camelia stared down at him, transfixed. She was suddenly acutely aware of the fact that Simon was very tall, which in truth seemed a rather odd thing to contemplate, given that they were lying together sprawled upon the floor. But Simon had managed to completely cushion her with his body as they fell, protecting her with the massive expanse of his chest and shoulders, and the lean, chiseled length of his legs. Her body had sighed and melted into the warm contours of him, molding to his granite-hard shape. It felt extraordinary to be lying against him so. It made her heart pound and her senses flame as she absorbed every detail of him. He smelled of spicy soap and something else, a wonderfully mysterious masculine scent that made her want to lay her cheek against his shoulder and breathe in the scent of him. His chest was rising and falling beneath her, his breaths deep and steady, and if she held very still, she could feel the steady beating of his heart against her.

Warmth flowed through her, pooling in her breasts and belly and between her thighs, a confusing, intoxicating sensation that made her feel strangely languid and aroused as she stared into the smoky depths of Simon's deep, unfathomable gaze.

"I think the lass is hurt." Oliver furrowed his white brows with concern. "She's nae movin'."

Camelia gasped and rolled off Simon with a thud. "I'm fine."

"Let me help you up, Tisha," Zareb offered. "You look flushed—are you sure you are well?"

"I'm just a bit winded, that's all." She briskly smoothed down the wrinkles in her gown, feeling flustered.

"I hope ye're nae thinkin' that slitherin' beastie is goin' to be stayin' in this house," Eunice reflected, eyeing Rupert disapprovingly.

"I'm so sorry Rupert frightened you, Eunice," Camelia hastily apologized. "I should have carried the basket myself—but I can assure you, there really wasn't any danger. Rupert's venom is not dangerous to people."

"Dangerous or no, I'll nae have him slippin' about my house scarin' me half out o' my wits."

"And you won't have to," Simon assured her. "Rupert is going to stay locked in Lady Camelia's room at all times—you won't even know he's here—isn't that right, Camelia?"

"Yes." In truth Camelia had hoped that she might be able to gradually acquaint Rupert with the members of the household, so that eventually they would feel comfortable having him around during their visit.

"What about that scraggy monkey?" demanded Doreen, rubbing her stinging scalp. "Will it be in the lass's chamber as well?"

"Unfortunately, Oscar needs a little more room than that," Simon explained, sensing Camelia's distress at the thought of locking Oscar up. "But I'm sure you will find that once he has become familiar with his new surroundings, you will hardly know he is there."

"That doesna seem likely," muttered Doreen, glaring at Oscar.

Oscar bared his teeth at her in a broad, mocking smile.

"Cheeky wee beggar!"

"At least the bird stays in her cage," Oliver interjected, trying to find something positive to say. "She's rare bonny, too."

"Actually, Harriet only uses her cage when she is traveling and sleeping," clarified Camelia. "She has to fly about and stretch her wings a bit during the day."

"And I'm sure she will find enough room for that in Lady Camelia's bedchamber," Simon added, realizing

Eunice and Doreen were not particularly warming to the idea of turning the house into a zoo.

"Well, now that that's all settled, shall we show Lady Camelia to her room?" suggested Oliver. "The lass has had a hard night, an' I'm sure she's most anxious to find her bed."

"O' course ye are, ye poor wee duck," clucked Eunice, abruptly forgetting her fright. "Come along upstairs, an' me an' Doreen will make ye cosy as a kitten, while Oliver sees to yer friend, Mr. Zareb."

Mr. Zareb. With those two simple words, Camelia instantly forgave Eunice for not liking Rupert. Since they had come to London, almost everyone Camelia had encountered had treated Zareb with varying degrees of distrust and condescension. While racist bigotry was also prevalent in South Africa, Camelia's father had always made sure that on his dig all men were treated with fairness and respect, regardless of the color of their skin. Of course Zareb had spent much of his life enduring the contempt of white people in places like Cape Town and Kimberley, but in Africa he was part of a population of millions, which meant he did not constantly arouse unwelcome attention. In England Zareb could not help but stand out, and everyone immediately assumed he was some kind of lowly servant to her. Most English people instantly felt superior to him, purely because of his color. But Eunice had referred to him as Camelia's friend, and had politely accorded him the title of "Mister." For that, Camelia would do her utmost to keep her animals out of Eunice's sight—at least until Eunice understood that they were mostly harmless.

"I will keep the animals with me tonight, Tisha," Zareb said, wanting to make things easier for Eunice and

Doreen as they settled Camelia into her room. "Do not worry."

"An' we have a fine bedchamber waitin' for ye as well," Oliver told Zareb, taking Harriet's cage from him. "If ye follow me I'll take ye to it."

Zareb gave his new friend a grateful bow. "Thank you, Oliver."

Simon watched as the strange party made their way up the stairs, with Oscar perched like a little hairy king on the throne of Zareb's head.

Then Simon turned and made his way into his study, feeling oddly disconcerted and badly in need of a drink.

Something had changed.

That was a bit of an understatement, Simon reflected ruefully as he stared at the amber liquid in his glass. Since meeting Camelia, his home had burned down, destroying everything he owned and, worse, every invention he had been working on. Then he had somehow been cajoled into letting Oliver, Eunice, and Doreen move in with him, completely eradicating the quiet solitude he absolutely required when he worked. And just when he thought his house and his life couldn't possibly be noisier or more crowded, Oliver decided to invite Camelia and Zareb and their pack of wild animals to join them. Pack was something of an exaggeration, he allowed, but given the propensity for trouble that a monkey, a bird, and a snake presented, not by much.

He took a swallow of brandy and stared at the crumpled sketches scattered across his desk, trying to concentrate on the steam pump he was attempting to develop. The challenge was to get the steam to expand gradually through a progression of chambers. Perhaps if he made the chambers smaller and increased their number . . .

"Forgive me—I didn't think anyone else was awake."

He looked up to see Camelia standing in the doorway to his study. She was dressed in a nightgown of ivory silk, which was trimmed at the neckline with a froth of finely stitched lace. She had carelessly draped the quilt from her bed over her shoulder but this makeshift cape only seemed to accentuate the delicacy of her form. Her sun-streaked hair was falling loosely about her shoulders and down her back, a shimmer of gold in the apricot spill of the lamplight. Simon stared at her, fascinated. His gaze moved slowly from the elegant curve of her cheek to the graceful line of her neck, across the sweet pulsing hollow at the base of her throat, then lower, to the lush swells of her breasts. He found himself remembering the feel of her as she lay against him earlier that night, all womanly heat and softness, her slender legs tangled within his, her body shifting and pressing as she stared down at him with those magnificent sage-colored eyes.

Desire surged through him, hard and hot and completely overwhelming.

"Is everything all right?" he demanded, clumsily knocking over his glass as he rose abruptly from his desk.

Get hold of yourself, he commanded silently, fumbling about for a handkerchief as brandy spilled across his sketches. Finding none, he picked up the sketches and shook them, effectively splattering brandy all across the surface of his desk.

For God's sake—what's the matter with you?

"Is your room to your liking?" he added awkwardly, still holding the dripping wet papers.

Camelia regarded him uncertainly, wondering at his apparent discomfiture. "Yes—my room is fine, thank you."

She noted that he was still dressed in his rumpled linen shirt and dark trousers, but he had removed his jacket and neck cloth and opened his collar, revealing just a hint of his muscled chest. His red-gold hair was tousled, and a shadow of dark growth grizzled his jaw, making him look even more disheveled than usual. In that moment he again reminded Camelia of a Scottish warrior, with his towering form and his enormous shoulders, and the piercing depths of his extraordinarily blue eyes. That was ridiculous, of course, she realized. Simon Kent was a quiet, bookish scientist who spent his life squirreled inside a laboratory, struggling to perfect new ways to wash clothes and mop floors and transform steam into power. He was scarcely the kind of man who would race fearlessly into battle wielding a heavy broadsword.

Instead he would toss a few children's firecrackers at the enemy and hope that the color and noise would scare them off.

"Are you hungry?" His desk now a complete disaster, he began to awkwardly lay his sopping wet sketches out on the floor to dry. "If you like we could go down to the kitchen and find something to eat."

"No, thank you. Eunice and Doreen very kindly made up a tray for me and brought it to my room earlier. They said they would take one to Zareb as well, which was most considerate of them. Zareb is not accustomed to being treated with such courtesy outside of our home—especially not here in London."

"Eunice, Oliver, and Doreen have always treated

everyone pretty much the same—for better or for worse. They are unimpressed with the trappings of titles and wealth, or even the color of a person's skin. All that matters to them is what lies beneath."

"Zareb is exactly the same," Camelia said, sitting in the chair facing Simon's desk. "I think he is pleased to have finally met some people here who share his view of the world. I'm afraid he was beginning to think that all British people were arrogant and stupid."

Simon smiled. "We're Scottish, actually. But I would hate to condemn the entire British people on the basis of Zareb's encounters. Perhaps he just hasn't met the right people."

"Perhaps." Camelia tucked her feet up underneath her legs. She had not been able to fall asleep as she lay on the soft bed that Doreen and Eunice had prepared for her. Despite her determination to be strong, the sight of father's home with all his precious possessions destroyed had affected her deeply. Worst of all was the use of his dagger to stab that vile note to her pillow. She did not believe in curses, she reminded herself firmly.

Even so, the fact that Zareb had been so adamant that they leave the house had disturbed her.

"How did you come to know Oliver, Eunice, and Doreen?" she asked, drawing the blanket closer around her shoulders.

"My mother took them into her home after they were released from prison," Simon explained. "But they were never servants to her. My mother was struggling to look after some children she had rescued from the prison and was badly in need of help. Eunice, Oliver, and Doreen became part of the family. They have remained so ever since."

"How many children did Lady Redmond take in?"

"There are six of us, in total." Simon's expression was contained as he sat behind his desk once more. "I expect, given how thoroughly you researched my background, that you have already heard that is how I came to be part of the Kent family."

"My interest in your background was focused purely on your achievements as a scientist and an inventor," Camelia returned. "I believe I had heard somewhere that you were raised as the ward of Lord and Lady Redmond, but I didn't really pay any attention to it. All that mattered to me was the fact that you were a brilliant scientist who I believed would be able to help me with the challenge of clearing water from my dig."

He stared at her a long moment. She returned his gaze with an easy, unaffected calm.

She was telling the truth, he realized, marveling at that simple, surprising fact.

For as long as he could remember, he had been ashamed of his past. Not in an overwhelming way, as it had been for his brother Jack. Jack had been forced to survive on the streets of Inveraray until he was nearly fifteen. All those years of violence and depravation had formed a wall around Jack, which only his wife Amelia's gentle love had finally managed to break through. But until Genevieve found Simon hunched on the floor of a prison cell at the age of nine, he had also been forced to survive on his own. He had no recollection of his real father, and his memories of his mother were vague. For years he had conjured up a childishly innocent image of her, a pretty woman with sable hair and wide, gray eyes, who would hold him close at night and gently stroke his cheek.

After Genevieve took him home and he was finally able to fall asleep knowing that he was safe until morning, his memories took a darker turn. The woman who invaded his dreams at night was filthy and foul-mouthed, with breath that stank of gin and grimy fists that beat him until he lay cowering on the floor. He would awaken suddenly, his heart racing and his mouth dry, shivering uncontrollably.

And then he would slip off his new, soft bed and curl up on the floor, pleading with God to dry his urine-soaked sheets by morning, so that Genevieve would not find out his terrible secret and make him leave.

"Is everything all right?" Camelia regarded him with concern, wondering at the shadows that had suddenly darkened his gaze.

"Yes," he assured her briskly. "Everything is fine."

He began to blot up the spilled brandy on his desk with his sleeve, avoiding her gaze. He could feel her staring at him, and wondered how much he had inadvertently revealed. He did not want Camelia to know about that filthy, cowering, thieving lad. For some reason he did not completely understand, he wanted her to think that he was better than he really was. He wanted her to see him as a man who was strong, and confident, and capable of solving problems. A brilliant scientist, as she had so extravagantly described him. Well, perhaps not brilliant, he amended, but at least reasonably educated and bright. A man who was capable of helping her when she needed him, be it scaring off the two thugs who tried to harm her, or offering her shelter when her own home was no longer safe. A man who was fully in control of both his emotions and his life. This was not so peculiar, he assured himself. After all, she was depending on him to help her. Although he had always been quick to help when it came to his own family, he could not remember a time when a woman had turned to him for assistance.

Then again, he hadn't known many women.

"May I have a glass of brandy?" she asked suddenly.

"Of course," he said, startled from his thoughts. "Forgive me for not offering you one earlier. I have sherry, too, if you prefer."

"Actually, I don't much like sherry. I find it too sweet. I suppose you find that rather unusual, a woman who would rather take brandy than sherry."

"I believe that, put against the fact that you travel with a monkey in your carriage and a snake in your trunk, having a sip of brandy rather pales by comparison," Simon reflected archly, handing her a glass.

Camelia took a sip of her drink and sighed. "I expect people in London find me rather eccentric."

"Do you care what they think?"

She shrugged her shoulders. "Not really."

"Good. Then you won't let anyone's opinion of you get in the way of what you want to do with your life. Not many women have that kind of courage."

"Elliott thinks it's foolishness. He thinks I'm naive and that I don't really understand the world around me, which is why he is so desperate to protect me."

"Is that what he was trying to do when I came upon you in the garden?" Simon's tone was wry. "Protect you?"

"In a way." Camelia stared into the depths of her glass, embarrassed by the fact that Simon had seen her in such a ridiculous situation. "Elliott wants to marry me," she added awkwardly.

So that was Wickham's goal. Simon supposed he

should have been relieved that the dullard's intentions were honorable, at least. But somehow the idea of Wickham marrying Camelia struck him as utterly wrong. Wickham would try to cage her, and Camelia was far too magnificent a creature to be locked up by that vacuous, arrogant fool.

"And what do you want, Camelia?"

"I want to return to Africa and excavate my father's site."

"Somehow I don't get the feeling that Elliott is entirely supportive of that plan."

"I believe his feelings are mixed," Camelia acknowledged. "Elliott came to South Africa right after he graduated from Oxford, because he wanted to work with my father. He was only twenty-one at the time, and he was filled with the energy and idealism of his youth. My father took him under his wing, teaching him everything he knew about archaeology. But as Elliott got older, I think he became rather disappointed that my father had not managed to lead him to a single spectacular find."

"In other words, he had thought the field of archaeology would be more lucrative than it turned out to be."

"Elliott is much more interested in being recognized for his achievements than in money," countered Camelia, anxious to defend him. "When his father died two years ago, he inherited his title and his holdings here in England, which are not insignificant. But Elliott wants to be known for his own accomplishments, and rightly so. That is why he has turned his attention to establishing his own business here in London."

"And he wants you to give up your excavation and stay here in London with him."

"He is concerned for my welfare," Camelia explained. "He is afraid that I am wasting my time and my money on a site that has already been exhausted. But that doesn't mean he hasn't been supportive of me. Elliott and I have been dear friends since I was a young girl. He went to Africa against the wishes of his family because he admired my father and his work, and over the years they became exceptionally close—like father and son, really. Other than Zareb, Elliott is the nearest thing I have to family. He will always try to help me, to whatever extent he can. That's why he wants to marry me." She took a sip of her brandy and sighed. "Elliott cares deeply about me, but on some level he also feels responsible for me, especially now that my father is dead. I think he believes my father wanted him to take care of me, and so he is willing to marry me, even though he knows I would make him an absolutely terrible wife."

Was she really so naïve that she didn't understand Wickham's desire to marry her? Simon wondered. As he studied her sitting curled up in his chair with her bare feet tucked up beneath her, sipping her brandy, Simon decided that perhaps she was. Camelia was an intelligent, independent woman of twenty-eight, but Simon sensed that her experience with men was extremely limited. She didn't seem to be aware of her extraordinary beauty, as well the easy, unaffected sensuality that permeated her every movement. On some level Wickham probably even appreciated Camelia's keen intelligence and her devotion to her father's work, even though he must have found it frustrating when she didn't agree to abandon the dig once he had decided the excavation was a failure. Camelia was as fine and rare as any artifact Elliott could ever have hoped to find, Simon decided. His lordship probably saw her as the ultimate prize for all those years he spent scrabbling about the dirt in Africa.

At least Wickham had enough brains to understand how special Camelia was, even if he couldn't grasp the fact that she was destined to be far more than some preening viscount's wife.

"He won't be happy when he finds out about what happened at your house this evening," Simon reflected. "I presume you didn't tell him about your little encounter with those two thugs in the alley?"

She shook her head. "It's actually better for Elliott not to know certain things, I find. He tends to get agitated, which doesn't help matters much."

"Once he realizes you aren't at your house, it won't take much for him to track you down here. Somehow I doubt he'll think your staying here with me is a particularly appealing situation."

"He'll be fine with it once I make him understand."

"Understand what? That someone has threatened to kill you if you return to your dig? Don't you think he will do everything he can to convince you not to return there?"

"I will not be frightened away from Pumulani," Camelia returned emphatically. "It was my father's dream to see that land properly excavated, and its relics carefully documented and placed in a museum for safekeeping. I have sworn to him in my heart that I will see his dream completed. I will not stop until I have done so."

Her sage-colored eyes were sparkling with a mixture of defiance and determination. They actually grew a little darker when she was angry, Simon realized, taking on the shifting greens of a forest.

"The excavation of Pumulani isn't really about you, is

it, Camelia?" he observed quietly. "It's about securing your father's legacy."

"My father's legacy is already secure." Her voice was proud, but there was a thread of defensiveness in it that told him she was well aware the archaeological world did not share her conviction. "He was a brilliant man and an outstanding archaeologist, who chose to go against the accepted conventions of his field and work on a continent where no others in his discipline had either his vision or his courage. During his years in South Africa he found countless important artifacts, rock paintings, and graves, all of which pointed to the highly intelligent, skilled, and resourceful tribes who have lived there since ancient times. He did not search the earth in the hope of finding fame or adoration, although the respect and support of his peers would certainly have been welcome. Nor did he devote his life to Africa because he hoped to make a fortune. My father was an explorer. For him, the journey itself was the reward. I want to continue that journey."

"For how long?"

"For the rest of my life."

"I'm not sure my pump will last quite that long," he joked. His expression grew more serious as he added, "I thought you said you were on the cusp of an important discovery at Pumulani."

"I am. But whatever I find will take years to be excavated, and when I'm finished I'll find another place in Africa to explore. Archaeology is in my blood, Simon, just as it was in my father's blood. I went on my first dig when I was ten. From the moment I had a bucket in one hand and a small pick in the other, I knew it was the only thing I wanted to do."

"I take it then your mother shared your father's passion for exploring Africa."

She sighed. "Unfortunately, my mother didn't know anything about Africa. She saw it as a hot, dirty, uncivilized place that would steal her husband for months at a time. My mother was the daughter of a viscount, and she had been raised to be a very proper, appropriately fragile English lady. I think sometimes she couldn't help but be disappointed in me, because she could see I was much more like my father than like her."

"If she despised Africa so much, then why did she let you go there?"

"She didn't. She died when I was ten, and my father returned to London, not quite sure what to do with me. I begged him to take me with him back to Africa. And he did."

"That must have been incredibly difficult for you. Leaving your home and everything you knew and going to a strange country."

"Losing my mother was agonizing. Going to live with my father was easy. As far as I was concerned, it didn't really matter where he took me, as long as we were together."

Simon was silent a moment, contemplating this. "And when did Zareb come into your life?"

"Zareb had been my father's friend for years before I went to Africa. On the day we arrived by ship in Cape Town, Zareb was there to meet us. He reached out and laid his hand against my cheek, and murmured a few words I didn't understand. Then he bent down, looked straight into my eyes, and told me he would always protect me." She laughed. "I must admit, at the time I was a little in awe of him, with his extraordinary robes and his warm, dark skin, and his intense way of looking at me. I had never met anyone like him in England. But Zareb was true to his word. He stayed by my side and watched over me more closely than my mother or father ever had, or even any governess I had ever known. He used to tell me the spirits had brought me to him as a gift, and that was why he had to take special care of me. I think that was his way of making me feel that I belonged in Africa. At that point, I only knew I desperately wanted to be with my father."

As she sat there loosely wrapped in her quilt, with her hair spilling in a honeyed tangle over her shoulders, Simon could well imagine the frightened yet determined little girl she had once been. Her father loved Africa, and she loved her father and wanted to be with him, especially after her mother died. Now that Lord Stamford was also dead, Camelia was determined to continue his work. Not just because she wanted to secure his legacy, as Simon had thought, although that was certainly part of it.

Camelia needed to continue her father's excavation at Pumulani because that made her feel closer to the man she had so adored.

"If you are determined to spend the rest of your life digging up Africa, where does that leave poor Wickham?"

"Elliott doesn't really want to marry me," Camelia assured him. "He feels an obligation to look after me because we have been so close for so many years, and because he loved my father. What he really wants is to marry his perception of what he thinks I could be, if only he could get me to settle down and be more like other women."

"Are you certain of that?"

"Yes—he just doesn't realize it yet. But I think he is coming to understand it a little better now that he sees how poorly I seem to fit in here in London. He was quite annoyed with me for the way I spoke to Lord Bagley earlier this evening. I honestly don't think I would make anyone a terribly good wife anyway," she continued irreverently, not sounding terribly bothered by this fact. "I know nothing of running a household, or entertaining, or raising children, and I'm absolutely hopeless at holding my tongue if someone says or does something I find insulting or offensive. I can't stay trapped in a house more than a month or two—I have to be out in the open, working. Then of course there is the matter of Zareb and my animals, who will always stay with me." Amusement lit her gaze as she finished, "Not many men would look at all of that and think I made a very appealing package!"

She was absolutely right, Simon reflected. Most men wouldn't think a headstrong young woman who spent her life digging up bones in Africa while traipsing around with her exotic animals would make a particularly appealing wife. But that was what made her so thoroughly fascinating. Camelia was living her life entirely on her terms, with her own goals and standards. She had no interest in what others thought of her, except as it applied to her achievements in the field of archaeology. And she was utterly dedicated to honoring the work of her late father, by pursuing his dream to its very end, regardless of the sacrifices and risks involved in doing so.

He took another swallow of his brandy, moved and bewitched by her. Why the hell couldn't Wickham just appreciate her for what she was, instead of trying to turn her into something she could never be?

"I suppose I should leave you to your work," Camelia

said, rising from her chair. "After all, the sooner you can get your pump built, the sooner we can leave for South Africa."

Simon stood. She was right—he really ought to get back to his work. Yet somehow the thought of remaining cloistered in his study, poring over his notes and drawings until early morning, no longer appealed to him.

"You miss it terribly, don't you?" he asked as he walked with Camelia to the door.

"I'm very anxious to return to my work."

"I didn't mean your dig. I meant South Africa."

She nodded. "Yes."

"What is it like there?"

"It's like . . . paradise," she returned simply. "It is a place of absolute contrasts, but the contrasts are magnificent. The cape is surrounded by the bluest, clearest, warmest strip of ocean you could ever hope to see— when the sun pours down upon it from the sky, you think that thousands of stars have fallen from heaven and are dancing on the waves. Around Cape Town there are trees and plants in every variation of green you could imagine, bearing the sweetest fruit you have ever tasted. And as you walk, a softness caresses your cheek and ruffles your hair, so gentle at first you may not notice it, until finally you realize it is the clean breeze off the ocean brushing against your skin. And then, as you travel inland, the land becomes hotter, drier, and more forbidding, but also more magnificent. The land flows around you like an endless sea of gold and green, dotted with resilient bushes and tufts of grass that care little that they may not taste rain for months at a time. There are ancient, towering mountains that stretch into the sky and try to touch the sun each morning, then turn into awesome jagged black peaks as the sky darkens and the moon rises at night. And when you stand under that brilliant pearl moon, all alone, and listen to the sound of your heart and your breath as the land settles into sleep, there is nowhere on earth where you could possibly find greater beauty."

The quilt she held around herself had fallen slightly, as if she were imagining the warm caress of that African breeze against her skin. And there was a moment of perfect stillness between them, as she stared earnestly into his gaze and tried to get him to feel what it was like to stand beneath an African moon.

Simon stared down at her, overwhelmed. He had never stood beneath an African moon, but he was quite certain it could not possibly compare to the extraordinary beauty of Camelia standing before him. She was an enchantress, he decided, even though his resolutely scientific mind knew there was no such thing. She had to be, because somehow she had woven a spell around him, powerful and exquisite and absolute, until he no longer remembered precisely who he was. All the tangled memories of his past and the relentlessly logical demands of his future suddenly melted away, until there was only that moment, with Camelia standing before him in her simple nightgown and faded quilt, her eyes sparkling with the memory of a world she loved and missed to the depths of her being.

Something within her was reaching out to him, he could feel it as surely as he could feel the silky breeze she had described brushing against his skin, the scent of exotic flowers drifting around him, the awesome quiet of the African night. He leaned toward her, closing the space between them, feeling as if he were losing his mind, and incredibly, not caring.

Just one kiss, he told himself fervently, holding her fast with his gaze as he dipped his mouth down to hers. She held herself perfectly still, not opening her lips to him, but not backing away from him either. Her breath fluttered softly upon the roughness of his cheek, as warm and gentle as the ocean breeze of which she spoke, and the scent of sunshine and meadows flooded his senses, until he no longer knew whether it was night or day, London or Africa. She sighed then, her lips parting ever so slightly, an invitation that Simon found heartbreakingly shy and inexperienced and beautiful. She was not his; he understood this completely as he drew his tongue along the brandy-sweet line of her velvety lips, slowly, gently, swearing that he would stop in another moment.

Just one kiss. Just one, and he would be satisfied. Then he would send her on her way, across the ocean to Africa, where she could have the freedom and the life she so desperately craved, with its mysterious relics and wild animals and oceans filled with dancing stars.

Camelia stood frozen, achingly aware of the warm caress of Simon's tongue against her lips, the soft roughness of his skin against her cheek, the potent promise of his hard body standing just beyond hers. Heat pulsed through her, hot and urgent, which was nothing like the horrified panic she had felt when Elliott had kissed her earlier that night. Instead she felt tense and strange and liquid, as if her body had suddenly been awakened from a deep slumber and now was flaming with need. She stood utterly still, her nerves taut with anticipation, her entire body flushed with a new and restless desire. This was what it was to want a man, she realized, confused and awed and overwhelmed by the intense sensations pounding through her.

And then, just as quickly as it had begun, Simon began to move away from her, breaking the searing touch of his mouth against hers, leaving her lost and alone.

A throaty plea escaped her as she reached up and pulled him down to her once more, pressing her lips hard against his. She opened herself to him, her tongue tentatively slipping into the dark, brandy-sweet mystery of his mouth. The quilt slipped from her shoulders and pooled onto the floor, leaving her in only the filmy veil of her nightgown. She moved closer to his warmth as she kissed him, desperate to feel his heat and the granite hardness of his body against her as she inexpertly twined her tongue with his, wanting only to be closer, and closer yet, until there was nothing between them but this magnificent, extraordinary longing.

A hollow ache bloomed inside her, tender and painful and frightening, opening the door to a fragile longing she had sometimes sensed but not really understood. But as she stood with her arms wrapped tightly around Simon's powerful shoulders, the only thing that mattered was that he not stop holding her, or touching her, or kissing her. Something had changed within her, and although she did not understand it, she knew with absolute certainty that she did not want it to stop.

Simon tightened his hold upon her, the last vestiges of his reason vainly protesting that this was wrong, that he should not touch her, that he had no right to put his hands and mouth upon her this way. But his body was afire with the most glorious need he had ever known, and he could not seem to summon enough rational thought to properly analyze just exactly why he shouldn't be prob-

ing the pink heat of Camelia's exquisite mouth with his
tongue, or roaming his hands across the soft curves of her
shoulders and waist and hips. She moaned and moved
closer, until the lushness of her thighs was caressing his
hardness.

He groaned and cupped his hands beneath her bottom
as he pressed against her, his mind lost to the citrus-
sweet scent of her, the tangy hot slickness of her mouth,
the incredible sensation of her lean softness shifting eagerly against him. He was not a man given to passionate
desires, yet in that moment he was so full of need he
didn't think he could bear it. Nothing mattered except
that Camelia wanted him, he could feel it in the desperation of her touch, could taste it in the sweet ardor of her
kiss, could hear it in the bewitching little pleas that were
escaping from her throat.

And he wanted her, with an intensity that was illogical and unthinkable and wholly, utterly unstoppable.

And so he devoured her with his mouth as he lifted
her into his arms, cradling her against him with fierce
possessiveness. He kicked the door to his study closed,
then lowered her onto the small sofa that rested against
the wall. He pulled his mouth from hers to rain hungry
kisses upon her sun-bronzed cheek, along the elegant
curve of her jaw, down the wildly pulsing hollow at the
base of her throat. The translucent layers of her nightgown melted away as he kissed lower, until his lips were
moving across the pale silk of her magnificent breasts. He
drew his tongue over one coral-tipped peak, then closed
his mouth over it and suckled long and hard, rousing the
firm, dark berry to life. He released his hold upon it and
moved to lavish equal attention to the other breast, licking and suckling and kissing while his hands moved

restlessly across the curves and planes of Camelia's beautiful body.

Camelia closed her eyes and threaded her fingers into the tangled red-gold waves of Simon's hair, wantonly holding him at her breast as he caressed it with his mouth. Her nightgown had slipped down to her waist and was cascading off the sofa and onto the floor, leaving her bare skin exposed to the warm night air. Somewhere in the farthest recesses of her mind she was vaguely aware that it was wrong to let Simon kiss her and touch her so, but she could not piece together why that should be. After all, she was not some blushing young girl who was being kept sheltered and pure by protective parents in anticipation of a handsome marriage contract.

She was an independent, grown woman of twenty-eight, who had long ago abandoned any childish notions of romantic marriage. From the time she was ten Africa had been her home, and the life her father had given her did not allow for a husband who would expect her to exist only to accommodate his needs. This realization had granted her an extraordinary amount of freedom, but it had also meant moments of staggering loneliness, especially since her father's death.

She pushed the thought away as she focused on the sensation of Simon nestling his face in the valley between her breasts, then showering kisses along the lean plane of her belly, gradually easing her nightgown further down her body. Down and down he moved, the roughness of his jaw grazing lightly against her hot skin, his breath warm and reassuring as it gusted softly against the dip of her navel, the rise of her hip, the creamy velvet of her thigh. Gradually her gown fell away and his breath was teasing the silky, aching triangle between her legs.

She held herself very still, suddenly unsure, but before she could protest he kissed her there, gently, reverently, his hands caressing her as he moved a little lower. Then the tip of his tongue slipped inside her, sending a surge of pure hot pleasure slicing through her.

She gasped in shock and stiffened, thinking she should push him away, but he anticipated her sudden modesty and grasped her wrists, gently holding them at her sides as he continued to lap at the dark hot pool he had discovered. Up and down he licked, flicking his tongue along the slick pink folds of her, tasting her and teasing her until her bones began to liquefy and her flesh was on fire. Pleasure sluiced over her, dark and shocking and intense, rinsing away all thought of modesty or control. She could have stopped him if she wanted to, she understood that completely, and somehow the bewildering realization that she didn't really want to eradicated the last fragments of her tattered reticence.

She sighed and sank deeper into the sofa, feeling the warmth of Africa wash over her even though the night was cool, and the open air of the plains surround her, even though she was in a small London town house. Pleasure was pulsing through her now, but with it came a kind of restlessness she couldn't understand. She began to shift and turn beneath Simon's tender assault, overwhelmed and yet vaguely dissatisfied as her flesh started to strain and stretch and reach for something more. She opened her thighs wider to him, inviting him to taste her more deeply, not caring anymore whether he thought her wild or wanton. He growled and sucked hard upon her, laying claim to the most intimate secrets of her body, and then he slipped his finger inside her and began to

thrust, slowly at first, then faster, filling her and emptying her as his tongue and mouth swirled over her.

Her breath began to come in shallow little puffs, her
breasts rising and falling as she tried desperately to fill
her lungs, but somehow there wasn't enough air, and her
body grew tense as she strained to fill the terrible emptiness now mounting within her. Never had she known
such wanting, but she had no idea what more it was she
wanted. Simon continued to ravish her with his mouth
and hands and fingers, devouring her as his fingers
slipped in and out of her, urging her to keep reaching
and reaching for whatever it was he was trying to give to
her. She shifted and arched beneath him, feeling feverish
and liquid and strange, and her breath continued to
come in desperate little sips, which sounded like pleas
upon the quiet night air.

Please, please, please, she implored silently, having no
idea what it was she was pleading for, except that he not
stop, not move away, not leave her when she needed him
so desperately. Farther and deeper she reached, enduring
his excruciatingly glorious assault upon her, the scalding
caress of his mouth and hands as he touched her and
tasted her and made her his own. She was losing herself
to him, losing herself to the dark passion he was showing
her, but if that was wrong then it was already far too late.
Farther and farther she reached, deep into herself and
beyond, until she thought she couldn't bear it anymore,
and yet she did bear it, and more and more, until finally
she couldn't breathe, couldn't move, couldn't think. And
then suddenly she froze, her entire being focused on an
exquisite explosion of pleasure and joy. She cried out, a
shallow, desperate cry, and Simon held her fast as ripples
of ecstasy pulsed through her, freeing her from every

constriction she had ever known, until there was nothing except Simon and her and the unbearable passion between them.

Simon held Camelia a moment, drinking in the velvety heat and scent of her, his heart pounding so hard he was certain a rib would crack. And then he rose and quickly shed his scuffed boots, his badly wrinkled trousers and creased shirt, until he stood naked before her, his skin bronzed by the spill of lamplight. She stared at him, her celadon eyes smoky with fascination, but he did not detect a trace of surprise or fear. No, Camelia had spent most of her life within the wilds of Africa, where she had doubtless seen hundreds of naked or near-naked men going about their lives with proud indifference to the dictates of Victorian modesty. Her unwavering gaze only added to the desire already roiling through him. Whatever doubt or hesitation he might have harbored about his need for her had disintegrated against the brilliance of her raw, honest passion. She wanted him with as much intensity as he wanted her.

Beyond that, there was nothing.

And so he stretched over her, covering her with the hard heat of his body, every fiber of his being on fire as he fought to keep himself from just burying himself inside her. Camelia sighed and wrapped her arms around him, welcoming him, enveloping him in her softness and her warmth, the honeyed dampness between her thighs grazing against him with tantalizing promise. He clenched his jaw, fighting for some semblance of control, trying to grasp at least enough steadiness of thought to permit him to go slowly with her.

She was the most magnificent woman he had ever known, not just because of her beauty, but because of the relentless determination that burned so brightly within her. There was a wildness to Camelia he found exquisite, a spirit that was exotic and bewildering and wonderful. She didn't belong in London, he understood that completely, but the thought of letting her go back to her beloved Africa and away from him was suddenly unthinkable. She wasn't his, and the realization made him feel hollow. He eased himself into her, slowly, gently, holding her tight within his embrace as he stared down at her, lost to the glittering depths of those magnificent sage-colored eyes.

Stay with me, he pleaded silently, knowing that it could never be, that Camelia would never permit herself to be bound or caged by anyone. *And I will keep you safe,* he vowed fervently, pressing deeper within her, thinking perhaps he could make her understand what he could never express in words. But safety was not what she sought, she had made that abundantly clear by her refusal to give up her excavation of the site she so cherished, despite the fact that there was grave danger in doing so. She sighed and began to shift restlessly beneath him, sensing that he was not giving himself to her completely. He held himself perfectly still. He was losing himself to her, he could see that now, he who had for years lived by the principle of reason over passion. He was losing himself to her and there wasn't a thing he could do to stop it, for she had already seeped into his flesh and his heart and his soul.

He withdrew a little, fighting to regain some shred of willpower, some semblance of control that would enable him to at least steel his emotions, if that was still possible. And then she wrapped her arms tightly around him and lifted her hips, stripping away the last remnants of his restraint as she sheathed him within her exquisite heat. Simon groaned, in ecstasy and despair, and buried himself as far into her as he could, kissing her deeply as he bound her to him, if only for a moment.

Camelia froze, startled by the sharp stab of pain that suddenly gripped her.

"Easy, love," Simon murmured, fighting to hold himself utterly, excruciatingly still. "Hold on to me a moment and the pain will pass."

He desperately hoped that was true. Given his complete lack of experience with virgins until that moment, he wasn't entirely sure.

Camelia buried her face against his neck, taking comfort in the warm shield of his body over hers, the tender kisses he was now raining upon her forehead and cheeks and lips, the gentle movement of him as he slowly began to stir within her. She focused on the warm marble of his back as she ran her hands over him, learning the masculine structure of his shoulders and ribs and spine, then slipped her palms lower, until she was caressing the muscled hills of his buttocks. Desire awakened within her once more, slowly at first, then faster, melting away her fear as her body sighed and stretched and rose to meet him. Simon kissed her deeply as he pulsed within her, gently, languidly, filling her and emptying her. His hand drifted down to where they were joined and began to stroke her, rousing her until she was once again restless and burning with need. She started to pulse with him, matching his rhythm, and then she tightened her hold on him and moved faster, drawing him deeper and deeper inside her with every aching thrust.

He was losing his mind. He had to be, because in that moment Simon could think of nothing except the unbearable torment of wanting Camelia. He wanted to stay like that forever, joined to her, bound to her, lost to her. Some piece of him was gone, he understood that now, whether stolen by her or given willingly he wasn't sure. All he knew was that nothing mattered except that moment, and the glory of her embracing him, the scent of sun-kissed meadows and exotic fruit surrounding him, the ancient drumming of Africa and Camelia's heart singing to him. She was not his, and the realization filled him with loss. Again and again he thrust into her, trying to bind her to him, trying to make her see that she belonged with him, however illogical and impossible that was. He needed more time, he realized, struggling to slow himself. He needed to make this fire burning between them last, so that she would understand. But there was no time, for Camelia was pulsing against him now, whispering frantic little pleas as she urged him to go faster, and faster yet. He fought to leash his desire, but it was like trying to stop a wave from crashing against a rocky shore. Camelia raised herself up to him suddenly and kissed him fervently, her silky hot body gripping him tight. He cried out, a cry of ecstasy and despair, and pushed himself deep into her. He held her fast and kissed her hard as he surrendered to her, feeling as if he were dying, and somehow not giving a damn.

Camelia lay in silence beneath Simon, feeling the powerful drumming of his heart against hers. She closed her eyes and thought of the African sun pouring over them, warm and clean and soothing. In that moment she was no longer cold, as she so often had been since coming to London. She sighed and held Simon closer, listening to the rapid gust of his breathing.

Nothing had prepared her for what had just happened between them.

She had long ago decided she would never marry, and therefore the concept of intimacy between a man and a woman had remained just that to her—merely a concept. She had been introduced to the specifics of the act years earlier when she and her father had come upon two lions mating. Although her father had been embarrassed, he had answered her questions with his typical, no-nonsense forthrightness. After all, he was an educated man of science, and he saw little benefit in keeping his daughter ignorant about a matter that she, in theory, might some day need to know about. After that Camelia took greater interest in the banter of the native women who occasionally accompanied their husbands to Pumulani. From them she was able to discern that the act itself was not altogether unpleasant—which was certainly her impression after watching the two lions—but that its purpose was chiefly for procreation. Since Camelia could not envision herself ever wanting marriage and children, she had dismissed the subject altogether.

Now she realized that there was much she had not been told.

Her body gradually cooled, and with it fear began to prickle along her spine. Was it possible a child might have been started after what had just occurred between her and Simon? She had no room in her life for a child. She needed to be free to excavate her site, which meant long, hot days spent working in the middle of virtually nowhere. A child would make her body swell as it grew inside her. And after it was born it would need her, and its need would take over her life. She couldn't afford that. She had to be free to fulfill her promise to her father, a promise which she knew could take months or even years to realize.

She pushed Simon away and leapt suddenly from the sofa, scooping up her nightgown from the floor.

"I must go," she said, hastily drawing the lacy froth over her head. She snatched up the quilt and wrapped it tightly around herself, trying to fortify the barrier she now wanted between them.

Simon regarded her in confusion, trying to think of something to say. What the hell could he tell her? That he was sorry? That he regretted touching her? That even though what had just happened between them had been the most magnificent thing he had ever known, that he was somehow remorseful it had happened?

To say such a thing would only cast a shadow over it, and her, and he refused to do that.

"Camelia," he began quietly, rising from the sofa.

"I'm sorry," Camelia interrupted, backing away from his impossibly handsome, distractingly naked form. Dear God, what had she done? She had potentially ruined her relationship with the only man who had offered to help her with her dig. In truth he hadn't exactly offered, but it scarcely mattered at that point. She desperately needed his help, and if he now refused and sent her away, she would never find the tomb before her money ran out.

"I didn't mean for that to happen, but it did, and I'm afraid there is nothing we can do to undo it, although I'm sure if such a thing were possible, we both certainly would," she blurted out, apologetic.

Simon stared at her incredulously. He had no idea what to say in response to that.

"The best thing for us to do in this situation is just acknowledge that it was a mistake, a moment of, say, total, utter madness," Camelia continued, anxious to mitigate the damage she had done. "I realize you are probably not given to such moments, but Zareb says that every now and then the stars align in such a way that people do things they would never otherwise do, and although I am not a great believer in myth and superstition, perhaps we could agree that in this particular case that is what most likely happened. The stars aligned in some peculiar way, causing us to do what we did. But it will certainly never happen again, I can promise you that."

She desperately wished he would say something, almost as much as she wished he would put his trousers on.

"You have no need to worry about me," she added fervently, struggling to keep her gaze focused on his face. "I can assure you that in the future I will have absolutely no problem exercising an appropriate amount of control over myself where you are concerned." She regarded him earnestly, wondering if she had managed to convince him.

Simon was completely out of his depth, he realized, feeling bemused and in truth, just a little bit insulted. Whatever reaction he might have expected from her, it was certainly not that she would bounce up off the sofa and start rattling on about Zareb and the stars and appropriate amounts of control, as if she believed she had just bloody well ravished him against his will.

"I'm impressed by your apparent resolve, Camelia," he muttered dryly, picking up his trousers from the floor. "But I suppose that is what has always separated you from other women—your extraordinary determination."

"Then you won't make me leave?"

He regarded her in surprise.

She was clutching the ends of her faded quilt so tightly her knuckles had been bleached white. Only then did he understand. Camelia was terrified that after what had just happened between them, Simon might decide to send her away. He didn't think she had anywhere else to go in London—except, of course, to Wickham. He supposed there was some comfort to be found in the fact that she actually preferred to stay with him, despite the fact that doing so was going to mean the stars would have to be realigned.

"Of course I won't make you leave," he informed her flatly. "Whatever would make you think such a thing?"

She regarded him uncertainly. "And you'll still build the steam pump, and come with me to Africa and train my men to run it?"

He stepped into his trousers and fastened them. He felt a bit less vulnerable now that he was at least partly covered. "Yes."

Relief poured over her, permitting her to ease her death grip on her quilt.

"Well, then, that's fine, then," she said. "I guess I'll leave you to continue with your work." She opened the door. "Good night."

Simon watched as she slipped quietly into the hall and shut the door behind her.

And then he went over to his desk and poured himself a generous drink, absolutely certain that he would not be able to get any more work done that night.

CHAPTER 7

"Where's the fire, lad?" Oliver demanded, scowling as he threw the door open.

Elliott regarded him in confusion. "What fire?"

"The one that has ye bangin' on the door like we're all about to be burnt to a crisp if we dinna make haste," Oliver returned acidly.

"I'm here to see Mr. Kent," Elliott informed him, deciding to ignore the old man's sarcasm. "You may tell him Lord Wickham wishes to speak with him."

"He canna be disturbed," Oliver replied, unimpressed. "The lad is workin' on one o' his inventions, and he doesna like to be bothered when he's hard at it."

"It is a matter of great importance," Elliott insisted.

Oliver regarded him skeptically. "Ye'll have to do better than that."

"It concerns the whereabouts of Lady Camelia Marshall," Elliott elaborated, bewildered by the fact that he was justifying his presence to a servant. This one was even more cantankerous than Zareb. At least the old

African made some effort to feign a modicum of deference in Elliott's presence. "I'm sure if you tell him that, he will be willing to speak to me."

Oliver scratched his head, considering. "If ye're wonderin' about Lady Camelia's whereabouts, why dinna ye just ask the lass herself? Seems to me that's simpler than botherin' the lad with it."

"Because I don't know where she is," Elliott explained, struggling for patience. "Now if you'll kindly let Mr. Kent know that I am here——"

"Come back here, ye cheeky wee beggar," railed a furious voice from the floor above, *"or I'll be turnin' yer scraggy hide into a hat!"*

Oscar bounded down the stairs with a voluminous pair of women's red flannel drawers billowing gaily behind him. He took one look at Elliott standing at the front door and screeched, whether with pleasure or irritation Elliott could not be sure. The fleeing monkey bolted toward him and climbed up onto his shoulder, draping the drawers across Elliott's head like a brilliant scarlet flag.

"I'll be grindin' ye into haggis!" Eunice threatened fiercely, huffing as she made her way down the stairs, "but first I'll be strippin' yer scabbit fur from yer bones an' usin' ye to polish my boots, ye rotten wee—sweet Saint Columba!" Pure embarrassment turned her wrinkled face nearly as red as her drawers as she saw Elliott standing there wearing them on his head.

"Forgive me, madam." Summoning as much dignity as he could muster, Elliott wrenched the drawers off his head. "I believe these are yours."

"They're nae mine," Eunice protested, hastily stuffing the baggy red banner into the pocket of her apron. "I was just gettin' ready to do some wash for one of the ladies down the street when that wicked beastie ran in and nicked them." She glowered at Oscar.

"What lady?" asked Oliver, frowning.

"Is Lady Camelia here?" managed Elliott, now trying to disengage Oscar, who was clinging desperately to his shoulder.

"A lady." Eunice shot Oliver a warning look. "Ye dinna know her, Ollie."

"I didna know ye was takin' in wash, Eunice," Oliver reflected, still confused. "Why would ye be doin' a thing like that, when there's so much to be done around here, what with the lass an' all her wild beasties runnin' about?"

"Is Lady Camelia Marshall here?" repeated Elliott, still wrestling with Oscar, who had evidently decided in that moment Elliott posed a safer perch than anywhere else.

"Elliott!" Camelia appeared from the door leading to the kitchen, with Harriet perched on her shoulder. "I didn't expect to see you here."

Elliott stared at her, confounded by her simple day dress and the fact that she was emerging from what he presumed was the kitchen wearing her ridiculous bird upon her shoulder.

"I went to see you at your house, but the curtains were drawn and Zareb didn't answer the door," he explained. "The first time I went I simply assumed you had gone out, but today I happened to come upon your postman, who said he had been unable to deliver your mail to you all week. Naturally I became worried that something might have happened to you. Since I last saw you leaving the Archaeological Society Ball last week with Kent, I thought he might know something, so I came here." Having finally detached Oscar from his shoulder, he set the mischievous monkey firmly on the floor. "Am I to understand that you are actually staying here, Camelia?" His tone was mild, but it was clear the possibility did not please him.

"It's only for a short while," Camelia assured him. "I'm afraid we had a few problems at my father's house, and Simon—Mr. Kent—very kindly offered to let us all stay here. So here we are."

Elliott raised a brow. "What sort of problems?"

"Just a few minor things that made staying at the house rather difficult," Camelia replied dismissively. She did not want Elliott to know her home had been broken into and that she had been threatened. If Elliott thought she was in any kind of danger, he would insist upon looking after her, and she did not want that. "Nothing to worry about."

"The lass's roof was leakin' somethin' fierce," Oliver supplied, trying to help her. "Like a great sieve, it was— ye could have washed yer tatties beneath it."

Elliott regarded him skeptically. "It hasn't rained in over two weeks."

"Aye, which means we're in for a fair soaker," Oliver retaliated gamely. "Canna leave the poor lass to fight that on her own."

"Camelia, what is this really all about?"

"I told you, I'm having a few problems at the house," Camelia insisted. "Once they have been taken care of, Zareb and I will be returning—"

"Help!" shrieked a voice from the kitchen. "He's after me!"

"Good God, someone is being attacked!" Elliott threw down his hat and raced toward the kitchen door.

"Tisha, have you seen Rupert?" called Zareb from the landing above them.

Camelia bit her lip. "I think he's in the kitchen with Doreen. Lord Wickham is going to see."

"Good afternoon, Lord Wickham," called Zareb pleasantly. "If you find Rupert, would you be kind enough to bring him back upstairs?"

Elliott stopped cold. "Are you referring to that snake?"

"Help!" Doreen burst through the kitchen door, her white hair poking out wildly from beneath her linen cap, wielding a heavy black frying pan. "He nearly bit me, he did!" she ranted furiously. "An' if he ever comes out from behind that stove, I'm goin' to crown him with this pan and fry him up for supper!"

"Oh, Doreen, I'm so sorry," Camelia apologized. "I was sure I had closed my door securely this time."

"You did, Tisha," Zareb assured her. "I checked it myself."

Oscar swung himself up onto the banister and snickered.

"Really, Oscar, that was very naughty of you," scolded Camelia. "You know Doreen and Eunice don't like Rupert slithering about the house—it makes them nervous."

"I'm nae goin' back into that kitchen 'til someone collects that slippery beastie an' locks him up proper," Doreen swore adamantly. "I've had quite enough of him poppin' out o' cupboards an' pots an' frightenin' me to death!"

"Rupert likes the kitchen because it is the warmest place in the house," Camelia explained, apologetic. "I'm afraid he isn't accustomed to the cool dampness of

London—he is much more accustomed to the warmth of Africa."

"If he doesna stop scarin' me out o' my wits, I'll be showin' him the warmth o' the hereafter," Doreen threatened sourly. "Now I'll thank ye, sir, to fetch him out o' my kitchen." She regarded Elliott expectantly.

Elliott retreated a few steps from the kitchen doorway. "Actually, I think Zareb will have better luck enticing him to come out than I."

"What the devil is going on here?" Simon scowled as he flung open the doors to the dining room. "I can't get any work done with all this yelling and shrieking—oh, hello, Wickhop. What brings you here?"

"It's Wickham," Elliott reminded him tautly. "And I came here to find out if you knew the whereabouts of Lady Camelia."

"She's right over there." Simon inclined his head toward Camelia. "Anything else I can do for you?"

"Elliott was concerned when he realized Zareb and I were not at our house," Camelia hastily explained, trying hard to appear as if everything between her and Simon was absolutely normal.

In the week that had passed since their extraordinary night of passion, Camelia had done her utmost to avoid Simon. This had actually proven remarkably easy, given that Simon had spent every day and night locked in the dining room, which he had set up as his new laboratory. Eunice and Doreen took trays of food and drink to him at regular intervals, and sometimes Oliver could be heard adamantly telling him enough was enough, and it was time for him to go to bed. Camelia didn't believe Simon ever actually heeded Oliver's advice, because no matter what hour of the day or night, the dining room doors were closed and Simon could be heard hammering and banging and muttering to himself within. If he slept, then it was only for an hour or two at a time, and he must have been lying on either the table or the floor.

Concern filtered through her as she took in his hopelessly disheveled appearance. Dark crescents had formed below his eyes, and his skin was pale and drawn from too many days spent without the benefit of sunshine, fresh air, or proper physical exercise. The silky hair she had passionately threaded her fingers through was now a wild tangle of red, and a week's worth of auburn growth shadowed the handsome lines of his jaw, giving him a faintly dangerous, almost savage look.

"So we were just explaining to him that I am staying here for a few days while we make arrangements for the repair of the roof," she finished, her tone artificially bright.

Simon frowned in bewilderment "The roof?"

"Aye, the one that leaks like a sieve," Oliver quickly explained. "I was tellin' his lordship here that we're in for a grand storm, an' that's why Lady Camelia here is stayin' with us."

"I see."

"Perhaps we could have a moment alone, Camelia," Elliott suggested, frustrated by the fact that everyone seemed to think he was a total idiot. "There is something I wish to discuss with you."

"What?" Although she could appreciate Elliott's desire to speak with her privately, the memory of his kiss in the garden made her reticent to be alone with him. She was not particularly eager to revisit the subject of marriage.

"It is regarding your site, Camelia," Elliott elaborated.

"I really think we should speak about this somewhere else."

Camelia glanced questioningly at Zareb.

"The dark wind continues, Tisha." Zareb's expression was sober. "We cannot fight that which we cannot see."

Camelia nodded, trying to suppress the dread blooming in her chest. "Let's go upstairs into the drawing room, Elliott. We can speak about it there."

"I'll bring ye some tea," Doreen offered.

"I will go with you, Doreen." Zareb's colorful robes rustled grandly around him as he moved down the staircase. "I will see that Rupert comes out from his hiding place so he does not frighten you."

"Why, thank ye, Mr. Zareb." Doreen smiled at him. "Ye're most kind."

"Perhaps you would also take Harriet with you, Zareb," said Camelia, handing the bird over to him.

"Do you want me to join you, Camelia?" asked Simon.

He stared at her intently. A ripple of fear had clouded her gaze when Zareb spoke of the dark wind. Simon could see she was afraid of whatever Wickham was about to tell her. However awkward their relationship may have become in the last week, Simon wanted her to know that he was still there to give her his support if she needed it.

Camelia looked at Simon in surprise. His blue eyes bored into her, stripping away the protective layers she had worked so hard all week to cultivate. A surge of heat shot through her, warming her blood and causing her skin to tingle with the memory of his touch.

"No, thank you," she managed. "I'm fine."

That was a blatant lie, of course. She wasn't fine at all. She was shaken by the effect Simon had on her, even though he was only looking at her. And more, she was afraid of whatever Elliott was about to tell her. But she didn't want Simon to know of her fear. She needed him to think what everybody else thought: that she was strong and able and utterly determined. If she demonstrated the least hint of weakness, then he might reconsider their agreement and stop building his pump. Without the pump, the site would remain flooded.

And unless she cleared it soon and found the tomb her father had been absolutely convinced lay buried there, her last remaining investors would withdraw their support, leaving her with a crush of debt and a barren piece of land she couldn't afford to excavate on her own.

She would be forced to sell it, or she would be left completely destitute.

"Very well." Simon turned abruptly and went back into the dining room, closing the door behind him.

"This way, lass," said Oliver, indicating the staircase. "I'll get ye settled while Doreen an' Eunice see to yer tea."

Squaring her shoulders for whatever Elliott was about to tell her, Camelia followed Oliver up the staircase and into the simply furnished drawing room above. She seated herself on the worn emerald velvet sofa and clasped her hands tightly together. Elliott paced the room until Oliver had left. Finally, he and Camelia were alone.

"Why are you really here, Camelia?" he demanded. "And please don't tell me any more nonsense about a leaky roof. I would think after all the years we have known each other and been close friends, you would at least trust me enough to tell me the truth."

His expression was wounded. A stab of guilt went

through her, making her feel small and ashamed. Elliott was right, she realized. He had been her father's protégé, associate, and dear friend for much of Camelia's life. In that time he had proven his loyalty and devotion to both her and Lord Stamford countless times. Elliott would do anything for her—even marry her as a way of protecting her.

He did not deserve to be lied to by Camelia.

"I'm sorry, Elliott," she apologized. "You're right. I'm here because someone broke into my house last week and ransacked it, destroying most of my father's precious art and artifacts. It actually happened the night of the Archaeological Society ball. Simon was with me when I went home, and when he saw what had happened, he very kindly insisted that I stay with him."

"My God." Elliott's eyes were wide with concern. "Have the police done an investigation? Do they have any suspects?"

"I didn't inform the police."

He regarded her incredulously. "Why on earth not?"

"Unfortunately, it wasn't just a simple robbery. As far as I could tell, nothing was actually stolen. It seems whoever broke in did so with the intent of frightening me, as opposed to actually stealing anything."

"What makes you think they were trying to frighten you?"

"They smashed everything they could get their hands on, Elliott. It was as if they were trying to destroy absolutely everything I cared about."

"It could just as easily have been drunken young hoodlums who thought it would be amusing to break whatever they found," Elliott argued.

She said nothing.

"Is there something else, Camelia?"

Reluctantly, she admitted, "They left a note."

"What sort of note?"

"A note warning me not to continue excavating my site."

His mouth hardened into a grim line. "What did it say?"

She shrugged her shoulders. "I don't remember, precisely."

He knelt down before her and took her hands, forcing her to look at him. "Tell me, Camelia."

She sighed. "It said something about death coming to those who disturb the sleep of Pumulani."

"Death?" Anger clouded his gaze. "They actually used the word 'death'?"

"It may have been something else," she amended, worried now that she had told him too much. "I don't really remember."

"We must inform the police of this immediately," he decided, rising. "I can't believe you have already let a week go by without doing so—and I can't believe that fool Kent hasn't insisted that you do so. If I had been with you that night, I would have made bloody sure the authorities were brought in so they could start searching for the scum who did this!"

"The police mustn't know," Camelia protested. "An investigation would be reported in the newspapers, and all of the British Archaeological Society would hear of it. That would make the few members who have reluctantly given me financial assistance worried about me, causing them to withdraw their support—ostensibly for my protection. They would also question the viability of excavating the site itself, which would destroy any possibility of my being able to solicit support from anyone else."

"They are men of science, Camelia," Elliott argued. "They aren't going to be frightened by talk of curses."

"You don't know that for certain, Elliott. I don't think archaeologists are entirely unaffected by the idea of curses, regardless of how much they protest otherwise. You and I both know there have been many bizarre accidents over the years as men have unearthed sacred tombs and treasures around the world. I think privately we all worry on some level that sometimes we may be unearthing something that is better left undisturbed."

"That doesn't sound like you, Camelia."

"I know." She traced her fingers along the faded velvet arm of the sofa and managed a small, forced laugh. "I don't think staying in London is particularly good for me. Sometimes I feel disoriented, here—like I don't know who I am."

"You have just been driven from your home under the most appalling of circumstances, and been forced to leave everything you love to come and stay in the house of a complete stranger," he reflected, seating himself beside her.

"You know you could have come and stayed with me, Camelia," he chastised gently as he took one of her hands in his. "I'm surprised you didn't ask me to come and fetch you right away. But I'm here now, and I'll wait while you pack up your things. You can even bring Zareb and your animals." His expression was faintly long-suffering as he finished, "I suppose I'll have to get used to them eventually."

Camelia regarded him blankly. "I didn't mean to suggest that I wanted to go and live with you, Elliott," she clarified. "It's London that feels strange to me, not this house. Everyone here is actually very nice to us, as long as Rupert isn't scaring poor Doreen out of her wits more than once a day. Of course Oscar has been tormenting dear Eunice something fierce, but I actually think that both of them secretly like each other. Eunice is always threatening to turn him into a polishing mitt, but at meals she's the first one to start fixing him a plate of all the choicest bits. I'm a bit worried that once we get back to Africa he's going to have cravings for oatcakes and sticky toffee pudding."

Elliott regarded her incredulously. "You cannot be serious, Camelia—you can't stay here."

"Why not?"

"For one thing, you have your reputation to consider—however much you may want to ignore it," he insisted, seeing she was about to protest. "As I'm sure you are aware, everyone believes Kent is somewhat mad—just look at the way he dresses and keeps himself, for God's sake. He's unshaven and unkempt. He looks as if he just stumbled out of Bedlam."

"He has been working night and day on my steam pump, Elliott," Camelia pointed out, feeling protective of Simon. "I think his ability to focus on his inventions to the exclusion of all else shows remarkable commitment and discipline."

"It shows he becomes abnormally obsessed about things," Elliott countered. "There is also the fact that he comes from a very unsavory background to consider. Lady Redmond found him in some filthy prison cell in Scotland, for God's sake, where he had been imprisoned for stealing."

"He was barely more than a child at the time, Elliott."

"He was nearly fifteen, Camelia, which made him virtually a man—especially for a young thug who had lived his entire life on the streets. It's well known that he has a dangerous violent streak in him—apparently while he was in prison he beat the warder so badly the poor fellow could never walk properly afterward."

"That was my brother Jack who beat the warder," drawled a low, untroubled voice. "I merely vomited on his boots."

Camelia looked up to see Simon standing in the doorway, leaning casually against the doorframe. His grease-streaked arms were folded across his chest, and the ink stains from his fingers had soiled the badly wrinkled folds of his shirt. His demeanor was relaxed, as if it didn't bother him in the least to come upon them in his drawing room clandestinely discussing the sordid details of his past. But his eyes had darkened to the steely blue color of a sky just before a summer storm breaks. There was anger there, yet Camelia could see there was vulnerability, too.

It was the same poignant vulnerability she had seen in his gaze the night she sought him out in his study.

"Please forgive us, Simon," she quickly apologized. "We should not be talking about your past."

Simon shrugged. "I don't care whether you talk about my past or not." That was a lie, but he'd be damned if he let Wickham think he had managed to upset him.

"Since you are so interested, Wickhip, I think I should at least clarify a few salient points. First of all, Lady Redmond took me out of prison when I was nine, not fifteen. I had been imprisoned for breaking into a cottage and gorging myself on a basket of apples and a bottle of spirits—it may have been whiskey, but as my appreciation of liquor was rather limited at that time, I cannot be sure. The apples, as I recall, were rotten and foul, but given the fact that I had not eaten in over three days, I did not particularly care. The spirits left me completely stewed, which is why I was still there when the owners returned home. I was thrown into the Inveraray jail, where I promptly vomited all over the warder's boots. This did little to endear me to him. I was given twelve stripes of the lash and sentenced to thirty days in jail, to be followed by five years at a reformatory school. Lady Redmond came to the prison some three weeks later and bribed the Governor to release me into her care, with the understanding that she would be responsible for me for the duration of my sentence. Is there anything else you would like to know?"

Camelia stared at him, unable to find any words. In that moment she understood with piercing clarity just how deeply Simon's past continued to haunt him. Whether that was because the ugly wounds of that past could never heal, or because the world around him refused to let him forget, she could not be certain.

"Forgive me, Kent," Elliott said, breaking the strained silence. "As you can appreciate, my concern is only for Lady Camelia and her reputation."

Simon tilted his head slightly. "Of course."

"And I have assured Elliott I need no such protection," Camelia added, trying to dissipate the tension that now filled the room.

"I'm afraid you don't understand the power of London gossip," Elliott returned. "But Kent here does—don't you?"

"I make a point of not listening to gossip, Wickhip,"

Simon told him, feigning complete indifference. "I have too many other things demanding my attention."

"Then your ability to disregard it is admirable. Unfortunately, Lady Camelia is a woman, and does not have the luxury of ignoring what is said about her."

"Nonsense, Elliott," protested Camelia. "You know very well I have never paid any attention to what people were saying about me."

"That was in South Africa. Things are different here."

"But I have no intention of staying here. As soon as Simon finishes building his pump, we will be setting sail for home."

"Regardless, for the next few months that you are here, you must pay greater attention to protecting yourself from vile gossip and innuendo."

"Actually, we will be leaving for South Africa in just a few days," Simon interjected.

Camelia regarded him in astonishment. "We will?"

He nodded.

A beam of pure joy lit her gaze. Simon stared at her, utterly captivated. For the past week he had been working like a madman, existing without more than an hour or two of sleep at a time, pausing only for the few minutes it took to eat and drink whatever food Oliver, Eunice, and Doreen had been kind enough to bring to him at what he could only assume were regular intervals. All because he was utterly determined to build Camelia her steam pump. He had told himself the sooner she returned to Africa and got her excavation underway again, the sooner he could come back to England and get on with his own bloody life. But as he stood there, feeling her pleasure wash over him like a great, calming wave, he realized that getting Camelia out of his life had not been his primary motivation, however much he may have liked to believe that. He had wanted to ease the terrible longing she felt for Africa.

The only way he knew to do that was to build her a pump and take her home.

"Are you saying you have managed to build a steam pump in just a couple of weeks?" demanded Elliott, incredulous.

"It isn't completely finished," Simon acknowledged, shrugging. "But the voyage to Africa will take more than three weeks by steamship, and then the journey to Pumulani will take time by train and wagon beyond that. I can finish assembling and adjusting the pump while we travel."

"That's wonderful!" Camelia jumped up to hug Simon, then suddenly stopped herself. "Really wonderful," she said, regarding him intently. "Thank you for working so terribly hard upon it."

"Well, this is good news." Elliott tried his best to sound enthusiastic as he slowly rose from the sofa.

Simon cast him a knowing glance. He knew Wickham was desperate to keep Camelia in London. After all, that was where his lordship was trying to establish his new business and life. He wanted Camelia with him, hovering quietly and devotedly by his side. It would be a bit difficult to court her and convince her to marry him when she was off happily digging in the dirt several thousand miles away.

"Perhaps, Camelia, you will reconsider staying with me, at least until you are ready to leave for Cape Town," Elliott suggested. "My mother is there with my three sisters, so you will have an appropriate chaperone. I really think that will be a much better situation for you than the one Mr. Kent has so kindly offered you here. I'm sure you don't want to impose upon him any more than you already have."

"Camelia has not imposed upon me at all," Simon assured him, affecting a remarkably credible expression. "In fact, I have barely noticed she is here. However, if she would prefer to go and stay with you, that is, of course, entirely up to her."

Camelia looked at him in surprise. His expression was utterly indifferent, as if it mattered not a whit to him whether she stayed with him or not. But a shadow veiled the clear blue of his eyes, masking whatever emotions may have been roiling within him.

She studied him a moment, taking in the paleness of his face, the dark bruises beneath his eyes, the wild red tangle of his unfashionably long hair. This was a man who had driven himself to the point of complete exhaustion to build her the pump she so desperately needed. He was a partner in her dig, and therefore he had a financial interest in helping her return to Africa and complete her mission. There was also the fact that until he supplied her with a pump and trained her men to use it, he couldn't go back to working on his other inventions. But Camelia sensed this was not the reason he had locked himself up in his dining room and toiled like a man possessed for the past week.

"It is better for me to stay here, Elliott," she said suddenly.

Elliott regarded her in disbelief. "Why?"

"That way I am available to Simon, should the need arise."

"What need?"

"In case Simon needs to ask me something." Camelia glanced at Simon. "You know—about the pump."

"Ah, yes, the pump." Simon nodded. "Pump questions do arise, Wickhip. I'm afraid it's rather inevitable."

"Well then, since I cannot convince you to come home with me, Camelia, I will not impose upon you any longer. Before I take my leave, let me give you this." He reached into his coat pocket and produced a stained, weathered envelope. "It seems the postman has been trying to deliver it to you for several days now. When I saw it was from Trafford, I knew it would be important, so I convinced him to give it to me, assuring him I would find you and give it to you promptly."

Camelia reached out and reluctantly took the envelope from Elliott. She had all but forgotten about Zareb's warning.

We cannot fight that which we cannot see.

Her chest tight with trepidation, she opened the envelope and quickly scanned the letter within.

Simon watched as Camelia's face paled. "What is it, Camelia?"

"There has been another accident at the site," she murmured. "An explosion."

"What do you mean?" demanded Elliott. "We don't use explosives."

"Apparently someone did. It was set off during the night, while most of the workers were sleeping. One of the men keeping watch was killed. The remaining workers are convinced the explosion was caused by the curse. About ten of them deserted the site that night, and Mr. Trafford says more are leaving every day. They believe I am too far away to have the power to protect them from the curse anymore."

Simon frowned. "What curse?"

"The natives believe Pumulani is cursed," Camelia reluctantly admitted. "That means whenever anything goes wrong, whether it be the weather turning against us or some part of the site collapsing, they blame evil forces, when in fact these are normal occurrences on an archaeological site."

"An explosion that kills a man doesn't sound like a normal occurrence," Simon reflected. "Have there been other accidents?"

"There are always accidents on a dig. It is, unfortunately, part of the job."

"But I take it the native workers don't share that view of them."

"I'm afraid it's a bit more complicated than Camelia is describing," Elliott interjected. "The land on which Lord Stamford chose to dig was believed to be an ancient burial place for a tribe that settled there hundreds, perhaps even thousands, of years ago," he explained. "About sixty years ago it was settled by a Boer family, who farmed it for barely two generations. But it was difficult—the land was dry most of the year, which made crop farming almost impossible, and the sheep and cattle they attempted to raise grew sick and died in the fields. The natives believed this was because of the curse. When Camelia's father came along and offered to buy the land from the Boers, the family was extremely eager to sell."

"And what was it about the land that so interested Lord Stamford?" Simon asked.

"My father had been working on a site where he had discovered a number of extraordinary cave paintings," Camelia explained. "These paintings depicted a very active tribal society that obviously spent a great deal of time in the area. After speaking with the elders of a nearby tribe, my father learned that the ancient tribe had practiced elaborate rituals in celebration of death, and that there was a place in which their tribal kings were believed to be buried. The area appeared to be on the Boer family's farm."

"You mean there is a tomb there?"

"Not a tomb like one finds in Egypt or China," Camelia qualified. "The African people do not tend to build grand structures in which to place their dead. But the elders described a 'Tomb of Kings,' where numerous kings had been laid to rest, along with articles they would need in the afterlife."

"What sorts of articles?"

"Typically they are very simple objects. There would be jewelry made of shells, grindstones, tortoise shells, bored stones, and sometimes ostrich eggshells made into containers."

"That hardly sounds like extraordinary riches."

"They are extraordinary from an archaeological point of view," Camelia argued. "They help us to understand the lives and beliefs of these ancient tribes."

"And I suppose they might seem extraordinary to the natives of the area, who might not appreciate your desire to dig them up."

"I am only trying to dig them up so that these things can be studied and preserved, instead of being destroyed by the elements."

"I understand that. But perhaps there are some natives who believe these things are better left where they are. Don't you think they might be responsible for your recent explosion?"

"No, I do not."

"Because you believe some rival archaeologist is trying to scare you off your site, in the hopes that he can then dig up these bones and ostrich eggs for himself."

"That is much more likely."

"Why?"

"First of all, the natives would not know the first thing about how to go about hiring thugs all the way across the ocean in London to ransack my home and intimidate me. Secondly, they would never resort to the use of explosives—they want to preserve the burial site, not risk destroying it."

"Compelling arguments," Simon agreed. "What's your thought on all this, Wickham?"

"Ultimately, I don't really care who is doing it," Elliott stated flatly. "The natives believe there is a tomb there that has been buried by the gods, and they think the gods are punishing them for trying to unearth it. I don't believe in curses, but I am concerned for Camelia's safety—especially given this recent attack on her home and the fact that she has been threatened."

"Elliott believes I should abandon my dig and just sell the land for whatever I can get for it," Camelia added. "Which I will never do."

"And just who do you propose Camelia should sell it to?" Simon asked Elliott. "If this mysterious rival archaeologist comes along and wants to buy it, I'm quite sure Camelia will feel even more compelled to hold on to the land and continue excavating it."

"That is absolutely correct," Camelia hastily agreed, giving Elliott a pleading look.

She did not want Simon to know the De Beers Company had made an offer to buy Pumulani. If Simon learned the diamond company was interested in her land, even though the site had never produced a single diamond, he might heartily agree with Elliott that it was best for her to simply sell it and move on with her life. Then he would be spared the time-consuming task of finishing the pump and making the onerous journey to Africa, which he had never wanted to do to begin with.

"There may be other possibilities," Elliott allowed vaguely, respecting Camelia's wish to not disclose any information about the De Beers Company's offer. "Unfortunately, Camelia chooses not to consider any of them, despite the fact that her ability to keep the excavation going becomes more and more difficult with each passing day. I devoted an enormous part of my life to excavating Pumulani, and I can tell you there is no tangible proof that the tomb exists—other than the rantings of a few old Kaffirs, who probably despised us whites and were lying anyway."

"We would not lie to see you dig up the earth, Lord Wickham." Zareb entered the room bearing a large silver tea tray, with Oscar sitting grandly on his shoulder. "We Africans have more respect for the land than that."

"I didn't mean you, Zareb," Elliott qualified. "I meant the natives who first convinced Lord Stamford to dig there."

"Lord Stamford made that decision himself," Zareb reflected. "His lordship was not a man who allowed others to convince him of anything he didn't truly believe in himself."

"Great convictions start small," remarked Oliver, entering with a plate piled high with oatcakes and cheese. Harriet was perched regally on his shoulder, gazing about like a faintly disapproving queen.

"An' slow fires make sweet meat," Eunice added, following him with some ginger biscuits.

"Sometimes it takes time to find a dream." Doreen was the last to enter, carrying a plate of sliced cake. "If Lady Camelia hasna found whatever her father was lookin' for, maybe the meat is nae ready yet."

"Well, now that Simon has nearly finished building a pump to drain the site and we're going home, I'm sure everything will progress very quickly," Camelia declared hopefully.

Zareb's expression was guarded. "Are we going home, Tisha?"

Camelia smiled at him. She knew Zareb was every bit as anxious to return to Africa as she was. "We'll be leaving within a week, Zareb."

"A week, ye say?" Oliver furrowed his brow, considering. "That'll give me just enough time to buy myself a new pair o' trousers an' boots."

"You're not going, Oliver," Simon told him flatly.

"Now lad, ye canna think Miss Genevieve will let ye go off to the wilds of Africa without someone watchin' over ye," Oliver objected. "Ye've nae been out o' Britain yer entire life."

"Neither have you," Simon pointed out.

"Then 'tis a grand adventure for both of us," Oliver returned cheerfully, rubbing his gnarled hands together. "I'm thinkin' the hot sun will do my achin' bones a world o' good."

"It'll fry ye up like a pan o' beef collops, more like," Eunice predicted.

"An' blister ye red as a lobster," Doreen added.

"Oliver will be fine," Zareb assured them. "I will get

him some robes and a good hat to wear, and he will be completely protected."

"There now, ye see? Mr. Zareb here will get me fixed up right, an' I'm sure he'll fix ye up too, lad, so that milky white skin o' yours doesna burn to a crisp."

"I'll be fine, Oliver." Simon disliked having his skin described as "milky" in front of Camelia. "And you're still not going."

"I'm thinkin' we should take one o' Jack's ships," Oliver continued, ignoring him. "I'm sure he must have one that goes all the way to Africa."

"Maybe he'll even be willin' to go with ye," Eunice suggested. "I'd feel better about all o' ye skitterin' across the ocean if I at least knew our Jack was at the wheel."

"Do you mean your brother Jack?" asked Camelia.

Elliott's eyes widened. "The one who beat the warder?"

"Aye—he owns a grand fleet o' ships, our Jack does," Oliver said proudly. "No doubt ye've heard of North Star Shipping?"

Camelia regarded him incredulously. "The little shipping company that took over the Great Atlantic Steamship Company a couple of years ago?"

"Aye, that's the one." Oliver was pleased that she seemed impressed. "That's our Jack that owns it, an' he's the finest sailor ye'll find on the Atlantic Ocean or any other. If he sails us to Africa, we can be sure we'll get there safe an' sound."

"I'll send word to his office manager that we'd like to book passage on one of his ships," Simon decided. "I'm not sure where Jack is right now—and it isn't necessary for him to actually steer the ship himself. I'm sure all of his crews are perfectly able."

"But Jack will keep it nice an' steady," Eunice pointed out, "which will be good for both of ye, since neither of ye have spent more than an hour on the water."

"I'll manage, Eunice."

"An' so will I," Oliver added.

"Oh, o' course ye will—like the time ye both went off for a sail on the lake with Charlotte and Annabelle, an' the lassies had to bring ye both back just a half hour later. Sick as cats, they were, an' Ollie here was beggin' me to dose him with poison, just to put him out o' his misery."

"I'd had a bite o' somethin' that didna agree with me," Oliver explained defensively.

"If ye're sayin' 'twas my cookin' that made ye ill, ye can think about makin' yer own supper," warned Eunice.

" 'Twas the lake that didna agree with ye," Doreen insisted, "what with all that bobbin' and slippin' about— I'm surprised ye both kept yer lunch inside ye 'til ye got back to dry land."

"At any rate, I'll be packin' ye some o' my special remedy for stomach sickness," Eunice told him. "If ye take it the minute ye're feelin' green, it'll help keep ye from spewin' out yer insides."

"That sounds wonderful, Eunice," Camelia said. "It's a long voyage to Africa, and although I've never been bothered by it, the ocean can sometimes be very rough."

"Fine, then, 'tis all settled," Oliver decided, smiling. "That's four tickets to Africa, on the first ship our Jack has ready to sail."

"I will also need a ticket."

Camelia regarded Elliott in surprise. "Surely you're not planning on going with us, Elliott. Isn't it far more important for you to stay here in London and take care of your business?"

"Nothing is more important to me than your safety, Camelia," he told her seriously. "Since you are determined to continue with your excavation, I'm going with you to help you. My business will simply have to wait until I return."

Simon regarded him curiously. Apparently Wickham was astute enough to realize that once Camelia was off digging up bits of bone on her site, he would be all but forgotten. Clearly that did not sit well with him. Even so, Simon could not help but wonder at Elliott's willingness and ability to abandon his fledgling import business on such short notice to go to Africa for several months. It seemed his devotion to Camelia ran far deeper than his concern for his business affairs. Or perhaps Elliott secretly nurtured the faint hope that the Tomb of Kings existed after all, and he wanted to be with Camelia in case she managed to find it. Simon suspected Elliott would not be pleased if someone else managed to unearth what he had failed to discover after so many years of trying.

Whatever the reason, the fact that Elliott was now coming left Simon feeling wary and faintly irritated.

"Fine then, five tickets it is." Oliver looked at Oscar, who had hopped off Zareb's shoulder and was now gorging himself on ginger biscuits. "I'm thinkin' maybe we should nae mention to Jack about the beasties. He may nae take kindly to the idea of havin' all these animals crawlin' about his ship."

"He doesn't have a thing to worry about," Camelia assured him. "I'll make very certain that Oscar, Rupert, and Harriet stay in my cabin for as much of the trip as possible."

"Best wait to tell him once ye're all on board," Eunice suggested. "Jack's very particular about his ships, and might nae fancy the idea of a monkey sharin' his plate, or a snake slitherin' about in his pots."

"Dinna fash yerself, lassie," Oliver said, sensing Camelia didn't like the idea that her animals might not be welcome. "Jack's been all around the world more times than I can count, an' seen things we can scarce imagine. He's nae likely to be bothered by a wee monkey, a skinny snake, an' a molting bird."

"Good, then it's all settled. I must go and write to Mr. Trafford, to let him know we are coming. If the letter goes out with today's post, he will at least have a few days' warning before our arrival. He'll be extremely pleased when he hears we are finally going to have a pump to clear the site. A machine is not going to be frightened away by a curse."

Oliver frowned. "What curse?"

"It's just nonsense, Oliver—you have nothing to worry about."

Oliver raised a questioning brow at Zareb.

"Don't fash yourself, Oliver," Zareb said, awkwardly attempting to use one of Oliver's expressions. "I will make you a powerful amulet to ward off any evil."

Oliver looked unconvinced. "Perhaps ye should make one for the lad here, too," he said, indicating Simon.

"That won't be necessary, Zareb. I don't believe in curses." Simon winced as Harriet suddenly landed on his shoulder in a flurry of gray feathers.

Zareb studied him a moment, contemplating the fact that Harriet had chosen that specific moment to go to him. "You may not need an amulet," he allowed. "But I will make you one anyway and carry it for you."

"While ye're at it, could ye make one for me?" wondered Doreen. "I could use it to keep that wicked snake away from me."

"Rupert isn't wicked, Doreen," Camelia objected. "He just likes you."

"Fine, then, make an amulet that'll keep him from likin' me quite so much. 'Tis either that or the fryin' pan for him."

"I will make you an amulet that will keep Rupert away, Doreen," Zareb offered. "But I must warn you, the smell of it may make it difficult for you to wear."

Doreen shrugged. "Then I'll just hang it over the kitchen door."

"Forgive me for taking my leave of all of you," Camelia apologized, "but I really must write that letter to Mr. Trafford."

"And I'd best get started on the medicines ye'll be needin'," Eunice decided. "I'm thinkin' a good supply of syrup o' violets to purge yer bowels now an' again will be handy. No tellin' what strange foods ye'll be eatin' over there."

"I'd rather ye give us medicines for keepin' food in us, instead of them that makes ye heave it out," Oliver reflected.

"I'll pack both," Eunice told him. "Just in case."

"I also have many matters to attend to before we leave," Elliott said.

"I'm happy to show ye the door, yer lordship," Oliver said pleasantly, leading the way.

Simon watched as the little party bustled out of the drawing room and headed noisily down the stairs.

Then he sat on the sofa and stared at Oscar, who was merrily gorging himself on the forgotten ginger biscuits.

"Give it over," Simon said, holding out his hand as Oscar greedily grabbed the last cookie. "Or I'll tell Eunice you were the one who tossed her good petticoat out the window."

Oscar shot back a defiant protest.

"You won't like being a polishing mitt," Simon warned. "Eunice uses a polish paste that smells really foul."

Oscar paused, considering. Reluctantly, he handed his precious biscuit to Simon.

"A very good decision," Simon assured him, preparing to bite into it.

Harriet squawked noisily on his shoulder in protest.

"You can have one of the oatcakes instead." Simon picked one up and offered it to her. "They are just as good."

Harriet took the oatcake in her beak and flung it irritably across the room.

"Fine, then," he conceded. "But you only get half." He broke the cookie into two pieces and gave her one of them.

Sinking back, he bit into his half of the cookie and sighed. After thirty-five years of never venturing farther than from Inverness to London, he was about to cross the ocean and trek deep into the wildest parts of Africa to find a tomb that was supposedly cursed.

At that moment, he could only pray for two things. One, that the pump he had just built would actually work.

The other was that he would survive the bloody voyage.

PART II

THE DARK WIND

CHAPTER
8

Camelia gripped the heavy iron railing and inhaled deeply, letting the cold, black spray of the ocean rinse away the filth and turmoil of London.

They were only a few days into their three-week voyage, but already she felt better than she had in months. The ocean air was fresh and pure, instead of being heavy with the stench of London's smoky fires, cloying perfume, stagnant manure, and sewage. She could not understand how she had managed to endure it for as long as she had without falling ill from some dreadful lung disease. Although they had not yet reached the coast of Morocco, she could feel Africa calling to her across the inky miles of star-flecked waves.

Come home, Camelia, it whispered with every crash of the ship's hull through the powerful, churning water. *Come home.* She closed her eyes and leaned out a little further, feeling free and reckless and guardedly hopeful.

Finally, she was going home.

When they had left Cape Town for England some three months earlier, Zareb had worried they might never return. He had cautioned Camelia that London was a wild and dangerous place, where one's spirit could be lost and never found. Camelia had dismissed his fears as those of an elderly African man who was afraid of a world he did not know—a world in which Camelia had forewarned him he might face even greater prejudice than that which he was forced to endure in his home-land. How could a gentle, honorable, intelligent man like Zareb, born to one of the most powerful tribes of the Cape, not fear their going to such a place?

But Zareb had been wrong. Camelia had not lost her spirit to London—had not even come close to it. The glit-tering balls and parties she had attended had paled be-yond her painful longing for the quiet beauty of an African night sky. The ornate, towering buildings and narrow, crowded streets had made her feel breathless and trapped. And the endless days of writing letters pleading for an audience with some potential investor, or attending some dull lecture or party in the hopes of se-curing a promise of either money or a pump, had left her feeling hollow and frustrated, as if she weren't really ac-complishing anything at all. Her father had been right about her, she mused as she leaned out even further.

She was happiest when she was playing in the dirt.

"I'd prefer it if you didn't lean out quite that far," said a low voice. "I don't particularly relish the idea of a late-night swim."

She turned to see Simon's brother Jack watching her from the shadows. He was leaning casually against a mast, his arms folded across his chest, his relaxed stance very much reminiscent of the way Simon often stood. From there the resemblance ended abruptly.

Jack Kent was about an inch taller than Simon, and his

handsome face was lined and bronzed from years of standing on a deck facing the wind and the sun as he steered his ships across the ocean. His hair was the color of well-polished wood, threaded with a few sun-bleached strands of gold, and his eyes were a steely gray that reminded Camelia of the gleaming blade of a dagger. At thirty-eight he was only three years older than Simon, but there was a worldliness to him that made him seem far more mature. Her gaze fell upon the thin white scar that snaked along the chiseled contour of his left cheek. She recalled Simon mentioning that Jack had been nearly fifteen when Lady Redmond finally rescued him from a prison cell in Inveraray.

She sensed that the years in which he had been forced to survive on his own had been extremely harsh.

"I love the scent and feel of the ocean," Camelia told him, leaning in a bit. "It makes me feel free."

"I understand completely," Jack assured her. "However, I do think Simon would be rather annoyed with me if I let you topple overboard."

"Where is he?"

"He's down in the engine room. He's trying to come up with a more efficient steam engine that will propel my ships faster than the current industry standard. He says he has a new idea that he will start working on for me the minute he returns from Africa."

"Then he must be feeling better."

"I'd say so, yes. It seems the seasickness finally ran its course."

"Or Eunice's medicine finally cleaned him out," quipped Oliver, joining them on the deck with Zareb. "Poor lad—for a moment I thought he was goin' to ask Jack to turn the ship around an' take him back to

England. He was afraid he was goin' to be green as a frog the entire journey."

"He would not have been so sick if he had allowed me to perform my healing ceremony," Zareb insisted. "Unfortunately, I was not able to convince him."

"He should still be resting in his cabin," Camelia reflected. "If he's weak he shouldn't be trying to work yet."

"Nae sweat, nae sweet," Oliver mused. "The lad has always been happiest when he's up to his ears in grease an' metal."

Jack nodded in agreement. "I remember when we first went to live at Haydon's estate, Simon was fascinated by all the clocks that were there. So one by one he set to taking them apart and trying to put them together again, to see if he could teach himself how they worked. But for some reason there were always a few extra parts left over after he had finished with them."

"For nearly a year we had clocks chiming somewhere in the house every minute of the day and night," Oliver continued, laughing. "Finally, his lordship had the whole lot of them packed up and sent to a famous clockmaker in Inverness, who worked for another year trying to make them all work proper again!"

Camelia smiled. She could well imagine Simon as a little boy, busily taking apart everything he could get his hands on. "Did Simon ever learn how to build a clock?"

"Ultimately Haydon hired the clockmaker to come to the estate and teach Simon how clocks and watches worked," Jack told her. "And after a week the man said Simon had an incredible aptitude for it, and should consider a career in clock-making."

"By then the lad was nae interested in clocks any

more," Oliver added, shaking his head. "He had set his mind to makin' other machines using the workings of the clock—only bigger."

"Like what?" wondered Camelia.

"One day when Eunice and Doreen had him and his brother Jamie washin' the supper dishes, Simon got it into his head 'twould be far better if a machine did it," Oliver began. "So he piled the plates and glasses into an old wooden tub with some soapy water and fixed some great contraption he had built onto the tub. When Eunice and Doreen came back to the kitchen a wee bit later, Jamie was turnin' a crank and makin' the tub shake somethin' fierce, while Simon urged him to go faster so the dishes would be done quicker."

"He was sorely disappointed when Eunice started pulling broken bits of plate and smashed glassware out of the tub," Jack continued wryly. "After that he was forced to reconsider his invention."

Camelia smiled. "But he never stopped inventing."

"He couldn't—'twas in his blood, the same as the sea is in Jack's blood," Oliver explained. "His lordship and Genevieve hired the best tutors they could find for him, an' they all agreed the lad was uncommonly clever— even the one who quit after Simon accidentally blew up his desk." He slapped his knee with amusement. "Singed the poor fellow's eyebrows clean off—his sister Annabelle had to draw them back on with a bit o' burnt cork afore he left. When Simon finally went off to university, we all worried he was going to accidentally burn the whole school down."

"And did he?" wondered Zareb.

"Only one science laboratory." Simon emerged from

below deck with Oscar perched comfortably on his shoulder. "It needed refurbishing anyway."

A soft spill of moonlight poured over him as he moved closer. He was dressed in a simple white shirt, dark trousers, and a loosely fitted coat. He seemed thinner to Camelia in the shadowy night air, and his skin had grown even paler over the last few days of his illness. A flicker of guilt pulsed through her. He had completely exhausted himself as he worked on the pump day and night before they boarded the *Independence*. She could not help but think Simon's weakened state had contributed to the illness that overcame him the minute Jack's great steamship left London. He would be better in Africa, she decided, watching as Oscar affectionately searched through Simon's tangled red hair for bugs. Once he was back on land, with the warm African sun and wind caressing his skin, he would quickly become strong once more.

"Jack and Oliver were just telling us about some of your escapades as a boy" she explained, smiling. "It seems even then you were always trying to improve upon things."

"I've always been interested in how things work," Simon returned, prying Oscar's questing little paws from his hair. "Once you understand how something works, then you can focus on trying to make it better."

"There's some things that need nae improvin' upon," Oliver reflected.

"Like what?"

"Like this sky." Oliver gazed upward. "All these stars have been about for thousands of years, an' they'll be about for thousands more. There's nae to improve upon there—ye just stand back an' enjoy it."

Simon looked up and frowned. "If we want to study the stars, we need the equipment to do so, and that is something that can always be improved upon. One day I will work on making a better telescope—one that allows you to see the planets more clearly."

"What do ye need to see planets for, when there's all these stars about ye?" demanded Oliver impatiently. "That's more than enough to fill yer gaze, I think."

"I would like to see even farther."

"Why?"

"Because I am curious about what else is out there. I want to know about the things I cannot easily see."

"Did it ever occur to ye there are some things ye're nae meant to see?"

Simon shrugged. "I suppose if I'm not meant to see something, then I won't be able to."

"Next thing ye know ye'll be tryin' to see all the way to Heaven, an' God himself will say 'Here now, that's enough, young Kent, ye keep yer eyes where ye're supposed to.'"

"When God says that, I'll just look somewhere else, Oliver," Simon returned easily. "There is a lot still waiting to be discovered."

"Good evening, everyone." Elliott stepped onto the deck from below. "It's a bit late for you to be out in the cold night air, Camelia, don't you think?"

"I'm fine, Elliott," Camelia assured him. "We were just enjoying this beautiful night sky."

"How is our course going, Captain Kent?" asked Elliott, not bothering to look up. "Are we maintaining our schedule?"

"We have made good progress these last few days," Jack told him. "But there's bad weather on the way, which will likely slow us down for the next day or two. Hopefully we'll be able to make it up after that."

"What do ye mean, bad weather?" scoffed Oliver. "The sky's as clear as can be."

"There is a patch of dark cloud off to the southeast."

"What, that wee bit o' shadow?" Oliver snorted. "That's nae more than a wee cloud that's lost its mother."

"The mother is right behind it," Jack returned, amused by Oliver's analogy. "And the father, too."

"The captain is right." Zareb's eyes narrowed as he stared into the distance. "There is a storm coming. I can feel it."

"Maybe we should pick up speed then," suggested Camelia. "Try to get past it before it hits."

"Unfortunately, with the course we're on, all we'll do is run into it even faster," Jack told her. "You needn't worry—the *Independence* has handled plenty of bad weather in her time."

"Yer ship may be accustomed to it, but the lad's stomach is nae so swack," Oliver said, inclining his head toward Simon. "If he spends the next three days with his face in a bucket again, he'll be nae but skin and bone by the time we reach Cape Town."

"Yes, you've had a bit of a rough time since we left, haven't you, Kent?" Elliott's tone was faintly superior. "Not accustomed to ocean travel, I take it?"

"I'm fine." In fact Simon felt like a wrung-out dishrag, but he saw no reason to share that with Wickham. It irked him that everyone else was apparently unbothered by the infernal shifting and rolling of the ship, while he had been reduced to a miserable, retching mess on the narrow bed of his cabin.

"I hope so. You'll need all of your strength for Pumulani."

"You needn't worry about me, Wickhip," Simon assured him. "Now that I've had a few days to get used to the motion, I find I'm quite enjoying being at sea. If you'll excuse me, I have to get back to my drawings. I'll see all of you in the morning. Good night."

He turned and headed below deck, whistling cheerfully.

He hated the bloody ocean.

That was his only thought as he lay sprawled on his bed, desperately gripping the sides of his mattress. His nausea had subsided, thank God, but the storm Jack had forecast had stirred the ocean into a roiling stew. The result was the *Independence* began rising and falling even more than she had already been, making Simon's insides plummet from his throat to his knees every minute or so.

How did anyone tolerate such relentless, torturous motion? he wondered furiously. And how was it physically possible that an enormous iron steamship could be rocked about as violently as if it were nothing more than a bloody cork?

If I ever manage to survive this sodding trip, I am never stepping onto a ship again. He watched in misery as his metal washbasin and jug slid off the washstand and clattered noisily onto the floor. *Not until I build a ship that doesn't rock about like a goddamn child's toy.*

He swallowed thickly and closed his eyes, which only seemed to make matters worse. He opened his eyes again and stared at his desk, trying to focus on the stack of books and drawings he had left there. Perhaps he should get up and try to work. That might help to take his mind off the movement. His books began to slowly slide from one end of the table to the other. He stared at them as they skittered back and forth, unable to decide whether it was worse to watch them and know how much the ship was shifting back and forth, or just close his eyes and feel the motion. Finally the books slipped right off the table, with his pen and inkwell following.

Right. That was definitely worse.

He closed his eyes, trying to block all sensation out. He considered going up onto the deck, thinking maybe the fresh air and the ocean spray would revive him a bit. There was also the fact that if he were going to be sick, it was much more convenient to just lean over the railing and spew right into the wretched ocean that was causing him so much grief. But the thought of dragging himself off the swaying bed, down the rocking corridor, and up a swinging flight of stairs was far more physical effort than he could possibly manage. So he simply lay where he was, holding fast to the mattress as he debated the consequences of taking yet another dose of Eunice's foul stomach elixir. If the ocean didn't kill him, Eunice's elixir surely would.

At that moment, that possibility was extremely appealing.

A sudden pounding on his door interrupted his misery.

"Mr. Kent! It is Zareb—please, you must come quickly!"

Somehow Simon managed to pull himself up off the bed, stagger to the door, and wrench it open.

Zareb stood in the corridor, his eyes wild with fear.

"She is dying, Mr. Kent, sir," Zareb whispered, his

voice breaking. "The dark wind has come, and I cannot send it away."

Fear sliced through Simon, eradicating all thought of his discomfort. "What do you mean, she's dying?"

"The dark wind," Zareb repeated, as if he thought Simon should know what he was talking about. "It has finally found her. I have tried to keep it from taking her, but it is too strong. Come!"

The aged African turned and flew down the corridor, his gaily colored robes fanning out behind him like the plumage of an exotic bird. Simon raced along behind him.

A thick, acrid cloud of smoke poured from Camelia's cabin as Zareb opened the door.

"Fire!" Simon roared, his breath frozen in his chest as he tore into the smoke-filled cabin. *"Camelia!"*

"No, no, not a fire," Zareb quickly assured him, following. "I am trying to drive away the evil spirits."

Simon blinked against the stinging haze. Camelia lay curled in a shivering heap upon the floor, dressed only in her nightgown, with Oscar, Harriet, and Rupert huddled protectively beside her. A caul of gray mist wafted thickly throughout the dimly lit cabin, enveloping all of them in its sickly sweet stench. A circle of sand had been drawn around her, and a half dozen smoldering containers were arranged by her head, arms, legs, and feet, each spewing a suffocating fog. Camelia weakly raised her head as Simon came in, barely managing to reach the chamber pot as her entire body was consumed with the most violent retching he had ever seen.

He rushed to her side and knelt down, gently moving her hair back and supporting her head as she was sick.

"Easy, Camelia." His voice was low and taut as he tried

to feign a calm he did not feel. When her retching had finally subsided, he cradled her in his arms, appalled by the ghostly paleness of her skin.

"I'm dying," Camelia whimpered, the words barely a thread of sound against the groaning of the ship.

"No, you're not," Simon countered firmly. "If I have to survive this goddamn torturous voyage, Camelia, then so do you." He began to lift her into his arms.

"You must leave her where she is," Zareb protested. "She needs to be protected from the curse!"

"She needs to be lying on her bed," Simon countered, taking her over to it and gently laying her down.

"But the bed is fastened to the floor—I cannot make a protective circle around her if she lies there!"

"Your protective circle isn't doing anything, Zareb," Simon argued, drawing the blankets over her. "Just look at her—she's freezing lying there on the floor!"

"Where's the fire, lad?" Oliver burst into the cabin, waving his skinny arms about and coughing. "Sweet Saint Columba, what's that filthy stink?"

"I am driving away the evil spirits." Zareb moved his pots of smoldering herbs closer to Camelia.

"More like ye're drivin' away every last bit of air," Oliver observed, hacking.

"Camelia!" Elliott raced into the room and stared in horror at Camelia lying limp and pale upon her bed. "My God, Zareb," he managed, choking on the smoky haze, "what have you done to her?"

"It is the dark spirits." Zareb's expression was tortured as he arranged his smoking vessels of herbs alongside Camelia's bed. "They have followed her across the ocean, and now they are going to take her."

"What the devil are you talking about?" Elliott

watched in horror as Camelia rolled her head over to one side and vomited into the chamber pot Simon was holding for her. His face blanched. "Sweet Jesus—what's wrong with her?"

"It is the curse," Zareb insisted, near tears. "The dark wind has found her."

"What the hell is going on here?" demanded Jack, appearing at the doorway dressed only in his trousers. "Is there a fire?"

"We need a doctor!" Elliott told him. "Now!"

"There isn't a doctor on board." Jack went over to where Camelia lay.

"That's outrageous—how the hell can a ship not have a doctor on board?"

"How long has she been like this?" Jack asked Simon, ignoring Elliott as he took in Camelia's shivering white lips and chalky skin.

"I don't know—I just arrived and found her like this." Simon reached for a cloth from the washbasin and gently wiped her mouth. His voice was low and strained as he asked his brother, "Do you know what's wrong with her?"

"She probably caught some hideous disease from one of these filthy bloody animals." Elliott glared furiously at Oscar, Harriet, and Rupert. "Maybe that bloody snake bit her—I've told her she shouldn't keep it around!"

Rupert raised himself higher and flicked his tongue at Elliott in warning.

"The dark spirits don't use animals to carry out their curses," Zareb countered, carrying another burning pot over to Camelia's bed. "They have the power to enter the body on their own."

"I'll take that, Zareb." Jack took the smoldering pot,

opened the window, and heaved it into the churning ocean. "Oliver, bring me those other burning containers, would you please?"

"No, Captain!" Zareb protectively grabbed hold of two pots. "We must fight the evil within this cabin!"

"The only evil within this cabin is the stench and smoke you have created," Jack argued, hurling another vessel out the window. "I can barely breathe, and I'm not sick—I can scarcely imagine the effect this poisonous air is having on Lady Camelia." He tossed another smoking container into the sea.

"You are fighting a dark power you do not understand," Zareb protested. "The curse of Pumulani is very powerful!"

"I may not know much about dark powers, but I sure as hell know a bad case of seasickness when I see it," Jack retaliated, grabbing another smoky container from Oliver and pitching it into the storm. "And I know you aren't helping her by forcing her to breathe that foul smoke when her entire body is trying to empty itself!"

Simon stared at him in confusion. "Seasickness?"

"Impossible." Zareb emphatically shook his head. "Tisha never gets seasick."

"Then I suppose there is a first time for everyone," Jack retorted.

Oliver scratched his head, mystified. "How can the lass be seasick now, when she's been fine these past three days?"

"The sea has become much rougher in the last four hours. Haven't you noticed how much the ship is lurching?"

"I thought it was always like this," Simon said ruefully.

"I thought 'twas the wee drop o' whiskey I'd had after supper," Oliver reflected.

"I wouldn't drink any more if I were you, Oliver—it will only make the ship's movement seem worse," Jack advised, handing Oliver the chamber pot. "Would you kindly rinse this out and have young Will, the cabin boy, fetch me two clean buckets, some fresh towels, a pitcher of drinking water, a spoon, and two more blankets. Zareb, you will need to stay by your mistress throughout the night, and keep a close watch on her. She will probably continue to be ill until she is so weak she can only sleep. Try to get a few small sips of water into her from a spoon—no more than one every ten minutes or so, or she will just throw it back up. If she gets worse or becomes feverish fetch me immediately. Do you understand?"

Zareb slowly nodded, struggling to focus on Jack's face as the cabin shifted and rolled.

And then he suddenly clapped his hand to his mouth and ran from the room, desperate not to be sick in front of everyone.

"I'll just make sure he's all right," said Oliver, who was also suddenly feeling anxious to get up onto the deck. "I dinna think Mr. Zareb will be much use to the lass tonight."

Jack sighed and turned his gaze expectantly to Elliott and Simon.

"I'll look after her," Simon said.

"No, *I'll* look after her," Elliott insisted. "I've known Camelia for years—I'm much closer to her than you are, Kent."

"Fine," said Jack. "As I was saying, Wickham, it's

important to try to get a little water into her, but go slowly with it. Once the vomiting has subsided, you can try to get her to take some weak ginger tea. Tomorrow, if Camelia is feeling well enough to sit up, she can have a little plain soda biscuit, broken into small pieces, and if that goes down well, then she can have some—are you listening, Wickham?"

"Of course I'm listening," Elliott asserted, fighting to keep his gaze focused on Jack as the cabin swayed back and forth. He braced his feet beneath him, struggling to find some degree of stability. "You were saying something about ginger biscuits and—" He reached out and grabbed the wall, trying to hold fast.

"Are you all right, Wickhip?" Simon frowned. "You look awfully pale—"

"I'm fine," Elliott retorted, swallowing thickly. "So I'm to give her biscuits and tea and . . ." He stopped, his expression panicked.

Then he charged from the cabin, barely making it into the corridor before he threw up.

"Bloody hell." Jack turned to look at Simon. "Are you all right, or are you about to boak as well?"

"I'm well enough to look after her," Simon assured him.

"Good. The main thing is to keep her as warm and comfortable as possible, and try to get a little water into her. The air in here is cooler and clearer now, but I think these animals should be removed, so there is less commotion around her. I'll put them in your cabin." He eyed Rupert warily. "On second thought, you pick up the snake. I'll get the other two."

Harriet flew up onto Simon's shoulder and squawked noisily as Jack approached her. Jack turned toward

Oscar, who scurried up Simon and planted himself firmly on his head. Rupert stayed where he was, his body raised and arched for striking.

Simon winced as Oscar gripped his hair. "Maybe the animals should just stay here."

Jack regarded his brother curiously. "I never knew you were fond of animals."

"I'm not," Simon assured him, trying to stop Harriet from digging her claws into his shoulder. "But for some strange reason they don't seem to sense that."

"Here are the things you asked for, Captain." A sleepy-looking lad of about twelve years of age entered the cabin weighted down with an armful of blankets, towels, buckets, and water. "That Lord Wickham ain't lookin' so good—I just saw him tryin' to get to his cabin and he was green with—bugger it—there's a snake in here!"

"That's all right, Will," said Jack. "That snake belongs to Lady Camelia. You can just put everything over there by that table."

"Does he bite?" demanded Will suspiciously, not moving.

"I've not actually seen him bite anyone." Having given up on moving Harriet, Simon was now trying to disengage a very stubborn Oscar from his head. "And even if he did, his bite isn't poisonous to humans."

"Why don't her ladyship keep him in a cage?" wondered Will, keeping as far away from Rupert as possible as he inched toward the table.

"Lady Camelia doesn't believe in cages."

"An admirable philosophy," Jack mused. "I'm not much fond of them myself. Come on, Will—let's see how things are going on deck. If this storm picks up, we'll have more to worry about than just a few sick passengers."

"What do you mean, 'picks up'?" demanded Simon, grabbing the water pitcher as it was about to topple over. "Aren't we in the storm now?"

"What, this? This is nothing. Wait 'til the ship starts listing until it nearly rolls right over—that's when you'll really feel alive!"

Simon held the sloshing water pitcher to his chest and groaned. "Does Amelia know you have this bizarre side to you when it comes to the sea?" he asked, referring to Jack's wife.

"Amelia knows everything about me. And for some reason I cannot fathom, she loves me anyway." Jack grinned at his brother, who in that moment looked utterly ridiculous with a monkey on his head, a bird on his shoulder, and a snake slithering over his feet. "Which leads me to believe there must be hope for all of us wayward thieves, Simon." He glanced at Camelia, who was lying quietly on the bed. "Her retching seems to have subsided a bit, which is good. Don't give her any water yet—just keep her warm. I'll be back in a while to see how she is." He left with Will, closing the cabin door behind him.

Simon stood in the center of the cabin, watching as Camelia's trunks and the chair at her small writing desk slid across the floor. Rupert hastily slithered out of their way, while Oscar bounded to safety on top of the desk, which was fastened to the floor. Harriet flapped her wings and tightened her grip on Simon's shoulder.

"Think of it as an adventure," he advised them, grabbing the wayward chair. "Something you can tell all the other monkeys and birds and snakes once you are back home."

Oscar frowned and vehemently shook his head.

"You're probably right—they wouldn't believe it. I know I bloody well wouldn't if someone tried to describe it to me." He planted the chair firmly beside Camelia's bed, then sat down. Pouring fresh water from the pitcher into the washbasin, he rinsed out a cloth and began to gently sponge her face.

Her skin was ashen, and crescent-shaped bruises had formed beneath her eyes. Her brow was creased and her lips were drawn in a tight line, as if she were still fighting the nausea coursing through her. An unfamiliar feeling of protectiveness welled within him as he slowly washed her face and neck. He dropped the cloth in the basin and laid his hand against her forehead, trying to determine if she was growing feverish. Her skin was cool. Remembering that Jack had told him to keep her warm, he rose to fetch the blankets that young Will had unceremoniously dropped on the cabin floor.

He returned to her side to find her watching him.

"You left me," she murmured softly. She seemed to struggle to form the words, as if it required great effort to speak.

"Only for a moment. I just went to get you these blankets." He carefully laid them over her.

"I'm dying, Simon," she whispered. "I'm sorry."

"You're not dying, Camelia. Although having just experienced something close to what you are currently going through, I realize at this moment you may not find that particularly reassuring."

She frowned, trying to make sense of what he was saying. "I'm not dying?"

"No."

"Zareb said the dark wind had come."

"I thought you didn't believe in curses." His voice was faintly teasing as he seated himself beside her and began to rearrange her sheets more to his liking.

"I don't." She stared at him, her eyes glazed with despair. "But I feel like I'm going to die."

Simon reached out and tenderly drew his fingers down the cool silk of her cheek. "It's dark, Camelia, and there is definitely a wind out there. And that wind has churned up the ocean, which is making this ship rise and fall like a bouncing ball. If you think you're sick, you should see poor Wickham," he quipped, smiling. "Right now he's probably hanging over the railing, debating whether he should just end his misery and jump in."

"And Zareb?"

"Unfortunately, he's sick, too. And I believe Oliver is right beside him."

"It's my fault," she said miserably.

"I don't think you can be held responsible for the weather, Camelia."

"They are here because of me."

"We are all here because we have chosen to be," Simon corrected her. "There is a difference."

She closed her eyes, too exhausted to debate the matter any further.

He sat beside her a long while, focusing on the pale weariness of her beautiful face as the cabin rose up and down and her trunks slid back and forth. He thought about how small and fragile she looked as she lay there, which was so at odds with the determined young woman who had marched into his laboratory unannounced and insisted that he should build a steam engine for her. She had traveled across this very same ocean to come into his life. Now she was finally going back to the land she loved. No dark winds or evil curses or mortal threats could keep her from going home to Africa. She would return to her site and clear it of water and resume digging, and either find the ancient tomb of which her father dreamed, or die in the process. If there was one thing he understood about Camelia, it was that she never gave up.

She fought with the heart of a warrior.

Her breathing had deepened slightly, and the lines on her brow had eased, suggesting her nausea was finally lessening. Simon thought he should probably fetch some of the ginger tea Jack had mentioned. When Camelia wakened, she should be encouraged to drink a little. He would also get her some biscuits, just in case she was hungry when she finally stirred. He rose and began to adjust her blankets so she would not grow cold while he was gone.

"Do not leave me," she murmured, her voice barely audible against the crashing of the ocean as it rocked the *Independence*.

"I'm not leaving you." He brushed a strand of sunkissed hair off her forehead. "I'm just going to fetch you some tea."

She frowned and reached for his hand, clasping it weakly within her fingers. "Do not leave me," she repeated, slower this time, as if she were struggling to make him understand. "Please."

He stared at the paleness of her slender fingers clinging desperately to his own. Her hand was small and soft against his, like the velvety petals of a flower. He remembered the feel of that hand caressing him, touching him and holding him until he thought he would go mad from it. He had felt as if he had lost himself to her on that night, lost some deep and secret part of himself that he could never reclaim, however desperately he might try. And he had tried, in the weeks that had followed. He had done his best to avoid her, to focus on his work, on the details of arranging this trip, and, for the past few days, on the overwhelming challenge of just surviving the misery of this bloody ship.

But as he stood there holding her hand, he found he was lost once more. *Do not leave me.* She meant only for that moment, while she lay sick and vulnerable and afraid. Yet somehow the words wound their way into the deepest recesses of his soul, binding him to her in a way she could not possibly understand. She had stolen a part of him. He understood that now. She had not meant to, but it scarcely mattered. She had taken a piece of his heart and his soul, and when he finally left Africa and went home, she would keep it with her.

He knew he could never convince her to return to London with him. Camelia belonged in Africa, with its sun-washed mountains and its wild animals and its mysterious bits of bone and shells. A banal life with a forgetful, distracted former thief in a crowded town house on some rainy, soot-veiled street in London could never compare to that.

And unlike Elliott, Simon cared enough about her to not try to convince her to live a life in which she could never be happy.

"I won't leave you, Camelia," he murmured, seating himself in the chair once more.

She squeezed his hand weakly, then sighed and

turned her head, finally allowing herself to slip into sleep.

And Simon sat and watched her, his hand resting against hers, guarding her against the dark wind while his heart began to tear in two.

CHAPTER 9

*Y*e take the stomach an' wash out the blood, then soak it for ten hours in cold salt water. That makes the pluck nice an' salty."

Zareb regarded Oliver in confusion. "What is 'pluck'?"

"Sheep's pluck," Oliver explained, plunging a raw stomach bag into a bucket of water. "The heart, liver, lungs, and windpipe."

Zareb regarded him doubtfully. "Windpipe?"

"'Tis more for the coarseness it adds than the taste." Oliver cheerfully bobbed the stomach up and down in the bloody water as if he were washing a pair of stockings. "I like my haggis nice an' rough, with a good strong pinch o' pepper an' allspice."

"Do you just put the pluck in and then add the spices?"

"First ye boil 'em up 'til they're nice an' tender," Oliver continued. "Then ye chop 'em fine—not too fine, mind—ye're nae makin' puddin'. Then ye mix it with toasted oatmeal, a good cup o' suet, some chopped onions and yer spices, an' ye stuff the lot of it into the stomach an' sew it up."

"And then you eat the stomach raw?" Zareb looked revolted.

"Ye boil it," Oliver replied. "Three hours in boilin' water on a low fire. Then ye serve it up hot with plenty o' whiskey an' smashed potatoes." He pulled the glistening stomach out of the bloody water and dropped it into the bowl of cold salt water. "I tell ye, there's nae like a big plate o' haggis to put some hair on yer chest!"

Zareb's eyes widened. "This will put hair on Tisha's chest?"

" 'Tis only an expression," Oliver assured him, wiping his hands on a rag. "None o' the lassies in Scotland have hair on their chests, an' they start eatin' haggis as soon as they're fit to take a spoon."

"Don't trust him on that, Zareb," warned Simon, his head bent over the crate he was using as a desk to work on some drawings. "It's highly unlikely Oliver has actually seen the chests of all of the lasses in Scotland."

"Here now, that's enough o' yer snash," Oliver scolded.

"The Khoikhoi only eat sheep's meat after they have been slaughtered for a ritual," Zareb reflected, wholly unconvinced of the merits of Oliver's haggis. "We keep sheep and cows mostly for their milk."

"What sort of meat do ye eat, then?" asked Oliver, curious.

"Whatever we hunt. Zebra, rhinoceros, antelope, buffalo. Ostrich meat is very good. We also eat some insects. You should try some while you're there—they are very tasty."

Oliver frowned. "What kind o' insects?"

"Different kinds. Termites, locusts, mopane worms. There are many there that make fine eating. Good for the digestion."

"I'm nae sure I'm braw enough to try that!" Oliver chuckled and heaved the bloody water from his bucket over the railing.

"When we get to the camp at Pumulani, I will prepare some for you," Zareb insisted. "It is good. You will see."

"You will see what?" asked Camelia, stepping up onto the deck from below, with Oscar following.

"Zareb is trying to convince Oliver that he should eat bugs while he is in Africa," Simon explained, rising from his makeshift seat on a crate as she approached.

Over two weeks had passed since that terrible night when her illness began. Her recovery had been slow. Simon had cared for her for nearly four days, while Zareb, Oliver, and Elliott had all lain groaning helplessly in their cabins. During that time Simon had remained by her side, trying to encourage sips of water, biscuits, and dry toast into her, and holding the chamber pot for her when her body rejected what little he offered.

Jack had kept assuring him that the length of Camelia's illness was entirely normal, but Simon had been worried nonetheless. When he would check on Zareb and bring him some drinking water and biscuit, Zareb would insist it was the curse that had made them all ill, and that he needed to light more fires in Camelia's cabin to protect her. Simon told him it was not a curse that had reduced them all to such a miserable state, but Zareb was unconvinced. He instructed Simon to smear Camelia with *buchu*, a fragrant African plant, to protect her, and was most annoyed when Simon flatly refused.

After four days the worst of it was over, but the illness

had taken its toll upon her. While the men seemed to re-cover their strength within a few days, a frailty had fallen over Camelia, enveloping her in a weariness she couldn't seem to overcome. The violet crescents beneath her eyes refused to fade, and her skin had lost its lovely sun-washed luster. She seemed cold all the time, and had taken to wearing a shawl wrapped around her even when the sun was bright and warm. Her clothes hung limply on her slender frame, and although she still talked about her site and her plans for when they finally ar-rived, Simon worried that in her current condition she would have trouble enduring the physical demands of her work.

"How are you feeling, Tisha?" Zareb's brow was fur-rowed with concern as he studied her.

"I'm fine, Zareb," Camelia assured him. "I'm feeling much better today."

"I'm makin' ye somethin' special that'll put some meat on yer bones and hair on yer chest. Only in a matter o' speakin', of course." Oliver cast Simon a warning look.

"What's that?"

"A nice, spicy haggis," he told her proudly. "I'm just soakin' the stomach now. By tonight it'll be stuffed an' cooked an' ready to eat."

Camelia regarded the bobbing yellow stomach in the bowl uncertainly. "I don't believe I've ever had haggis."

"It's windpipe and lungs." Zareb gave her a warning look. "Chopped up with animal fat."

"It sounds worse than it actually is," Simon inter-jected, wondering if the sight of the sheep's stomach would make Camelia queasy. "But you don't have to eat it if you don't want to."

Oliver regarded him in bewilderment. "Why wouldn't

the lass want to eat it? Any lass who's accustomed to chewin' on bugs an' worms canna be frightened by a wee bag o' good Scottish haggis."

"Actually, I've never eaten any bugs or worms," Camelia told him. "And while I'm sure your haggis is wonderful, Oliver, I'm not really feeling that hungry just yet."

"Wait 'til ye see it piled on yer plate with a fine hill of smashed tatties smeared in butter. Ye'll think ye've died an' gone to Heaven."

"Or you'll be wishing it," Simon quipped.

Camelia stared at the glossy raw stomach and swallowed hard, fighting the queasiness threatening to overcome her. "Does one actually eat the stomach, or do you just eat what's inside?"

"Don't worry, Camelia. If you don't like it, I'm sure Simon, Oliver, and I will make short work of it," Jack said, smiling as he joined them on the deck. "When we were lads we loved Eunice's haggis."

"Aye, an' when they came to Miss Genevieve ye'd nae seen a scraggier pair o' cubs," Oliver added. "Filthy an' half starved, an' lookin' like they could be blown away by a puff o' wind. Then we filled them up with haggis an' tatties an' hotchpotch an' pudding, an' ye can see for yerself how big an' swack they've grown!"

"No matter how much Doreen and Eunice served him, Simon was always hungry for more." Jack glanced with amusement at his younger brother. "Ten minutes after breakfast he'd be wondering about lunch, and right after lunch he'd be asking Eunice if it wasn't time for tea. Then when we'd have tea, he was always bartering with one of us to give him one of our biscuits or buns in exchange for something else."

"Me an' Eunice couldna believe one small lad could eat so much, so we were convinced he was hidin' the food in his napkin for later," Oliver added. "His sisters Annabelle, Grace, an' Charlotte would do that when they first came, as they didna quite trust there'd be another meal on the table in just a few hours. But every time we checked, Simon's napkin was clean. Then Doreen thought he was squirrelin' it around the house, but she never found so much as a crumb. Finally, we decided the lad had been born with hollow gams, an' no matter how hard we tried, we never could fill them up!" Oliver slapped his knee and laughed.

Camelia watched Simon smile as Oliver and Jack told their story. He was dressed in his usual rumpled white shirt and dark trousers, with his sleeves shoved carelessly up to his elbows and his shirt unfastened at his neck. Somehow the casual outfit seemed entirely natural on the sun-drenched deck of the ship, even though it did not fit within the standards of appropriate public attire. The ocean breeze was playing with the red-gold waves of his hair, which had lightened during the voyage, and the sun had turned his skin a healthy bronze. He seemed utterly relaxed as he stood with his sketches strewn around him, surrounded by the sea and sun and fresh air, with his brother and his old friend teasing him about his youth.

She had worried about him on those first few days of the voyage when he had been too ill to venture from his cabin. But not only had he fully recovered from his bout of seasickness, he actually looked stronger and more invigorated than she had ever seen him. Simon's life in London was spent largely indoors, she reflected, forever buried beneath mountains of books and papers and dozens of inventions. When he was working on something he often lost track of time, sometimes for days, as he had the day she marched into his laboratory. Until Eunice, Doreen, and Oliver had gone to stay with him, Camelia suspected there were many times when he actually forgot to eat. Yet in that moment he looked wonderfully strong and handsome and relaxed.

"The fresh air agrees with you," she remarked, moving closer to him.

"It does now that the sea has grown calmer." Simon moved his sketches off his crate desk and gestured to it. "Would you like to sit down?"

"Thank you." She drew her shawl tighter around herself as she sat and stared out at the endless expanse of sparkling sea. "It's beautiful, isn't it?"

He kept his gaze on her. "Yes."

"I think we are getting close to the coast," Camelia mused, tilting her face up to the warm rays of sunlight.

"How do you know?"

"I can feel it. I know that's not very scientific, but it's really the only explanation I have."

"Many scientific discoveries begin with little more than a feeling," Simon assured her. "Sometimes our intuition is the only thing we can trust. What do you feel, Camelia?"

She closed her eyes, absorbing the soothing heat of the sun, the scent of the ocean, the extraordinary feeling of the ship gently moving up and down as it carried her closer and closer to her home.

"I feel warmer," she began, enjoying the sun pouring its hot rays over her. "And the air smells sweeter, somehow—not the same salty crispness that it has out in the middle of the ocean. But most of all, I feel my heart is starting to beat slower. There is a sense of calm that I feel in Africa more than anywhere else. It's as if when I am home, nothing bad can happen to me." She opened her eyes to find him staring at her.

"There is still a dark wind blowing, Tisha." Zareb's expression was sober. "This I know."

"It seems there is always a dark wind blowing." Camelia pulled her shawl tighter around herself and stared at the horizon. "If it is still there when we return to Pumulani, then I will simply deal with it, Zareb, as I always have."

"I'm afraid it may be different, this time, Camelia," Elliott reflected, appearing from below.

Unlike Simon, Elliott had made a point of being fashionably attired at all times during the voyage. That morning he had chosen to wear a pair of well-cut charcoal trousers, a yellow-and-cream-striped waistcoat, and an immaculately tailored slate-colored coat. As befit any gentleman, he was also wearing white gloves and a round charcoal felt hat.

"With all the accidents that have been occurring at the site," he continued, "we may well arrive and discover there are no more natives left there to dig."

"There are many men who have stayed with me because they loved and respected my father, Elliott," Camelia pointed out. "I do not believe they will be easily frightened away."

"Not easily, no. But if the accidents continue . . ."

"If the accidents continue and everyone is frightened away, then I will continue to excavate the site by myself," she insisted stubbornly. "You know as well as I do that my father always said you could never discover anything unless you were willing to put your heart into it, Elliott. My heart is in Pumulani."

"Set a stout heart to a steep hillside, an' ye're sure to set the heather on fire," Oliver mused approvingly. "I may be old, lass, but I can still pick up a shovel an' a pickax, if ye need me to."

"Thank you, Oliver." Camelia smiled at him fondly. "Although I don't think it will come to that. Not all of the workers are frightened by the idea of a curse."

"Why don't ye make each o' the workers one of yer special amulets?" Oliver asked Zareb. "The ones ye made for me an' the lad here seem to be workin' fine."

"It wasn't working so well when I was sick," Simon pointed out.

Oliver frowned. "Ye didna die, did ye?"

"No."

"Well, then, what are ye complainin' about?"

"I would have preferred not to get ill at all."

"Then you should have stayed home," Jack told him, amused. "Getting sick is part of being on the ocean, Simon—at least until you get used to it."

"The workers are not all Khoikhoi—they come from many different tribes," Zareb explained to Oliver. "They each have their own way of fighting evil spirits, and prefer to make their own charms and amulets."

Oliver scratched his head. "Well, I guess that makes sense. In Scotland ye'll find at least a dozen different ways to ward off witchcraft."

"Look!" Camelia rushed over to the railing, her heart pounding with excitement. "Land!"

"Are ye sure, lass?" Oliver squinted hard at the horizon. "I dinna see anything."

"Yes, I'm sure," Camelia insisted, pointing. "It's hard

to see—just a thin strip of gray at the edge of the ocean, but it's land—I'm sure of it!" She turned to look at Jack, her expression almost imploring. "Isn't it?"

Jack smiled. "It is. We've moved closer to the coast. By my calculations I'd say we should be docking at Cape Town in a few hours, providing the ocean stays calm and the wind is steady."

Simon watched in fascination as pure joy spread across Camelia's face like a brilliant beam of sunlight. She turned to focus on the barely discernible sliver of land, her entire body taut with anticipation. The shawl she had kept wrapped so tightly around herself for the last two weeks slipped down to the small curve of her back as she leaned into the wind, straining to be closer to the shadowy emerald coast. He found himself overwhelmed with the need to stand beside her, to wrap his arms around her soft form and feel her body sigh against him, to know the lush curves of her pressing into him as they stood together watching the sun cast thousands of sparkling stars upon the warm turquoise waves of Africa. Desire surged through him, sudden and unexpected, heating his blood and tightening his loins, until he could think of nothing except the exquisite memory of pulsing deep within Camelia, with the scent of sunshine and wildflowers floating around him as he held her close and slowly made her his.

He inhaled a steadying breath, fighting to regain control of his reeling senses.

What in the name of God was the matter with him?

"A few hours?" Oliver regarded Jack with exasperation. "What about my haggis?"

"Don't worry, Oliver. Once we arrive in Cape Town I'll have to arrange for our train tickets to take us to Kimberley, and the train won't leave until tomorrow morning at the earliest," Camelia told him, seeing his disappointment. "You'll have lots of time to finish your haggis and eat it."

"Well, that's fine, then." Clearly relieved, he gave the slimy stomach he was soaking a loving pat and finished brightly, " 'Twould be a crime to waste a perfectly good sheep's pluck."

"Godamercy, why don't ye just kill me now and have done with it?" moaned Bert, hanging over the railing of the *Sea Star*.

"The cap'n says ye'll be feelin' better in a day or two, Bert," Stanley told him cheerfully.

"I'll be dead as a herring in an hour," Bert countered, weakly clutching the rail. "I'd rather God just bloody well strike me dead now an' leave it at that."

"Ye shouldn't talk that way, Bert." Stanley took a bite of the enormous pickled tongue in his hand before adding, "I don't think God likes it."

"An' who the hell cares what God likes?" demanded Bert, scowling. "If ye wants me to snuff it then do it now, ye soddin' old shanker, do you hear?" he railed at the sky.

"Ye're just upset on account of ye havin' the collywobbles for so long," Stanley decided, sympathetic.

"I'm dyin'," Bert insisted. "I ain't goin' to make it to Africa. Ye'll have to toss me overboard an' leave me to the bloody fish."

"Maybe if ye ate somethin' ye'd feel a bit better. Do ye want a bite o' pickled tongue?" He held the gray slab of vinegary meat out to him.

"Get that away from me, ye great bloody simkin!" Bert snapped, cuffing Stanley's hand. "Are ye tryin' to kill me?"

"I'm sorry, Bert." Chastened, Stanley dropped his gaze to his badly worn boots. "I didn't mean to make ye mad at me."

Guilt stabbed at Bert, only adding to his misery. He hated it when Stanley stood like that, with his great big shoulders all hunched forward and his grizzled chin drooping down to his bloody chest. It wasn't Stanley's fault that God had seen fit to give the poor clod pole the brains of a baby. If Bert did kick it and ended up in heaven, he was going to have a word with God about that. What was the use of having all that power if God couldn't fix Stanley's brains so that the great looby could take care of himself, at least?

"Never mind, Stanley," Bert said. "I'm just a bit cagged from being sick, is all."

Stanley cautiously raised his head. "Ye ain't mad at me?"

"No, I ain't mad at ye." He sighed. "I'm just tired o' bein' sick, is all."

"Ye'll feel better once we get to Africa. Ye just need to get some land beneath yer feet."

"We won't be reachin' Africa for another week at least," Bert reflected miserably. "'An' once we get there we'll have to head for that place the old toast told us to go to—that Poomoolanee. It's probably out in the middle of the bloody jungle, where the flies are big as bats an' there's savage animals hidin' behind every tree. If God's plannin' to keep me alive just so some buggerin' tiger can eat me, then He might as well finish me now and be done with it."

Stanley's face paled. "The flies are big as bats?"

"Probably not all of them," Bert amended. It wouldn't do to scare Stanley. It had been hard enough to convince his friend to get on the ship in the first place. It seemed most unjust that after all that pleading and arguing and ordering, Stanley appeared to be actually enjoying the voyage, while Bert was suffering so mightily. Another one of God's bloody jokes, he mused acridly. Like his whole life had been.

"It can't be too bad, or Lady Camelia wouldn't be goin' there in the first place," he added. "She's only a woman, after all."

"I guess you're right about that, Bert." Stanley took a big bite of the pickled tongue. "Although she don't seem like most ladies."

"An' how would you know, since the only ladies you know are the wenches an' doxies from Seven Dials?"

"I've seen ladies," Stanley insisted. "Sometimes I go to Mayfair and watch 'em walkin' with their gentlemen, or ridin' in their fine carriages. They look like pretty dolls—like they might break if ye held 'em too tight. But none o' them is like Lady Camelia. She's a real spanker—an' smart, too."

"If she was smart, she'd have stayed in London like she was supposed to, instead of makin' us chase her across the soddin' ocean," Bert mused sourly. "We could be well breeched by now, livin' in a nice little flat in Cheapside, havin' beefsteak-an'-kidney puddin' with gin every day, and sleepin' on a nice clean bed at night."

"We'll still have that, Bert. You'll see. It's just goin' to take a little longer to get it."

"If that first bloody captain had only agreed to take us on his ship, we would have been nearly there by now.

The sooner we get there, the quicker we can finish the job an' get back home."

"That's all right, Bert. The old swell said it didn't matter if we got there a few days after her. He said once she got there, she wasn't goin' nowhere."

"The old bastard should've paid us for what we've done, instead of makin' us sail all the way to bloody Africa," Bert countered, scowling. "We done everything exactly as he told us to, an' she still didn't scare off. How was we to know she wouldn't pike it after we wrecked her house?"

"That's what I mean about her not bein' like other ladies." Stanley smiled. "She's got pluck."

"Once we get to her bloody Poomoolanee, we'll make her wish she'd done like she was told an' stayed in London." Bert's expression grew dark as he finished grimly, "She won't have much pluck after we've finished with her—I promise ye that."

PART III

THE GLOW OF THE FIRES

CHAPTER
10

$\mathcal{S}$imon stepped off the train with Oscar perched happily on his shoulder and looked around in astonishment.

"How can they have electricity here in the middle of nowhere," he asked, indicating the wires strung between the street lamps and the houses, "when they didn't even have it in Cape Town?"

"Kimberley grew out of the diamond mining," Camelia explained, setting Harriet's cage on top of her valises. "Fifteen years ago it was nothing but dirt and rough shacks. Then huge fortunes started to be made overnight, and those who had money wanted proper homes and stores with electric lights."

"That has been one of the positive elements of the mining," Elliott pointed out. "It has turned a godforsaken piece of uninhabited land into a modern, productive town."

"The land was inhabited, Elliott."

"By a few Boer families and a handful of wandering, half-starved tribes. If the diamonds had not been discovered, no one would have ever known or cared about this part of Africa—except, of course, your father," he swiftly added, seeing a familiar flash of irritation in Camelia's eyes.

"And the natives who lived here."

Elliott sighed. When had he and Camelia fallen into this pattern of always disagreeing with each other? he wondered wearily. It seemed they were almost constantly at odds, despite the fact that he was trying his damnedest to appear supportive of her. She had always been an independent thinker, and was never one to shy away from a debate. Her passionate nature was part of what had attracted him to her in the first place. Lately, however, he found himself wishing that she would start to see things differently.

His life would have been infinitely simpler if she had grown disenchanted with Pumulani at the same time he had.

"Ultimately, diamonds will make South Africa rich," he insisted, knowing she would certainly want to argue that point.

"They will make the white men who send others down into the earth rich," Zareb corrected. "For the African men who crawl into the darkness to find the diamonds, there will be little."

"But that's nae fair," observed Oliver, who was carrying the basket with Rupert inside it. "Why dinna the natives just stake out a piece o' their own land an' search for their own diamonds?"

"They aren't allowed to," Camelia told him. "Initially there were some native claim owners, and some claims owned by *Griquas* or 'Cape Coloreds,' who are people of mixed blood. But the European claim-holders didn't like it. Within a few years a law was passed prohibiting natives or colored men from having a digging license."

"So the natives are only allowed to work for the white claim owners, without any possibility of benefiting from the stones they find in their own land." Simon shook his head, appalled by the injustice of it. "It is easy to see how they would view such an arrangement as unjust."

"They are paid for their work," Elliott argued. "Most of them come from tribes that are starving, so to get a job working in the mines is a godsend. It means they can return to their tribes with the money to buy hunting rifles, ammunition, ploughs—and to make an offering to a prospective bride's family. The mines have given them a chance for economic independence. Now they have money for purchasing goods, whereas before they had only their animal skins or a few primitive weapons to trade."

"An animal skin can keep one warm or protect one from the sun, and a weapon can save one's life," Zareb quietly pointed out. "These things are useful for whoever carries them. Coins have no value until they are exchanged for something else. And the Africans are paid with very few coins."

"You must be tired, Camelia," Elliott said, changing the subject. "We should go over to the hotel and see about getting some rooms for the night."

Camelia shook her head. "I don't want to spend the night here. If everyone is willing, I would like to go on to Pumulani."

Elliott regarded her incredulously. "It is after seven o'clock, and we have been on that blisteringly hot train since early this morning. I'm sure everyone is exhausted.

We should stay here for the night, and then head out to the site in the morning."

Elliott was right, Camelia realized. But somehow she couldn't bear the thought of not going on to Pumulani. She hated Kimberley. To Simon and Oliver it probably seemed like a reasonably prosperous town with electric lights and a decent hotel—all welcome features after nearly three weeks on a ship and twelve hours on a train. But Kimberley was built on the blood and sweat of the African natives who slaved in the mines. For Camelia it represented another link in the long chain that was being tightened around the African people. Also, a number of white investors had committed suicide there recently, as the diamond market plummeted due to an overabundance of stones and newly made fortunes swiftly collapsed. The air was heavy with desperation and greed.

She couldn't bear to be there a second longer than necessary.

Simon watched Camelia closely. Her face was shadowed with fatigue, yet he could see she was most reluctant to spend the night in Kimberley. Although the prospect of a hot bath and a decent night's sleep on a real bed was immensely appealing, he found himself loath to stay there when it was so clear that Camelia did not want to.

"How long is the drive to Pumulani?" he asked.

She regarded him hopefully. "Only about two hours."

"Or less," Zareb added. "We will be traveling in the evening, so the air will be cooler. The horses will be able to move faster and not need to stop as much."

Elliott shook his head. "It isn't wise to travel in the dark."

"But it will still be light for at least another hour," Zareb observed.

"And what about after that?"

"I know the way, Lord Wickham," Zareb assured him calmly. "I do not need the light to find Pumulani. The stars will guide me. If Lady Camelia wants to go there tonight, then I will take her. You can take Mr. Kent and Oliver there in the morning."

Simon shrugged. "I'm quite willing to go on this evening. What about you, Oliver?"

"I'm feelin' as spry as ever," Oliver returned cheerfully, rubbing his gnarled hands together. "Must be this warm African air."

"Good. So we'll go on with Camelia, and you can join us whenever you like tomorrow, Wickham, after you've had what I'm sure for you is a much-needed rest—all right?"

"If you're all insistent upon going on, then I'll go with you." Elliott would be damned if he was going to let Kent somehow appear more resilient than he was. "You're going to need me for protection anyway—unless, of course, Kent, you know how to fire a rifle?" He raised an enquiring brow.

"Actually, no, Wickham, I can't say that I've ever fired one," Simon admitted easily. "But I'm sure I could manage it if necessary. My understanding is you just point the thing in the general direction of whatever you want to shoot and squeeze the trigger—isn't that about it?"

"I'm afraid it's a little more complicated than that—"

"I can teach you," Camelia offered.

Elliott grimaced. Inspiring Camelia to spend time teaching Kent how to shoot was not precisely what he had intended.

Oliver knit his white brows together. "How does a bonny wee lass like ye know how to fire a great big rifle?"

"Knowing how to handle a weapon is a necessity in Africa," Camelia told him. "My father taught me how to shoot a rifle when I was fifteen."

Oliver scratched his head, bemused. "What are we goin' to need protection for?"

"The land we will be traveling through is filled with wild animals," Elliott explained. "And they are always hungry."

"Is that all?" Oliver scoffed. "Then ye needn't worry about me, lad. I can throw a dirk as swift an' true as any bullet."

"What about you, Kent? Can you throw a dirk?"

Simon scratched Oscar's head. "I can manage, if I need to."

"The lad can hit a tree at twenty paces," supplied Oliver proudly. "I taught him myself when he was nae more than a stripling, an' he took to throwin' like a flea to a dog!"

"That will certainly be helpful if we find ourselves being threatened by a tree," Elliott observed dryly.

"Then it's all settled." Now that the decision was made, Camelia was eager to get going. "Zareb, would you be kind enough fetch our wagon and our weapons from the livery, and load everything onto it while I go to the store and purchase some supplies?"

"Of course, Tisha." Zareb bowed his head to her. "I will take care of it."

"I'll go with you, Camelia, and help you with the supplies," Simon offered.

"An' Rupert an' Harriet an' I will stay here an' watch

our things 'til Zareb gets back with the wagon." Oliver slowly seated himself on an enormous valise before the small mountain of trunks and the canvas-wrapped steam engine that had been unloaded onto the platform from the train. "Ye can leave Oscar here with us, too, if ye like."

Oscar shook his head and wrapped his arms tightly around Simon's neck.

"I think Oscar wants to stay with me," Simon observed, trying to ease the monkey's grip upon him. "What are you going to do, Wickham?"

"I'm going to see about buying a horse for myself," Elliott returned. "The wagon is going to be full as it is, and I prefer to have my own transportation."

"That's a good idea." Camelia knew Elliott didn't like traveling by wagon. It was better to have him on horseback anyway, given how much room their luggage, the supplies, and Simon's precious pump were going to occupy. "We'll meet back here in one hour. Then we'll load the wagon and leave for Pumulani."

Everything was going to be fine.

This was the thought she focused on as she leaned against the hard sack of ground corn she was using as a makeshift chair. The wagon had but one bench for the driver and a passenger, which Zareb and Oliver were occupying. Elliott had purchased a handsome black mount for himself at the livery. Unfortunately, the animal was proving to be as spirited as he was strong, and poor Elliott was spending much of the journey galloping off in one direction and then another, fighting to bring the lively steed under his control. Camelia doubted Elliott would have enough time to forge an understanding with the beast before he had finally had enough of Pumulani and decided to leave.

Despite his insistence on accompanying her back to Africa, Camelia knew Elliott didn't really want to be there. He had come solely because of her. She was deeply touched that he had been willing to sacrifice the many demands upon him in London in order to return with her to Pumulani. For years Elliott had watched over her like an older brother, indulging her in small gifts, trying to make her smile, listening to her when she needed someone to talk to other than her father or Zareb. Camelia had grown up loving Elliott for his serious, patient, practical nature, perhaps because it was so completely different from her own. When he had first told Camelia after her father's death that he was giving up archaeology to start an export business in England, she had been disappointed, but not entirely surprised. Elliott was intelligent and ambitious. He had a right to pursue goals in which he believed he had a greater chance of success. It was only when he tried so fervently to convince her that she should sell the land her father had left her and go to England with him that she realized how little he understood her. Her father had spent his entire life dreaming of finding the legendary Tomb of Kings.

Camelia was determined to make that dream come true, not just out of love for her father, but out of her love for Africa and its people. By celebrating the past, Camelia hoped to help the world understand the richness of Africa's history and culture. Perhaps then some of her people's dignity, which others were working so hard to strip away, could be restored.

"I can feel it."

She looked at Simon in confusion. He was in the back of the wagon leaning against an enormous basket of sweet potatoes, with his feet propped casually on a sack of rice and his arms folded across his chest. He looked completely comfortable, even though the wagon was jostling back and forth and the basket he was leaning against was digging into his back. Simon seemed to have a unique ability to adapt to his surroundings, even when those surroundings were far from hospitable.

Camelia wondered if he had had that skill when he went to prison, or if it was prison itself that had forced him to hone it.

"You can feel what?" she asked.

"What you were trying to describe to me that night in my study." His blue gaze was intense as he added in a low, faintly teasing voice, "You do remember that night, Camelia, don't you?"

A ripple of heat pulsed through her. Of course she remembered that night. She remembered everything about it as if it had happened just an instant ago, despite the fact that she had spent countless sleepless nights desperately trying to erase it from her mind. A moment of madness, she had called it, thinking if she dismissed it as such, it would never happen again. But her body did not seem to understand what her mind had decided, especially now that she had recovered from her seasickness. Honeyed warmth spread through her as Simon held her with his gaze, stirring her blood and making her skin prickle with anticipation.

"I remember." She focused on straightening the hopelessly wrinkled mess of her skirts, grasping for some semblance of formality. "I was trying to describe South Africa to you."

"That's right." The corners of his mouth lifted slightly. Simon found himself arrogantly pleased by the effect the memory was having upon her. "You were telling me about the feel of the breeze against your skin, and the towering black mountains, and the brilliant pearl of the moon. I thought I could feel it then, just by the way you were describing it, but I was wrong." He watched the coral flush of her cheeks and neck seep down to the pale skin covering her collarbone as he finished quietly, "This really is one of the most peaceful places on earth."

A bullet sliced the air just above his head.

"Get down!" he roared, throwing himself on top of her.

Another shot shattered the blackness around them, then another. Oscar shrieked and leapt down from Zareb's shoulder, then scooted beneath the canvas covering Simon's pump.

"Let me up, Simon!" Camelia ordered, struggling beneath him, "I need to get my rifle!"

"Here now, what's this about?" demanded Oliver crossly as he snatched his dirk from his boot. "Why in the name o' Saint Columba would someone be shootin' at us?"

"Stay down, all of you!" Elliott reined in his horse beside the wagon and aimed his rifle into the darkness.

"Do not fire, Lord Wickham." Zareb had not stirred from his seat. "These bullets are not meant for us."

"What the hell do you mean, they aren't meant for us? Who the hell do you think they're for?"

"They are not for us," Zareb repeated, insistent. "But if you kill one of the men who fires them, then the bullets will be for us."

"If you think I'm going to bloody well just sit here and be shot at—"

"Listen." Oliver frowned and cocked his head to one side. "The shots have stopped."

Zareb nodded. "Yes. They have warned us they are there. It is good."

"You don't need to shield me anymore, Simon." Camelia pushed against him, confounded by the way her body had eagerly molded to his muscular form. "Zareb says it's good."

"Forgive me if I don't quite see what's so good about nearly being killed," Simon muttered dryly, still shielding her. "How does Zareb know they aren't just moving closer so they have a better chance of hitting us?"

"Zareb knows. If Zareb says it is good, then it is good."

"How can you possibly be sure?"

"Because Zareb always errs on the side of caution where I am concerned," Camelia explained. "If he says we are safe, then I trust him."

Simon regarded her skeptically and continued to cover her with his body.

"I am Zareb, son of Waitimu," Zareb announced solemnly, standing. "I am returning to Pumulani with friends. Be assured we come in peace."

There was a moment of utter silence.

"Welcome back, Zareb!" called an elated voice suddenly. "We have waited long for your return!"

Simon peered over the edge of the wagon to see two black tribesmen emerge from the darkness into the moonlight. They were draped only in a few leopard and antelope skins, with magnificent black crane and ostrich feathers fluttering from their shoulders and waists. Pale ivory cuffs glowed against their dark, muscular arms, and several heavy loops of beads made out of bone and shell gleamed against their chests. Each man had a formidable dagger sheathed against his calf, and an enormous rifle cradled against his chest.

"Badrani, Senwe, I am pleased to see you both again." Zareb smiled as he climbed down from the wagon. "I have brought Lady Camelia back, as I promised I would." He glanced at Camelia, who was still struggling to extract herself from Simon's protective hold. "You can let her go, Mr. Kent. There is no danger."

"Thank you for protecting Pumulani so well, Badrani and Senwe," Camelia said, standing up in the wagon. "I am pleased to see you."

"Welcome home, Lady Camelia." Badrani respectfully bowed his head. He was a handsome young man who appeared to be in his late twenties, tall and well muscled, with a strongly cut jaw that spoke of determination. "And to you, too, Lord Wickham," he added, recognizing Elliott.

"We are pleased to have you with us again, Lady Camelia." Senwe was younger and shorter than Badrani, but the muscled contours of his chest and arms indicated that he was no weaker. "We feared you might not return."

"Nothing could keep me from returning to Pumulani," Camelia assured them. "I have brought a mighty teacher with me—one who can help solve the many troubles we have suffered. I present to you Mr. Kent." She indicated Simon as he rose from the wagon floor with Oscar clinging to his shoulder.

Badrani and Senwe stared at Simon, their eyes rounding with awe.

"It is a pleasure to meet you." Simon wondered why

they appeared to be so dumbfounded. He decided Camelia must have overwhelmed them with the term "mighty teacher."

"He has hair like fire!" Badrani turned to Zareb in amazement. "Does he have special powers?"

"Yes." Zareb nodded solemnly. "Good powers."

"Not really." Simon did not want the natives to think he had special powers just because his hair was red.

Senwe's expression instantly hardened. "Your powers are not good?" He pointed his rifle at Simon.

"No—I mean yes—that is, I'm here to help you, but I don't have any special powers," Simon hastily explained. Oscar bounded nervously out of his arms and over to Zareb. "I'm an inventor."

The two tribesmen regarded him blankly.

"Mr. Kent is here to fight the curse," Zareb explained. "He will bring good fortune to Pumulani once more."

"I will try," qualified Simon, wanting to manage their expectations.

"If Zareb says it, then it must be so." Senwe was still staring at Simon's hair incredulously.

"And this is Oliver," Zareb continued. "He comes from a faraway land called Scotland, and is an honored friend."

"A pleasure to meet ye, lads." Satisfied that the two strange-looking natives were not going to shoot Simon after all, Oliver lowered his dirk. "Have either of ye ever heard o' Scotland?"

Senwe and Badrani shook their heads.

"'Tis a grand place—though not quite so warm as what ye have here in Africa. Ye'll have to come for a visit some time."

"Thank you." Badrani solemnly bowed his head to

acknowledge the invitation. "We will take you now to Pumulani. The men will be very pleased to see that Lady Camelia has finally returned. They feared the dark wind had blown her away forever."

"How far from Pumulani are we?" asked Simon.

"Pumulani lies just at the base of that mountain." Badrani pointed to the jagged black peak they had been moving steadily toward since leaving Kimberley. "If you look carefully you will see the glow of the fires. The flames are keeping the evil spirits away."

Camelia stared at the soft orange haze radiating at the base of the mountain. "We're nearly there." Anticipation bloomed within her, making her feel better than she had in months.

She was almost home.

"We will lead you there now, Lady Camelia," Senwe said. "But you must be careful. The spirits have been very angry since you left. Do you not have your rifle with you?"

"I do." She bent down and retrieved her weapon from the bottom of the wagon. "But all will be well now, Senwe." Nothing could dampen the elation she was feeling at finally returning to her site. "You will see."

"Even so, you must take care," Badrani insisted. "You all must."

She nodded, acknowledging his concern. "Thank you. We will."

She seated herself against her sack chair once more and focused on the pale ring of saffron light at the base of the mountain, feeling stronger and more whole as she slowly approached the brilliant fires of Pumulani.

CHAPTER

11

"Lady Camelia is back!" announced Senwe happily as they approached the stillness of the camp.

Joyful shouting cut through the quiet of the night. Elated tribesmen began pouring out of the tents pitched around the campsite, smiling and waving their arms in welcome. Most of them were dressed in animal skins, feathers, and beads, but Simon noticed that a few of them also sported the odd pair of well-worn trousers, or a ragged coat or waistcoat. They crowded around the wagon yelling and chanting excitedly. Simon stood and extended his hand to Camelia, to help her disembark from the wagon.

A gasp of shock silenced the natives.

"This is Mr. Kent, a mighty teacher who has traveled all the way from England to come to you," declared Camelia, gesturing to Simon. "He is going to help us battle the forces that have made excavating Pumulani so difficult."

"Do you have to use the word mighty?" muttered

Simon as he smiled stiffly at the wary tribesmen. "I'm not sure that's helping."

"They need to trust you, and your hair is making them nervous."

"He has hair of fire!" shrieked one native man, pointing fearfully at Simon.

"See what I mean?" Camelia smiled and took hold of Simon's hand, trying to demonstrate that he was not dangerous. "They've never seen anything like it."

"Wonderful. Had you forewarned me, I would have done something about it."

"Like what?"

"Like shaved it off."

"I don't think you would have found being completely bald beneath the African sun very practical. Also, you would still have red hair on your arms, legs, and chest—"

"I'm flattered you remember."

"—and I doubt you would have wanted to shave your entire body," Camelia finished tautly, resisting the urge to wrench her hand away. "I understand when it grows back it can be rather itchy."

"I'm touched by your concern."

"Mr. Kent's hair is a sign of his great power," Zareb announced solemnly, standing to face the crowd. "There is a fire within him that burns hot and pure, which will drive the evil spirits of Pumulani back where they came from!"

"Oh, for God's sake—it's just hair!" Elliott swung down from his disobedient horse, tired and irritated by all the attention Simon was commanding. "Where the devil is Trafford?"

"Right here, Lord Wickham!" A stocky, powerfully

built man burst out from one of the tents, fumbling with the buttons of his badly stained coat as he cut through the crowd of workers.

"Welcome back, Lady Camelia." He hastily raked his fingers through the curly bush of his graying hair. He appeared to Simon to be about forty-five years of age, with leathery sun-browned skin and a deeply grooved face that spoke of a life full of adventure and challenge. "I'm pleased to see you have finally returned. You have been sorely missed by all the men here, myself included."

"Thank you, Mr. Trafford." Camelia smiled at him warmly as she stepped down from the wagon. "Simon, this is Mr. Lloyd Trafford, the foreman of my site. Mr. Trafford, this is Mr. Simon Kent, the renowned inventor, and his trusted friend and associate, Oliver. Mr. Kent has built a steam pump for us which we will use to finally clear the site of water, and Oliver has come along to help."

"A pleasure to meet you both." Lloyd shook hands with Simon and Oliver. "We have all been anxiously awaiting your arrival."

"Have ye now? Well then, we'll have to make sure we dinna disappoint ye with our work." It was clear Oliver was enjoying immensely the attention they were commanding.

"You must be tired after your long journey," Lloyd continued. "Let me show you to your tents—they're not fancy, but they're relatively clean. If you're hungry, I'm sure we could quickly make something for you to eat—although I'm afraid we're down to mostly antelope and zebra meat."

"We have brought grains and fresh vegetables with

us," Camelia told him. "I'm sure the men will find that a welcome addition to their diet."

"Then let's get the wagon unloaded." Lloyd signaled to the natives, who immediately began to unload the heavy sacks, baskets, and boxes filled with precious food and supplies.

"Badrani and Senwe, would you please take Harriet's cage and that basket there to my tent?" Camelia asked. "Rupert is in the basket."

"Be careful with that!" Simon shouted as a few men clumsily hoisted up his canvas-wrapped pump.

The men gasped and froze, nearly dropping the pump in the process.

"I dinna think ye should shout at them, lad," Oliver reflected. "What with yer red hair an' all—ye seem to have given them a wee bit o' a fleg."

"I mean, please be careful," Simon amended tautly, trying to sound reassuring. "It's nothing dangerous—you just need to be careful with it as you carry it."

The men eyed him nervously and nodded. Tentatively adjusting their grip, they gingerly began to move the pump again.

"You should take the pump to Mr. Kent's tent," Camelia directed.

"It can just stay outside," Simon told her. "I doubt I'll be doing much of anything tonight except sleeping."

"Even so, the pump is safer with you," Camelia insisted. Why don't we all go to the dining tent and have some refreshments, and you can tell me what is happening, Mr. Trafford? I'm anxious to have a full report."

"That would be fine, Lady Camelia," Lloyd said.

He led the little party through the maze of heavy canvas tents until finally they came to the dining tent. Inside there was a relatively good table and chairs for working and dining, sheltered from the African elements.

"I'm afraid we have made little progress since you left for England," Lloyd reported soberly as Senwe and Badrani laid out a simple meal of dried antelope meat, hard corn biscuits, steamed bananas, and water. "We have tried to clear the water by hand, but unfortunately, such a method just isn't practical for such a large area. So much rain fell during the rainy season, it basically turned the dig site into a small lake. Then the accidents began and men started leaving, which meant fewer hands to tackle a task that could barely be accomplished with the work force we already had."

"How many men do we have left?" asked Camelia.

"Thirty-eight, at last count, which was at supper-time," Lloyd answered. "But every morning I find another one or two have packed up and left."

"And how many do ye need?" wondered Oliver.

"When Lord Stamford first began work on the site, we had well over two hundred," Lloyd told him. "That was just enough to keep the dig progressing at a steady rate, given the size of the area. At thirty-eight, we are extremely short-handed."

Elliott scowled. "Those natives were under contract. How could you let them just get up and leave, Trafford?"

"How could I stop them, your lordship?" Lloyd countered. "This is an archaeological site, not a prison. If the men choose to leave, they forfeit their pay. That is the only hold we have over them. Unfortunately, with all the accidents that have occurred, the natives believe the site is cursed. For many, their pay is no longer enough to keep them here. They even believe the rains were sent by the spirits to flood the site and keep us from digging."

"That's ridiculous," protested Camelia. "It rains a huge amount here every year during the rainy season—surely they must know that."

"It doesn't matter, Tisha," Zareb quietly argued. "Men who are afraid see things differently. To them, the rain is part of the curse. No amount of money can convince those who are truly afraid to stay."

"If you're insistent upon continuing with this excavation, Camelia, you simply cannot afford to lose any more men." Elliott's expression was grim. "You have to implement a better system for controlling the workers."

"My father did not believe in compounding the natives, Elliott, and neither do I," Camelia returned adamantly. "The men who choose to work for me are employees, not prisoners."

Simon regarded her in confusion. "What is compounding?"

"It is a system developed by the mining companies a few years ago to counter the problems of stealing and desertion," Elliott explained. "It simply requires that the natives live in a walled compound for the duration of their contracts, which is generally a period of three months. There are huts within the compound in which they sleep and eat, and an entrance from the compound into the mine. That way no natives can steal any of the diamonds they find and run off with them, or leave before their contract is finished."

Oliver frowned. "Why canna they just hide the diamonds 'til their contract is over, an' then walk out with them?"

"They are searched."

"In the most degrading way you could imagine." Camelia's voice was taut.

Elliott sighed. "In a way that is, unfortunately, necessary."

"'Tis a terrible thing, to strip a man of his freedom," Oliver reflected soberly. "I know. But 'tis far worse to take away his freedom when he's nae done anythin' wrong."

"The men who are still here are loyal to Lady Camelia," Zareb insisted. "They do not need to be penned like animals and treated like slaves."

"Once they see Simon's pump working, they will realize the water is not part of some curse," Camelia added. "The pump will do the work of fifty men or more, which means we can make good progress even though we have so few workers left." She regarded Simon hopefully.

"How well the pump works remains to be seen." Although he appreciated her faith in his abilities, Simon did not want to raise Camelia's hopes too high. "I can't make any promises until I've had a chance to get it running and see what sort of adjustments it's going to need."

"We should all get to bed, then," Camelia suggested, rising from her chair. "We will need to begin work early tomorrow."

Oliver stifled a groan and stretched. "A wee rest, an' I'll be as swack as ever an' ready to work."

"I'm afraid you may not find your bed quite as comfortable as what you are used to, Oliver. I hope it won't keep you from being able to sleep."

"I can sleep almost anywhere, lass, an' so can the lad here," Oliver assured her. "Once ye've lived on the streets an' been in prison, ye learn to make do with whatever comes along."

Badrani's eyes widened. "You've been in prison?"

Oliver shrugged. "A time or two."

"For what crime?" Senwe was also regarding Oliver with new interest.

"For fleecin'."

The two men regarded him blankly.

"Stealin'," Oliver clarified. "I was one o' the best thieves in Argyll county, an' still could be, too, if I wanted to. These old hands can nick a watch as quick as a whip, an' I'd wager there's nae a lock in London I canna get past."

"Really?" Badrani was clearly impressed. He raised the tent flap for Oliver to get out as he continued, "How do you get through a lock, Mr. Oliver?"

"Well, now, there's different ways o' goin' about it," Oliver began, pleased to have found such a fascinated audience. "With most locks all ye need is a couple o' pieces o' good, straight iron an' a wee bit o' patience..."

"I will show you to your tent, Simon," Camelia said. "It's just at the other side of the campsite."

"I can show Kent his tent," Elliott quickly offered.

Simon smiled. "That's very kind of you, Wickham, but I'd hate to impose upon you after such a long journey—especially after all the trouble you had with that horse you bought."

"Have a good sleep, Elliott," Camelia added. "I'll see you in the morning."

Elliott smiled stiffly, frustrated that Kent somehow managed to find time alone with Camelia when he could not. "Very well then. Good night."

The air was sweet and cool as Camelia stepped out of the tent. It was laden with the scent of rich African earth and tender young plants, laced with the unmistakably musky smell of the wild animals existing just beyond the perimeter of the camp. Despite Mr. Trafford's bleak report about all the men who had deserted her, she felt happier than she had in months. She was back at Pumulani, and she had brought Simon and his steam pump with her. A renewed optimism pulsed through her veins as she walked along with Simon, making her feel excited and eager to get to work.

If not for the fact that it was the middle of the night and everyone else was exhausted, she would have asked Simon to unwrap his pump and get it working immediately.

"This is your tent," she said, raising the heavy canvas flap of a tent pitched near the edge of the camp. "I'm afraid it isn't much, but I hope you'll find it adequate."

She stepped inside and frowned at the narrow wooden cot, the small table on which a battered metal washbasin, jug, and oil lamp had been placed, and the single rickety chair. The canvas-wrapped steam engine took up nearly half of the available space, leaving only a narrow path for Simon to practically climb over his trunks to get to his bed.

"Maybe you should have my tent." She suddenly disliked the idea of his being confined in such a tiny, crowded space. "Mine is bigger, and you're going to need more room—"

"It's fine, Camelia," Simon assured her. "I'm sure I'll be very comfortable. I can sleep just about anywhere, you know."

She nodded, unconvinced. She wished she had thought to tell her men to put Simon's things in her tent instead, and she could have taken this smaller tent. Somehow she had forgotten how Spartan the accommodations were at Pumulani. Perhaps they had simply never struck her as being uncomfortable or spare until that moment.

"Well, then, unless there is anything else you need, I guess I'll say good night."

"Good night, Camelia."

She moved toward the tent opening, then stopped.

"Was there something else?" Simon wondered.

She regarded him uncertainly. "I wanted to ask you something."

"What is it?"

She was silent a long moment. "What was being in prison like?" she finally asked, her voice small and tentative.

Simon tensed. He supposed it was only reasonable that she would be curious. She had assured him when she first met him that she was interested only in his abilities as a scientist and an inventor. But much had happened between them since then. There had been the most extraordinary passion he had ever known, but more, there had been the quiet, steady blossoming of something that went far deeper than his desire for her. It was this that made him reluctant to answer her question.

On some level he did not completely understand, he wanted Camelia to think only the best of him—at least as much as that was possible, given his sordid past, his obsessive preoccupations, and his eccentric ways. And so he hesitated, as if he did not quite understand what she was asking, when in fact he knew exactly what she was searching for.

"I know it must have been terrible." Camelia didn't want him to think she was some sort of sheltered woman who had no concept of the cruelties of the prison system. "I don't mean what were the conditions like. What I would like to understand is, how did you survive it? You were just a boy, yet somehow you managed to endure years of living on the streets and being in prison, and— just look at you."

"I'm not sure just what part of me, exactly, you are looking at." His voice was faintly teasing as he tried to deflect her interest in his childhood.

"All of you. You're disciplined and brilliant—"

"I'm not brilliant, Camelia," Simon protested. "I just look at things differently from the way other people do."

"You *are* brilliant," she insisted. "One has only to look at your academic success and all the wonderful papers you have written to see that."

"Lots of people graduate from university and write papers, and I can assure you, most of them are complete idiots. In my experience, some of the most intelligent people I know have never been inside a schoolroom."

"What makes you brilliant is that you see possibilities where other people see the end," Camelia explained. "You don't look at something and think, 'What a great thing that is,' the way most of us do. You look at something and think, 'That's not good enough—how can I make it better?' And it doesn't matter what it is— whether it's a perfectly good mop that has been around for a hundred years, or the latest engines of a steam- ship—you're able to come up with ideas for improving everything."

"Not everything." His expression was unreadable as he quietly reflected, "Not when I see something that is already perfect."

"Nothing is perfect."

You are.

He studied her as she stood before him, her brow

furrowed as she struggled to delve beneath the protective layers he had wrapped around himself for so many years. Her champagne-colored hair had nearly escaped the last of its pins and was falling across her shoulders in golden disarray, and her skin was bathed in the apricot cast of lamplight. Copious wrinkles and grime covered the dove gray silk of her traveling outfit, and a smudge of dirt streaked the velvety perfection of her cheek.

She had never looked more beautiful to him.

Something had happened to her since she stepped onto African soil, and whatever it was had increased a hundredfold the moment they arrived at Pumulani. She seemed stronger to him, stronger and more confident, like an animal that had been caged and then is finally released back into its own environment. It amazed him that Camelia could actually blossom in such a harsh and isolated environment, but then, she was utterly unlike any woman he had ever known. It was this realization that began to erode the wall he had built around himself since he had kissed her so long ago in London. That and the magnificent dark pools of her celadon eyes, the faintly citrus scent that seemed to waft about her wherever she went, and even that dusky smudge upon her sunburnished cheek.

He inhaled a steadying breath, feeling as if he were entering a place where he was afraid to go, yet somehow he found he could not turn away.

"Being in prison was like being in hell," he told her quietly.

She regarded him soberly, her expression not filled with pity, which would have unmanned him, but with acceptance and compassion. He took some shred of comfort in that, if there was any comfort to be taken when one is asked to expose scars that have long been hidden from view. No one had ever asked him directly about his past before. Not even Genevieve and Haydon, who believed that their children should lift the bandages off of their old wounds only if they chose to. But as Camelia stood there staring at him, Simon felt something within him change. She was reaching out to him, because for some reason he could barely comprehend, she wanted to understand what had made him who he was.

And for the first time in his life, he actually wanted to open the door to the hell he had fought so hard to escape—if only for a moment.

"I was barely nine at the time," he continued in a low voice, "but I was already well schooled in the art of survival. And still I found prison to be far more terrifying than anything I had ever known. For the first time in my life, I had absolutely no control over what was to happen to me. And when I realized I was to continue in that state for a period of five years, I wanted to die."

He stopped.

"I'm sorry, Simon." Camelia voice was soft and laced with remorse. "I didn't mean to bring up such painful memories for you. I had no right to ask."

"You have every right to ask, Camelia." He moved toward her and brushed a wayward strand of hair off her cheek. "I want you to know."

She stared up at him, mesmerized by the warmth of his fingers against her skin, the burning intensity of his silvery blue gaze, the low cadence of his gentle voice. She wanted to wrap her arms around him and hold him close, to somehow absorb the pain of the memories he was delving into only because she had asked him to. And yet something within her told her no, that to enclose him in her arms would start something she would not be able to stop, something that would only confuse her when she desperately needed to be focused and clear. It was this that kept her where she was, quietly accepting the gentle caress of his fingers as they languidly began to trace a path along the curve of her jaw.

"And then Lady Redmond came and took you out," she said softly, trying to ignore the path of flame he was creating everywhere his fingers caressed.

"She rescued me." His fingers were moving lower now, down the slender column of her neck and across the silky hollow at the base of her throat. "But it was years before I truly believed that someone wouldn't come to the door and drag me back, or that my circumstances wouldn't suddenly change and I'd find myself out on the street again. Once you have lost control of your life, you do everything you can to protect yourself, because you know it could happen again. You're afraid to trust anyone. You're afraid to believe in anyone. Everything in your life is shadowed by the belief that there is nothing out there that is truly good and beautiful and pure." He wrapped one arm around her and pulled her close, still tracing the silky paleness of her throat and cheek. "But there was something I didn't know then, Camelia."

"What?" Her voice was a wisp of sound against the pounding of her heart.

He lowered his head until his lips were barely grazing hers. "I didn't know about you."

He closed his mouth over hers, trying to make her understand. One kiss, he told himself desperately, and then he would stop. Just one simple kiss, to ease the fire that had been raging within him ever since that night in London. He could be disciplined, he swore, even as a little moan escaped her throat and she opened to him, inviting him into the sweet darkness of her mouth. He swept his tongue inside, eager to reclaim the secrets she had shared with him once before.

It was only a kiss, he told himself fervently as his hands began to roam across the lush curves of her breasts and waist and backside. It was really nothing more, he reasoned, pulling her closer until the soft mound between her thighs was pressing against his aching hardness. Just a simple, passionate kiss, he insisted, unable to comprehend how his fingers had begun to unfasten the buttons at the front of her jacket. He peeled the garment off her and then did away with the blouse underneath, still telling himself this was nothing, merely a loosening of some garments that she didn't need anyway. Her skirt slid to the floor in a puddle of crushed gray silk, and was quickly followed by the ivory layers of her petticoats.

And still he insisted to himself that this was just a kiss, that he could easily stop it if she wanted him to.

He swept her up into his arms and laid her down upon the narrow cot, telling himself he would kiss her for another moment and then no longer. But her hands were upon him now, stripping away his shirt and his trousers, exposing his skin to the warm African night air and the desperate heat of her touch as she explored the muscled contours of his body. His kisses began to move lower as he swiftly unfastened the hooks of her corset, exposing the beauty of her coral-tipped breasts and creamy belly inch by glorious inch. He slipped her drawers down her legs and eased her stockings off next, until finally she lay magnificently naked beneath him.

He rained reverent kisses along the pale silk of her thighs, then dipped his tongue into the hot pink slickness between. She moaned and shifted against the cot, opening herself to him, threading her fingers into his hair as she held him between her slender legs. He tasted her deeply, lapping at the sweet dark pool of her until her breath was coming in frantic little gasps and her thighs were squeezing against him. He eased her legs open more and slipped his finger inside her, slowly, languidly, seeking out the most intimate secrets of her body while his tongue stroked and swirled against her.

She writhed upon the cot, accepting the pleasure he was giving her and wanting more. He slipped another finger into her and increased his rhythm, licking and suckling harder and faster as his fingers moved in and out. He could feel the pleasure mounting within her as surely as if it was his own, her body growing tauter and her breaths coming faster. Frantic whispered pleas filled the quiet of the tent, as she desperately reached for what he was trying to give her.

Over and over he kissed her and licked her and filled her, feeling as if he would surely go mad from the raw desire surging through him as she responded to his impassioned touch. Her body went taut suddenly, and she cried out, her pleasure so intense that it nearly shattered what little remained of his control. He stretched over her, burying himself into her as the tremors of her climax squeezed him again and again.

Then he began to shift within her, fighting for some semblance of control as she wrapped her arms around him and pulled him close, kissing him deeply.

He wanted to go slowly, to make it last, to somehow make her understand whatever was happening between them, even though he barely understood it himself. But his body was treacherous. Having waited so long for the wonder of being inside Camelia once more, he found he could not go slowly, any more than he could have stopped night from turning into morning. And so he moaned and kissed her fervently, caressing her everywhere he could as he pulsed deeper and deeper inside her.

He wanted her with a desperation that was overwhelming, more than he had wanted anything before in his life. And the realization was agonizing, because at his very core his mind was still rational enough to recognize that she would never be his. Camelia belonged in Africa, with all its exquisite harsh beauty, living a life that was utterly foreign to him—a life in which he could never belong. Deeper and deeper he thrust, holding her close and kissing her hard as he pressed her against the creaking cot. And she moved with him, rising and falling with every aching thrust, matching his rhythm and urging him to go faster.

Suddenly he was falling, down and down, into a vortex of darkness and light. He cried out, a cry of ecstasy and despair, because he knew when it was over she would retreat from him once more. He wrapped his arms around her and crushed his mouth to hers, kissing her with desperate possession, wanting to make her understand that she belonged with him far more than she belonged in Africa. But as he lay against her, covering her with his heat and strength and desire, he could feel her begin to withdraw from him, as surely as he could feel his own heart begin to slow. He buried his head against her neck and held her fast, unwilling to move off of her.

Stay with me, he pleaded silently, knowing it was a hopeless request. He gently brushed a golden strand of hair off her forehead, then traced the sweet curves of her

cheek and nose and chin, trying to memorize every wondrous detail of her. It was a small torture to caress her so,
but he did it anyway, so that when he finally had to let
her go, he would be able to remember what it was to lie
against her and brush his fingers over her satin skin.

Camelia lay beneath Simon, her heart pounding
against the hard wall of his chest. Powerful emotions
were sweeping through her, making her feel fragile and
afraid. This was not what she had wanted, she told herself, but even as she thought it she knew it was a lie. For
weeks now she had been haunted by the memory of
Simon's caresses, the velvety press of his lips upon her
mouth, the scorching heat of his hands upon her skin. It
was wrong, of course. She understood that completely.
He did not belong to her, any more than she belonged to
him. Her heart and her life were in Africa, and his were
back in London, where he could be happily locked away
for weeks at a time in some stuffy, overcrowded laboratory, with no one to bother him with the mundane demands of meals or conversation or companionship. There
was no room in his life for marriage and children, any
more than there was room for such conventional trappings in hers. She realized all of this with painful clarity.

And still she did not stir.

"I should go," she finally ventured quietly, not really
wanting to go at all, but feeling she should say it all the
same.

Simon raised his head and looked down at her. Tears
were glittering in the pools of her eyes, and her gaze was
filled with regret.

"It was not the stars, Camelia," he said, his voice low
and rough. "Not this time."

She stared up at him, mesmerized by the gentle

cadence of his voice, the tenderness of his hold upon her, the wonderful feel of his beautiful body pressing her into the thin mattress. "What is it, then?"

He reached down and captured a silvery tear with his fingertip as it leaked down her cheek. "I'm not sure."

She closed her eyes, unable to look at him. She was losing part of herself to him, she realized, and she couldn't bear it. "I cannot leave Africa, Simon," she whispered raggedly. "I cannot."

Her tears began to fall faster, trickling down her sun-bronzed cheek and into the honeyed silk of her hair. It had cost her a great deal to admit that to him, Simon realized, feeling his heart clench. She was trying to be as honest with him as she could be. But whether she had spoken the words or not scarcely mattered. He already knew about her deep connection to this strange, wild place.

If he thought he could weaken that connection by trying to bind her closer to him, he was wrong.

"I would never ask you to leave, Camelia," he said, gently stroking her hair. "But you must also understand that I cannot stay here. I have my own work, and my family, and the life I have built for myself in England and Scotland. I cannot abandon all of that to live in the middle of nowhere in Africa. This is your world and your life, not mine."

She swallowed thickly, holding fast to him. "I understand."

He looked down at her, unconvinced. "Do you?"

She nodded. "I should go," she whispered.

"Stay with me, Camelia," he urged, his voice tender and coaxing. He did not want her to leave. Not then. Not ever. "Just a little longer."

She shook her head. She could not stay with him another instant. Her heart was slowly tearing into two, and she did not think she could bear it. "Let me go, Simon." She moved to get up, but he did not shift to accommodate her. "Please."

He had no choice. He rolled off of her and retrieved his trousers, keeping his back to her as he stepped into them and gave her a moment to dress herself.

Camelia fumbled with the hooks of her corset and the strings of her petticoats, struggling to get dressed as quickly as possible. When she was finally ready, she moved to the entrance of the tent.

Simon turned to say good night to her.

But she was already gone, leaving only the tent flap rustling slowly after her, and the faint scent of citrus and meadows floating upon the cool African night air.

This was not as it was meant to be.

Zareb frowned as he watched Camelia race from Simon's tent, her hair cascading down her back and her hands clutching her jacket closed over her half-buttoned blouse. Although it was too dark for him to see her face clearly, there was no mistaking the despair he felt emanating from her.

This was wrong.

He was getting old, he realized, feeling anger and frustration sweep through him. That was the only explanation for the fact that he had not foreseen the pain Kent had caused his beloved Tisha. He had not expected his powers to diminish with age, but then, he had never fully understood them. His mother had warned him that they might be weaker or stronger at different points in his life, depending on what was happening with him. That was one of the reasons he had chosen never to marry. The myriad demands of a wife and children would have sapped his strength and clouded his vision. And although it was sometimes a curse to be able to sense the forces around him, there were other times when it gave him indescribable pleasure. It was as if he were more fully connected with the powers of the heavens and the earth than even the greatest shamans who had come and gone before him.

But what was the purpose of having such abilities, he wondered angrily, when he seemed unable to prevent the suffering of the one who mattered most to him?

"Go to her," he told Oscar, who was sitting on his shoulder eating a biscuit. "She needs you."

Oscar jumped down and scurried toward Camelia's tent.

Zareb studied Simon's dark silhouette through the canvas veil of his tent in wary silence. Had he been wrong in thinking that this strange white man with his fiery hair and his wrinkled clothes would be the one to help fight the dark wind at Pumulani? And even if Kent was the one to battle the forces that Lord Stamford had unwittingly unleashed when he first began to break the ground there, what cost to Tisha did his presence demand?

Zareb watched as Simon stripped the covering off the steam pump in his tent, then lifted a tool and began to make some adjustment to the machine. At least he seemed intent upon providing Camelia with the means to clear the site of water.

That was good.

He shook his head, confused by the swirl of good and

dark powers churning around him. Sometimes it was not easy to make sense of the forces. Perhaps, he reflected reluctantly, his advancing age was responsible for that as well.

He retreated into the darkness once more, tired and confused as he sought out the sanctuary of his own tent.

And wholly unaware that he had not been the only one crouched in the shadows, watching as Camelia fled half dressed into the night.

CHAPTER 12

There's good news and there's nae so good news," Oliver reported soberly.

Simon clenched his jaw and gave the screw he was tightening one final turn, completely stripping it in the process.

"For God's sake," he muttered, "that's the fifth bloody screw I've ruined trying to put this bloody thing together!" He sat up, cracking his head against the edge of his pump in the process. "Christ!"

Oliver frowned. "That's enough o' yer blasphemy, lad, or I'll be scourin' yer tongue with a good chunk o' Eunice's soap!"

"It can't taste worse than that stringy dried meat we ate for breakfast," Simon returned irritably, rubbing his head.

"That was biltong," Zareb informed him, insulted. "Spiced and wind-dried antelope meat. Very good for your strength."

"It's taking all of my strength just to digest it," Simon

muttered. "I feel like I've eaten an old boot. What's the good news?"

Oliver's expression brightened. "The good news is, I've asked around an' everyone agrees the rainy season is well over. Nae but bone dry days from here to next October."

"Wonderful," Simon drawled. "At least we don't have to worry about any more water filling this mud-choked hole." He rooted around in his box of tools, impatiently searching for another screw. "What's the bad news?"

"Well, lad, I'm afraid I've come into a wee bit o' a snag when it comes to the firewood ye asked me to get for ye."

"What sort of a snag?"

"There is none."

Simon looked up, incredulous. "What do you mean, there is none?"

"Take a look around ye, lad." Oliver gestured with his scrawny arms. "There's a wee bit o' grass an' plenty o' bushes, but there's nae trees—unless ye count those wee shoots that'll nae be ready for fellin' for at least another few years."

Oliver was right, Simon realized, amazed. Other than a few green saplings and some scrubby looking bushes, there were no trees within sight. He looked at Zareb in confusion. "Where are all the trees, Zareb?"

"There were trees, once, a long time ago," Zareb answered. "But the tribes who lived here cut them down to make their huts and their fires."

"Then the Boers came," added Senwe, "and they took down even more trees, so the land would be clear for farming."

"Then the diggers came," Badrani continued, "to

search for diamonds along the Vaal and Orange Rivers, and they felled trees for their huts and their fires."

Zareb nodded. "Then the lumber haulers came, and cut the trees that were left so they could drive them to the mines and sell them to the diggers."

"Then the rains came," began Senwe, "and the—"

"I understand—there are no trees left." Simon rubbed his temples, trying to fight the throbbing in his skull that had been plaguing him all morning "Then what were the men burning in all those fires last night?"

"Dried dung."

He regarded Badrani in disbelief. "Dung? As in animal excrement?"

Senwe nodded. "Exactly."

"And that's what I'm supposed to burn to make my pump work?"

"We cannot say what you're supposed to burn in your pump," Zareb returned. "All we can tell you is that we do not have any wood. We have dried bullock's dung."

"And how well does bullock's dung burn?"

"The fire is low and rather smoky," Badrani admitted.

"And unfortunately, if the dung is not well dried, it can sometimes smell unpleasant," Senwe added.

Wonderful, thought Simon sourly. *This day really couldn't get any better.*

"Fine, then. Oliver, Senwe, and Badrani, please bring me as much bullock's dung as you can manage, and let's get started on building a fire. Have some of the others help you carry it, if necessary. I need the fire to be really hot to heat the boiler properly. It will probably take a few days for the pump to clear out the water, so we'll go through a lot of it."

"Yes, Mr. Kent." Senwe bowed.

"Dinna fash yerself, lad," Oliver said, sensing Simon's frustration. "We'll bring ye the very best dung we can find."

"I'm not fashed," Simon assured him. "I'm just anxious to get this pump working."

"Well, then, why are ye wastin' yer time talkin'?" Oliver scolded. "Get back to work."

Simon watched as the old Scotsman cheerfully headed off with his new African friends. Dried dung. He shook his head in disbelief. Then he wiped away the sweat trickling down his brow with his grimy sleeve and lowered himself back down onto the ground, preparing to work once more.

He had been unable to sleep after Camelia left his tent, and so he had spent the rest of the night trying to assemble his pump. Unfortunately, the task was proving to be much more difficult than he had anticipated. Three weeks of damp salt air during the voyage had corroded some of the parts, and several blades of the wheel were dented. Simon supposed that must have happened at some point during the journey there. It had taken him hours to repair the damage, and he was not sure that he had straightened the dented pieces sufficiently so their movement would not be compromised.

It was just one more thing to challenge his already dark mood.

"Everything going all right, Kent?"

Simon squinted up into the sun to see Elliott standing above him. Wickham was dressed in a handsomely tailored suit, with cream-colored trousers, an amazingly crisp shirt, a perfectly knotted tie, and an ivory-and-gray-checked coat. A stylishly broad-brimmed straw hat completed his debonair attire. He looked as if he were about to attend some sort of picnic or lawn party, Simon mused, instead of working on a mud-filled dig in the middle of South Africa.

"Good afternoon, Wickham," he said pleasantly. "I trust you had a good sleep last night?"

"I slept fine. And you?"

"Like a baby," Simon lied.

"How is your pump coming?" Elliott asked, studying the machine Simon was putting together. "It seems like you have been working on it a long time." He raised a querying brow. "Is everything all right?"

"It's coming along perfectly. I should have it up and running in another few hours."

"That's good to hear. I know Camelia is most anxious to continue with her excavation. The sooner we can get the water out, the sooner we can start to dig again."

"You seem uncharacteristically eager to get going, Wickham. I've always had the distinct feeling that you weren't particularly supportive of Camelia continuing with her work here."

"I'm not supportive of Camelia bankrupting herself while she chases her father's dream," Elliott returned. "So the sooner we get the water out and the natives can continue digging, the sooner Camelia will realize there is nothing more here for her to find."

Simon regarded him curiously. "How can you be so sure there is nothing here?"

"This dig was my entire life for nearly fifteen years. Camelia was barely more than a child when I came to help her father. For years I was utterly convinced of the existence of the Tomb of Kings, mostly because Lord Stamford believed in it so passionately. But as the years went by and we didn't find it, I gradually began to question the probability that the tomb ever existed. At the time of Stamford's death, I had already made the decision that I was not going to waste any more of my life chasing what I now believe is nothing more than a Kaffir fairy tale."

"Most fairy tales are built around some kernel of truth," Simon observed. "That is part of the reason why they endure."

"You are talking about a people who have stories for everything, including how the sun and the moon came to rule the sky. They are childish myths, nothing more."

Simon shrugged. "It is not so unreasonable to believe that a tribe had a special place for burying its kings."

"If it did, it is not going to be anything more than a pile of disintegrating bones and a few broken shells. As fascinating as that might be to Camelia, it will not be enough for her to raise sufficient funds to keep paying these natives and keep the dig going. She should just sell the land for whatever she can get for it and go home."

"Camelia believes she is home."

"This piece of godforsaken land in the middle of nowhere is not her home," Elliott argued. "It is her folly—just as it was her father's."

"If you are so convinced that the site has no value, then why are you here again?"

"Because Camelia needs me—whether she realizes it or not. I am the only one who can help her come to terms with the fact that there is nothing more here for her to find. She needs to understand that before she completely goes through what little assets her father left to her, and finds herself destitute."

"And what do you expect her to do, once you have helped her come to that realization?"

"There are lots of things she could do," Elliott assured him. "London is full of committees of women who are raising funds for various charities, museums, and the arts. A woman of Camelia's intelligence and determination should have no trouble finding ways to occupy her time."

"But she doesn't like London, Wickham. Surely you must realize that."

"She doesn't really know London," Elliott argued. "She went there solely to secure a pump and raise more funds to enable her to continue with her dig, not with any thought of actually making friends and enjoying the city. Once she and I are married, she will come to enjoy it. And if she finds the city too overwhelming, she can always stay at my estate in the countryside."

"I see you've thought this out."

"Yes." Elliott regarded Simon intently. "I have."

He brushed a speck of dust off the front of his immaculate jacket and adjusted his hat. "I'll leave you to it, then, Kent. The sooner you can get your pump running, the sooner we can get Camelia to realize there's nothing here. Then we can all stop wasting our time and go home."

Simon watched as he walked away, then picked up a wrench and set to work adjusting the tension of a bolt. Wickham really didn't understand her at all, he realized.

I cannot leave Africa, Camelia had told him the previous night. And as Simon had looked down into her pain-filled eyes, he had known with utter clarity that she was speaking the truth. Camelia may have been wrong about the Tomb of Kings, but it was not the tomb that held her there. On some level he couldn't understand, the heat and beauty and rawness of Africa flowed through her. It was what gave her energy and life, and filled her with purpose. And deep within, she understood herself well enough to realize she could never be happy anywhere else.

Elliott was a fool if he couldn't see it.

But Simon was an even greater fool, for losing his soul to a woman who would never choose him over the place she loved more than anything.

PART IV

EVERY WHISPERED WORD

CHAPTER 13

Camelia sat on the ground, studying the enormous rock that stood just beyond the staked perimeter of her site.

It was an impressive piece of stone, standing over six feet in height and more than twelve feet across at its widest point. Its edges had been worn smooth from thousands of years of exposure to the powerful wind and rain that swept across Pumulani in the summer months, and the painted etchings upon it had also weathered and faded. In many ways it was not unlike the hundreds of other examples of African rock art her father had discovered and documented over the years.

But once Lord Stamford had stumbled upon this particular stone, he became convinced it held the secret to the location of the Tomb of Kings.

"I don't have any more nuts," she told Oscar firmly as the monkey jammed his little paw deep into the pocket of her wrinkled linen jacket. "You ate them all."

Oscar sat back on his haunches and pointed accusingly at Harriet and Rupert.

"Harriet ate a few, and I only had about five," Camelia said, poring over the sketches of the stone contained in her father's record book. "And Rupert doesn't like nuts. That means you must have eaten all the rest, Oscar. You'll be lucky if you don't get a stomachache."

Oscar jumped up and began to turn in swift circles, demonstrating how fit he was feeling.

"Well, good. But I don't suggest you eat any more, unless you want Zareb to put you in his tent and start building fires around you and dosing you with one of his foul medicines."

"My medicines are not foul," Zareb objected as he approached.

Oscar ran over to Camelia and climbed up onto her shoulder, seeking protection from the possibility of having to drink one of Zareb's elixirs.

"How are things progressing with the pump?" asked Camelia, looking up from her father's book.

"The same as it has been for the last week. It works for a few minutes, sometimes long enough to draw out several buckets of water. Then something happens and it stops working."

"Does Simon know why?"

"He isn't sure. The water is heavy with mud, so it requires greater strength for the pump to pull it up. And although he believes he has created a steam engine capable of greater strength, he is challenged by the fact that the fire burns low, because it is fuelled by dung. That is affecting his ability to create steam, which in turn is affecting the power of the pumping mechanism."

She resumed her study of her father's journal, trying hard not to let her disappointment show. "I see."

Zareb seated himself on the ground beside her, adjusting his robes until they rippled around him in a brilliant pool of scarlet and sapphire. He studied her in silence a moment, taking in the lines of worry that had formed between her eyebrows, and the determined set of her jaw. She had changed since they first went to London, he realized, feeling both pride and anguish at the thought. There had been sadness within her when they left, of course. There was emptiness and loss after her father's death, and the trepidation one faces when one is going to a place far from the home one loves. But Zareb could see the pain she carried within her now was not the same as that which she had carried when she left.

"Does it speak to you yet, Tisha?" he asked quietly.

She looked up from her father's book in confusion. "Does what speak to me?"

"The stone. Has it whispered its secret to you yet?"

Camelia managed a small laugh. "If it had, I wouldn't be sitting here in front of it day after day, as my father used to, trying to make out the meaning of these figures."

"Let us begin with the figures, then. What do you think they are telling you?"

She studied the stone a moment. "It looks like a simple hunting scene, with this herd of antelope surrounded by these warriors. But the stars above it indicate it is night, which suggests the scene has a mythical interpretation There is this lion facing the herd, which may mean danger for the antelope, or the warriors, or both. Or, it may be the lion himself who is in danger—either of being trampled by the antelope, or shot by the hunters." She shook her head in frustration. "My father was convinced this stone was the key to the precise location of the Tomb of Kings, but he was never able to decipher it. Sometimes

I can't help but wonder if we are digging in the right place."

"That depends on what you are looking for."

"You know what I am looking for, Zareb. I want to find the Tomb of Kings, which my father spent his whole life searching for."

"Your father searched for many things, Tisha. The Tomb of Kings was only one of them."

"It was the one that meant the most to him. He would have given anything to have found it before he died."

Zareb stared at the stone and said nothing.

"I miss him." Camelia's voice was small and soft as she ran her fingers over the worn pages of her father's journal. "I wish he were here to tell me what I should do."

"Your father never told you what you should do, Tisha. It was his way only to love you, and to give you the freedom to find out for yourself what it was you truly wanted."

"What I wanted was to be an archaeologist like him. To spend my life unearthing the secrets of Africa."

"Some secrets are not meant to be unearthed. They will either come to you of their own accord, or stay hidden. The choice is not yours to make."

She regarded him in confusion. "Are you saying I'm not meant to find the Tomb of Kings?"

"The Tomb of Kings will either permit itself to be found, or it will not. All you can do is decide how much of yourself you choose to devote to that quest."

"I will devote all of myself to it. Just as my father did."

"Your father had other things in his life, Tisha. His search for the Tomb of Kings was but one small part of it."

"He made other discoveries over the course of his career, but none of them was ever deemed significant by the archaeological world—largely because they were all in Africa."

"I'm not speaking of his work, Tisha. I am speaking about his life."

"His work was his life."

Zareb shook his head. "When I first came to know Lord Stamford, he was a man torn between his work and his soul. The natives called him Talib, which means 'one who seeks.'"

"That makes sense, given that he was an archaeologist."

"They had no concept of what being an archaeologist meant. They could not understand why a white man would dig up that which has been left behind by those who came before. They called him Talib because they sensed unhappiness in him. They believed he had come to Africa to find that which he was missing."

"He wasn't missing anything— except the recognition of the archaeological world."

"You are looking at him through your eyes. You cannot help but see his love for you shining back at you. Before you came to live with your father, he was a different man. There was a terrible emptiness within him. Not even his love for Africa could ease the pain of that emptiness."

"But he had everything," Camelia objected. "A title, his work, a wife and child—"

"A wife and child who lived an ocean away."

"I suppose he missed being with us," Camelia allowed. "But his work was very important to him. He found enormous fulfillment through it."

"Yet he was prepared to give it up for you."

She regarded him in surprise. "He never told me that."

Zareb fixed his gaze upon the stone and said nothing.

She was much like her father, this beloved girl who had been placed in his protective care so many years ago. Strong-willed. Intelligent. Determined. Perhaps even just a little bit selfish, in the way that those who are destined to achieve great things must be—protective of their time, their responsibilities, their hearts. But there was an unhappiness growing within her, and its shadows had only deepened in the week since Zareb had seen her fleeing into the night from Simon's tent. Zareb sensed unhappiness growing within the white inventor as well.

A fire had raged between them, and neither time nor the wall they had erected between each other had succeeded in diminishing the flames.

"Before your mother died," he began quietly, "Lord Stamford knew his work was exacting a terrible price from you. And there came a time when he no longer wanted you to pay that price. Then your mother died, and he brought you here—not because he intended to raise you in Africa, but because he intended to abandon his dig and go home with you to England."

Camelia frowned. "If he was going to abandon the dig, then why did he bring me here? Why didn't he just leave me in England until he came back?"

"You were just a little girl, Tisha, and you had just lost your mother. You were lonely and afraid. Your father understood you needed to be with him at that time. There were those who said you should be sent away to school. Your mother had an aunt who insisted she should take you in, assuring his lordship that she would raise you to be a proper young lady while he pursued his work. But your father wouldn't agree to it. He loved you, and he

wanted to care for you himself, even if that meant giving
up his work in Africa."

"Then why didn't he?"

"Because once you were here he saw that Africa called
to you, Tisha. Just as it had to him."

"I guess it was obvious," Camelia reflected. "From the
moment I arrived here, I felt as if I had come home."

"And it was at that moment that your father felt as if
he were home—once he knew you were happy here. But
it was not the place that made it home for him, Tisha. It
was you."

"I suppose I may have been part of it," Camelia allowed. "But my father belonged here. He would never
have been happy if he had been forced to return to
England."

"His choice was to be with you, Tisha, wherever that
was. You were his home."

She regarded him uncertainly "Why are you telling
me this, Zareb?"

"Something has changed in you, Tisha." His expression was sober. "There is a sadness that was not there before, and it pains me to see it."

"I miss my father."

"And you will for the rest of your life. But the sadness
I feel from you is not that of a daughter missing her
father."

She looked away, suddenly feeling vulnerable and
exposed.

"My life is here, Zareb," she insisted quietly. "Nothing
can change that."

"This is but part of your life, Tisha," Zareb countered.
"It was the part that formed a powerful bond between
you and your father, and that is good. But it is not your

entire life. There is much to come. Much that has yet to be written. That is the part you can change."

He rose, brushed the dust from his robes, then raised his gaze to the sky. "The wind is beginning to shift," he mused, watching as a scattering of gauzy clouds settled in a delicate veil around the jagged peaks of the mountains.

"Does that mean that the dark wind is finally going to stop blowing?" Camelia tried to keep her voice light. "I think we could use a little good luck around here."

Zareb stared at the sky in silence, trying to sense the forces swirling around him. Something was coming toward them, he realized, feeling it as surely as he could feel the steady beating of his own heart.

Something powerful.

He closed his eyes and sharpened his senses, until he was acutely aware of the blinding brilliance of the sun pouring down upon him, the warm caress of the wind blowing against his robes, the pungent, smoky scent of Simon's dung fire drifting slowly through the air.

Beware, the wind whispered, its voice so soft Zareb was uncertain he was hearing it correctly.

Beware.

Sweat began to trickle down his brow as he strained to listen, trying to understand.

Beware of what? This place? A man? A spirit? The tomb?

Tell me, he pleaded, spreading his arms wide until his robes were draped around him in a great banner of slowly rippling color. *Tell me . . .*

"What is it?" Camelia demanded suddenly, her voice sharp with concern. "What do you hear?"

The wind was abruptly silenced.

Zareb opened his eyes to look at her. Her eyes were wide and shadowed with fear. Clearly she, too, had heard something.

"We must tread carefully, Tisha." His voice betrayed none of the anxiety that had unfurled within him. "The dark wind still blows."

"What did you hear, Zareb?"

"Only a warning," Zareb told her truthfully. "The spirits remain protective of this place. We must move carefully, so as not to displease them."

She stared at the painting on the rock, considering Zareb's warning. "If the Tomb of Kings truly did not want to be found, then it would have driven me away by now."

"There are those who would say it has killed several men and frightened away most of your workers. It has sent you months of drought followed by months of rain and flooding. Passages that took weeks to build have collapsed, machinery has been destroyed or doesn't work, and the money you need to keep excavating is all but gone. You were attacked in London, your father's home was ransacked, and on the voyage here you were stricken with an illness so severe I feared you would not survive." His expression was almost beseeching as he asked, "Do you not think these obstacles are meant to drive you away, Tisha?"

"Perhaps," Camelia allowed, still staring at the rock painting. She raised her hand to trace her fingers around the figure of the lion. "Or perhaps they are a series of challenges—a test to see if I am truly worthy to be the one who finally discovers the Tomb of Kings."

Zareb regarded her in silence. Of course she would interpret it that way. Lord Stamford's blood coursed through her veins, and her father had never been one to walk away from a challenge.

Even when that challenge had been a lonely, fragile ten-year-old girl who had begged her father not to send her back to England.

"What's that sound?" Camelia wondered, shifting her gaze in the direction of the dig site.

"It sounds like cheering," Zareb mused.

Camelia rose from the ground and shielded her eyes against the sun. "Is that Oliver dancing?"

"Yes—with Senwe and Badrani." Zareb smiled. "I believe they are celebrating because Mr. Kent's pump is finally working. Listen—you can hear the noise it makes."

Camelia tilted her head to one side and listened to the steady, rhythmic chuffing of Simon's pump. "He did it!" she cried, elated. "I knew he would!"

"Shall we go over and see?"

She ran a few steps, then stopped suddenly. "You go, Zareb. I still have much to do here."

"Are you sure, Tisha?"

She seated herself back down upon the ground in front of the rock and opened her father's journal once more. "I'm sure. You can tell me about how well it works later."

He regarded her uncertainly, torn between his desire to watch over her, and the knowledge that at that moment she needed to be alone.

"Very well. You stay with Tisha," he instructed Oscar, who had climbed down from Camelia's shoulder and was about to climb up Zareb. "Make sure to fetch me quickly if she needs me."

Oscar obediently settled himself on a rock nearby.

Zareb turned and began to make his way back to the

dig site, where Oliver appeared to be trying to teach
Badrani and Senwe the steps to some kind of Scottish
dance. The two Khoikhoi men doubled over with laughter as they mimicked Oliver's odd, jerky movements,
much to the amusement of the other native workers.

Zareb decided he would check on the performance of
the pump, to see for himself that it was truly working.
Then he would return to Camelia and escort her back to
the campsite. The wind's warning had been clear.

Danger was coming, and it was moving closer.

CHAPTER 14

"Honestly, Oscar, look at the mess you are making," scolded Camelia. "Do you have to eat those oatcakes on my desk?"

Oscar crammed the rest of the biscuits into his mouth, causing a shower of dry crumbs to rain over her books and papers.

"Where on earth did you get these from, anyway?" she muttered as she picked up her father's journal and shook the crumbs onto the ground. "I don't remember packing oatcakes in my trunks."

Oscar picked up one of Harriet's dropped feathers and held it over his brow.

"If you're getting them from Oliver, then I'll thank you to eat them in his tent," Camelia instructed sternly. "Come on, Harriet, see if you can clean up some of these crumbs."

She held a morsel of biscuit out to the bird, enticing her to abandon her perch on the back of Camelia's chair and start daintily pecking at the fragments on the desk.

"From now on we're going to have a strict no-eating

rule in my tent. I can't have you making such a mess when I'm trying to work."

Oscar regarded her mournfully.

"Rupert never eats in my tent." Camelia glanced at the snake, who was lying curled up in the center of her cot. "He goes out and catches a nice little lizard or a fat mouse, then comes back here to curl up and digest it. He never makes any mess whatsoever."

"I didn't realize snakes were so tidy," drawled a low, faintly amused voice.

Camelia gasped and turned to see Simon standing at the entrance to her tent.

"I'll have to let my younger brother Byron know about that," he reflected. "He can add that to the list of attributes he is compiling for my parents on why a snake would make him a marvelous pet." He raised an enquiring brow. "May I come in, Camelia? Or are you determined to keep avoiding me?"

"I haven't been avoiding you," she returned innocently, turning her attention to straightening up the books and papers on her desk. "I've just been very busy."

"So Zareb keeps telling me. Even so, I would have thought that you might take time out of your busy schedule to see that I finally got the pump to work. I've been wrestling with it night and day for over a week now. For a while I was afraid it might not be able to handle the muddy water in your dig after all."

Weariness edged his voice, causing her to stop tidying her desk and look at him.

Dark shadows circled his eyes, and his brow seemed more deeply lined than before. His hair was a wild tangle

of sun-streaked red-gold, which must have been of endless fascination to the native workers, as it now resem-
bled the color of fire even more than it had on the night
they arrived. The African sun had bronzed his skin, but
Camelia could see by the redness on his nose and cheeks
that he had spent too much time beneath its harsh rays.
Several days of beard growth grizzled his jaw and there
was an unmistakable gauntness to his cheeks, suggesting
he had not bothered to take the time to shave or eat. He
wore his usual outfit of a wrinkled white shirt with the
sleeves rolled up, exposing a bandage wrapped around
his left forearm. His trousers were heavily creased but
clean, indicating he had taken the time to wash and
change before he came to see her.

"I'm sorry," she apologized, feeling contrite. "When I
heard the pump finally working and everyone cheering,
I wanted to rush over and see for myself. I was so relieved and excited and happy—I wanted to cheer, too. I
think if I had come over, I would even have tried that
ridiculous dance Oliver was teaching to Badrani and
Senwe."

Simon regarded her curiously. "Then why didn't
you?"

She turned away. "I suppose because I didn't know
how to face you."

"I would think you would have faced me the same
way you did after the first time we were together in my
study in London," he pointed out. "You didn't seem to
have any trouble facing me then."

"You were the one who avoided me in London,"
Camelia argued. "You locked yourself in your dining
room and didn't come out for a week."

He raised his brow in surprise. "Is that what you think I was doing? Avoiding you?"

"Weren't you?"

"I was working on my pump. When I am working on an invention I completely immerse myself in it, to the exclusion of everything else, including eating, sleeping, and interacting with the rest of the human race. It is one of the things my family is constantly trying to tell me isn't normal." He ruefully shook his head. "I suppose it isn't really normal—it's just normal for me. Just as living in a tent in the middle of the African plains digging around for some mythical ancient tomb is normal for you."

Camelia regarded him uncertainly.

"We can't change what has happened between us, Camelia." His voice was low and heavy with resignation. "And even if we could, as ungentlemanly as this may seem of me, I wouldn't. The only thing we have the power to control is how we react to it. And I, for one, am not going to let this—" he paused, searching for the right word, "*force*," he supplied awkwardly, "that seems to ignite between us whenever we are together, compromise your work here. I told you I would build you a pump and train your men to work it. I intend to fulfill that commitment to you—regardless of whether you choose to avoid me for the rest of my stay here or not. That's all I came here to say." He lifted the tent flap to leave.

"Wait."

He stopped and regarded her expectantly.

"What happened to your arm?"

"I cut it on one of the pump's blades," he told her, shrugging. "It's nothing."

"Did you have Zareb look at it?"

"Zareb very kindly offered to smear it with dung and antelope fat. I declined his offer."

"What about Oliver?"

"Oliver decided I needed to be bled. After I ordered him to put his dirk away, he asked Zareb if he knew where they might find some good thirsty leeches. Zareb offered to find maggots instead, which he said would suck the blood out of me just as well as any English leeches might. At that point I left to bandage it myself."

"Let me look at it."

"It's just a scratch, Camelia."

"Even a scratch can be deadly here, if it isn't cared for properly. Sit down and let me look at it."

Simon sighed and reluctantly seated himself in the chair.

"Did you wash it, at least?" she asked as she carefully unbound the linen strip.

"Yes."

"You'd never know it." She frowned as she looked at the exposed wound. "It looks filthy."

"I was in a hurry."

"It needs to be cleaned again, and I think it's going to require a few stitches to hold it closed," she decided. "Otherwise it will just keep pulling open, and it's liable to become inflamed."

"I'm not letting Zareb or Oliver come near me: Oliver is liable to slit my other arm open while Zareb covers me in maggots. I prefer to take my chances with the possibility of inflammation."

"I will do it."

He regarded her incredulously. "You know how to stitch a wound closed?"

"Yes. Does that surprise you?"

"No more than everything else I have come to know about you, I suppose," he reflected, shrugging.

"My father insisted that I learn how to tend to wounds when I was fifteen. He was like you—a bit squeamish."

"I'm not squeamish," Simon protested, insulted.

"Well, he didn't trust the natives' methods for healing," Camelia amended as she poured some water from a metal pitcher into her washbasin. "So once when we were staying at our house in Cape Town, he had a doctor come over to give me lessons on how to tend to wounds, sprains, burns, and the like." She dropped a small washcloth into the basin and retrieved a piece of soap. "He thought it would be helpful for me to know about basic wound care when we were living on an excavation site." She went over the large trunk at the foot of her cot and began searching through it for her medicine chest.

"That was extremely pragmatic of him."

"My father could be very pragmatic when he wanted to be." She opened her medicine chest and extracted a needle, thread, some clean strips of linen, and a jar of liniment. "Except when it came to his work. Then he refused to be daunted by whatever obstacles came his way—even when everyone else insisted he should just give up."

"Sometimes it's easier not to give up."

She regarded him in surprise. "Why do you say that?"

"Giving up means you have to turn your time and energy to something else. If you are giving up on a relatively small project, that is not too difficult. But if you are giving up on the pursuit of something that has been a lifelong obsession, admitting defeat and moving on is far more difficult."

"My father was not wrong to devote so much of his life to his search for the Tomb of Kings. Some of the most important discoveries in the world have been the result of years and years of hard work and unwavering determination. You know that."

"There have also been countless cases of individuals who have searched for something their entire lives and never found it."

"The Tomb of Kings exists, Simon. I'm certain of it."

"I'm not suggesting it doesn't."

"And I won't stop looking until I have found it."

He regarded her steadily. "I know."

She turned away, suddenly unable to meet his gaze. "You should probably lie down on my cot while I do this," she said, placing all of her supplies on the small table beside her cot.

"I'm fine in this chair. I promise you I won't faint."

"I was thinking of me."

"If you're going to faint, then you should have the cot," he offered gallantly.

"I can assure you I'm not going to faint," Camelia retorted, moving Rupert to the pile of soft clothes in her trunk. "Stitching your arm will take a few minutes, and it will be easier for me to do it if I can sit on that chair while you lie on the cot."

He sighed. "Very well." He went over to the cot and stretched out upon it. The bed creaked in protest beneath his heavy frame.

"You've given yourself quite a nasty gash," Camelia mused as she gently sponged the wound clean. "We'll have to be careful to keep it clean and change the dressings often, so it doesn't fester."

Simon raised himself onto his other elbow so he could see the wound himself. "It doesn't look that bad to me, Camelia. I don't think you need to stitch it. Just put a clean bandage on it and I'll be off."

"If you develop a fever, Zareb will put you in your tent and burn fires around you," Camelia warned sternly. "And then he will fill your arm with maggots when you aren't looking."

"I suppose if it's a choice between you brandishing a sharp needle and a horde of hungry maggots, then by all means, stitch away." He lay back against her cot and closed his eyes, resigned to his fate.

"You shouldn't dismiss the maggots so quickly," Camelia reflected as she threaded her needle. "They have been known to be of benefit in healing for centuries. Wounded soldiers who had maggots infesting their wounds had a greater chance of survival than those who didn't. By eating the dead tissue, the maggots helped to keep the wounds clean."

Simon scowled at her. "Is this your idea of making idle conversation while you jam a needle into me?"

"I haven't touched you with the needle yet."

"If you keep talking about maggots, you won't get the chance."

"Fine. I just thought you might find it interesting, given that you are a scientist."

"There are lots of things I find interesting. Hearing about maggots eating dead tissue from festering open wounds is not one of them."

"There, you see?" Her expression was triumphant. "I was right—you *are* squeamish."

"I'm only asking that we find something a little more uplifting to talk about while you stitch me up," Simon argued. "Is that too much to ask?"

"Not at all. Now please lie back, before you put weight on your arm and cause it to start bleeding again."

Simon reluctantly lay back against the cot once more and closed his eyes.

Camelia studied the gash in silence, determining how best to stitch it together. The wound was deep but fairly straight, which was good. She thought she should make a series of small stitches, leaving just enough room between each for any further blood to seep through. . . .

"What are you waiting for?" he demanded irritably, sitting up.

"I'm trying to decide how I'm going to close it."

"I don't require anything fancy, you know. It isn't a quilt you're working on."

"I've never worked on a quilt, so I don't have any fancy stitches," she returned archly. "The gash has to be closed properly or it won't heal nicely. You don't want to have an ugly scar, do you?"

"I don't really care what it looks like. I would just like you to get this done before it's time for me to be buried in a tomb."

"If you would stop bolting up every two minutes and interrupting me, I would have been finished by now."

"It doesn't really need to be stitched anyway," Simon decided. "Now that you've cleaned it, all you need to do is put a bandage around it and I'll be on my way." He started to get up from the cot.

Camelia rose from her chair to block him. "If you don't lie back down this instant, Simon Kent, I shall have to force you."

He looked down at her, his eyes lit with amusement. "That's a very impressive threat, coming from a woman who barely reaches my chest. Just how, exactly, do you intend to force me?"

"Don't assume just because I am a woman that I can't," Camelia warned.

"The fact that you are a woman has nothing whatsoever to do with my assumption," Simon assured her. "It is more a question of our difference in size."

"That's not a very scientific way for you to look at it," Camelia argued. "After all, even a mighty elephant can be felled by a tiny bullet."

"Are you planning to shoot me?"

"No—then I'd have two wounds to deal with instead of only one."

"Quite sensible."

"Lie back down, Simon."

"Really, Camelia, as tempting as your offer is, I honestly believe my arm is looking much better now that you've washed it. A quick bandaging, and I'm sure it will heal splendidly."

"I'm not bandaging it until it is stitched closed."

"Fine, then, I'll do it myself." He started to move around her.

"I'm terribly sorry, Simon." She grabbed the little finger of his right hand and jerked it up hard.

"Sweet Jesus—" he swore, stumbling backward and falling onto the cot.

She released his finger and regarded him calmly. "Now are you ready to be stitched?"

He glowered at her. "Where did you learn that nasty little trick?"

"From Zareb," she told him, rinsing out her washcloth. "He thought it would be handy for me to know a few defensive tactics, in case I ever found myself in a situation where I might need them."

"Judging by the way you just did that, I'd say you've had a few opportunities to put it to the test."

"Actually, you were my first time." She began to gently sponge his wound clean once more. "I've only practiced on Zareb before now, so of course I never could do it very hard." She tossed her cloth in the washbasin and smiled. "He'll be very pleased to hear about how well it worked."

"I think I'd prefer it if you just kept this between us. I believe my manhood has suffered enough, without your announcing it to the entire camp."

"As you wish." She picked up her needle and thread once more. "Is there anything you'd like before I start?" she asked sweetly. "A shot of whiskey, perhaps—or maybe a bullet to bite on?"

"Actually, there is one thing."

"Yes?"

He grabbed her, hauling her on top of him as he crushed his mouth against hers.

Camelia gasped and struggled against him, but Simon held her fast and kissed her deeply, his hands roaming possessively over her back as his legs tangled with hers.

He only wanted to assuage his wounded pride and even the score between them. Childish, perhaps, but in his mind completely understandable. But the feel of Camelia in his arms was overwhelming, unleashing the extraordinary passion he had tried to bury beneath the endless sleepless nights and hours of struggling with his work. He held her close and kissed her tenderly, his tongue exploring the sweet dark slickness of her mouth, coaxing, entreating, trying to get her to understand what he could not seem to put into words.

Camelia held still a moment, feeling the last vestiges of her restraint erode.

And then she moaned and pressed against Simon, her slender softness molding into his hard planes and curves, which seemed so wonderfully familiar and arousing. She threaded her fingers into the sun-washed tangle of his hair, feeling as if she had been starving for his touch, his kiss, his desire. If the fire that burned between them was wrong, then everything about her life was wrong. That was all she could think as she tore her lips away to press kisses against the elegantly chiseled line of his jaw, her fingers frantically unfastening the buttons of his wrinkled linen shirt.

She wanted him with a desperation that was absolute, more than she had ever wanted anything in her life. And so she focused only on the feel of his powerful body shifting beneath her, the masculine scent of him flooding her senses, the salty-sweet taste of his beautiful bronzed skin tantalizing her tongue as she nibbled and licked and kissed her way down the corded column of his neck.

I want you, she confessed silently, although she scarcely needed to say it aloud. She peeled his shirt open and pressed kisses along the hard ridge of muscles sculpting his chest.

I need you, she added, overwhelmed by the intensity of her desire. Her kisses moved down and down, across the taut flat of his belly. His hold upon her gentled slightly, his touch growing reverent and tender.

Whatever this force was between them, it was more compelling than anything she had ever known in her life. More powerful than her need for independence.

More mysterious than the secrets of the Tomb of Kings. And more terrifying than the dark wind that had cast its shadows around her ever since her father died. It was a force she could not fight. A force that on some level she did not want to fight.

She inhaled a ragged breath and lay her cheek against the hard flatness of Simon's belly, searching for some way to tell him how she felt.

Loud snoring suddenly filled the tent.

She raised her gaze in confusion. Simon's expression was nearly boyish as he lay with his head pressed blissfully into her pillow, completely oblivious to both her emotional turmoil and her passionate kisses. He must have been utterly exhausted, she realized. Clearly he had spoken the truth when he said he had been working night and day to get his pump to work.

Moving slowly so as not to wake him, she eased herself off the cot, gently covered him with a blanket, then quickly stitched and bandaged his wound.

And then she sat at her desk and stared at her father's journal through tear-glazed eyes, wondering how she would find the strength to bear it when Simon finally left her.

CHAPTER 15

"Wake up, lad," Oliver urged.

Simon groaned and buried his head deeper into his pillow. "I don't want any maggots, Oliver. And no dung, either. Now go away."

"We need to speak to you," insisted Zareb.

"Speak to me when I'm awake." Simon jerked the blanket over his head and flopped onto his side.

"I know ye're tired, lad," Oliver acknowledged soberly, "but I really think ye'll want to hear this."

"Just by the way you're saying it, I'm quite certain I don't want to hear it," he drawled. "What's the problem? Have we run out of dung already?"

"'Tis worse than that, I'm afraid."

"Wonderful. What is it?"

"Unfortunately, yer pump has had a wee bit o' an accident."

Simon whipped the blanket off his head and regarded him in disbelief. "What do you mean, 'an accident'?"

"It has fallen over," Zareb explained. "And it suffered some damage—"

Simon leapt from Camelia's bed and raced out of the tent into the early morning light, not bothering to listen to whatever else Zareb was saying.

The native workers were crowded around the muddy banks of the excavation site, their expressions grave. As Simon got closer he realized they were watching Camelia, Badrani, Senwe, Lloyd, and Elliott wading in the muddy water, apparently searching for something. He shifted his gaze to the ground beside them.

And saw the mangled remains of his steam pump lying in pieces upon the ground.

He stared blankly at the ruined piece of machinery. It wasn't possible. He walked over to it, slowly. Surely he must be dreaming. He reached out and tentatively laid his hand upon it. Warm steel pressed against his palm.

Not a dream, then. Real.

Pure, hot fury surged through him, so intense it momentarily stripped him of the ability to speak.

"Can you fix it?"

He turned to look at Camelia. Her hair was a tangle of gold around her shoulders, her gown was soaked with muddy water, and her cheeks and forehead were heavily streaked with dirt.

"Here." She opened her dripping wet hands to reveal a motley assortment of screws, nuts, bolts, and other small, broken pieces from the machine. "I found these in the water. The others have found a few pieces as well." Her voice was taut. "We'll keep looking for more while you begin your repairs."

Simon stared down at her in helpless silence. Her beautiful face was pale beneath the smudges of dirt, and lines of dread creased her elegant brow. Yet her sage-colored eyes remained wide and hopeful, lit by the magnitude of her own determination and perhaps even by the incredible faith she seemed to have in him. And as he looked down into the depths of those extraordinary eyes, he suddenly felt overwhelmed, both by the wonder of her belief that he could fix the disaster before him, and the absolute certainty that he could not.

"Camelia," he began, his voice low and rough, "I cannot fix this."

"I promise you we'll find all the missing pieces," she told him fervently. "We'll search all day and all night, if we need to. Once you have everything, you'll be able to put it back together again."

Simon shook his head. "Even if we find all the missing pieces, I cannot do it. The valve mechanisms are badly damaged. The boiler is cracked. The expansion blades are severely dented and the shaft is broken. I cannot repair it."

"We can order whatever parts you need from Cape Town." She pressed her collection of screws and bolts into his hand, unwilling to accept what he was telling her. "Make a list, and Zareb and I will ride out to Kimberley this morning and see if there is anything we can get from there. Then we'll order the rest from Cape Town."

"It isn't that simple, Camelia. Most of these parts I designed and had made especially for me by a steel welder in London. They are unique."

"Then we'll send a letter to your welder and have him make us more."

"That will take months, Camelia."

She met his gaze evenly, struggling to appear strong and determined. But her bottom lip was trembling as she clutched at the filthy wet folds of her skirts. She was just as devastated as he was, Simon realized. Her workers were watching her in grave silence, waiting to see how she would handle this latest disaster. It was this that kept the slender thread of her emotions from snapping. She was a fighter, but at that moment, she was also a leader. She could not afford to let fear and disappointment overwhelm her, or her few remaining workers would believe she had finally been defeated.

And then they would leave.

"I am sorry, Mr. Kent." Badrani slowly approached Simon and Camelia, his head bowed in shame. "It is my fault. I was on watch last night." He knelt in misery before Camelia. "You must punish me as you see fit, my lady."

"I'm not going to punish you, Badrani," Camelia assured him. "Please get up. I just want to know what happened."

"It was the dark spirits," Badrani told her, rising to his feet. "They came late, after everyone in the camp was asleep. They cast a spell on me to make me sleep also. When I awoke, they had broken the pump into pieces and thrown them down into the water."

Oliver regarded him incredulously. "Ye mean ye just fell asleep when ye were supposed to be on watch?"

"It was the dark spirits," Senwe insisted, loyal to his friend. "They cast a spell on him."

"More like drink cast a spell on him," Oliver countered, frowning with disapproval. "What were ye drinkin' afore ye went on watch?"

"Only milk with honey," Badrani told him.

"Now, lad, ye canna expect me to believe a great strappin' lad like ye is only nippin' on milk at night."

"We Khoikhoi all drink milk from the time we are born," Zareb interjected. "It keeps us strong."

"If you do not believe me, look in my container—I haven't rinsed it out yet." Badrani removed the ostrich eggshell container looped around his chest and handed it to Oliver. "It is not good for drinking now, but last night it was fresh."

Oliver took the drinking vessel and glared into it, unconvinced. A subtle scent assailed his nostrils as he glanced at the white liquid inside. Frowning, he held the vessel closer and sniffed again.

"What is it?" asked Simon.

Oliver regarded him soberly. "Laudanum "

"You're sure?"

"Aye."

Badrani drew his black brows together in confusion. "What is laudanum?"

"Somethin' to make ye sleepy, lad. Someone put laudanum into yer milk to make ye sleep."

"The honey probably countered its bitterness," Simon added. "That's why you didn't notice it."

"Did you fill your container yourself, Badrani?" asked Lloyd, who had climbed out of the water to join them.

Badrani nodded. "But then I left it in my tent, so it would stay cool until I was ready to begin my watch."

"It would have been easy for someone to go into your tent and add a few drops of laudanum," Camelia reflected.

"So it wasn't the dark spirits?"

"No," Camelia assured him. "Not dark spirits."

Relief spread across the handsome warrior's face.

"Whether we blame it on dark spirits or not, we have a big problem," Sim mused grimly. "The pump is broken and the site is still flooded."

"I'm thinkin' the problem is even bigger than that,

lad," Oliver added. "There's some spineless cur around tryin' to drive us away from here."

"Oliver is right." Muddy and dripping wet, Elliott climbed out of the excavation site and gave Simon another handful of screws and nuts from the pump. "The previous pumps Camelia leased were also damaged, but never on this scale. Whoever did this was determined to be extremely thorough." He swept his gaze over the remaining workers. "Did any of you men see anyone going into Badrani's tent yesterday, before it was his time to go on watch?"

The natives eyed each other nervously, then vehemently shook their heads.

"I don't believe it was one of my men, Elliott," Camelia objected. "They are all good men and hard workers, who respected my father. None of them would do such a thing."

"They've made no secret of the fact that they believe this site is cursed," Elliott argued. "If they actually believe the Tomb of Kings exists, they certainly don't want you to find it. They're happy just to waste your time, collecting money from you while they secretly go about sabotaging your efforts."

"When we Africans fight, we fight openly, Lord Wickham." Zareb's voice was deceptively mild. "It is not our way to lie and deceive as you have suggested."

"I'm sorry, Zareb, but the simple fact is not all natives are like you," Elliott countered evenly. "Clearly someone did this, and it wasn't any bloody dark spirits. It was someone who wants to stop this dig from progressing."

"Whether the cur is here amongst us or off somewhere watchin' over us, he'll nae stop 'til he's won," Oliver reflected. "That's plain enough, I think."

"Which is why we have to catch him," Elliott insisted.

"I can increase the number of men watching the camp at night, but not by much," Lloyd said. "With every available man working from dawn to dusk, they are just too tired to then stay awake and guard the camp at night."

"Then let's have six men stop and sleep in three different shifts during the afternoon, so they are able to stay awake for three different shifts during the night," suggested Camelia. "If they are guarding the camp in pairs, one can always raise the alarm if something happens to the other."

"That's a good idea." Elliot turned to Simon. "So what do you think, Kent? Can you fix this pump of yours? If so, I'll climb back into the water and see what other pieces I can find."

Simon regarded Elliott in surprise. He would have thought Wickham would be pleased that the pump was ruined. It was just one more failure for Camelia, and therefore one more argument in favor of abandoning her dig. But Elliott met Simon's gaze with determination, apparently eager to help in whatever way he could. It occurred to Simon that he was merely trying to demonstrate to Camelia that he wanted to be supportive of her. After all, he was far more likely to win her affection if he at least pretended to champion her dream. Or maybe Elliott secretly nurtured the hope that she would actually succeed in finding the Tomb of Kings. Despite his assertion that he no longer believed in its existence, it was possible that deep within he actually allowed that it might. Whatever the reason, instead of telling Camelia that she should just give up, he was trying to help, at a time when Camelia needed all the assistance she could get.

For that, Simon momentarily forgave him for being such a pompous idiot.

"I might be able to fix it." He didn't want to raise Camelia's hopes too high, only to disappoint her. "I won't know until I've had a chance to really inspect it and see how severe the damage is. But even if I can, it's going to take weeks, Camelia—or even months. You have to understand that."

Camelia nodded. Weeks. Months. Time in which she had to go on paying her workers, and using up what precious little money she had left. Lord Cadwell had reluctantly invested some money in her dig before she left London. She had also managed to convince her creditors in London to give her just a little more time, assuring them that she would be able to start making payments against her mounting loans shortly. She had hoped with Simon's help, she would be able to clear the site of water quickly and finally find the precious Tomb of Kings.

The destruction of his pump was a devastating setback.

"I understand." Somehow she managed to feign calm, when inside she felt like screaming. "If you can provide me with a list of what you think you need, Simon, then Zareb and I will take the wagon to Kimberley this morning and order it. In the meantime, we will continue to clear the water from the site with buckets, as we did before."

"All right, men," Lloyd called out. "We need every bucket and container available in the camp brought back to the edge of the bank here. As we get the water level down, we'll search the bottom for more of the missing pieces from the pump. Let's look sharp—the morning is half gone already!"

"You go and get dry, Camelia," Elliott urged gently. "I'll continue looking for more of the machine's pieces."

"There's no reason for me to change until it's time to go to Kimberley, Elliott," Camelia told him. "Until then, I'm staying here and searching."

Simon watched as she climbed back down into the excavation and began groping around once again in the muddy water. Elliott sighed and climbed in after her.

"That lass has a braw heart," Oliver mused, watching as she plunged her arms up to her shoulders into the murky pool. "I'm thinkin' she must be a wee bit Scottish."

"Tisha has an African spirit," Zareb informed him. "That is why I gave her that name. It means 'strong-willed.' I knew it the moment I first saw her."

"How did Lord Stamford react to your calling his daughter that?" Simon wondered.

"His lordship was happy to hear I believed she had such strength," Zareb replied. "He was very afraid for his young daughter when she first arrived in Africa. She was small and pale and lost—like a delicate flower. He feared she would not be able to endure living so far away from the world to which she had been born. And so he planned to take her back to the land she knew, to England."

"Then why didn't he?" wondered Oliver.

"Because he soon realized Africa burns in Tisha's heart. Africa, and her father, and the search for the Tomb of Kings. For many years, there has been nothing else. But the heart can change," he reflected soberly. "And what fills it one day may not necessarily fill it the next."

"Camelia will never leave Africa, Zareb," Simon told him with absolute certainty. "She belongs here, and she knows it."

"I was not speaking of Tisha." Zareb regarded him intently.

Simon looked away, suddenly uncomfortable. "If I'm to get that list to you, I'd better get started." He cast one final glance at Camelia, who was still doubled over in the murky pool of her dig, searching for more pieces of his pump. "Excuse me."

Camelia inhaled a deep breath and dove into the river's cleansing embrace, washing away the day's layers of mud and dust and despair. She closed her eyes and cut through the soft, cool blackness with swift strokes, her arms reaching and reaching as her legs propelled her forward, gliding through the star-studded swath of ebony. She tried not to think of anything except the sensation of the water around her, the feeling of it holding her up as she moved through it. Farther and farther she swam, away from the banks where her towel and nightdress lay, away from the rock on which Zareb, Harriet, Oscar, and Rupert sat guarding her, with one small lantern as their beacon.

Away from the dig and Simon's ruined pump, and the fearful looks of the native workers who worried that they, too, would soon fall victim to the curse of Pumulani. Away from Elliott's anger and Simon's frustration, although Simon had done his best to hide it from her. Away from Oliver and Zareb, who had both tried to cheer her and help mitigate the crushing sense of failure that threatened to overwhelm her the moment she saw the pump lying in the muddy grave of her father's dig.

And away from the painful memory of her beloved father, who died not knowing whether his life's work would prove to be a brilliant discovery or a ludicrous folly.

She broke the surface of the water and gasped for air. The sound she made was more a sob than a breath. She followed it quickly with a few more breaths, trying to make them loud and even, because she was afraid Zareb might have heard her cry and worry that something was happening to her.

"Are you well, Tisha?" Zareb called, his voice edged with concern.

"I'm fine." She could see him standing on the riverbank, with Harriet on one shoulder and Oscar on the other, staring out into the darkness. "I just lost my breath, that's all."

"You should not swim out so far," he objected. "You should come in now."

"I'll be there in a moment. I want to swim a little more."

"The air is cold, Tisha. You must not let yourself get chilled, or you will get sick."

"I never get sick."

"You were sick on the voyage over here."

"I'm not going to get seasick from swimming in the river at night."

"You may catch a chill and a fever." He picked up her towel and held it out. "Come in, Tisha. It is late."

"I'll be there in a minute."

She turned to float on her back, letting the water pull the silky wet tangle of her hair into a veil around her, unable to hear whatever more Zareb was saying. She didn't want to defy him, but she didn't want to leave the river yet, either. There was no sound except the whisper of the water, like the call of a seashell as it weeps for the ocean. She sighed and closed her eyes.

Look up.

Frowning, she opened her eyes.

A silky cape of black stretched over her, scattered with a handful of shimmering silver stars. The moon had slipped behind a froth of clouds, softening its pearly light. This made the stars glitter even more than before, like tiny jewels against the velvet African night sky.

The stars will guide you.

She started suddenly and looked around. Zareb was seated on the rock once again, offering some nuts to Oscar.

"Did you say something, Zareb?"

"I said you should come in, Tisha. The river is cold."

"I mean did you say something about the stars?"

"No. But they are very bright tonight. If you want to look at them, you should come in."

"I'll be there in a minute." Cautiously, she lay back against the water once more.

The river surrounded her again. She held herself very still, her senses keen, straining to listen.

The stars will guide you.

"Did you hear that?" she demanded suddenly, looking toward Zareb.

"Hear what?"

"That voice."

"I heard nothing, Tisha." Zareb looked around. "There is no one else here. Perhaps you are hearing the men singing at the camp."

"It isn't singing."

"Maybe an animal?"

"No."

Zareb was silent a long moment. "What is this voice saying to you, Tisha?" he asked quietly.

Suddenly she felt uncertain and foolish. She had probably just imagined it. Maybe she had spent too much time in the sun that day.

"Nothing."

She waited for Zareb to question her further, but he did not.

She lay back once again in the water. A few more minutes and she would get out. Then she would head straight to her bed. Clearly she needed to sleep.

Let the stars be your guide.

This time she did not move. She stayed as she was, floating on the water, trying to decide if she was going mad. She didn't think that she was, since everything else around her seemed entirely normal. *Let the stars be your guide.* Zareb had always relied on the stars to guide him. It was one of the reasons he had disliked London. The city's relentless caul of smoke and soot and clouds had not only blocked out the sun, but had also prevented Zareb from seeing the stars at night. It didn't matter that they were in a city organized around streets and squares and thoroughfares, with gas lamps and signs.

Without the stars, Zareb was lost.

Camelia lay there a moment, barely breathing. The river continued to gently lap around her. She strained to listen, but there was nothing more. Confused, she turned over to swim in to Zareb.

And then she heard a lion roar.

"What is it, Tisha?" Concern was carved deep into

Zareb's features as she scrambled out of the river in her sopping wet chemise and drawers and grabbed the towel he was holding for her. "Did something frighten you?"

"I have to see the stone." She hastily wrapped the towel around herself and pulled on her boots.

"It is late, Tisha," Zareb objected. "You can see the stone in the morning. It will not have moved."

"I have to see it now, Zareb."

"At least dry yourself and put on these warm clothes, Tisha. I will not go until you do." He turned, giving her privacy so she could get dressed.

And then shook his head in bewilderment when Oscar and Harriet started to screech, telling him she had gone on without him.

CHAPTER 16

"Wake up, Simon!"

Simon cracked open a bleary eye and scowled. "What is it about the way I sleep that makes everyone feel obliged to wake me?"

"We've been digging in the wrong place," Camelia informed him.

"Wonderful. Tell me about it tomorrow." He closed his eye and slumped back into his pillow.

"We've been digging in the wrong place, Simon! Don't you care?"

"The only thing I care about at this point is getting a few more hours of sleep."

"You have the rest of your life to sleep, Simon." She grabbed his shoulders and shook him roughly. "Wake up!"

He rolled onto his back and glared at her. "If this is how you are going to wake me up, Camelia, then I can see that our mornings are going to be rather difficult."

"I need you to listen to me."

"Fine. I'm listening."

"Are you awake enough to understand what I'm saying?"

"I'm awake enough to understand that if I don't give you my attention you're going to keep on shaking me. That will have to suffice."

"We've been digging in the wrong place, Simon."

"So you keep saying. I take it then you still believe there is a tomb?"

"Of course there's a tomb!"

"Just checking. Any idea where it is?"

"I'm not sure. I was hoping you might be able to help me solve that puzzle. You're good with things like that."

"Things like what?"

"You know—thinking strangely."

"Are you trying to insult me into helping you?"

"I'm not trying to insult you," Camelia assured him. "I've told you before, you don't look at things the way most people do. Where most people see boundaries, you see possibilities. That is what makes you brilliant."

"If I were brilliant, I would have made a pump that could withstand being tossed into a giant mud hole," Simon reflected dryly. "Or at least I would have developed some kind of reasonable secondary plan, in the event that the pump was destroyed practically beyond repair. That would have been the actions of a brilliant strategist—something which I obviously am not."

"You can't be expected to anticipate every little thing that can go wrong."

"I would call having a steam engine smashed to pieces and heaved into the mud a rather big thing."

"Forget about the steam engine, Simon!" Exasperated, she marched toward the opening of the tent. "Are you coming or not?"

"That depends. Do you really think I'm brilliant?"

"Yes. Incredibly. Now come on!" She jerked open the flap of his tent and disappeared into the darkness.

Sighing, Simon climbed out of his bed and wearily pulled on his boots.

". . . and then if you look at this lion, there are different ways of interpreting it as well," Camelia continued earnestly, pointing to the lion figure on the rock as Zareb held the lantern. "The lion may be about to attack one of the antelope, or one of the warriors, which means he symbolizes danger. But it is also possible that it is the lion himself who is in danger, because he could just as easily be trampled by the antelope, or shot by one of these warriors. Or perhaps he isn't really a lion at all, but a shaman who has taken the form of a lion. That would mean he can't be killed, and therefore he really isn't in any danger, because shamans are believed to be able to transcend the animal forms they sometimes take. But if that's the case, then why is he here at all?"

Simon yawned.

Camelia shot him an exasperated look. "Have you been paying attention?"

"Amazingly, yes. And that's despite the fact that I've been dragged from my bed in the middle of the night after working sixteen hours to repair your steam engine. I think that must grant me a least a little bit of leniency when it comes to yawning."

"What do you think it means?"

"It means I need more sleep."

"Not that—the rock painting!"

Simon sighed. "I don't really know, Camelia. Archaeology is your area of expertise, not mine. What I don't understand is, why did you feel compelled to bring me here now so we could debate the meaning of this rock painting in the bloody dark? Couldn't it have waited until morning?"

"No."

"Why not?"

"Because there are stars in this painting." She pointed to the faded yellow stars above the antelope and warriors. "For years I've been looking at it and thinking as my father did: that the stars symbolized the mythical element of the painting. But now I think my father was wrong. I don't think the stars are meant to symbolize the spirituality of the animals or a shaman. I think the stars are meant to be used as a kind of guide—maybe even a map—to show the viewer where the tomb is."

"How?"

"I don't know," she admitted. "That's why I wanted you to look at it. Zareb and I studied it for over an hour before I finally went to wake you—we couldn't sort out what the stars meant."

"They may not mean anything, Camelia."

"Yes, they do," she insisted. "They are a guide. I'm certain of it."

"What makes you suddenly so sure?"

She hesitated. Somehow she did not think that was the right time to start telling Simon she had heard strange voices whispering to her in the river. "It's a feeling I have—like knowing when we had reached the coast of Africa. You told me sometimes our intuition is the only thing we can trust."

Simon turned to Zareb. "What do you think, Zareb?"

"I believe Pumulani has spoken to Tisha tonight," he

answered seriously. "It may be the Tomb of Kings is finally going to permit itself to be found."

"Then why doesn't it give her something a bit clearer
to go on than all this veiled stuff about stars and lions
and shamans?"

"Pumulani has had its own reasons for staying hidden.
When it finally reveals itself, it will have its reasons for
that also. We cannot be expected to understand."

Simon sighed. Since it was quite clear Camelia was not
going to let him go back to bed, he figured he might as
well at least try to understand what the hell she and
Zareb were talking about.

"All right, then," he began, focusing his attention on
the enormous stone. "Here we have the lion, here we
have the antelope, and here we have these warriors, who
actually look a bit skinny, if you ask me. Then, if we look
up, we can see a scattering of stars. I count— let's see . . .
four, five, six."

"Five," Camelia corrected.

"I see six."

"There are only five," Camelia insisted. "Look—see?
That's how many are drawn in my father's journal." She
opened her father's book to show him.

"He may have only drawn five, but that doesn't
change the fact that I see six," Simon countered. "Zareb,
would you please bring the lantern closer?"

Zareb moved closer, casting a golden wash of light
across the worn surface of the ancient stone.

"There, you see? Six stars," Simon affirmed, pointing
to each of them.

"That last mark you pointed to isn't a star," Camelia
objected. "It's just a place where the surface of the rock
has faded a bit—maybe it was chipped by something."

"It was chipped by the person who was making it a star," Simon insisted. "Fresh eyes see things differently. Here, run your finger over it—you'll see it is definitely a star."

"It might be," Camelia allowed, lightly grazing her finger over the rough surface. "But even if it is, what does that mean?"

"I'm not sure it means anything. I'm just saying I see six stars, not five."

"Fine, then. Six stars. What else do you see?"

He drew his brows together and stared at the simply drawn scene. "I don't believe the grouping of stars follows any of the accepted recorded constellations, so it's hard to determine if the artist was trying to render something specific in the sky."

"Whoever drew this would not have known about the accepted constellations," Zareb pointed out. "They had no telescope to see beyond what their eyes told them."

"So it could just be a random assortment of stars, just telling us that this hunting scene is taking place at night."

"But hunters don't hunt at night," Camelia argued. "They hunt during the day, when animals are grazing and the light is good. So the fact that whoever drew this included stars is important. The stars mean something. I tried imagining lines drawn between them, to see if they made some sort of pattern, but I couldn't come up with anything that made any sense to me."

"It looks like they are in the shape of a kite," Simon reflected. "But I doubt the ancient tribes had kites."

"Where do you see a kite?" asked Camelia. "If you join the stars in order, they form a triangle."

"I'm including this other star you thought was just a

scratch in the rock. If you draw a line from star to star, this last one forms the top point of a kite." Simon traced an imaginary line between the stars to show her. "There, you see? A kite."

Camelia's eyes widened. "It's a shield," she breathed softly.

Simon shrugged. "If you prefer. Personally, I think it looks more like a kite than a shield."

Exhilaration lit her face. "Of course! Why didn't I see that before? It's a shield, hovering in the sky between the antelope and the lion!"

"Wonderful. So what does that mean?"

"The shield represents guardianship—trying to keep something or someone safe," Camelia explained excitedly. "And it's angled toward the lion, which means the shield is there to protect the lion."

"Since when does a lion need a shield?"

"The lion is symbolic," Zareb told him. "He represents a powerful spirit."

"And he's facing those warriors and the antelope dead on," Camelia continued, "and has no intention of running away—because he's guarding something—he's guarding the Tomb of Kings!"

Simon raised a brow, intrigued. "So if he's guarding the Tomb of Kings, where is it?"

She bit her lip, unsure. Tentatively, she reached up and skimmed her finger along the pattern of stars on the rock. Her finger grew warm as it reached the last star, which was the one at the top of the shield. She hesitated, uncertain.

And then her finger slowly began to move down of its own accord, until it stopped at the lion.

"It's behind the lion," Camelia said softly.

Simon glanced at the endless surrounding darkness. "Which is where? Unfortunately, the painting doesn't give us any clues for that—or if it did, they have been worn away."

Let the stars be your guide.

Camelia tilted her head back to see the sky. "Look," she whispered.

Simon looked up. Six stars in the shape of a shield glittered against the inky sea of black.

"That's strange," he said, bewildered. "I don't remember seeing that star formation before."

Zareb stared at the stars and smiled. "It would only show itself when the moment was right."

"If we take the star at the tip, and imagine a line coming down from it like the one you traced on the rock, Camelia, then that would put the lion somewhere over there." Simon pointed to a dark cluster of bushes and rocks near the base of the mountain.

"Come on!" she urged, racing toward the bushes.

"Couldn't we do this in the morning?" Simon pleaded. "If we're going to have to start digging around in the dirt, I think I'd rather have a bit more light and a lot more sleep."

"We have to do it *now*," Camelia insisted, swiftly studying the bushes and rocks around her. "The stars are pointing us in the right direction."

"And now that we know what that direction is, we can just leave some kind of marker here," Simon pointed out as he joined her. "It would be much easier to do this when there is light."

"It may be that Pumulani was not meant to be found in the light." Zareb approached with Oscar and Harriet riding grandly on his shoulders. "We need to respect the signs that have been given to us tonight."

"If we don't search for the opening to the tomb now, the opportunity might be lost to us." Camelia began riffling through the bushes, looking for some clue as to what she was supposed to do next. "Look around, and move everything you see. But be careful—we don't want to damage any artifacts we may find."

"Since you're here, you might as well look around too, Oscar." Simon pulled the monkey off Zareb's shoulder and set him on the ground. "If you find something, there might be an oatcake in it for you."

Oscar obligingly scurried over to an enormous rock and began to make a great show of pretending to push it with his paws.

"That's strange." Camelia frowned at a thick clump of bushes growing before the rock. "This cluster of bushes seems thicker than the rest."

She went over to it and began to search through them, trying to see if they were covering something underneath.

Satisfied that he had done enough, Oscar climbed up onto the rock he had been pushing and thrust out his paw, demanding his reward.

"You didn't work for very long," Simon observed.

Oscar regarded him innocently and stretched his paw out a little further.

"Well, I suppose you deserve something for at least trying." Simon leaned against the rock, fished into his pocket, and retrieved an oatcake, which he broke in half. "Half for you," he said, giving it to Oscar, "and half for Harriet, just because she's out past her bedtime." He moved away from the rock to give Harriet her piece of the biscuit.

"The lion," Camelia whispered.

Confused, Simon looked back at the rock.

There, faded but unmistakable, was the crude outline of a lion's head. It had been hidden beneath countless years of dirt, which had partially fallen away when Simon leaned against it.

Camelia ran over and swiftly brushed off the rest of the dirt with her hands. "Look, it's all here—the lion—exactly as it appears on the other stone!"

"The warriors probably covered the drawing with mud, and then planted those bushes in front of it to help hide it," Zareb mused.

"We have to move this rock." Camelia wrapped her arms around it and started to push. "Come on, grab hold!"

"Camelia, wait—you'll never move it that way." Simon studied the heavy rock a moment, thinking. "We need something to lift it up, like a pry bar."

"But we don't have anything like that here."

"We can use some of these smaller rocks as tools instead," Simon decided, looking around. "We'll dig out some of the dirt beneath the stone and make it less stable. Then between the three of us we should be able to shift it off balance and knock it over."

Zareb nodded with approval. "Sometimes the simplest tools work best."

The three of them fell to their knees and began swiftly digging at the soft, crumbly earth beneath the rock with their stones. After a while they had scooped out enough dirt to satisfy Simon.

"Okay, grab hold and keep the rock steady," he instructed. "Now, when I say three, I want everyone to throw their weight against it, and keep pushing until it goes over. Ready?"

Zareb and Camelia nodded.

"All right then, here we go. One . . . two . . . three!"

The rock shifted slightly.

"Push!" commanded Simon. "Come on, *push!!*"

The rough surface of the stone ground painfully into Camelia's hands, and her body began to shiver against the crushing weight of the rock. She squeezed her eyes shut and clenched her jaw.

Push, she chanted silently, throwing every ounce of her weight and strength against the heavy stone. *Push, push, push . . .*

The rock shifted a little more.

And then suddenly it slipped away from her, toppling over in a thunderous crash.

Camelia stared at the narrow opening cut into the base of the mountain that had been hidden behind the rock. A black stream of enormous spiders poured out in an agitated wave, racing across the ground like a small attacking army.

Oscar shrieked and scurried up onto Simon's shoulder.

"I don't suppose you'd be willing to hold off going inside until it's morning and we can bring some decent lanterns in with us?" asked Simon, wincing as Oscar pulled his hair.

Camelia shook her head. "I have to go in now, Simon. But I don't think there's any danger. The spirits wouldn't have shown me the way unless they wanted me to enter."

"It isn't the spirits I'm afraid of. It's all the nasty little things in there that slither, crawl, creep, bite, and sting that are making me feel uneasy."

"Fine. You wait here." She picked up the lantern and disappeared through the opening.

Simon sighed. "I was afraid she might say that. All right, Oscar, are you coming?"

Oscar wrapped his paws tightly around Simon's neck and buried his face in his hair.

"I'll take that as a yes. What about you, Zareb? Feel like crawling into a tiny black hole full of spiders and God knows what else in the middle of the night?"

"I go where Tisha goes," Zareb informed him solemnly. "That is my destiny."

"Excellent. I'm thinking things will be much jollier in there with the three of us."

Simon dropped to his knees and squeezed through the dark hole, following the faint glow of Camelia's lantern.

"Look at this!" Camelia said excitedly as she pointed to the drawings on the rock walls of the narrow passageway they had climbed into.

A faint rustling sound caused Simon to look up. "What are all those nasty-looking things hanging up there?" he asked warily.

"They're bats," Camelia told him, distracted. "Look at these drawings, Simon—they show warriors carrying in bodies, while these men following them are bearing gifts and riches."

Still keeping his gaze on the bats, Simon wrinkled his nose at the dank air. "Let's hope they thought to bring something more than a few slaughtered animals—this cave smells like rotted old skins and bones."

"Even skins and bones will still be significant in terms of helping us understand the ancient people," Camelia assured him.

"The warriors who used this passage must have been

very thin," complained Zareb, grunting as he forced his way in. "Harriet and Rupert are not used to such small places."

He opened the leather bag he wore looped around his shoulder and withdrew Harriet, who flew up onto his shoulder in an agitated flurry of gray feathers. Rupert popped his head out, guardedly flicked his tongue at the cool darkness of the cave, then permitted Zareb to place him on the ground so he could stretch out and explore.

"Bloody hell!" swore Simon, nearly stumbling over a skeleton lying on the ground with a spear beside it. "Is he one of the kings?"

Camelia went over to take a closer look. "No, he is probably a guard. He would have been left behind to protect the tomb."

"Couldn't have been much fun for him after they rolled that rock in front of the opening," Simon mused. "If this is the tomb, then where are all the bodies and riches?"

"This is only a passageway. We must go further." Holding her lantern out in front of her, Camelia began to make her way deeper into the cave.

"Stop flicking your tail around, Oscar—you're tickling my back," complained Simon as he trudged behind her.

Oscar looked down and shrieked, then clambered up onto Simon's head, covering Simon's eyes with his paws.

"Come on, Oscar—quit fooling around!"

"Hold still," commanded Zareb, swiftly brushing his hands over Simon's back.

Simon pulled Oscar's paws from his face in time to see a waterfall of giant black beetles dropping from his back and scuttling away from his feet.

"Why couldn't I have had a nice, ordinary woman come into my lab?" he wondered wryly, struggling to avoid crushing the ugly insects as they crawled over his boots. "Someone whose idea of a pleasant outing was a carriage ride on a sunny afternoon through the park?"

"That was not your destiny," Zareb told him.

"You believe it's my destiny to be creeping through this dark, foul-smelling cave with a panicky monkey gripping my head and nasty little creatures I can barely see creeping all around me?"

"You did not have to enter. That was your choice."

"I didn't want to miss all this fun," Simon muttered, brushing aside a sticky veil of spiderweb.

"Simon! Zareb! *Come quick!*"

Simon raced down the passageway, trying to ignore the bats swooping over his head and the bugs squishing beneath his boots.

He turned a corner and found Camelia standing in the midst of a large chamber, lit only by the soft wash of gold from her lantern.

"Sweet Jesus," he murmured, awed.

Eight skeletons lay in a circle around the room, wrapped in disintegrating capes of leopard, zebra, and lion skins. The arms of each skeleton were heavily adorned with cuffs of ivory and gold, and ropes of beads made of bored stones and bits of shell were draped over the remains of their chests. Magnificent shields, spears, daggers and masks were carefully arranged around each body. The walls of the chamber had been intricately painted with numerous scenes depicting tribal life, including warriors in battle, women preparing food and caring for children, and animals racing across the African plains.

Simon shifted his gaze to the earthenware jars carefully placed at the head of each deceased king. "What is in those jars?"

"They are probably just bits of quartz and other rocks that the tribes thought were pretty," Camelia speculated, glancing at the mounds of rough pebbles. "Look at these paintings, Simon—they are extraordinary!"

Simon picked up one of the milky stones and examined it against the glow of the lantern Camelia had set upon the floor. Curious, he took the pebble and dragged it against one of the lantern's panes.

A deep scratch marred the smoky glass.

Simon stared at the scratch in disbelief. "This is a diamond."

Zareb arched an incredulous brow. "Are you sure?"

"Not quite." Looking around, Simon found a plain rock fragment on the ground. He took it and rubbed it hard against the stone, trying to scratch it. Slowly, he raised his head. "Now I'm sure."

Camelia turned away from the paintings. "How can you possibly be sure?" she demanded, skeptical.

"Because a diamond can scratch any other mineral, but it cannot be scratched by any other," Simon explained. "And given the similarity of the other stones in those pots, I'm almost willing to bet they are all filled with rough diamonds." Guarded excitement filtered through him as looked at Camelia. "Do you know what that means, Camelia?"

"It means I'm finally goin' to be well breeched," drawled Bert, stepping into the chamber holding a pistol.

Simon instantly moved in front of Camelia, shielding her with his body.

"Hello, Bert," he said pleasantly, closing his fingers around the diamond in his palm. "You're rather a long way from London, aren't you?"

"Leave yer hands where I can see 'em, nice and steady," Bert ordered. "Me an' Stanley here ain't afraid to shoot all of ye, make no mistake."

Zareb frowned. "Who is Stanley?"

Bert cautiously glanced back over his shoulder, then scowled. "Stanley! Get yer great big arse in here, ye puddin'-headed oaf—can't ye see we're doin' a job?"

"Sorry, Bert." Stanley lumbered in from the passageway, holding a half-eaten potato in one hand, sheepishly rubbing his head with the other. "This cave here is awful small, Bert—I keep crackin' my napper on the ceiling."

"I told ye not to stand up, ye great clod pole," Bert snapped.

"But I've got to stand up, Bert—otherwise how am I supposed to walk?"

"For cryin' out loud—ye just walk hunched over, like that monkey over there on the inventor's shoulder—can't ye do that?"

"Sure, Bert," Stanley said, trying to be agreeable. "I'll try."

"Good." He frowned. "Now then, where was I?"

"I believe you were just reflecting on how all these diamonds were going to make you well breeched," Simon reminded him, still gripping the diamond. He was fairly certain if he whipped it into Bert's head, he could knock the beefy little prigger down.

Unfortunately, that would still leave him Stanley to contend with.

"Right," Bert said, nodding. "I'm thinkin' there's enough here for us to get a nice little place—"

"In Cheapside, right, Bert?" interrupted Stanley eagerly.

"Cheapside ain't good enough for us no more, Stanley," Bert scoffed. "What with all these diamonds, we'll be rich enough to live wherever we wants—even St. James Square, if we like."

"I want to live in Cheapside," Stanley insisted. "There's a nice pie shop there."

"We won't be goin' to no greasy pie shops, Stanley— it'll be stewed lamb an' boiled beef an' chicken with cream sauce three times a day!"

Stanley hunched his shoulders, disappointed. "I like pie."

Bert rolled his eyes. "Fine, then, ye can have pie, too. Now take yer rope an' tie up those three over there," he orderd, indicating Camelia, Simon, and Zareb. "I don't want 'em givin' us any trouble while we takes these diamonds out o' here."

Stanley moved toward Camelia. "Sorry, yer ladyship," he apologized. "I'll try not to make yer bindings too tight."

"That's very considerate of you, Stanley." Camelia smiled sweetly at him as she slowly reached for the dagger she kept sheathed in her boot. *I'll take that into consideration when I stab you.*

Stanley stopped suddenly, troubled. "An' then after we take the diamonds out o' here, we untie 'em, right, Bert?"

"Of course we don't untie 'em, ye great hulkin' pigeon! Then they'll just come after us!"

"But if we don't untie 'em, how are they supposed to get out? They ain't goin' to fit through that little hole we come through all tied together."

"That's right, they ain't," Bert agreed, struggling for patience. "That's the plan, Stanley. We takes the diamonds and go back to London, and her ladyship gets to stay here with her skeletons an' old bits o' junk forever." His mouth split into a crooked yellow grin. "Everybody's happy."

Stanley soberly shook his head. "That ain't right, Bert. The old toast that hired us back in London never said nothin' about leavin her an' her friends all tied up in a cave. He just said we was to follow her to Africa and make trouble for her so she would want to leave an' go back to London."

"He never said nothin' about *not* leavin' her all tied up in a cave, neither," Bert pointed out reasonably.

"But if we leaves 'em all in this cave, then what are they supposed to do for food an' water, Bert? They're goin' to get hungry."

"For the love of—o' course they're goin' to get hungry, ye giant simkin! That's the whole point, ain't it? They stays here an' they can't blow the gab on us on account of they're goin' to be dead!"

Stanley's eyes widened in shock. "We can't do that, Bert! That ain't right! Besides, what would the old toast think?"

"He won't know about it. The scraggy bugger could never pay us what we got here in diamonds, anyway. The way I sees it, we come all the way to Africa on account of her ladyship here didn't have the sense to stay put in London like she was supposed to." He glowered at Camelia. "I nearly snuffed it comin' over here, an' I've hated every soddin' day in this bloody Poo Moo Lanee since. Now I've found these diamonds, an' I ain't leavin' without them."

"Actually, I believe Lady Camelia found the diamonds," Simon pointed out amiably.

Bert sneered. "Well, she won't be needin' them in here."

"You're right about that." Camelia tried to sound resigned as she shifted her stance slightly.

Somehow the idea of plunging her blade into Stanley didn't sit well with her. Besides, she reasoned, it was Bert who was the real threat, since he was the one with the pistol. As soon as Stanley moved out of the way, she would whip out her dagger and hurl it at Bert.

But first, she wanted to find out who had hired them. "Who is this 'old toast' you keep referring to, Stanley?" she asked conversationally, trying to distract him as she moved into a better position for hitting Bert.

"He's the old swell that hired us to follow you," Stanley explained. "He wanted to know everywhere you went."

"Is he Lord Bagley, the archaeologist?" Her voice was soft and persuasive as she reasoned, "There's no harm in telling us now."

"He never gave us no name. He saw me an' Bert one night at the Spotted Dick, an' said he had a lady what needed watchin'. An' then each time we reported to him on what we seen, he'd give us another job to do—like scarin' ye in that alley, or settin' fire to the inventor's house."

"Those were the actions of men without honor," Zareb observed disdainfully. "The spirits will judge you as cowards."

"Here, now, I ain't no coward," Bert countered, insulted. "We're just a couple o' sharpers tryin' to make a livin', same as everyone else."

"More like a couple o' filthy scalawags," declared a low, brittle voice, "who are about to get a hole blasted into their scurvy arses if ye dinna drop yer pistol now!"

"Oliver!" burst out Camelia, smiling. "However did you manage to find us?"

"Now, lass, I may be old, but I can still sense trouble a mile away," Oliver assured her immodestly as he stepped into the dimly lit burial chamber. "That's what comes from havin' raised the lad here, an' all his brothers an' sisters." He began to chuckle. "I remember one time they all decided to fleece a wee shop——"

"I'm sure Camelia would love to hear that story another time," Simon interrupted, deftly relieving Bert of his pistol. "In the meantime, Stanley, I hope you don't mind if I use that rope of yours to tie you and Bert here together?"

"I don't mind," Stanley said cheerfully, handing Simon the rope. "Just try not to make Bert's lacings too tight——he gets a bit cagged if he ain't comfortable."

"Ye can't just leave us here to snuff it in this cave!" Bert protested as Simon bound his wrists together. "That's murder!"

"I have no intention of leaving you here," Camelia assured him.

Bert regarded her in surprise. "Ye don't?"

"Of course not. This tomb is an extremely important find, and it will take years for me to analyze it and remove its artifacts for study and safekeeping. I can't have you two sitting around complaining and getting in my way while I am working here."

"I wouldn't complain, yer ladyship," Stanley promised. "If ye like, I could help ye," he added shyly. "I'm good at liftin' things. I pushed that steam pump o' yours clean over, an' it was awful heavy."

"Thank you, Stanley. That's very kind of you to offer."

"What are ye goin' to do with us?" demanded Bert.

"You should be judged by the Khoikhoi chief," Zareb growled angrily. "He would send you out into the desert with no food or water, and demand that you not come back until you have found wisdom!"

"That seems a little harsh, Zareb," Camelia mused. "I think I shall be satisfied with turning them over to the police in Cape Town."

"Camelia!" Elliott rushed into the chamber suddenly, his face flushed and his chest heaving with exertion. "What on earth is going on here?"

"We found the Tomb of Kings, Elliott!"

Overwhelmed with a surge of emotions, Camelia ran over and wrapped her arms around him. After a lifetime of searching, she had finally succeeded in fulfilling her father's dream. She was glad Elliott was there to share the excitement and joy of that moment, although at the same time a painful stab of loss pierced her heart. Her father should have been there with them. She laid her head against the comforting warmth of Elliott's chest and closed her eyes, inhaling a shuddering breath. Somewhere, high above the six glittering stars in the night sky beyond the cave, she was certain her father was looking down upon them and smiling.

"Isn't it magnificent?" she murmured, speaking to her father as much as to Elliott. "It's everything we thought it would be."

"My God, Camelia—yes, it's wonderful, but all I care

about is you!" He closed his arms tightly around her. "Are you all right?"

"I'm fine." She brushed away the tears pricking her eyes and managed a shaky smile as she looked up at him. "This is Stanley and Bert," she continued, gesturing to the pair, who were now safely bound. Realizing Elliott probably required a bit of explanation as to what was going on she continued, "They are the ones who have been giving me trouble both here and back in London. It seems they followed us here, and have tried to undo all our work by destroying the pump."

Elliott glowered at the two men. "So this is the scum that tore apart your home and stabbed your pillow with that filthy note?"

Confusion seeped over her. Slowly, she extricated herself from Elliott's embrace and regarded him uncertainly. "What did you say?"

"The note you told me about—you said it had been stabbed to your pillow with your father's favorite dagger. Are these the two that did that?"

Her chest tightened as she stared at him. *No,* she thought to herself. *It can't be.* Assuring herself there had to be some logical explanation for Elliott's statement, she quietly pointed out, "I never told you it was stabbed to my pillow, Elliott."

"Of course you did," he insisted. "You told me everything that happened."

"No, I didn't. I didn't want you to know my father's dagger had been used, because I was afraid of how you might react. You knew about its supposed powers, and you knew how much my father loved it. I thought if I told you it had been used to threaten me, you would have done everything you could to keep me from returning to Pumulani."

"Well, someone here must have told me," Elliott returned dismissively. "Maybe it was Kent."

Simon shook his head. "Sorry, Wickham. I've never discussed anything about that night with you."

"Then I suppose I heard it from Zareb."

"I do not discuss Tisha's affairs with anyone." Zareb's expression was hard. "Not even you, Lord Wickham."

Elliott regarded them impatiently, as if he thought it was patently ridiculous that they were making an issue of something so trivial. "Fine, then, I suppose I heard it from Oliver."

"I'm sure I never told ye, either, lad." Oliver's white brows were twisted into a frown. "I know 'tis better to hold yer tongue when ye dinna know from where trouble is callin'."

Slowly, Elliott's gaze returned to Camelia.

She stared back at him, her silvery green eyes wide and shimmering with fragile hope. He could see she was fighting to keep calm, fighting to maintain the belief that there was some plausible, logical explanation for the fact that he knew about the dagger in the pillow. In that moment he was overwhelmed, both by her fierce desire to guard her faith in him, which had burned in a slow but steady flame from the time she was a little girl, and by the sudden painful realization that he had failed her completely. He hadn't meant to, but that scarcely mattered. What had begun as a heartfelt desire to protect her and make a life for her with him had somehow evolved into this terrible, impossible moment. Shame pulsed through him, tempered with a helpless anger, making him feel bitter and frustrated.

Where had that beautiful young girl who used to look
at him with such wonder and admiration gone? he wondered painfully. When had she started to slip away from
him, moving further and further beyond his grasp, until
finally nothing he said or did or thought aroused anything in her except impatience, or a kind of brittle defiance? There had been a brief time, right after her father
died, when Camelia had turned to Elliott for comfort. He
had felt her love for him then. He had thought she understood his feelings for her. She had certainly understood how much he loved her after he kissed her in Lord
Bagley's garden.

It wasn't enough for her, he realized, feeling something inside him begin to shatter. He had offered her
everything he had to give, including his name, his home,
his heart.

And still it wasn't enough.

"I'm sorry, Camelia," he managed thickly. His voice
was rough with regret. "I never wanted to hurt you."
There was truth in that, at least. But as he looked down
at her and saw the last shreds of her trust slowly disinte-
grate, he realized it didn't matter. He pulled his pistol
from the waistband of his trousers and pointed it at her,
fighting to keep his hand steady. "I'm afraid I'm going to
have to ask you to give me the dagger you keep in your
boot."

He watched as she numbly bent and removed the
blade, then tossed it on the ground at his feet.

He cleared his throat. "If you don't mind, Kent, I'd like
you and Oliver to lay your pistols down over here, and
then untie my friends Stanley and Bert."

"I ain't yer friend," Stanley protested, confused. "I
don't even know ye."

"Shut yer gob, Stanley—can't ye see his lordship is tryin' to help us?" Bert snapped.

"Why is he tryin' to help us when he don't know us?" wondered Stanley.

"Because I do know you, you stupid, gutless pair of clod pates," Elliott informed him tersely. "I'm the old toast you keep referring to—although I realize without my customary disguise, crouched like an old drunkard in some filthy corner of the Spotted Dick, I don't particularly resemble the elderly man who employed you."

Bert stared at him in amazement. "Ye're the old toast?"

"Yes. And I must say, Bert, I am very disappointed to hear about how you planned to rob me of these diamonds—especially since I'm the one who paid for you to be here in the first place."

"I was just havin' a bit of a joke, yer lordship," Bert hastily assured him as Simon removed his ropes. "I hope ye ain't thinkin' I was serious!"

"Ye sounded serious to me," Stanley reflected.

"Shut yer potato trap, Stanley, an' give yer tongue a holiday!"

"Oh, I gets it now—ye was bein' sarky. That's when Bert says somethin' that he don't really mean, only he says it like he does mean it," Stanley explained to Oliver, who was slowly untying him. He frowned. "It's a bit confusin', for sure."

"Why, Elliott?" Camelia swallowed hard, fighting to keep the tears glazing her eyes from spilling onto her cheeks. "All those years you worked alongside my father. He loved you like a son, Elliott. He taught you everything he knew. How could you betray him like this?"

"I didn't mean for it to end like this, Camelia," Elliott assured her. "You've got to believe that. For years I believed just as passionately as your father that the Tomb of Kings existed. But after fifteen years, we weren't any closer to finding it. Workers were leaving. Funding was drying up. And then my father died, leaving an extraordinary amount of debt. Suddenly I had my mother and three unmarried sisters to support, several homes to run, and servants to pay for and bills to be met—and no sufficient source of income to pay for it."

"That's a hard lot, to be sure," Oliver drawled mockingly.

"Your father died a year before mine did, Elliott," Camelia pointed out. "You could have left right away and gone back to England to start your business. You didn't have to stay here."

"I know. And I planned to. But the night I went to tell your father I was leaving, I found him in his tent examining some diamonds he had found."

She regarded him in disbelief. "You're mistaken. My father never found any diamonds here at Pumulani."

"Yes, he did, Camelia. But he didn't want anyone to know—not even you. He was afraid if word got out, the site would be overrun with prospectors fighting to buy or steal a stake from him. And he knew mining Pumulani for diamonds would have destroyed everything here of archaeological significance."

She shook her head, unwilling to accept what Elliott was telling her. "If what you are saying is true, then what happened to those diamonds in his tent? They weren't among his things when he died."

"I took them—for safekeeping."

Oliver snorted in disgust. "Is that what ye call it? In my day, we called that fleecin'."

"I just needed more time, Camelia," Elliott insisted,

trying to make her understand. "I knew the diamonds were rightfully yours, but I also knew you would see things the same way your father had. I needed time to help you realize the merits of properly mining the land, as opposed to endlessly scraping away every bloody inch of it with little brooms and shovels—and never finding anything of real value."

"I would never have consented to mining the land, Elliott. I always believed in the existence of the Tomb of Kings. I would not have done anything to imperil it."

"He knows that, Camelia." Simon regarded Elliott intently, debating whether to heave the diamond in his palm at him then, or wait until he was certain Zareb and Oliver were in a position to relieve Stanley and Bert of their pistols. "That's why he never showed you the diamonds. He didn't want to try to convince you to sell the land to De Beers because of its potential value as a diamond mine. He knew you were too much like your father to ever agree to such a thing. He wanted to scare you off it, while convincing you that the land was virtually worthless anyway."

"But why?" Camelia regarded Elliott imploringly. "Even if I did finally decide to give up and sell the land, how would that have profited you?"

"It wasn't my initial intention to drive you away." His voice was gentle as he continued, "You know I cared for you, Camelia. I hoped you would marry me, and then after that I planned to tell you about the diamonds. I believed I could make you understand it would be better for us to sell the land and make a life for ourselves in England." A shadow fell across his gaze. "But you absolutely refused to accept my courtship of you. Then I realized I would have to take firmer measures to get you

KARYN MONK

to give up Pumulani and turn to me. Yet no matter how many accidents I arranged here, or how much I paid these two harebrained fools to frighten you, you simply would not surrender your father's dream."

"Here now, who are ye callin' harebrained?" demanded Bert.

"The lass has a stout heart." Oliver observed, gazing fondly at Camelia. "She doesna shrink—she shakes off the water."

"Tisha is African." Zareb looked at her meaningfully. "She is a warrior."

"That must have been very frustrating for you, Wickham," mused Simon. "I'm guessing by that point you had already approached the De Beers Company and told them about the diamonds."

"I made some overtures to them," Elliott admitted. "And after they saw the diamonds, they were naturally very interested in acquiring the land. I promised to get Camelia to agree to sell it to them at an extremely desirable price, in return for which I would be paid a generous fee for my services."

"I'm surprised you didn't negotiate for a percentage of the mine as well."

"They offered that, but in exchange for a smaller fee. As I had no way of knowing whether the land would produce more than the few stones Lord Stamford had already found, I preferred to have my money immediately."

"Very pragmatic. I see you aren't much of a risk-taker."

"I have devoted most of my life to taking risks, Kent," Elliott informed him tersely. "My father vowed to disinherit me when I told him I wanted to be an archaeologist. He said I was an idiot, and promised I would never receive a penny from him in support. Before I left for Africa he threw me out and cut off my allowance, convinced I would never have the courage to go to Africa without his financial assistance."

Camelia's eyes widened in surprise. "You never told me that, Elliott."

"I never told anyone—except your father. I had to tell him. Lord Stamford had agreed to train me, but suddenly I had no way of securing passage to Africa. I asked your father if he would lend me enough money to buy my ticket. Instead he gave me a ticket as a gift and offered to pay me a modest salary. He enabled me to stand up to my father and follow my dream. For that I was forever indebted to him."

"And yet you betray him by damaging his site and hurting his daughter." Zareb's voice was laden with fury. "The spirits will not be pleased."

"I repaid him by staying with him for years, believing him when he kept assuring me that we were on the brink of an incredible find," Elliott insisted. "And all it got me was a mountain of debt and the amused contempt of the British Archaeological Society. They thought I was a fool to have wasted so much time digging up Africa with Lord Stamford." His mouth tightened into a bitter line as he looked at Simon. "But it wasn't until Kent came here that I realized just how much of a fool I had been."

His meaning was unmistakable. "Be careful what you say, Wickham," Simon warned, clenching his fists.

"Do you honestly think I don't know what game you two have been playing in your tent at night?"

"Here, now," said Oliver, scowling, "we'll have none o' that snash!"

"I advise you to hold your tongue, Lord Wickham,"

added Zareb, barely containing his rage, "or else I might be forced to hold it for you."

"Ah, yes, the ever-loyal Kaffir comes to Lady Camelia's defense, even though he has two pistols pointed at him," drawled Elliott acridly. "You're part of the reason she turned out as she did."

"I have spent my life protecting her from the dark forces." Zareb regarded him with forced calm. "And from you."

"She didn't need protection from me, you old fool! I would have taken care of her!"

"She was never yours to care for, your lordship," Zareb countered. "You were not deserving of that privilege."

Elliott shifted his gaze to Camelia. "There was a time, Camelia, when I truly believed we were meant for each other." He reached out and trailed his fingers slowly across her dirt-smudged cheek. "But now that I understand the kind of filthy, common scum you are attracted to, I consider myself lucky you rejected my marriage proposal."

"Is he sayin' her ladyship is attracted to me?" wondered Stanley, bewildered.

"Actually, Stanley, I believe his lordship is talking about me," Simon returned.

"But ye ain't common. Ye're bang up sharp, what with all yer inventions an' all."

"Thank you."

"Shut up, Stanley!" snapped Bert. "Can't ye see we're doin' a job here?"

Stanley regarded him sheepishly. "Sorry, Bert. What do ye want me to do now?"

Bert looked at Elliott questioningly.

"Tie them up over there," Elliott ordered, "and start carrying these pots of diamonds out. Hurry, damn it! I want this cave emptied and sealed back up before anyone can find them."

"So that's it?" Camelia's voice was cold as Stanley and Bert reluctantly began to do as they had been told. "You just seal us up in here and leave us?"

"I'm sorry, Camelia, but at this point I really don't see any alternative. I never dreamed you'd actually find this tomb. Now that you have, you must admit, it does seem rather fitting that you and your friends stay here. You've spent your entire life trying to find this place. Now you'll stay here for all eternity."

"But I already told Bert, that ain't right," Stanley protested, pausing in his binding of Oliver's wrists. "I ain't leavin' 'em here to snuff it in this cave—there's spiders in here!"

"You'll do as you're told, you great big pudding-headed oaf, or I'll leave both of you in here as well," Elliott threatened furiously. "Do you understand, or do you need your scrubby little friend here to explain it to you?"

Stanley regarded Bert imploringly. "It ain't right, Bert."

"Shut yer cake-hole an' do as yer told, Stanley," advised Bert, nervously eyeing Elliott's pistol.

"Sound advice," Elliott mused dryly.

Camelia stood frozen, her hands fisted at her sides. An icy gust of air was wafting around her, making her acutely aware of the rapid pounding of her heart, the cool prickle of her skin, the powerful surge of blood pouring through her veins. She had found the Tomb of Kings. In doing so she had discovered that dearest Elliott, who had been a son to her father and an older brother to her, was willing to cast aside the years of friendship and devotion in exchange for a few vessels of diamonds.

Nothing was as it seemed, she realized painfully.

Let the stars be your guide.

"It is time, Tisha," Zareb said quietly.

Camelia glanced at him in confusion. He gazed back at her with extraordinary calm, his dark eyes glittering with love and grim determination.

"The spirits have spoken, Tisha," he whispered softly. "It is time."

"You never give up, do you, Zareb?" muttered Elliott. "All your idiotic nonsense about evil spirits and dark forces and curses. Really, it baffles me why Stamford chose an ignorant old Kaffir to look after his daughter." He glared at Camelia as he finished, "Things would have been much different if your father had left you in England under the care of a good English governess."

"You're right, Elliott," Camelia agreed softly. "Things would have been much different. But there is something I don't believe an English governess could have taught me."

"What's that?"

"This." She grabbed the little finger of his left hand and jerked it back as hard as she could, snapping it from its socket.

Elliott howled in pain and staggered back, accidentally firing his pistol.

Oscar shrieked and leapt onto his head, momentarily blinding him. As Elliott fought to tear off the attacking monkey, Harriet flew to Oscar's assistance, flapping her wings as she pecked violently at Elliott's face and head.

A flash of orange and black rose from the ground as Rupert sank his fangs deep into Elliott's leg.

"Help! Get them off me! *Help!!*" Elliott raged, stumbling blindly over the skeletons of the dead kings and knocking over the vessels of diamonds. "Help!"

All at once the bats hanging from the cave's ceiling squealed and took flight, stirring up a frigid wind as they deserted the chamber.

"I guess they didna like the blast from that pistol," mused Oliver, scratching his head.

A thunderous cracking sound shook the cave. Bits of stone and clouds of dust began to rain upon them.

"It's going to collapse!" roared Simon, racing over to Camelia and grabbing her hand. *"Everyone clear out!"*

"Come on, Stanley—pike off!" shouted Bert, running toward the passageway as fast as his short little legs would carry him.

"Right behind ye, Bert!" Stanley said as he swiftly untied Oliver and Zareb.

"Oscar, Harriet—that's enough!" Camelia scooped up Rupert as he slithered toward her, and looped him around her neck. "We have to get out of here now!"

Harriet gave Elliott one last hard peck before flying back to Zareb's shoulder. Oscar angrily whacked Elliott on the head, then jumped off him and climbed up onto Simon.

"Are you all right, Elliott?" asked Camelia urgently. "Can you make it out of here?"

Elliott regarded her in confusion as dust and chunks of rock fell around him. "My diamonds!" He fell to the ground and began to rake his hands across the cave floor, trying to gather up the scattered stones and stuff them into his pockets.

"For God's sake, Wickham, leave them!" Simon shouted.

"They're mine!" Elliott scrabbled frantically through the dust on his hands and knees.

"Elliott, please," Camelia pleaded, "we've got to get out now!"

"Just one more minute!"

An ominous crack began to streak through one of the walls, creating a fissure in the painting between a group of warriors and the lion they were trying to slay.

"Come, Tisha," said Zareb. "It is time for you to leave this place."

"Elliott, I'm begging you—leave them!" Camelia's voice was ragged.

"Just a few more," said Elliott, groping his way across the floor.

"It's his choice, Camelia." Simon took her arm. "Let's go!"

"I can't just leave him here!"

"If you stay, you will die," Simon informed her brusquely. "And while that outcome might seem acceptable to you, I can assure you it is absolutely unacceptable to me."

With that he swung her up into his arms and raced down the disintegrating passage, with Oliver and Zareb following close behind.

"Come on, Stanley—move it!" commanded Simon as they found him wedged in the cave's entrance.

"I can't—I'm stuck!"

"This night really couldn't get any better," Simon muttered, setting Camelia onto her feet. "Bert, are you out there?"

"I'm here!" Bert answered. "But he's stuck tighter than a mouse hole, an' I can't get him to budge!"

"All right, we're going to pull him back a bit, and then see if we can't get him angled better so he can get out. Oliver and Zareb, each of you grab one of his legs. Camelia and I will take his torso. Everybody ready? Pull!"

"That's it!" shouted Bert from the other side of the entrance. "He's movin'!"

"All right, Stanley, I want you to twist your right shoulder down and bring your left shoulder up, so you're more sideways—got it?"

"I think so," Stanley gasped. "I feel like I've a bit more breathin' space."

"Excellent. Now pull your stomach in, and make yourself as small as you possibly can. When I say 'three,' I want you to pull hard, Bert, and we'll push. Ready? One . . . two . . . three!"

There was a chorus of grunts and groans as everyone strained to free Stanley from the grip of the rock.

"'Tis like tryin' to shove an elephant through a bloody keyhole!" growled Oliver, his aged arms quivering with exertion.

More dirt and rock began to fall down on them. A sea of bugs and snakes surged over them as they sought to escape the rapidly crumbling cave.

"Come on, Stanley," Simon grated out, "think small!"

"He's moving!" Camelia cried.

Stanley shifted an inch. And then an inch more.

And then he popped from the opening like a giant cork, landing heavily on Bert.

"Go!" Simon commanded Camelia after he pushed Oscar and Harriet out the hole.

"But Zareb and Oliver—"

"Will be right behind you," he promised, unceremoniously shoving her and Rupert through the opening. "All right, Oliver, you're next!"

"Dinna tarry, lad. I'm of nae mind to be sufferin' that trip back to England alone!" The old Scotsman scrambled awkwardly out of the cave.

"You're next, Zareb."

Zareb regarded him gravely. "The spirits have spoken."

"Right, they're telling us to get the hell out of here—so move!"

Zareb stared at him, then solemnly bowed his head. "She is yours, now. Guard her well."

His dark eyes glittering with tears, he turned back toward the crumbling passageway.

"For the love of God—"

Simon grabbed him by his shoulders and whipped him around. "Do you really think I'm going to leave here without you, Zareb?"

"You must," Zareb insisted. "Tisha needs you."

"I'm flattered you think so. She needs you, too."

Zareb shook his head. "My time watching over her is finished. It is your turn now."

"Is this some sort of crazy African belief of yours? Because Oliver would *never* think his job of watching over me was finished. He still watches over my mother, and she's married and has nine children, for God's sake! The way he sees it, his job only gets bigger each year!"

Zareb's eyes widened. "He does?"

"I'd love to chat with you more about this," Simon drawled, ducking as a huge chunk of rock fell beside him, "but I'd really prefer to do it outside of this cave. Are you coming?"

Zareb stared in surprise at Simon's outstretched hand.

And then he laid his palm against it, absorbing its warmth as Simon's strong fingers closed around his aged, weathered ones.

"Of course." He smiled. "Tisha is waiting."

"Nothing like holding off until the last possible second," muttered Simon as he helped Zareb squeeze through the narrow opening.

A heavy shower of rock and dirt cascading around him, he dove through the shrinking entrance, landing hard upon the ground.

Then he grabbed Camelia and rolled on top of her, shielding her with his body as the Tomb of Kings sighed and collapsed, burying its secret chamber once more.

CHAPTER 17

"I don't have anything more for you to eat," Camelia told Oscar as he nudged her arm.

She sat cross-legged upon the ground, her father's precious journal open upon her lap, solemnly contemplating the rock painting of the lion and the warriors.

"If you're still hungry, go and see Oliver. Maybe he will give you one of his last oatcakes before he and Simon leave."

Oscar continued to pull at her arm. Sighing, Camelia lifted it. Oscar scooted in beside her and gazed up, his dark little eyes troubled.

"It's all right, Oscar." She gently stroked his head, trying her best to sound reassuring. "Everything is going to be fine."

"Zareb said I would find you here."

She turned abruptly to find Simon standing behind her. He was dressed in his usual outfit of a loose-fitting linen shirt and rumpled trousers, both copiously wrinkled but clean. Rupert was looped carelessly around his neck, while Harriet was perched regally upon his shoulder.

"It seems Rupert and Harriet have taken a liking to my things," Simon said, carefully removing the snake from his shoulders and setting him down upon the ground. "Harriet keeps hauling items out of my trunk and flinging them around my tent, while Rupert just keeps slithering into it and burying himself in my clothes. He gave me quite a start just as I was about to close the lid."

Camelia watched as Rupert coiled himself beside Simon's boot, patiently flicking his tongue as he waited to see where Simon would go next. Harriet flapped her wings in protest when Simon tried to remove her from his shoulder. On some primitive level, they seemed to understand he was leaving.

Camelia bit her lip and turned her gaze back to the painting on the rock.

"What will you do now, Camelia?" Having given up on trying to detach Harriet from his shoulder, Simon seated himself on the ground, not quite touching Camelia, but close enough that she was achingly aware of him.

She continued to gently stroke Oscar's head. "I'm not sure."

"You could try to excavate the Tomb of Kings once more. It would take time, but at least now you know exactly where it is."

She shook her head. "I don't want to find it again."

Simon regarded her in silence. Her sage green eyes were shadowed with sadness, and the violet crescents underneath told him she had barely slept since the collapse of the cave the previous night.

"What happened to Elliott last night was terrible," he

began gently, "but it was his choice, Camelia. He could have left the tomb with the rest of us. He chose to stay until it was too late."

"I don't think he was consciously making a choice, Simon. There were other forces in that tomb—forces that you and I can't understand."

"Don't tell me you're starting to believe all Zareb's talk about dark winds and curses. That isn't a very scientific approach for an experienced archaeologist like you."

"Some things defy the tenets of science," Camelia reflected. "Zareb has always said there are things we cannot know, because we are not meant to know them—at least not until the time is right. Last night the Tomb of Kings revealed itself to me. In doing so, Elliott was revealed to me also. The two things were intrinsically linked. I don't think the spirits would have let Elliott leave that cave even if he tried to. That's why they buried it."

"The spirits didn't bury the cave, Camelia," objected Simon, "Elliott did. He fired his pistol and the cave collapsed, either because he created a fault in the ceiling or because the resonance from the blast caused tremors in the structure. For every action there is a reaction—and in this particular case, the physical reaction was the collapse of the cave."

"I broke Elliott's finger, which caused him to fire his pistol in the first place," Camelia pointed out. "If everything is just action and reaction, then I am responsible for the destruction of the tomb."

"If you hadn't broken Elliott's finger when you did, Zareb, Oliver, and I would have done everything in our power to knock him down, which would also have caused his pistol to fire. I think even Stanley and Bert

would have ultimately helped us. All morning Stanley
has been trailing after me, asking if there is anything he
can do to repay me for helping to get him out when he
was stuck. And Bert offered to help Oliver with his
trunks—although I think he just meant he would get
Stanley to carry them. So you mustn't torment yourself
with the thought that you are responsible for the collapse of the tomb and Elliott's death, Camelia. I'm glad
Zareb showed you that little trick with the finger—although I must admit," he finished, smiling, "I didn't
think so when you tried it out on me."

"Elliott never would have attempted to harm us if we
hadn't found the cave with all those diamonds in it—and
we never would have found the cave if I hadn't heard
that voice whispering to me at the river."

Simon frowned. "What voice?"

"It doesn't matter." Camelia closed her father's journal
and set it aside, trying to make sense of her ragged emotions. "All I'm trying to say is, maybe there are some
things that are better left undisturbed, Simon. To excavate this site would mean countless years of tearing up
the ground—and for what? To remove the artifacts from
their rightful home so they can be hauled across the
ocean and placed in a museum in England? Where they
would be put into glass cases and exposed to thousands
of gawking people who couldn't begin to appreciate their
importance?"

"This doesn't sound like you, Camelia. You have always believed in the value of sharing information about
the past with the rest of the world."

"The bodies and artifacts in that cave weren't placed
there with the intention of their being removed and exposed to the world. It's a burial chamber, Simon. Those

artifacts belong to Africa, and to the African people descended from the chiefs buried within, and even to the spirits who are guarding them. It would be wrong for me to remove them."

"What about your father's dream?"

"My father dreamed of finding the Tomb of Kings. We did that."

"If you don't provide the archaeological world with proof, they'll never believe you. It will just be a story that will be dismissed as either grossly exaggerated or pure fiction."

"I know. And it pains me to think my father's work will never be celebrated, when he struggled his entire life to earn the respect of his peers. But I know if he were here, he would agree with me. My father loved archaeology, Simon, but he loved Africa more. Ultimately, he would want to do what was best for Africa, not what was best for his legacy."

She had changed, Simon realized, moved and humbled by the quiet acceptance and maturity emanating from her. The quest that had consumed her every thought and breath from the time he had first seen her sprawled in a sopping wet tangle of petticoats on his laboratory floor had just been taken from her. And although sadness shadowed her gaze, he sensed she was at peace with her decision.

"You could always mine the land for diamonds," he suggested. "Away from the site of the tomb, of course."

She shook her head. "I won't ravage the land in search of a few useless white pebbles. Diamonds are of no interest to me—they have no redeeming value."

"Actually, being one of the hardest substances on earth, I believe they do have some redeeming value, at least from a scientific point of view," countered Simon. "They could eventually prove to be of considerable importance in the fields of science and technology. Even if I can't convince you of that, there is something else you should consider. Elliott took the diamonds your father found to the De Beers Company, who have remained discreet about it because they hoped to buy the land from you. It is only a matter of time before rumors about the diamonds of Pumulani spread. When they do, how will you stop others from coming here and digging up the land?"

"Pumulani is mine. I will not permit anyone to dig upon it."

"Which is admirable—you might succeed in protecting it for as long as you are able to keep men here to constantly guard it. But where will you find the money to pay those men? And what will happen to this place after you die?"

"I will make arrangements for it," Camelia insisted.

"Even if you succeed in protecting the land for the next hundred years, eventually someone is going to come along and try to mine it," argued Simon. "The question is, how careful will they be with the earth, how well will they treat the workers, and to what use will they put the profits they make here?"

"I don't know. I can only control how I treat the land and the people who work for me. I cannot control what others will do."

"Which is exactly why you should consider mining the land yourself. Think about it, Camelia," he urged. "First of all, you could mine the land as carefully as you pleased, making sure you kept well away from the site of the tomb, and preserving any artifacts you might find as you sifted through the earth. Secondly, you could ensure the native workers were well treated and fairly paid, while providing them with much-needed work. And thirdly, you could use some of your profits for the good of the African people."

It was a sound argument, Camelia reflected. She had always despised the mining companies, because they destroyed the land and abused their native workers, all for the sake of making a fortune for the investors. But if she were mining her own land, things would be different. She could ensure the land was excavated carefully, preserving any artifacts they might find along the way. She would treat her workers with integrity and respect. And any profits she made could be used to help the surrounding tribes when food was scarce, and to prepare them for the new world that was swiftly and inevitably descending upon them. A school could be built. Perhaps even a small hospital could be erected, for when the powers of burning herbs and shamans were not enough. Searching for diamonds at Pumulani was not necessarily a betrayal of all she believed in, she realized. Not if it meant bettering the lives of even just a few African people.

Even so, she found herself strangely reluctant to take on this new venture.

"I don't know." Her voice was hollow as she tentatively added, "I'm not sure I'm going to stay here."

Simon regarded her in confusion. "You don't have to live here at the site, if you don't want to. As long as you hire capable workers whom you trust, and a good overseer, I'm sure you can run things from your home in Cape Town."

"I was thinking of going a bit further away than that, actually."

Simon arched his brow. "Where were you thinking of going?"

She inhaled a long, steadying breath. "To London."

His eyes widened in amazement. "Why?"

Because I cannot bear to stay here without you, she thought, feeling vulnerable and afraid of the feelings coursing within her. *Because nothing I ever do or see or feel or touch will ever be the same if you are not with me. Because if you leave and I remain here, I will live the rest of my life feeling that my heart has been torn in two.*

"I just want to go there." She had hoped he would be pleased by the thought of her going to London with him. Instead he looked completely dumbfounded. "Is that so strange?"

He shrugged. "For most women, probably not. For you, who despise London and love Africa with all your heart, yes."

"I could learn to like London."

"That's doubtful. But even if it were true, why on earth would you want to, when everything important to you is here?"

"Because everything important to me isn't here. Something extremely important to me is in London."

"What?"

She turned her gaze to him. Summoning up every fragment of her courage, she solemnly whispered, "You."

He regarded her in astonishment.

And then, to Camelia's profound irritation, he began to laugh, causing Harriet to abandon his shaking shoulder in flurry of disgruntled gray feathers.

"I'm not going to London, Camelia," he finally managed.

She regarded him blankly. "You're not?"

"Well, I suppose if you are, then I'll have to, but I'd suggest we go only for a short visit. I know my family is most anxious to meet you, especially after the stories they've no doubt heard about you from Doreen, Eunice, and Jack. But you have to promise me we can take Rupert with us—my little brother Byron will never forgive me if we don't. He's been trying to convince Genevieve that a snake would be a marvelous pet."

"But I'm only going to London because you are," Camelia objected. "Badrani told me you were packing. He said he and Senwe were taking you and Oliver to Kimberley to catch the train to Cape Town this afternoon."

"Aye, an' if ye both keep sittin' here blatherin' away, the day will be gone an' I'll have missed the train," Oliver added sternly as he approached.

"It would be better for you to leave tomorrow," Zareb insisted, walking slowly beside him. "I have not yet prepared *mopane* worms for you."

"There's a reason to stay if ever I heard one, Oliver," quipped Simon, amused by the flash of revulsion on the old Scotsman's face. He rose and extended his hand to assist Camelia to her feet.

Oliver scratched his grizzled chin, pretending to think about it. "I fear I've already been away too long," he finally said, sighing. "As fine as those worms sound, Zareb, they'll have to wait 'til I come back again. Maybe I'll be able to convince the lad's family to try to manage without me for a few months next summer."

Zareb solemnly bowed his head to his friend. "Then I will do my best to find the very best worms in time for your visit."

"Oliver is leaving," Simon explained to Camelia. "He

believes I can finally be trusted to get along without him for a while. I think after all the excitement last night, he's just about ready to be back in Scotland, where he won't be dragged through bat-filled caves and subjected to nearly being murdered."

" 'Twas nothin'," Oliver scoffed. "I've been in worse scrapes with yer brothers an' sisters, an' still lived to tell the tale."

"But Badrani said you were both packing and going to Kimberley," Camelia said, still confused.

"I've been helping Oliver pack, and I'm going to accompany him to Kimberley, just to make sure he gets on the right train," Simon told her. "And then I'm coming back here."

"Why?"

"Because although I consider myself fairly open-minded, I am not so liberal in my thinking that I want my wife living on one continent while I live on another." He tilted his head to one side and regarded her with mock seriousness as he finished, "I'm afraid I'm going to be quite adamant about that, Camelia."

She looked at him incredulously. "Are you asking me to marry you?"

He grinned. "By any ceremony you choose, in any place you like."

"I will perform the ceremony now, in front of this ancient rock," Zareb quickly offered, stepping forward. "The spirits who brought you together are watching. They will make your union sacred."

"Here now, that might be fine an' well for the spirits, but the lad an' lass need a proper ceremony in a church before a clergyman," objected Oliver. "I'm nae tellin' Eunice an' Doreen they were married by you in front of a rock with a monkey, a bird, an' a snake for witnesses. Eunice will be on the next ship to Africa with a Scottish minister in tow."

"But your life is in London," Camelia persisted, wondering if Simon fully understood what he was giving up.

"No, Camelia." Simon regarded her tenderly. "My life is with you. I've seen you in London, sweetheart, and you were miserable. You belong in Africa, with all its sunlit beauty and open spaces and opportunities for you to do something that really matters. Besides, there isn't just you to think of—there's Oscar, Harriet, and Rupert to consider." He gave the trio a long-suffering look. "I'm not sure I'm up to living with them in a small London town house again."

"But what about your work?"

"The wonderful thing about being an inventor is I can work just about anywhere," he returned, shrugging. "Although you'll have to promise me we will visit my family for a couple of months every year. That way you can spend some time getting to know them, and I can keep abreast of the new technology in Europe, and purchase enough equipment to keep me productive here. My family will probably insist on registering patents for anything I invent while I am away. They are convinced that one day I might actually invent something important."

"'Tis nae more than the truth." Oliver's wrinkled face beamed with pride. "The tattie masher he made for Eunice was pure genius."

"Simon is brilliant," Camelia agreed softly as she stared at him. "I've always known that."

"Perhaps you and I should load the wagon, Oliver," Zareb tactfully suggested, seeing how Camelia and Simon were now gazing at each other.

"We can do it faster with the lad's help," Oliver said, oblivious.

"I'll be along in a minute, Oliver," Simon told him.

"That's what ye said over a half hour ago—"

"Come, my friend," said Zareb, gesturing to Oliver. "Tell me again how to make that fine haggis of yours—in case Simon wants to grow some hair on his chest while you are gone."

"Why, certainly," Oliver replied, pleased that Zareb remembered. "The most important thing is, ye've got to start with good, meaty sheep's pluck. Rinse it well, makin' sure ye've washed away all the blood, then soak it for ten hours in cold salt water . . ."

Simon waited impatiently for the two elderly men to disappear against the sun-washed bands of coppery earth and sapphire sky. Finally, he and Camelia were alone.

"There's something I've been meaning to tell you." He stopped, suddenly unsure.

"Yes?"

He reached out and brushed a silky lock of hair off her forehead. "I love you, Camelia," he said hoarsely. "I think I've loved you from the moment I turned in my laboratory and saw you sprawled across the floor wearing that ridiculous hat. I don't give a damn whether we live in London, or Cape Town, or even here in a little tent on the grounds of Pumulani. All that matters is that I'm with you. Although," he added, pulling her into his arms, "if you want to stay here during the rainy season, I hope you will at least consider the practical merits of building ourselves a house, and permit me to have some wood brought in. I'm not sure I want to spend the rest of my life eating food cooked over burning dung."

Camelia looped her arms around his neck and smiled. "You haven't given the dung enough of a chance," she teased. "After a while, you might start to actually like the unique flavor it imparts."

"Fine. I'll eat dung-smoked biltong, if you eat the hair-growing haggis Zareb is planning to make for me." He lowered his head and began to nuzzle her cheek.

"Actually, I'm thinking we should make our home in Cape Town," Camelia quickly returned, threading her fingers into the red-gold tangle of his hair. "I have a house there with a lovely big wood stove, and as far as I know, Zareb has never tried to burn dung in it."

"A sound compromise," Simon mused, raining lazy kisses along the pulsing hollow of her throat. "Marry me, Camelia," he urged, his voice low and husky as he grazed her lips with his. "Marry me, and I will spend the rest of my life doing everything within my power to make you happy."

Pure joy washed through her, making her feel strong and sure and whole. "Yes," she whispered fervently. "As long as you promise me one thing." She sank against him, molding her body to his.

"Anything," Simon murmured, fighting to control his desire to ease her down against the warm African soil and bury himself inside her. His hand drifted up to her breast and began to stroke her, rousing the peak to life. "What would you like, my love?"

"Promise me you'll never stop loving me this much." She captured his mouth with hers and kissed him deeply, tasting him and shifting restlessly against him until Simon thought he would go mad from desire.

"Get your things," he finally managed roughly. "You're coming with me to Kimberley."

She regarded him in confusion. "Why?"

"Because there is a church there," he explained. "And hopefully a minister who will satisfy Oliver."

"You want to get married today?"

"I want to get married this *instant*. But since Oliver objects to Zareb's performing the ceremony, it seems I have no choice but to wait until we get to Kimberley." He regarded her uncertainly. "Would you prefer to wait and arrange a more elaborate wedding?"

Camelia laughed. "I was quite content with the idea of our being married right here by Zareb." She bent to retrieve her father's journal. "Let's go."

Simon glanced at Oscar, Harriet, and Rupert, who were watching them intently. He sighed. "Fine. You can all come, too."

Squealing happily, Oscar bounded forward and scrambled up onto Simon's head, while Harriet flew onto Camelia's shoulder and Rupert slithered over to her leg, enabling her to pick him up and drape him over her shoulders.

"Very fetching," Simon said, unable to resist planting a quick kiss on Camelia's nose. "I'm probably the only groom in the world whose bride wore a snake and a bird to their wedding."

"I'll be sure to remove them before the actual ceremony," Camelia promised.

"As long as you don't cause the poor minister to faint, I don't really care," Simon assured her, offering her his arm. "Shall we?"

Camelia's eyes twinkled with mischief. "Does that mean you don't care what I wear tonight, either?"

"You're a saucy lass," Simon chided. "My only stipulation is that there are no animals in our tent tonight. I don't want to be distracted."

Camelia laughed and pulled him down for a long, heated kiss, making it clear she intended to hold his attention, both in the coming night and in all the years ahead.

ABOUT THE AUTHOR

KARYN MONK has been writing since she was a girl. In university she discovered a love for history. After several years working in the highly charged world of advertising, she turned to writing historical romance. She is married to a wonderfully romantic husband, Philip, who she allows to believe is the model for her heroes.

Readers can find out more about Karyn at
www.karynmonk.com

Experience the enchanting wit of *New York Times* bestseller

Betina Krahn

"Krahn has a delightful, smart touch." —*Publishers Weekly*

~

The LAST BACHELOR
___0553-56522-2 $6.50/$9.99 Canada

The PERFECT MISTRESS
___0553-56523-0 $6.99/$9.99 Canada

The UNLIKELY ANGEL
___0553-56524-9 $6.99/$10.99 Canada

The MERMAID
___0553-57617-8 $5.99/$7.99 Canada

The SOFT TOUCH
___0553-57618-6 $6.50/$8.99 Canada

SWEET TALKING MAN
___0553-57619-4 $6.50/$9.99 Canada

The HUSBAND TEST
___0553-58386-7 $6.99/$10.99 Canada

NOT QUITE MARRIED
___0553-57518-X $6.99/$10.99 Canada

The ENCHANTMENT
___0440-24267-3 $6.99/$10.99 Canada

Please enclose check or money order only, no cash or CODs. Shipping & handling costs: $5.50 U.S. mail, $7.50 UPS. New York and Tennessee residents must remit applicable sales tax. Canadian residents must remit applicable GST and provincial taxes. Please allow 4 – 6 weeks for delivery. All orders are subject to availability. This offer subject to change without notice. Please call 1-800-726-0600 for further information.

Bantam Dell Publishing Group, Inc.
Attn: Customer Service
400 Hahn Road
Westminster, MD 21157

TOTAL AMT $_____
SHIPPING & HANDLING $_____
SALES TAX (NY, TN) $_____

TOTAL ENCLOSED $_____

Name _____

Address _____

City/State/Zip _____

Daytime Phone (_____) _____